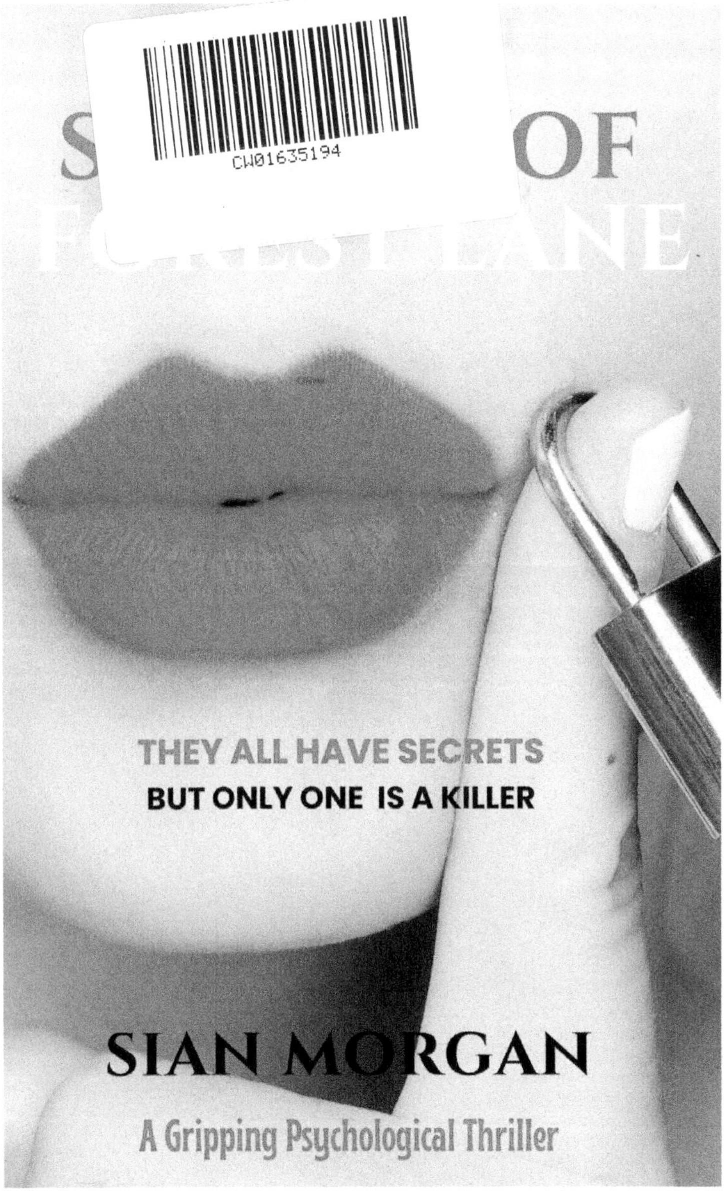
CW01635194
OF
THEY ALL HAVE SECRETS
BUT ONLY ONE IS A KILLER
SIAN MORGAN
A Gripping Psychological Thriller

THE SECRETS OF FOREST LANE

SIAN MORGAN

ISBN: 978-1-0369-2255-9

Dedication

I dedicate this book to my husband and my six children. It was not easy, but we got there. When Mummy was writing, they were helping around the house, getting on with their schoolwork and asking about my progress every step of the way. They are my biggest support.

I also want to thank my Instagram and TikTok Followers. They have been so supportive. Even though I am a new author and they have never heard of me before! Giving me advice and tips along the way. I never expected to feel so supportive, and you have made a Welsh girl very happy.

Lastly, I want to thank my ARC team for spotting my mistakes and giving me tips to make the book better. As well as promoting my book alongside me. I thank you from the bottom of my heart.

Contents

ONE

LATER

Peering out from behind a bush, he wasn't where he should have been. He was gone. Running from him had made her legs start to cramp, and the fear that was swelling through her body was also making them feel like jelly. That was too close. Kneeing him in the balls was all she could think of to get him to release his grip. And to her surprise, it had worked. Crouching on the floor, she panted. She was gaining her breath back slowly, but he was out there, and soon, the running would have to start again. He was still out there lurking in the darkness. He was still on the hunt to kill her.

Her eyes were wide with panic as she searched for her attacker. She licked her lips and swallowed. A soundless breeze swept through the woods that was just a little more than a whisper. It was quiet. All except for her breathing, which was loud in her ears. There was no controlling the sound or the heavy panting. She had been running for her life, and her lungs had worked hard to pump fresh blood through her muscles.

She gripped the bush tightly, unaware it was pressing painfully into her palms. She looked down and saw the blood dripping down her hand, tainting the orangey leaves below in a rich red instead. A dull pain crept over her, nagging away at her hand. Moving her hands off the bush, she quickly learnt how tender they were. She clenched her fist tightly and moved her head closer to the bush as she crouched lower. The smell of the leaves reminded her of a freshly sharpened pencil and comforted her.

She continued to look around, her eyes glancing around the darkness in fright, fearful that she might see her perpetrator. Fear dripped from her tears as they poured down her face. It was a black, inky night. The clouds had disappeared, and all that remained was the darkness that blasted throughout the sky. Her mouth was dry as if sandpaper had found its way onto her tongue, and she dreamed of guzzling down a gallon of water.

There. She spotted his back looking across the park in the distance. Trembling, she ducked back down. He didn't know where she was hiding. How could she have been so wrong about him?

Her muscles tightened, striking every inch of her body as if the grim reaper himself already had a hold of it. She wished more than anything she was back home where she was safe. Where she was protected. Instead, she was alone in the dark. It was so dark. The fear of death was too overwhelming for her to take.

Leaves rustled behind her. It was followed by a loud scream in the distance, like a woman was being attacked. She jumped. Hurdling back down a slope, she hit her head on a tree that was placed a few metres behind, hidden in the darkness. Sitting up, she rubbed her head to overcome the dizziness. The wind pushed against her face as she leaned forward. Scrambling to get back to her hiding place, she dusted her bum. Mud and grass stains clung to her sore knees. Suddenly, she realised she had heard that sound before. It was a fox. They were not alone in the park. No doubt, there were hundreds of creatures lurking about in the darkness. She was in their territory.

Pain shot into her stomach, and it began to tighten again. Bending over, she gripped her stomach in an attempt to make it stop. She heaved uncontrollably. Sweat burned onto her face. Nausea was infecting her body. Tears continued to run down her face, and the sobbing came with no control on her part. A shiver went down her spine, and her body started to quiver. She clenched herself tightly using her arms, rocking back and forth in an attempt to soothe herself from the misery that surrounded her. Maybe it would be better if she just ended it? How long could she keep up this running? What he would do to her when he finally caught her was too much for her to bear.

She exhaled deeply. Get a bloody grip, girl. You can make it. She decided her only chance for survival was to run. Preparing for her next dash across the park, she pushed off her muddy stilettoes and tossed them on the ground. Still shaking, she pushed herself off the ground and, grasping her head, looked straight towards the trees before her. She attempted to hold it steady but struggled to focus and stumbled slightly. She could make it. She had to make it. She gulped, trying to swallow the overpowering horror that consumed her. She needed to move, and it needed to be now. Then, before she knew it, she was running barefoot as fast as her legs would carry her. Her tight dress made it hard to run, but she kept going. Her feet stung on the brambles beneath her. Run, she told herself. Just Run.

As she looked back over her shoulder, there was only a deep darkness. The park seemed so different, so alien-like. What had once been so familiar to her, so friendly, was now replaced with despair. Nothing was left, just a grimness that flooded the park, chasing her everywhere. Her chest was sore, and she gasped for air as she ran. She was desperate to escape, but her legs were crying at her to stop. How long would they carry her for?

She wailed as she tripped over a branch on the ground. Jumping onto her knees, she spun around in every direction, searching. Shit. Where is he? She could not see anything. Where the hell was he? Had he gone? She clambered to her feet, clutching the cold dirt as she got up. Convulsions penetrated straight through to her core. Had she escaped? Sweat was dripping from her face, and with a trembling hand, she wiped it away from her eyes.

Leaning on a tree, she tried to take a breather. Her legs were like jelly, and she wanted to crash to the ground, but she managed to hold them up. Her body was screaming for her to give up. Her muscles were tight, and each breath caused her bones to ache. She vomited. Cocktails from earlier that night surged their way out of her stomach. Her body went limp with weakness. She looked down at the Blue Lagoon drink she had previously consumed. Her mouth was so dry. Screw the water; she would give anything to have an ice-cold can of Coke; her mouth started to drool, thinking the impossible would never happen.

She looked down at her hands. They were covered in blood. They throbbed so hard. Her fingers had turned blue. She just wanted to give up. But she had to keep moving. She looked up and could see the road up ahead. She could see light. *Yes.* Maybe someone would see her if she could only get onto the main road. A faint glimmer of hope came over her. She could make it.

Suddenly, she felt something grab her from behind, forcing a hand across her mouth. She spun around screaming, but no sound came out. She was facing her killer. Her pulse raced faster than ever, bracing for what would come next.

TWO

NOW

Lily

Lily closed her front door behind her. The sun was bright, and she squinted as she stepped out. Oh God! The sun is shining today, thought Lily. Still, it was nice to have some warmth in the air for early September. The cardigan she wore today was a good choice. There was no need to dig the winter coat out yet, although some leaves were starting to turn from their leafy summer green to a hint of orange, ready for the Autumn weather ahead.

'Fresh air,' Lily said out loud as she inhaled deeply. She was grateful to be out of the house, released from the same four walls as if she were being held there against her will.

'The wheels on the bus go round and round....round and round!!' Meghan sang loudly.

'Not this morning, please, Meghan,' irritation dripping from every word Lily spoke. But she almost immediately regretted snapping at her. Was she being too harsh?

Lily couldn't help it, though. She was so miserable lately. But Meghan didn't deserve anger being thrown her way. She was only four. Anxiety shifted through Lily like a wave had flooded over her entire body. Her heart rate doubled, and sweat seeped out of her body, pouring all over her face. It felt like excitement for a moment until her stomach began to flip. Meghan was growing up, and there wasn't a damn thing she could do about it. Lily's mother had reminded her of this earlier that morning, right before she took a picture of Meghan on her first day at school.

Taking a deep breath, she tried to slow down her thumping heart. Her mother was right, of course. Meghan looked grown-up in her new uniform on her first day at school. As Lily smiled at Meghan, her anxiety subsided. When Jackie raised her phone to take the picture, Meghan blushed. Meghan always blushed when the attention was on her. Lily was the same. Seeing a part of you in someone else was a weird feeling, yet there was also some pleasure in it.

Wouldn't it be great if she could keep Meghan four forever? If only she could keep Meghan with her always, she could keep her safe and protect her from getting hurt. The world could be cruel; Lily knew that better than anyone else. Lily's heart began to race again. The anxiety was back. The blood pooled down her face. She was about to raise Meghan alone as a single mum.

The anxiety surged over her as if a bolt of lightning was hitting her repeatedly, causing her heart to beat faster. More sweat poured from her face. How had she got here? There had never been a baby in her life plan, let alone single motherhood. But then her life plan had never banked on meeting a boy called Chris, who would be responsible for stealing her heart. Then breaking it.

Stupid Fucking Chris. He was why she was living back home with her mother and sister, in her new poxy apartment. Along with their four-year-old daughter. With no degree. And with no bloody job. All thanks to Chris.

Her anxiety turned to anger. This was now her life at twenty-two. Shame stuck to Lily as if tattooed across her body. She hadn't achieved any of her aspirations. But then Lily, at the same time, felt guilty for feeling so angry that her life and the plans she'd made for her future were gone. If it hadn't been for Chris, she wouldn't have had Meghan, whom she loved more than anything.

'Sorry, Mummy,' said Meghan, interrupting Lily's thoughts.

'That's okay, darling, Mummy's sorry too. I shouldn't have snapped at you.'

'What do you think my friends will be like Mummy?'

'I think they will all be lovely Meg,' rubbing her daughter's shoulder, trying to reassure her.

Meghan continued to natter, and her babbling soothed Lily into a daydream. Thoughts trailed back to five years earlier, when she was an excited eighteen-year-old full of hopes and dreams, with no care in the world and nothing to hold her back. Lily was accepted to study Law at the University of Surrey. She'd wanted to be near her home in Kent and was over the moon when she got the acceptance letter. Ever since Lilly was little, Law has been her passion. She loved solving a good mystery and used to love watching "Midsummer Murders" with her nan, where someone would die in every episode, and the local detective would solve the case. That was one village she didn't fancy living in! Surely, no one was left to kill in such a small and quaint English village!

As they turned the corner, Lily was taken aback by all the posh houses. It was like going from Old Kent Road to Mayfair. There were substantial detached houses elegantly placed side by side. It looked like something out of Wisteria Lane. Except this was Forest Lane, the nicer part of the street. At the end of the bottom stood the gates to the school. One house in particular caught her eye. It was painted in a shade of white, not a bright white, but it was in no way dreary. In the middle of the house stood a beautiful, elegant archway and a big porch to sit out on, surrounded by an impeccable white picket fence. In front of the house lay an immaculately cut lawn. It was the quintessential dream house. It reminded her of the doll house she had many years ago.

Lily admired the house and spied intently through the window. Wonder who lives there? Lily thought. Inside, she could see the perfect doll family, too. A woman was kissing her husband goodbye for work. Lucky cow, living in the perfect dream house with the perfect husband. The man then turned to his two daughters and wrapped his arms around them before swinging them in the air. They were all laughing. They looked so happy. There was even a Labrador in there playing with its rope.

The husband left the front door and headed to his car parked in the driveway. Lily crouched down behind a car. She looked up and saw Meghan still singing up ahead on the street. Lily knew she should have caught up with her, but this man intrigued her somehow. Just one minute, Lily thought. Lily continued to hide as she turned back to the man, simpering to herself; she wished she had a husband like that. He wore a smart grey suit with a white shirt and tie. It looked expensive. He looked handsome. He was your very own Ken doll. Every inch of him was dressed and styled to perfection. Lily bet he was the man in charge at work and was probably the boss everybody in the office adored. Lily couldn't help but stare at the guy, almost in awe of him. Lily had a thing for a man in a suit. They were hot.

The man leaned his briefcase onto the ledge of the boot. The man turned around sharply, and Lily jumped from the car to a tree on the pavement behind her. He didn't see her. Lily leaned closer, intent on seeing what he was doing. He flicked around with the combination lock of the case. What was that inside? It couldn't be, could it? As he opened it, there were knives. A lot of knives. All different shapes and sizes. Some looked like hunting knives, others like standard kitchen knives. Next to them was a thick, cream-coloured rope, some gaffer tape and what seemed like cable ties. He took out the knives, rope, and tape before stuffing them into his boot.

What was he doing with all this stuff in his car? Especially as he clearly didn't look like he was getting his hands dirty at work today. He looked more business-like as if he was off to the office in that suit. Lily pondered for a moment. Well, he is probably the man around the house, too and needs that sort of stuff, Lily reasoned to herself. She knew there would likely be a reasonable explanation. She needed to stop watching so many crime dramas and leave the house more often. Maybe it was time to get a hobby?

Lily glanced back in the direction of the school. Meghan had trotted on up ahead and was still chatting with herself. Oh crap! Lily jogged so she could catch up with her. Once back at her side, Lily's mind returned to her daydream and her first week at university. She had met Chris at a fresher's party. They hit it off straight away, and she was excited when she found out he was living opposite her in the halls where she was staying. Lily remembered that feeling of being totally and completely consumed by Chris; it had been love at first sight, if such a thing exists. Such a stupid notion.

After dating for two months, things became more complicated when she found out she was pregnant. Her initial reaction had been to run for the hills, as there had been no plan to have a baby at eighteen, especially during her first term at university. Lily dreamed of becoming a lawyer, conquering the world, and fighting crime. But being the trusting girl she was then, she had believed the man she was madly in love with. When he'd said they would be a family and he'd take care of them both, he would. That was her downfall, and he knew it. The word "family". Ever since she was a little girl, Lily had craved the perfect family. When Lily was nine, her dad was done with the marriage and left her mum. He also left Lily with a big, empty hole in her heart. Her mum had done a good job raising Lily and her baby sister, Jasmin, but she never got over it. She would not be making the same mistake with another man in a hurry.

'Mum!!' shouted Meghan at the top of her voice.

With her heart nearly jumping out of her skin at Meghan's urgent cry, a young boy around the same age as Meghan appeared from nowhere.

Having nowhere to go, the boy stared up at Lily with fear. One minute, she stood upright as she was meant to be, and then the next, Lily spun around before falling. As their bodies collided, she landed with a thud on the cold, hard pavement below. Her thong shot right up her arse crack.

What the hell just happened? If there was ever a time to look ungainly, this was it. Remarkably, however, the boy landed on her lap without a scratch.

But all was not lost. As Lily looked up, bewildered, she saw a handsome man running across the road to save her. Lily blinked. She must be dreaming.

'JACK,' he shouted at the boy. 'What have I told you about running off without me?'

The man was a little out of breath and had clearly been running to catch up with the boy she now knew to be Jack. Oh, right, yes. He was running over to save Jack. Not her. How stupid of her. Lily blushed. She assumed the man must be Jack's father.

Suddenly, Jack jumped up from her lap and appeared fine as he stood up. A look of relief quickly came over the man's face; Lily, on the other hand, could feel the bruise on her arse already starting to blossom.

Jack's dad turned from his son to look upon Lily. The concern he once had for Jack was now squarely all on her. In an instant, her thoughts of hating men disappeared from Lily's mind as she was entranced by this beauty before her.

'Are you okay?' he asked, bending over and lending his hand to help her up.

'Yes, I'm fine,' Lily lied through her teeth as her arse continued to throb from the unexpected fall.

As Lily took his hand, she could feel the softness as it touched her.

'Hi, I'm Tom,' he said, his eyes glistening in the sunlight. He pulled her softly upwards, but as he did that, she could feel the intensity of the pain increase as gravity pulled at her bruised body. He had more strength than she expected. He was not a skinny man, nor was he a big guy. He looked into her eyes. Wow, they were intense. He was mesmerising. His emerald green eyes locked her into a trance, and her heart pounded hard as he continued to stare at her.

'Lily,' she said, finally finding her voice.

'Sorry about Jack, he can be a little boisterous. Plus, it's his first day of school, and he is full of energy this morning,' he said, flashing a smile at her, full of subtle charm. A cold chill swept down her body and through her arms, leaving her with goosebumps. There was something mysterious about this man that Lily couldn't quite put her finger on. Tom had an aura around him, like a darkness inside him. She could feel it. This intrigued Lily, and this intrigued her a lot, even though her brain was screaming at her to proceed with caution.

'No, I'm so sorry. I wasn't looking where I was going. Is he okay?' Lily finally broke the gaze they had between them.

Lily couldn't take her eyes off him, though, taking quick glances, making sure he didn't notice her staring. As Tom faced his son to wipe some dirt off his trousers from the fall, Lily looked at him once more, drunk with curiosity. He was quite smartly dressed for a school run. He had a Ralph Lauren polo shirt on, with expensive-looking trouser bottoms.

'Yeah, he's fine,' Tom said, brushing off the remaining bits of dirt from Jack's trousers. 'Aren't you, buddy?'

'Yeah, fine, Dad,' he said, not even looking up at his dad.

'And this is Jack,' Tom shook his head in amusement as he looked up at her, giving her that mind-blowing grin again. A surge of electricity ran through Lily's body, and she let out a small giggle as if she were a little girl. She was completely under his spell. Lily swallowed and took a deep breath, struggling to return to reality.

'Meghan,' Lily called over to her daughter while looking around to get her bearings. She saw Meghan running back to her.

Lily walked back in the direction of the school with Tom by her side.

'So, I assume by the uniform you are going to Kitterton too?' Tom said to her.

'Yes, the first day.'

Tom nodded in agreement. 'Mind if we walk with you?' asked Tom as Meghan grabbed Lily's hand. They were surprisingly cold. How could they be freezing on such a warm morning? She should have packed gloves in Meghan's bag. A bit late now, though. She should be okay as they would be mostly inside anyway, thought Lily.

Lily brushed a strand of hair behind her ear, 'Of course! This is Meghan.' She tried to sound relaxed, although Lily wasn't sure if she was pulling it off.

'Hi, Meghan,' Tom gave Meghan a wave. Meghan moved behind Lily and buried her face shyly into Lily's coat.

Wow, he smelled so good; he was killing her with his mix of aftershave and good looks. Falling for this man was a big mistake. He had to be married. *Right?* Lily looked down, searching his hand for a ring. But she was walking to his right and was sure it was the left hand that wore a wedding ring. There must be a ring there.

As they approached the school gates, Lily instantly became overwhelmed as she watched the other parents drop their children off. They were all pulling up in their flash cars, Mercedes, Range Rovers, SUVS, you name it. The green-eyed monster almost immediately lurked into her as if smacking her in the face. Such arseholes. With their flash cars. What twats! Lily didn't even have a car, never mind a hot car!

As Lily stepped through the school gates, her irritation grew at the sight before her. She noticed a group of women in their late thirties, deep in conversation.

'Well, I told them....I won't be back at your spa anytime soon with that attitude!..... Who do they think they are, making me wait?' Lily heard one of them say.

'I'm telling you, Val, use Julian. He does wonders. He charged me £800, which was worth every penny,' her friend replied. £800! Were they for real? That amount of money would pay for Lily's first term at uni.

They looked masterfully sporty, as if they were ready for the gym. Yet they were plastered in the most ridiculous amount of gorgeous make-up. They were disgustingly glamorous. Stupid, perfect mums.

Lily jolted back in time to high school and saw them as the popular girls who were idealised. Could she be a part of this mummy group? However, Lily had a feeling she was not their cup of tea. Nonetheless, an impassioned sense of curiosity towards them invaded her. They had the life. "The life". *What would that be like?* Amazing, of course, she thought.

Lily looked down at her clothes. She was far from glamorous. More like a tramp compared to them. As if she had just rolled out of bed that morning and chucked on the first thing she saw. Which was not far from the truth. Lily had grabbed a plain white top from her drawer before wearing her favourite pair of pale blue jeans, which she had owned for the past three years. It had an old ink stain near the crotch, but it didn't bother her much. She paired it with her favourite black and brown cardigan that she always wore. She hated wearing heels and felt much more comfortable in her black flat pumps, although they were now starting to wear on the sides due to their everyday use. Yeah, she was no Grace Kelly.

Lily thought back to that morning when she had picked up a random hair bobble on the living room mantelpiece and lazily scrunched her long, thick brown hair into a ponytail. She was now regretting the decision not to put on any make-up that morning; the result had left her looking more like one of the ugly stepsisters. If only she knew. *Damn it!*

Now, seeing the mums in their perfect clothes made Lily want to run to the nearest Karen Millen shop, then pop to Debenhams for a complete makeover, hoping to feel more presentable around them. Not that she had that kind of cash to compete with them. She was like Julia Roberts in Pretty Woman; they would probably laugh her out of the store.

What was the point? She was an unemployed, young single mother living with her mother. All her friends had recently graduated from university and were now off travelling. The only excitement she had to look forward to was watching Strictly Come Dancing on Saturday night. Woohoo. Not.

One woman joined their group, and Lily immediately recognised her as the one from the perfect doll house they had passed on their way to school, kissing her husband goodbye. The woman was tall and slim, a lot skinnier than Lily was. A good size 8, if she were to guess. *Did this woman ever eat?* Lily wasn't particularly overweight but suddenly felt terribly conscious of her size 12 pear-shaped figure. She should add a gym membership to that list, too. Lily had never entirely lost all her baby weight after having Meghan, nor did she make that much effort. Lily was too busy scoffing down a Chinese every Saturday to care. A takeaway was all she had to look forward to.

Now, which way should they go? Lily stopped and asked an older woman standing on her own.

‘Excuse me, do you know which way the reception is, please?’ Lily asked her.

‘It’s that door there. The kids usually line up outside until Miss Norton blows the whistle, ready for them to go in.’

‘Okay, great, thanks,’ Lily said. She was grateful for the help. Lily and Meghan walked towards the reception door area, closely followed by Tom and Jack.

As they stood and waited, Lily took her phone from her back pocket and automatically opened Facebook. As she flicked through, she saw a picture of Chris and some of his friends. “LOCATION: Malia, Greece”, she read. Uhhh....what a dick! A sensation of jealousy coursed through her, and utter disgust at his betrayal. How dare he live it up while she’s looking after their daughter. Why had she opened up Facebook? Lily shook the thought out of her mind and pushed the phone back into her pocket.

Lily thought Chris was different, but after they moved in together, it seemed like he used his money far more for partying than he did on buying nappies or paying bills. The tears welled up again in Lily’s eyes, and then came an overpowering perception of being unable to breathe. But this was quickly replaced with rage as Lily focused her energy on the father of her child. Lily wished she hadn’t promised to stay friends with Chris. Every time they met, it made it so hard. Although Lily had no choice, she couldn’t stop Meghan from seeing her father. They won’t be hearing from him soon, though. By the looks of things, he’s too busy living it up in Greece. *Damn him, and damn bloody Greece!*

Lily sighed, pushing the thoughts to the back of her mind as she bent down to face Meghan. She took a deep breath to stop the blood from boiling over inside her.

‘Ready?’ Lily said to Meghan calmly.

‘Ready, Mum,’ Meghan replied. She was such a brave girl.

‘I love you so much,’ Lily crouched to Meghan’s height.

‘I love you too,’ Meghan repeated back and tightly threw her arms around Lily’s neck. Lily took the full brunt of intensity from her daughter’s squeeze as if Meghan were trying to crack Lily’s ribs. Despite this, Lily was pleased to feel the overwhelming amount of unconditional love they had between them. Meghan always had the power to make her feel better. Meghan was her world, and Lily’s heart would not beat without her. That prick Chris had at least done one thing right in their short relationship.

‘Right, come on, you, go and line up,’ Lily told Meghan, still feeling the warmth between them.

Lily watched Meghan walk into the classroom, waving intently goodbye. After she watched Meghan disappear, Lily spun around and caught Tom rubbing his face. She was initially oblivious to what she was looking at. Still, it registered that Tom’s wedding ring was tactfully placed on his finger. And on his left hand. *Great! Of course, he’s married.* Just her luck.

As Lily walked away from the reception, she looked around the school at the crowd of parents in front of her, fascinated by what their world was like. She looked back at Tom, who smiled back at her. Although Lily didn’t know it then, the people who lived on Forest Lane were about to give her more drama than she could ever imagine.

THREE

Katherine

Katherine was face down; head squashed against the soft Egyptian cotton sheets of the bed as her husband James continued to plunge his penis inside her. Back and forth. Back and forth.

It wasn't that she minded having sex this way. But it didn't really make her feel all that special. It was almost like a transaction, more than anything else, like one of her wifely duties that needed to be ticked off. It would be nice if James actually took it upon himself to kiss her once in a while. Not some crazy little peck on the lips, but an actual, real snog with tongues and all.

Katherine couldn't remember the last time they had sex where it was missionary style or any position other than doggy style, where she was planted face down on the pillow like some dirty whore. Was this the way she was going to have sex for the rest of her life? Katherine had tried to kiss him in bed that morning. But before she had a chance to, James had flipped her over onto her stomach using his strong muscles. God, he spent more time at the gym working on those stupid biceps than anything else, probably just so that he could drag her around in bed.

He grabbed her arse and pushed himself inside her like she was some lifeless doll he could shag how he pleased. She wondered how much those diamond earrings he bought for her birthday were worth. How much had he paid so she could endure this shit sex they were currently having? No foreplay. No groping. No love. This must be what it was like to be a prostitute, Katherine speculated.

Like a job. In and out. *Come on, James!* A girl has needs. And this was not it!

James moaned behind her. He was clearly enjoying himself. At least someone was.

'Oh yeah, Oh, yeah baby...You like that, don't you?' James muttered.

He lunged himself inside her, again and again. How long would it take for him to cum? Not too long, she hoped. His body odour was fumigating the room, and Katherine was now thankful she had the pillow to soften the scent.

Suddenly, James jumped off her. Katherine looked over her shoulder, surprised. Was *that it? Were they changing positions?* James stood up, placed his feet on the floor, and positioned himself at the foot of the bed. He grabbed her by the legs, dragging her arse towards his penis. James pushed himself back inside her vagina, deep into her. Nope. *Still the same position.* But when it slipped back inside her, Katherine couldn't help but cry out. His movements were hard, and his force was making her sore.

James continued to moan and then quickened his pace. He grabbed hold of her hair, pulling her head back towards him. Was this his way of trying to show dominance? James paused for a moment. But Katherine knew he was finished when his penis decided to spasm inside her. James groaned loudly before collapsing on top of her. He let out a massive sigh in her ear.

Salty drops of sweat dropped against her back, and the overpowering smell of his odour sprang into her nose. *Ew*! Katherine buried her nose into her hand. Her stomach tightened, and she gagged. Waiting for him to get off her seemed like a lifetime. Finally, he pulled out and headed to their en-suite bathroom. *Thank God!*

She reached around the bed searching for her knickers. After finding them, she pulled them up quickly. She swung her legs around the bed as she sat on the edge. Katherine put her hand in between her legs in an attempt to soothe her vagina. It had somewhat pleasured her, but she was equally sore from the powerful thrusting her husband had given her. A wave of shame filled her as if she had just asked him to leave the money on the nightstand. Why did he not want to kiss her during sex? Why did he not even want to see her face? In the public eye, James was so different. He was so respectful and always kissed her goodbye. Yet, during sex, it was like he was someone else.

James appeared from the bathroom, drying his golden blonde hair with a towel. He walked over to his drawer and grabbed a pair of boxers. Slipping them on, he wandered over to their wardrobe and looked inside. James had around ten suits that were all exactly the same colour: grey! Katherine had tried to get him to buy a different colour whenever they went shopping, but every time she and James left the shop, he was left holding the same colour suit he already owned. But that was him to a tee; predictable. Katherine didn't see the point in it. Why would you wear the same colour suit every day? *Complete madness.*

Katherine got up from the side of the bed. She looked at the clock on her bedside table. The girls would be up soon. Katherine headed to the bathroom.

'I'm just going to jump in the shower, love,' she said to James, who was still staring at his suits.

'Yeah, okay. Don't be too long. The girls will be up soon, and I need to get ready for work.'

'Yeah, I won't,' Katherine replied as she walked into their en-suite bathroom.

Turning on the knob of the shower, she slowly pulled down her knickers and slid in. The hot water was an enormous release of comfort on her skin. Katherine picked up the soap and scrubbed her body hard, caressing her body intently. Her vagina was still pulsating. Still waiting to be quenched. Katherine slowly moved her hand towards her vagina, scrubbing herself before dropping the soap. Screw it, she thought. If James couldn't give her an orgasm, she would give herself one. Katherine casually moved her hand over to her clit and started to move her fingers in a circular motion. She closed her eyes, relaxing her shoulders. Insane pleasure shot through her, and she quivered slightly. Picking up her pace, she started to groan quietly, moving her body to the rhythm of her motion. She placed two fingers inside her body deeply, leaning back on the shower wall, eyes still closed as she enjoyed the pleasure.

'Mummy!' Katherine was interrupted by a voice from the other side of the bathroom door. 'I'm hungry!' *Shit*! Katherine quickly stopped what she was doing and turned off the water. Springing out, she wrapped a towel around herself.

Katherine opened the bathroom door and witnessed her younger daughter, Sophie, staring up at her. Katherine bent down to match her height.

'Hi, honey. Go downstairs with your sister. She will make you some breakfast. I will be there in a minute.'

'Okay, Mummy,' Sophie replied, running out of the bedroom and down the hall. 'Ellie!!!' Sophie screamed as she went into Ellie's bedroom.

James was now nowhere to be seen in the bedroom. *Whew*! Katherine took a deep breath and let out a sigh. As she leaned back on the wall, clutching her towel, she knew she better get dressed and face the reality of the day. After composing herself, Katherine wandered over to her drawer to put on some clothes.

Katherine was due to go to the gym after the school run. She really didn't want to go. It was something about the sweat of others that always grossed her out. Nonetheless, Katherine had promised James she would go. It might make her feel better anyway.

Katherine grabbed her jogging trousers and top from the drawer. She slipped them on. Looking in the mirror at her dressing table, she took out her makeup. Katherine breathed out heavily. She looked a mess. There were severe bags under her eyes. And were those wrinkle lines, too? No wonder James didn't want to look her in the face whilst he was having sex with her.

Katherine huffed. This situation needed to be rectified. Katherine took out her foundation and plastered her face as much as possible. She carefully stuck on her fake eyelashes before polishing her favourite bright red lipstick on her lips. Looking at the finished product in the mirror, Katherine smiled. She was satisfied with the results. Thank heavens for make-up. Now she looked good.

Katherine walked down the stairs into the kitchen to find the two girls eating cereal. Sam, their Labrador, was hovering to see if they dropped any crumbs.

'Mine is better than yours!' Ellie teased Sophie.

'No, it's not. They are both the same,' Sophie whined.

'I spat in yours. Mine is the best,' Ellie snarled.

'Girls, what's going on?' Katherine asserted herself, trying to take control of the arguing brats. James was reading the paper and drinking his coffee. He hadn't even acknowledged their argument.

'Mum, Ellie said she spat in my cereal when she made it,' Sophie sobbed, snot rolling down her face and tears rolling down her small, freckled cheeks.

'Ellie, don't be so nasty to your sister,' Katherine scolded her oldest child. 'I am sure you were just kidding, weren't you, Ellie?' Katherine scowled at Ellie.

'Of course not,' Ellie muttered slyly.

'Ellie!' Katherine raised her voice at her. She couldn't be dealing with this nuisance right now because there were other pressing matters to deal with. The smell of coffee trailed its way to her nostrils and lured Katherine in, like a moth to a flame. Katherine couldn't function until she had a nice cup of coffee inside her.

'Mummy! It's my first day at the big school,' Sophie exclaimed.

'Loser,' Ellie muttered again. Katherine ignored her comment.

'I know love,' Katherine replied to Sophie as she walked over to the coffee pot.

'So, Mummy,' James piped in, 'What are you going to do with yourself now both Sophie and Ellie are in school?' James looked at Katherine straight in the eyes. Katherine looked down.

'Well, I thought I might sign up for that gym you mentioned, the one Susan goes to,' Katherine continued to look at the floor.

'Good idea. Glad you took my advice.' James looked up smugly from his newspaper. 'You could do with losing a bit of weight. Especially around the tum,' James said, reaching his arm across and patting Katherine's stomach. She jumped back.

'Yeah, okay!' Katherine wrapped her arms around her stomach self-consciously, hurt by his remarks. How dare he? She wasn't that fat, was she? Katherine hadn't been running much lately. So maybe she did need to go to the gym.

'You know I am only joking, dear. Right, girls?' He looked at the girls, smirking. They both giggled. James leant towards Katherine and kissed her on her cheek, grinning cunningly at her.

'Okay, girls, Daddy's got to go to work now. Come here.' James went up to Ellie and Sophie and gave them a huge hug. Katherine smiled. He may be a dick sometimes, but he really did love his family.

'Okay, bye, ladies,' James said one final time before leaving the kitchen.

'Have a nice day, love,' Katherine called after James as she watched him disappear behind the front door.

Katherine leaned on the counter, watching the girls finish breakfast before getting out their sandwich boxes. The mountain of washing, followed by a mountain of ironing, was left for her in the corner. But they would have to be tackled after the stack of dishes that lay in the kitchen sink is dealt with. It was impossible to see from this situation that Katherine actually had a law degree and was a trained solicitor.

Katherine hadn't even wanted children. It had been James's idea. He wanted a family so much to make up for his own troubled childhood. Katherine tried to please him and so gave in.

However, Katherine hadn't counted on being a stay-at-home mum, looking after them full-time. Katherine assumed she would continue with her career and follow the path to becoming a barrister. Katherine had just received the acceptance letter to take the bar professional training course when she learned she was pregnant. Despite them trying to conceive, Katherine had been naive about the situation, thinking it would take much longer to fall pregnant. Instead, she became pregnant in their first month of trying. Katherine honestly didn't believe she was that fertile. It was a shock, to say the least. Katherine had secretly hoped it would take a lot longer than that for it to happen. She hadn't felt ready to be a mum at the time.

However, her boss, Richard Cunningham at Cunningham and Sons, had been more than understanding and said her job would be there for her after she had the baby. She managed to complete the course but never took the bar exam. Assuming she could take it on her return to work after the baby.

However, there was one small problem. James. He had interjected, saying that there was no point as Katherine would be looking after the children. It wasn't something she had thought about before they started trying. Katherine just assumed he wouldn't have an issue with her continuing to work after having children.

'You don't want to be one of those mums who neglect their children by working all hours of the day,' James said to her. James had been scarred by his own childhood; his parents were rarely around to even notice him, most of the time. Katherine was sure he was the victim of neglect as he appeared to spend more time with his stuffed dinosaur than with his parents.

This was probably why James had convinced Katherine to agree with him. So she decided to give up work, there and then and devote her life to looking after her two girls. Despite their arguments, especially with Ellie, Katherine was so glad she had them. They brought a lot of joy to her life.

'Okay, girls, it's time to get dressed,' Katherine said, picking up their empty cereal bowls before following them up the stairs. She walked into Sophie's bedroom and picked up her uniform, which was hanging on the handle of her wardrobe. After Katherine dressed her, she stood back to truly admire her.

'My girl is so grown up, not a baby anymore.' Katherine took hold of Sophie's arms, looking at her proudly. Sophie swung her arms around Katherine, gripping her tightly. Katherine smiled. The love of a child was definitely special. James had been right; being at home full-time with them had probably been the best decision at the time. After all, you can't get that time back with them.

But now that Sophie was in school full time, maybe it was time she got her career back on track and did something for herself. Katherine sighed. But she would need to approach the subject with James first.

'Okay, let's brush your teeth, and we can get you into your first day at school,' Katherine said, stroking her soft face.

***

Katherine firmly opened the door handle to the gym. Inside, warmth swept throughout the building. Katherine was immediately gratified to be saved from the gale-force winds that were blowing around outside.

It had been a long time since Katherine had gone to the gym. Times had changed. The gym looked different from the one she used to attend. Katherine relaxed her shoulders as she followed her friend Susan towards the reception desk. A sudden waft of disinfection flooded the area into her nostrils. Katherine scrunched up her nose, taken aback by the smell. *Why did they feel the need to go so overboard?* Guests don't want to faint whilst working out.

The gym was Susan's thing. She was a size eight and had an amazing figure. Unequivocally more sculpted than Katherine's body. But Katherine would never tell her that. Katherine didn't have the same enthusiasm for the gym as Susan. She would prefer to run out in the fresh air. Susan was also only her friend because they had met through James and her husband, Bruce. So here she was, signing up for the amazing gym that everyone kept banging on about.

'Hey, it's my friend's first time joining the gym,' Susan said to the young, bleached blonde girl behind the desk. The girl looked up, shining her veneers at her with the biggest, cheesiest grin Katherine had ever seen. She stared at the girl. Her name badge read "Claire". Her skin was an orangey streaky colour, probably as a result of using too much fake tan. Katherine narrowed her eyes. Stupid girl, Katherine thought. If you are going to fake tan, do it right. This also meant her teeth stood out more, as if she were some weird cartoon character.

Katherine beamed a big smile at her whilst Claire explained what she needed to do. 'Hi, could you fill in your details on this form for me?' Katherine grabbed

Claire's form, which was attached to the clipboard, before she could reply.

'Okay, I'll see you in there,' Susan said, looking back at Katherine as she swiped herself in.

'Yeah, okay,' Katherine waved to Susan and started to fill out her details. Once she had finished, Katherine passed the form back to Claire. Katherine wrapped her coat tightly across her stomach as she observed the buff men and women walking about. *What were they all looking at?* Had they never seen a woman in a winter coat sweating like a monkey in an extremely hot gym before! And yes, she was trying to hide her body, even if the inside temperature was a hundred degrees. She wasn't a frumpy fat woman like some of the other women in the gym. She looked after her appearance; she used Estee Lauder moisturiser daily to get her skin looking this good for Christ's sake. Fat good it did her though, when her dick of a husband preferred her from behind.

'Here's your pass,' Claire said, passing the gym pass to Katherine.

'Thanks,' Katherine looked down at her pass. It read "Katherine Lippet". So, she was now officially part of the gang. *Screw it.* Let's do this, she thought.

'Just swipe in and out as much as you like. You will get billed at the end of each month. If you have any issues, please let me know.'

'Okay, thank you, Claire,' Katherine stated, scanning her pass and entering the changing room. Katherine dumped her bag and coat in a free locker. Her stomach turned, making her queasy as she walked into the gym room with all the equipment. An overpowering stench filled the air. It reminded Katherine of her sweaty old gym teacher in high school, Mr Walker. The gym hall would continue to smell long after he had departed. Katherine shuddered at the thought of him. Katherine spotted Susan on the treadmill. She brushed the thought out of her mind. Katherine walked over to join her friend on the treadmill next to her.

'Hey!' Susan waved.

'Hey,' Katherine looked around the room nervously, her lip quivering as she watched the other women running effortlessly on the surrounding treadmills. Breathing all in time, matched with their perfect young skin complexion and brilliantly tight abs. Katherine huffed, and she turned the machine on.

Jogging on the treadmill, Katherine picked up the pace to match the young girl next to her, competing with her. The girl was clearly half her age, and even though Katherine still went for walks with Sophie, this was different.

As they both sped up on the treadmill, Katherine started to pant. Her chest was burning, crying out for her to stop. She had only just started. But she was determined to beat her. There was no way Katherine was going to let this girl get the better of her. *Who did this girl think she was?* Strutting her stuff about. She was no better than her.

The girl looked at her, smiling. Anger illuminated in Katherine. She didn't like to lose. Losing was not an option. Certainly not against this stupid smug bitch with clumpy mascara. Katherine's face screwed up with sheer perseverance. Her arms flapped vigorously by her side, desperately trying to keep up the pace as she jogged. Katherine turned to face the girl, who was still not really breaking that much of a sweat. Katherine's face burned like a hot iron had been placed onto it. Sweat poured down her face. Must not lose, she told herself. *Must not lose*. She kept convincing her body to keep going. But her legs were stinging, ready to collapse at any second. Her muscles started to cramp, and before Katherine knew it, she had jumped onto the side of the treadmill. Her body had given up. *Shit*!

Katherine guzzled down her water, spraying it relentlessly over her head to ease her burning face. Katherine looked beside her, and the girl high-fived her friend. Katherine's blood boiled. Well, of course, she would win - she looked like a professional bloody athlete or something, Katherine thought.

'What were you thinking?' Susan turned to Katherine disapprovingly, eyebrows raised. 'You are meant to be warming up, Kath, not going into a battle with a girl half your age. '

'I know, I got carried away,' Katherine looked over and saw the weights in the corner. 'I think I will work on my stomach and tighten my abs. I will be over by the weights if you need me.' She would do anything to get away from the shame that lay where Katherine had been running.

'Yeah, sure, crack on,' Susan replied, shaking her head in disbelief.

Katherine walked over to the corner and picked up the weights.

The girl from the treadmill came over and looked down at her. Katherine's body strained. *Oh great. What did she want?*

'What's the matter? The treadmill wasn't enough for you, Granny. What do you think you were doing trying to compete with me?' The girl cackled.

Katherine was shaking, adrenaline pumping, coursing its way through her veins. She was vexed. Katherine watched the girl snickering with her friend next to her. Katherine lifted the weights over her head. Suddenly, Katherine let go, and 15kg of weight landed on the girl's foot. *Oops*!

'Ow!' The girl cried out, hopping across the floor, clenching her foot with her hands. 'You did that on purpose!' yelled the girl.

'Oh, sorry, it was an accident,' Katherine lied. A slight sense of victory built up inside her, but she was quickly crushed by the sound of her pumping chest. Her heart rate had suddenly increased at a phenomenal pace. Grabbing her water, Katherine abruptly sprang up and ran towards the changing room.

'Fucking lunatic!' She heard the girl call behind her.

In the changing room, Katherine was leaning on a locker, trying to catch her breath. Katherine was frozen to the spot. The colour drained from her face, with her mouth open in shock. Her mind buzzed at the realisation of what she had just done to that girl. Bitch or no bitch, she probably didn't deserve that. Something had just snapped inside her, and Katherine had just seen red. Maybe the gym wasn't such a good idea after all. She was much better suited to running where she could be alone. Who knows what she could be capable of when pushed far enough?

FOUR

Tom

Shit. Tom was going to be late. He stepped outside his house and ran down Forest Lane towards Kitterton Academy. He didn't want to pick Jack up from his first day at school late. Timekeeping really wasn't his strong point. His recent ex-employer had told him that. He probably had a point.

Except Tom was a perfectionist. *What's wrong with wanting things done right?* Sweat dripped down his face. He looked down at his watch. 3:15. He slowed from his jog to a brisk walk. He inhaled deeply, trying to catch his breath and wiped the small particles from his forehead. The kids didn't get let out until 3:20, so he still had plenty of time.

He was now almost at the gates. He really needed to start leaving earlier. But Tom found it challenging to be organised. It came so much more naturally to women. As he entered the school gates, plenty of parents strolled in like they had all the time in the world. Not dripping in sweat like they had just run a marathon like him. Tom watched one mum pull about six kids from her minibus. *Screw that!* That was absolutely crazy, he thought to himself. *How did she cope with them?* She must be like a super mum. Tom couldn't imagine anything worse. One was enough for him.

Tom walked through the school playground. Now, which way was it again? He looked around the school, but he was clueless. This morning, he had just followed Lily. The school wasn't big, but all the doors looked the same. *Was it this way?* Tom walked to his right through the playground and around the side of the building. Yup, he had no idea. Hopefully, one of the other mums could help him.

'Excuse me,' Tom tapped a blonde lady on the shoulder.

She spun around to face him. 'Hi,' she said, her eyes lighting up as she looked at him. *Wow!* She was pretty for an older woman, he thought. Well, not old, but older than him. Maybe late thirties or forty, even.

'I'm looking for the reception class?' said Tom, giving the woman his best charming smile. Oh my, what he'd love to do with her right now. Tom bet she had some stuffy accountant for a husband who didn't know what to do with her. Bet she had not had an orgasm since her early twenties. Or most likely ever.

'I did drop my son off his morning, but now I can't remember which door he comes out of,' he blushed, a little embarrassed. It sounded stupid saying the words out loud. Tom's pulse raced as he looked her over; he was starting to feel horny, and he tried to control the bulge that was now growing in his pants.

'First day?' she asked, smirking devilishly at him.

Fuck, her smile. She's hot. Smoking hot.

'Yeah,' Tom replied in his most charming voice. Was there a connection between them? Or was it just him with his wishful thinking?

'I'm Katherine,' she said, touching his shoulder slowly, 'My daughter is in reception too. I'll walk with you.'

Katherine's touch made Tom shiver.

'I'm Tom,' he said, waving at her.

'Nice to meet you, Tom,' She gave him a wicked smile as if she was flirting with him.

Tom followed Katherine's lead towards the door of the reception. 'They're not out yet.'

Tom couldn't make eye contact with her. His heart was racing like the clappers. He looked around instead, pretending to be interested in the reception door.

'So, what's your daughter's name?' Tom asked her, accidentally meeting her eyes. His heart leapt, and the lust consumed his body. *Those eyes! They were absolutely lush.* Bright blue, which sparkled like crystals.

'Sophie,' she replied, meeting his gaze intently. There was definitely a spark.

He wanted the conversation to end. He was picking up his son at school, for God's sake. She may leave in a minute.

'Is he in Miss Norton's class?'

'Yes, I think so,' replied Tom, nodding at her.

The door opened to the reception class, and a young, geeky woman with glasses started to call out their names.

'That's Miss Norton's class,' Katherine whispered, leaning towards his ear. *What was this woman doing to him?*

'Daisy....Ben.....Dylan,' Miss Norton called each child individually. Different mums and dads stepped forward to collect their child as their name was called. 'Sophie, ' Katherine stepped forward, waving her hand at someone who appeared to be her friend.

'See you again,' she said, smiling coyly at him. 'I have to go and pick up my eldest, Ellie.'

Tom watched Katherine walk off and out of sight. Fuck me, Tom thought. Has it been that long since he'd had sex, or was she having some effect on him?

The teacher continued calling out names, but none were Jack's. 'Come on, mate,' Tom said under his breath.

He could picture Jack now, at the back of the queue in a daydream.

Parents continued to collect children, and now there were just a few left in the crowd. As Tom looked at the parents, he noticed someone. Lily. The girl he had met that morning. Thank God Jack hadn't done severe damage to her when he went crashing into Lily. She was standing there looking like a lost soul. *Poor girl. I know how you feel, love.*

'Hi, again,' Tom smiled at her.

'Oh...Hi,' Lily responded. 'Sorry, I was in my own world.'

'How are you after your fall this morning?'

'Oh, I'm fine,' Lily replied, looking at the floor. She seemed a little shy. Either that or she didn't want to talk to him.

'Sorry about Jack, he can be a little boisterous sometimes,' Tom tried to pull a conversation out of her.

'No, it's fine. Honestly, I wasn't looking where I was going,' Lily looked back at the school door. She certainly came across as if she were uninterested in him.

'Jack,' Miss Norton called, finally. Followed by, 'Meghan.'

Jack ran out towards Tom. *About time.*

'Dad, I met a friend called Dylan, and we played tag. There was a drawing, and we had cake.' Jack couldn't quite get the words out fast enough. He was jumping up and down on the spot as he spoke.

'Looks like you had a nice day then,' Tom said to him, smiling.

'Oh yes, Dad, can I come back tomorrow?' Tom looked around, but Lily had disappeared.

'Yes, of course, you will be here all week.' Tom grabbed Jack's hand and started to head out of the playground. Tom continued to search the area as they walked. Where the bloody hell did she go? Lily was like Houdini. One minute she was there, and the next, she was gone. Jack suddenly broke free of his grip.

'I want to run,' Jack called as he ran ahead of Tom.

'Don't run. Stay where I can see you, Jack,' Tom called after him. *Kids!* They have so much energy. Jack had been in school all day, yet he wasn't even knackered.

'Okay,' Jack shouted as he ran flat across the playground.

How do the teachers cope with him? They must think he is a handful, Tom thought. Tom had never met a kid who was so energetic. His brother's girl would sit there and colour when he used to visit him. All nice and quiet. She made parenting look easy. *Why couldn't Jack be like that? It would be so much fucking easier.*

As Tom moved around the other parents, he noticed Lily walking ahead. Jack was running full speed down the street towards them. God help that kid if he knocks Lily over again. But luckily, Jack passed them without bumping into either Lily or Meghan. Tom picked up his pace so he could catch up with Jack. He was really getting fed up with running to and from school already. Jack then abruptly stopped and started to talk to Meghan.

'Which way are you heading?' asked Tom, joining Lily's side. He was trying his best not to pant.

'Oh Hi.' Lily mumbled. She was probably starting to think Tom was stalking her. She clearly didn't want to talk to him. 'I'm heading to Forest Lane,' she said hesitantly. 'Where the apartments are.'

'Me too, I'm on Forest Lane. Just behind you.'

'Those posh new houses?' she marvelled.

Tom chuckled. 'Well, I guess so; we just moved in.'

Was he posh? Him? It somehow made him feel important. He tried hard not to smile at her compliment. They were nice five-bedroom detached houses. But they were by no means mansions. The truth was, his wife Carol was to thank for their house. Not him. She had been promoted to a speciality surgical registrar, which allowed them to buy this house. This meant she could now boss around all the junior doctors in her team as she trained for next several years to become a surgeon. She extended this courtesy to Tom, too, when Carol was home. The new job also meant they were able to afford the new house. Since she had taken the job, she was working crazy hours and seeing Carol was a rarity for both Tom and Jack. He sighed. Disappointment oozed through him as he thought of it. She was beginning to feel like a ghost to him.

As they all walked down Forest Lane and around the bend towards their homes, there was not much conversation from Lily. Tom studied her and couldn't work out if she was shy or just didn't want to speak to him. Maybe she didn't like him? Well, that would be the first. Tom could usually charm most girls to come around to his liking.

'Okay, so I'm down here,' Lily reluctantly told Tom. 'Come on, Meghan,' Lily started rushing towards the block of apartments.

'Okay, bye,' Tom called after her. 'Say bye, Jack.'

'Bye,' Jack waved before walking a couple of doors down to their house. Tom shook his head. She was a strange woman. He only assumed he would see her tomorrow.

As they approached their house, he noticed Carol's car was not in the driveway. *Not home again*. His heart sank, and an unpleasant weight of disappointment imploded over him. Carol should have been home by now. Tom put his key in the door and looked down at the floor, taking a deep, disappointed breath as he walked in. He was initially glad she got the job. It meant they could afford this house and be in the catchment area for the school they wanted Jack to attend. After all, Kitterton Academy was one of the best schools in the area. As Jack ran to his room to change, Tom entered the kitchen and clicked the kettle on.

Coffee was what he needed. His head sagged down to his chest as he sat thinking, leaning on the kitchen counter, waiting for the kettle to boil. A wealth of shame filled him. He was such a loser, letting his wife take care of him. This hadn't been the plan. Tiny streams of frustration circled their way through him. He was the one who was meant to be taking care of his family. A lump caught in Tom's throat, and he gulped it down.

He took a cup from the cupboard above, grabbing the coffee jar from the counter before him. He scooped in a large teaspoon of sugar. Then another. He was so tired. He hadn't slept properly the night before, mainly because he was tossing and turning all night, thinking about his lack of career success.

Moreover, it was becoming apparent that he was also failing miserably at being a husband. The lack of sex between him and Carol was getting him down. Sex was one thing that they succeeded in. There were only so many jerking-offs he could take. The kettle clicked.

He filled up his cup and chugged down a mouthful of coffee. He burnt his throat on the hot liquid, and he put it down to cool.

Tom was not a child either, and the fact that Carol thought she could boss him around as if he were a kid like Jack made the situation even worse. *Where had the woman he'd married gone?* She didn't usually behave this way. They had once been equals, but now everything revolved around her. Carol's job meant bossing people about at work, which had clearly gone to her head. But that didn't mean she had to talk like shit to him. He was her husband.

'Can I play on my tablet?' Jack came up to him as Tom sipped some more coffee. 'Yeah, sure, buddy,' Tom walked into the living room and picked the tablet up from the bookshelf. Tom keyed in the code and passed it to Jack. 'There you go.'

'Thanks,' Jack said, his eyes locked onto the computer screen while he plonked himself on the sofa.

Tom's phone suddenly vibrated in his pocket. A text from Carol:

'Sorry, love, emergency at work. I will be home in time for tea.'

Carol had been gone before Tom had woken up that morning. But she had promised the night before that she would be home before Tom returned home with Jack. Ready to greet Jack on his first day at school. Of course, that was just a joke.

'Okay,' Tom replied to her text. Then chucked the phone with fury onto the sofa. Tom wandered back to the kitchen and looked inside the fridge. Not much in there, he said to himself. Just sausages.

'Sausages for tea?' he called to Jack, who was still sitting on the living room sofa.

'Yeah,' Jack called back, not looking up from his tablet. Jack wasn't really a fussy eater. He was actually entirely laid back about most things. Tom shoved the sausages into the oven and clicked on the timer.

Tom's phone vibrated again. What the fuck is it now? Tom strolled back into the living room and grabbed his phone from the sofa. It wasn't her. A text from Damian, his brother.

'How are things, brother?' Tom read, sitting down on the sofa.

'Yeah, okay,' Tom lied. 'How are you holding up?' Tom wrote again. He chucked the phone next to him and took out his laptop. Popping the lid open, he looked at his e-mails, his eyes scrolling down the page. Junk, Junk, Junk. Great, no proper leads. Well, that's shit. His phone vibrated.

'Not good, bro,' Tom read. It vibrated again. 'Fancy a drink later? I'm off tomorrow.'

Excitement came over Tom. A drink sounded good. Screw that. It sounded fucking amazing. It would get him out of this shit tip. But the truth was, he could never go.

'Can't sorry. I have Jack,' Tom typed into his phone.

His phone vibrated. 'Can't she babysit?'

Tom laughed. His brother had never really liked Carol. 'She's a moody bitch,' Damian always said.

This thought made Tom laugh again. 'She's not here,' he typed.

'Typical,' his brother wrote back.

Damian was so right. His brother was having such a shit time lately, too. He was going through a divorce from his wife.

The oven timer started to beep, and Tom headed over to check on the dinner. He looked up at the clock on the kitchen wall. It was a bit early to start serving dinner, and Carol said she'd be home for teatime. Supposedly. He would leave it to simmer a little longer and then dish it up.

Half an hour passed, and still no sign of Carol. *Fuck it.* He was going to dish up for just him and Jack. Why should they starve just because she couldn't keep a promise? He was a mug for thinking she would actually make it on time.

'Jack, dinner's ready,' he called out.

'Okay, Dad!'

Tom put the peas to boil and took the Bisto from the cupboard. Jack strolled in just as Tom was pouring the gravy over their plates. Jack glanced up at him.

'Okay, mate?' Tom asked him.

'Yup....I'm hungry,' Jack looked around the room. 'Where's Mum?'

'Still at work, Jack.'

'Okay.' He mumbled, sitting down in his seat and slouching his shoulders down. Jack was not used to her not being there. Carol spent most of her time at work and little at home.

'How was school?' Tom asked, trying to have a conversation with him.

'Yeah, good...I made friends,' Jack said, sitting up straighter in his seat. His words filled with enthusiasm. 'One boy... um... can't remember his name. He let me play tag,' Jack was scoffing down his dinner in between his words. 'He is my best friend. Remember, I told you earlier, Daddy?'

'Nice!' Tom laughed. The mind of a child was so simple. Adults were the ones who made things much more complicated than they needed to be. Tom looked up at his son and smiled as he watched Jack eat. At least Tom had done one thing right: his son.

His thoughts turned back to Damian's text. God, he could really do with a drink right now. He hadn't had a proper drink in ages. Scrap that, he hadn't gone out drinking on a night out in a long while. *What the fuck happened?* He used to be such a party boy before they had Jack. Thought, Jack wasn't the reason. Carol and her job meant she couldn't go out much. Which meant he couldn't go out. Loneliness dominated the shell of the man Tom once was. Where was that fun person he used to be? Who was he these days? A sense of worthlessness invaded his thoughts. Tom was basically just a house husband.

'Can I be excused, Dad? I've finished.' Jack interrupted him from his thoughts.

'Yeah, sure, mate,' replied Tom, putting on the fakest smile he could give his son. 'Take a biscuit from the barrel if you want.'

'Can I have two?'

Tom chuckled. 'Yeah, sure, crack on,' Jack disappeared from the kitchen.

***

It was almost eight o'clock when the front door slammed shut. Tom looked up at the clock. Where the fuck had she been?

'Sorry, love,' Carol said apologetically. She kicked off her shoes in the doorway and entered the living room. Tom was sitting on the sofa, looking at his computer. He gripped his beer tightly as she walked towards him. Carol kissed Tom on the cheek, but he flinched away from her.

'My dinner in the oven?' asked Carol, ignoring his hesitance and walking automatically into the kitchen. Was she literally going to ignore the fact that she was late again?

Tom stood up, walking into the kitchen to join her.

'Unfortunately, yes,' replied Tom, rage beginning to eat him up inside.

'Sorry, love, a patient crashed on the table, and he needed emergency surgery to save his life,' Carol stated.

Tom tutted. Okay, that was a good excuse. But there were other doctors at the hospital. Surely one of them could have stepped in?

'Having a beer, dear?' Carol said.

'Yes,' Tom replied coldly.

'Make sure you don't have too many. Jack's in bed,' she lectured.

'Don't you think I know that? I put him there.'

'What's the matter?' she said, surprise ran through her voice.

'You're never fucking here, is what's the matter,' Tom blurted out. He took a large gulp of his beer, practically necking it. His hand started to tremble as he tried to hold back the anger that was building up towards his wife.

'Well, someone's got to pay for this house,' Carol snapped, venom dribbling from every word she uttered.

Was this woman for real? What a condescending bitch. 'Yeah, and don't we know it,' Tom snapped back at her.

'It's not my fault you lost your job. You did that all by yourself, dear!'

'You were the one who said it was for the best, and I would become a freelance graphic designer. Or was it all a ploy to get me at home where you can keep an eye on me and have a full-time nanny for Jack?'

'No! That's not true!' Carol bellowed.

Tom looked up at the wall and saw the photo of Carol and him at their wedding. 'Where has the woman I married gone? The fun-loving girl I met at university, who would drink any guy I knew under the table? When did you become a fucking manipulator instead?'

Carol opened her mouth, but he wouldn't let her speak.

He pointed to the picture. 'Two young kids, so happy and in love. Where did it all start going so wrong? You might as well be a guest in our house, popping up occasionally. Whenever it suits you.'

Tom's heart ached. Could they be those people again? Not likely, he thought. He could only detect a hollow hole of nothingness between them now. Were they just beating around the bush and staying together for Jack's sake?

'That's not fair! I'm working my arse off. Around-the-clock shifts! We have responsibilities, Tom. A mortgage. A son,' Carol stopped for a moment. 'Plus, you know how important my job is if I want to become a surgeon....'

'Yes, I know, you need to put in the hours.'

Usually, Tom would go to bed at this point. Tom couldn't even be bothered to argue with Carol. *What was the point?* She was oblivious to how he felt, as long as everything suited her. She didn't really care about anything else or anyone else.

Tom didn't want to be in the same house as her, never mind the same room. Carol made his skin crawl at the very thought of being near her at his very moment. *Fuck it.* She could deal with it all. He'd had enough.

Tom downed the last of his beer, stood up and screwed up the can as hard as he could. Taking a deep breath, he chucked it into the living room bin. Grabbed his phone from the coffee table and snatched his keys from the key holder before taking one last look at the woman who used to be his wife.

'I'm off,' Tom called to Carol, heading towards the door.

Adrenaline pumped around his body like a possessed human. He pulled his coat from the coat hanger at the door and swung it around himself.

'What!' She ran after him, jumping in front of the door and blocking his exit. 'What about Jack?'

'You deal with him, you're his mother.' His tone was cold. His eyes were full of steam; they blazed up like a savage fire, full of hatred as he stared at her.

'Get out of my way!' Tom shouted at her. His face was close to hers. Carol looked up at him, her eyes wide with surprise and even fear. Carol stepped to the side. Pulling the door open, Tom slammed it hard behind him.

Outside, the cold air seeped into his bones and down his spine. He gave an uncontrollable shiver and rubbed his arms vigorously with both hands. Fuck. Had he really just done that? Tom took a long, hard, deep breath. What was he going to do now?

FIVE

Tom

Tom's hand shivered as he scrolled through his contact list. He was still standing outside his house. Shock continued to unfold throughout him over what he had just done. He found the number he was looking for, pressed his bright red finger onto the name: "Damian", and clicked the dial. Pressing the phone between his ear and shoulder, he rubbed his hands together to bring back its warmth. The night was pretty cold. The sky was a clear black, with an exquisite array of stars glistering into the night. Beautiful, yet cold. The number kept on ringing. 'Come on, Damo. Please answer,' Tom prayed. Shit, he wasn't going to answer.

'Hey Bro, you okay?' Damian finally answered.

'Thank God! You picked up,' Tom replied, 'Well... I'm not okay.'

'What happened?'

'I kinda stormed out of the house.' Tom heard his brother's laughter through the phone.

'You? Mr calm and collected? Stormed out of the house?' Damian continued to laugh.

'Yeah, I know. She is just being such a fucking idiot. I had to get out of there, man. You still up for that drink?' Tom asked.

'Yeah, of course. Where are you?'

'I'm still standing outside the house.'

'Okay. Get the fuck away from there and wait on the corner of your street. I'll come pick you up. I'll be about 15 minutes.'

'Okay, do hurry up. It's freezing!'

'Peace out,' said Damian, and ended the call.

Tom put his hands in his coat pocket. The cold air hit his face as he started to wander down the street. His cheeks were on fire as the cold burrowed into every bit of skin that was on show. He walked past Lily's apartment and looked over to see if he could spot which one was hers, but there was no sign of her.

Tom took a deep breath in and composed himself. It had been a while since he had been out after dark; the darkness reminded him that summer was now truly over. Tom liked the summer. It reminded him of fishing with his father as a child. This was his happiest memory. Before things turned sour. The lampposts were brightly lit against the dark night. He could see the flicker of televisions as he walked past the houses. He was utterly alone outside in the silence. Yet, the silence was peaceful.

Sighing deeply, Tom reached the corner of the street. Would Carol be okay with Jack? Should he go back? But she was his mother after all. Tomorrow Carol has the morning free, so there was no reason why she couldn't take Jack to school. Tom was her husband, not her bloody nanny for god's sake. But they just seemed to be living like strangers these days. What was the point in that? Something had to change.

Tom leaned back onto a street sign and snuggled up into his coat as much as he could. A chill shivered down his spine, and his hands were now going numb despite being huddled in his pocket. He took them out and made a fist, blowing warmth into them, before placing them back inside his coat pocket.

What was taking Damian so long? His balls were going to turn into ice at this rate. Tom curled his toes up inside his shoes. A cigarette would be nice right about now. Not that he was a smoker. The last time he smoked was at university. That was a very long time ago. But right now, anything that could calm his nerves would be appreciated.

Tom thought back to the time when he first saw Carol. She was slim with long brunette hair. Her hair was nothing like that now; a short bob which made her look like some sort of lesbian. Not at all attractive. Tom would love her to grow her hair long again. It suited her, and she was so pretty like that. But how could he tell Carol that without upsetting her? He couldn't.

Tom had met Carol at a club in London on a student night out, a decade earlier. Carol was there with all her medical students, and it just so happened that Tom and his group of friends decided to join in. Carol was dancing on the dance floor when he met her. They sat down and chatted until the lights came on in the club, signalling it was the end of the night. He remembered sitting there listening in awe of her and her passion for medicine. Carol was so vibrant, so full of life.

Carol was at St George's University of London training to be a doctor, while he was studying Graphic Design at the University of Arts, London. Although their worlds and passions were completely different, they fell completely in love with each other. Carol had made Tom feel so alive when he was with her. She had the power to make him do things he would have never dreamed of doing before. Like one time, they broke into the university. Tom couldn't help but widen his smile as he thought back to that moment. It was so wild.

Carol graduated from her medical training, and Tom became a graphic designer at a magazine company.

However, Carol's dream of becoming a surgeon meant an increasing number of working hours, and this started to take over after they got married. Piece by piece, she became less of the person Tom fell in love with and more of a stranger.

When Carol became pregnant with Jack shortly after getting hitched, Tom had been naïve enough to think she would slow down her career. He thought Carol would enjoy Tom and Jack whilst on maternity leave so much that she'd understand where she was needed more.

But only three months after having Jack, Carol was back at work. Carol had just finished her post-graduate foundation course at the time and was keen to become a speciality surgical registrar, which meant doing her core training too. Now four years later, she was two years into her training and would be a consultant before she knew it. Tom was proud of her. But wished more than ever that Carol would just take notice of him more. That she would become that fun, loving, go-getter she once was.

It wasn't like her passion had changed much, that was still there, it's just Tom didn't see it anymore. Tom's throat became scratchy, and he tried to stop his eyes from filling up with tears.

Enough thinking about the past. Tom pushed his thoughts to the back of his mind. He was going to have a good night with his brother and forget about his troubles for the night. A white Porsche 911 Carrera suddenly spun around the corner and abruptly stopped in front of Tom. That sound was like music to his ears. What a sound! What a car! *Fucking bastard.* Tom jumped in, greatly appreciating the warmth of the car after being out in the cold.

'Hey bro,' Damian grinned at him. That grin was trouble. That grin meant Damian was up for a big one tonight. However, Tom was secretly pleased. That was just what he needed.

'Hey, thanks for getting me. It's freezing out there,' said Tom, clenching his fists and blowing into them once again. "Some car, bro!"

'No problem,' replied Damian. "The best part about getting divorced. You don't need permission to get the car you want," he grinned, turning the heating up in the car. Tom laughed.

His hands started to burn as the hot air was blasted onto them. He let out a huge shiver as his body adjusted to the warmer temperature. Damian slammed his foot onto the accelerator, and they both jolted forward from the thrust. Damian screeched out of Forest Lane and towards the main road in the direction of the city. Tom pushed himself back into his seat and grabbed hold of the car door, hoping it would help him from his brother's lunatic driving.

'Geez! Take it easy,' Tom exclaimed.

'Oh, don't be such a baby,' Damian laughed. 'You know your problem? You need to get out more. She's got you under the thumb.'

'Well, we can't all be living the single divorced life like you,' Tom said, sarcastically.

Damian laughed. 'Hey, I'm free, single, good-looking, and I've got money. What woman wouldn't resist me? I just need my wingman. I would look a bit sad by myself.'

Tom chuckled. Damian was not good at expressing his true feelings. Tom knew he was secretly devastated by his recent divorce from Lauren.

'Well, I haven't been your wingman for a long time. But I will give it a go.' Tom's hands jittered, and he clenched his fist in an effort to hide it. He noticed his heart rate had sped up. Was it just Damian's erratic driving through the town? Or was he nervous about the night's events? A thrill of excitement washed over him as if a part of his soul was being unlocked. The anticipation drove into him, and butterflies soared in his stomach. His leg began to shake uncontrollably. Tom just wanted to get there and have a drink. Hopefully, that would calm his nerves.

'So, Smoking Gun?' Damian said, distracting Tom's thoughts.

Smoking what?' Tom exclaimed.

'It's a new bar that's just opened near Old Street Station, meant to be the place to hang out at,' Damian said compellingly, waiting for Tom's response of approval.

'Yeah, wherever. I haven't a clue, just as long as I get a good drink down me.' They pulled up to the car park. Damian took the ticket from the machine, and they drove in. 'Oh yeah, I've brought a few shirts with me. You can't go in looking like that. In fact, they probably won't let you in looking like that.

'It's a Ralph Lauren top!' Tom exclaimed.

'Yeah, but too casual. Also, what size shoes are you?' Damian asked.

'10, but I've got shoes on,' Tom replied.

'Yeah, but mine are better. They are 10 and a half, so it should fit you.'

'Okay, if you say so.'

'I do so,' Damian asserted. Tom changed into Damian's white shirt and put on a smart pair of brown shoes that Damian had handed him. They were actually quite nice. Damian was right. He did look better.

'There, you scrub up well.' Damian said, looking him up and down. 'Suits you. Keep them.'

'No, it's fine. I'm not a charity case.'

'Yeah, I know. But it looks good on you. So keep them. I have plenty more.'

Tom raised his eyebrows. *Cheeky Twat!* 'Okay, thanks,' Tom mumbled.

They headed over to the car park lift and down onto the streets of Cardiff. Tom yawned as they approached the bar.

'Hey, don't flake out on me,' Damian snapped at him, 'In fact, I've got something that will wake you up.' He took out a bag of cocaine and waved it at Tom.

'What are you doing? Put that away' Tom ordered, looking around to make sure no one was watching. Tom should've known Damian would have brought drugs. The last time Tom did cocaine, Carol was pregnant. Before Carol had got pregnant with Jack, Carol and Tom liked to party a lot. But Carol had made him promise not to touch it anymore as they were starting a family. Family. She wouldn't know the meaning of the word even if it smacked her in the face.

'Nah, I'm good, bro. 'I will stick to the alcohol,' Tom said.

'Okay, buddy,' Damian replied. They walked further down the cobbled street and across to the bar. Once inside, there were a few couples and a small number of groups. It wasn't overly packed.

There was a band set up ready in the corner in front of what looked like a dance floor, but there wasn't anyone playing yet. On the left as they walked in, stood the bar, and they headed across to order their drinks.

'Can we have two Budweisers, when you have a minute?' Damian said, shouting over to the barman, who was talking to a brunette woman in her twenties at the other end of the bar.

'Also bring us a few shots of Sambuca,' added Damian and turned to face Tom. 'Let's get this party started,' Damian exclaimed.

'Is there a band on tonight?' Tom asked the barman as he poured their drinks.

'Yeah, they'll be starting in a minute,' the barman replied, 'It's student night tonight. So, we usually have a local band on. It's a group of guys from uni playing, I think.'

'Oh, brilliant,' Tom said and sat down on the stool near him. He loved a good band. A tumultuous rush of sensation started to build up inside of him. He was out at night like a proper grown-up. A touch of guilt also washed over him. Would Carol be worried? Was she wondering where he was? This was not like Tom. He was a good boy normally and always did as he was told. He never left Jack. So why did it feel like he had abandoned him?

'Here you go, bro,' Damian said, passing him a beer and an unexpected shot of Sambuca. *Yuck, Sambuca.* Tom hated that drink but needed something strong to calm his nerves, allowing him to relax more. *Fuck it.* Tom picked up the Sambuca and necked it back as fast as possible, hoping his taste buds wouldn't notice the vile-tasting thing the Italians call a drink. Tom almost gagged as it went down, but swallowed instead. He let out a huge burp, louder than he expected. It had been a while since he had done shots. His body was out of practice. Tom took a sip of his beer. But it wasn't enough to take the taste away. He drank some more. Although vile, the Sambuca did its trick. Tom's shoulders relaxed, and he was now much more at ease.

'Ah...,' Tom said, downing a big part of his beer.

Damian looked at him and laughed as he easily necked back his Sambuca. As Tom turned around, he watched more people come in. This was usually Tom's bedtime, and people had only just started to arrive. Tom was not as young as he used to be. What was he saying? He was only twenty- eight. Yet, the last four years appeared to have aged him dramatically. Having a kid will do that to you.

'Two Sex on the Beaches,' a girl called to the bartender beside Tom. Still sitting on his stool, Tom turned to face her.

'Hi,' Tom blurted out before he could stop himself. She was clearly young. Possibly a student at university. Considering it was a student's night, the bar had a mixture of ages, from youngsters in their late teens to an older crowd in their forties.

'Hey,' she smiled at him. Her lips were soft and a sweet red. They immediately drew Tom in. Wonder what it would be like to bite those succulent lips? Tom shivered at the thought. She had cute little dimples to match. The girl flashed her gorgeous velvet-black eyelashes at him. Tom's body tingled with delight. Wow, she was stunning.

'I'm Tom,' he said, giving her half a wave.

'I'm Damian,' Damian said as he leaned over Tom and held his hand for her to shake it. She giggled and shook his hand back.

'I'm J,' she said, staring intently into Tom's eyes. She was beautiful. She reminded him of someone. She had a familiar look about her. Maybe someone he had met? Or someone on TV, perhaps?

'J?' Damian said to her. 'Ummm....that's a very cool name. She giggled again, cupping her hand over her mouth.

'Thanks. This is my friend, Chloe,' J said, and she pointed to her friend. Chloe's friend half heartily waved at them before walking off with her cocktail. Not very interested in them.

'I'm going to see Dave before he plays,' Chloe said to J.

'Okay, I'll wait here,' she called to her. Chloe disappeared across the dance floor towards the band.

'Her boyfriend, Dave, is playing in the band tonight,' J informed Tom, sipping her cocktail through her straw.

Tom gazed at her pressingly, fixed on her face. She had long brunette hair with a few streaks of purple in it. Tom was digging it. Her hair also had a slight wave to it and was styled to perfection, moving effortlessly in time with her body. It slightly went in front of her, not completely showing her entire face. It gave her a look of mystery. He was instantly fascinated by her.

Was she waiting for a boyfriend, too? There was no way this girl was single. Not that anything could happen between them. Tom was still married, even if his wife was a bitch.

Tom looked at the counter, took a big gulp of beer, and glanced back up at J. She placed her hair behind her ear. He could see the full beauty of her face; it exposed her deep hazel eyes. He stared into them; her eyes looked like a part of autumn had been imprinted into them. They were incredibly intense. He had never seen eyes so big as hers before. Tom's stomach fluttered, and his heart raced. He really wanted to fuck her. Damm it! Tom sighed in frustration.

'Same again.' Tom could hear Damian behind him talking to the bartender. Oh shit. He was getting drunk tonight. Was that such a good idea? Should he leave now? Go home and make up with his wife. But his feet didn't move.

'Do you want one love?' Damian called across to J.

'Yeah, sure! Why not?' J replied, lifting her arms bashfully.

To be young. To be free. To be wild. Or, in Damian's case, to be free and wild.

He might as well ask the question. 'So, are you meeting your boyfriend here too?' Tom said, trying to sound casual.

'Oh no, I don't have a boyfriend. I just came with Chloe so she could see Dave play,' she smiled at him, taking another sip of her cocktail.

'Here you go, mate,' said Damian as he passed Tom another Sambuca. 'Here you go, beautiful.' J giggled shyly at the compliment.

J picked up the Sambuca and necked it back, slamming it down on the counter.

'Woooo!' J exclaimed. 'Thanks,' she chuckled at Damian.

Tom laughed to himself. What a girl!

Just then, the band started to play.

'Hey, want to dance?' Damian shouted as he leaned over Tom to speak to J.

'WHAT?' J shouted back, holding her hand to her ear. Damian drank up his Sambuca and slammed it back.

Then, he moved around Tom so he was face to face with J. Damian took her hand and pulled J towards him as he walked backwards onto the dance floor, where people were already starting to crowd.

Tom was green-eyed as he watched them. Surely J wasn't interested in his brother? Damian was a complete phoney! Tom snatched the shot glass from the counter and downed it. He then picked up his beer glass and held it tightly, trying not to break it. Tom watched them as they danced. This was stupid. He was married. So there was no reason to feel jealous of his recently divorced brother going off and dancing with a young, pretty girl they had just met. Why shouldn't he? Yet the irritation poured over him. He needed something more to chill himself out.

Tom walked over to Damian.

'Hey, can I have some of that stuff, bro?' he whispered into his ear.

'Yeah, sure,' Damian laughed, 'Decided to finally loosen up, huh?

'Something like that,' Tom replied. Damian took out the bag of cocaine from his pocket. Holding it low between his fingers, he discreetly passed it to Tom. Tom quickly shoved it into his pocket, ensuring no one was watching. Except, J was looking. She smiled at him. Tom put his finger over his lips as if to shush her. Tom spun around and walked towards the bathroom, leaving them to it.

Tom opened the men's toilet and found it was completely empty. Good, he thought. He walked over to one of the empty cubicles and locked the door behind himself. Tom took out his wallet and placed a card down on the toilet. He opened the cocaine bag and poured the powder carefully into a line. Taking out a £10 note from the back of his wallet, he rolled it up, bent down over the cocaine and sniffed hard. Electrifying intensity ran up his nose and straight to his head. His mind was utterly blown. *Fucking hell!* He forgot how good this stuff was.

Tom's heart tripled its beats almost instantly as if trying to escape his chest. Adrenaline was now in charge of his body. *This was good. Really good.* He wiped the rest of the coke up with his finger and licked it. He grabbed his cards and shoved them back into his wallet, along with his £10 note. He pushed the wallet and cocaine back into his pocket. He sniffed intensely to ensure it had all gone up his nose. Tom opened the cubicle and peered outside. The toilet was still empty. He pushed his shoulders back and grinned to himself before exiting the bathroom.

Tom stepped outside the toilet and bumped into someone in the process.

'Oh, sorry,' Tom said, firmly grabbing the person's shoulders and stepping back. He looked up. It was J.

'Hey,' Tom said to her, grinning.

'Hey,' J smiled back at him. She moved closer towards him. A thrill of excitement ran through him. Tom wanted to grab hold of her.

'Can I have some of that?' J smirked. Were they flirting? If they were, it was dangerous territory.

Without warning, Tom grabbed J's hand, and she flung forward with him as he pushed the toilet door back open. He took her over to the toilet cubicle and locked it behind them. Tom took out the cocaine, placing it in his hand. He passed J the note. J looked a little awkward.

'Have you done this before?' he asked her.

'Yeah, of course,' she said, lifting her chin. J placed the note over the cocaine firmly and sniffed it up. J flicked her head back up and looked at him. Tom looked into her eyes. A fierce surge of sensations consumed him.

J bit her bottom lip as she gazed back at Tom. God, those lips. Tom grabbed hold of her hips and pulled her towards him. A flutter of resistance ran through him before he kissed her intently on her lips. Tom's mouth quivered with pleasure as he continued to feel consumed by her kiss. Tom's erection grew with every kiss, and he placed his hand inside her knickers. He felt the wetness he hoped to find, and his skin tingled with gratification. Tom lifted up J's top and was pleasantly surprised by her erect, perky nipples. He blissfully stared at them for a moment, grinning at the sight of them. It had been a long time since Tom had seen breasts like these. He grabbed her hands, pushing them up over her head and delicately running his fingers down her arms. Tom leant in and moved his tongue gently across her nipples. J gave out her first moan. Tom smiled. He sucked harder, his lips locking onto her breasts.

Tom pushed her hands more intensely against the cubicle wall. He considered stopping for a moment. He didn't even have a condom. But there was no way his pumping hard-on would let him stop now. Tom pulled down his trousers and quickly pulled off her knickers as his lips moved to her neck, slowly at first, then harder. He picked her up, gripping her tightly underneath her bum, and she wrapped her legs around his body, ready to straddle him.

Tom hoped she was on the pill as he pushed his hard cock inside J. Tom gripped her smooth arse hard as he continued to jab her, repeatedly slamming her against the cubicle wall. He gently brushed her hair so that he could see the true beauty of her face. Tom wanted to see her face as he fucked her. He continued to kiss her neck hard, his breathing getting more profound. An abundance of pleasure shot through him as he continued to plunge inside her vagina, their two bodies colliding together. Tom put his hand over her mouth as she made pleasurable noises in an attempt to shush her. By God, this felt good! Tom had forgotten how good sex could feel. The excitement was in full swing inside him. He wanted all of her. No matter how hard he tried, he couldn't get enough of her. Tom's breathing became harsher. He was panting as he moved quicker and quicker. His orgasm was building, but he didn't want it to end. As Tom thrust deeper inside J, he felt her cum dripping as he was inside her.

Oh fuck. He was going to climax. Then it happened. An explosion imploded through him, giving him an oh mighty ecstasy thrill. Tom felt J tighten, and he held himself there for her to finish. Her eyes were tightly closed as she let out a scream. Liquid dripped down his limbs as he pulled out. Their gaze met, and they both giggled. Tom grabbed some tissue and passed some to J. He pulled up his trousers and watched as J pulled her knickers back up, their gaze still not broken. Tom admired her petite figure as she straightened up her dress. Tom could not believe what had just happened. He had not done anything that wild since...well, ever.

The toilet door opened, and footsteps walked over to the urinal. Tom gently placed his hand back over J's mouth. Her breathing was still deep, and he could feel her breath in the palms of his hands. The toilet door swung back open. They were alone again. Tom took his hand from her mouth. J beamed at him. She was so mesmerising. Tom kissed her passionately.

'You go first,' Tom said, stroking her soft brunette hair. 'I will follow after you.'

Tom looked at her beauty one last time before she headed out of the cubicle. Tom straightened his shirt and stepped outside the toilet after her. Tom headed back to the bar to find Damian.

A sense of thrill and excitement washed over him. Euphoria travelled throughout his body as if he were floating. The old Tom was back. He was alive.

Damian was standing at the bar.

'Hey bro, where have you been? Did you have the whole bag?'

'Here you go,' Tom laughed, discreetly slipping it back to him.

'Order some drinks, I will be back in a minute,' Damian told him.

'Yeah, sure, I am going to get wasted,' replied Tom as he leaned his back against the bar, grinning. He looked around the room to see if he could spot J.

But she was gone.

SIX

Lily

Lily walked across the school playground after dropping off Meghan at school for her second day. Lily shook her body uncontrollably as the chill ran up and down her spine. But with autumn came cooler weather, and it was assuredly cooler today. A complete turnaround from the previous day. Lily stopped and zipped up her coat to gain some warmth. Thank God she had decided to put on a coat today. Lily had nearly decided against it.

Lily shuffled through the mob of mums, chatting frantically with each other. Stay-at-home mums are on one side, working mums are on the other.

As Lily turned around the corner of the playground, she froze. She had spotted him. It was Tom. Lily had been hoping to avoid him ever since they first met. She felt awkward around him, and although Tom was cute, her heart raced every time she saw him. But the last thing Lily wanted to do was get involved with an older married man. Perhaps a wave would be okay, though.

'Hi,' Lily waved as Tom rushed past, trying to get Jack into Miss Norton's class behind her.

Tom looked up at her. He had a baseball hat on, and his eyes had dark circles and bags underneath them.

'Hey,' he mumbled. Nice to see you too, Lily thought to herself. She wished she hadn't bothered making an effort now.

Lily reached the gates of the school. Lily could smell the musty aroma surrounding her and the fruits ripening in the hedgerows beside her. A gust of wind brushed some of the remaining summer leaves from surrounding trees along the pavements, and they made their way to the ground. Lily sniffed the air. It was fresh. She breathed deeply, filled her lungs with the clean air, and exhaled. Although it was chilly, Lily did like this time of year; Halloween was coming up, and then Christmas was coming. Plus, all the TV dramas were on. There was undoubtedly something about this time of year. It had its own kind of smell, like the leaves were giving off an earthy smell, as summer departed.

'Hey Lily, wait up,' a voice shouted behind her. Lily glanced over her shoulder. Tom was briskly walking to catch up with her. Lily stopped, allowing him to catch up with her.

'Not avoiding me, are you?' Tom asked, giving her a lopsided grin.

'No, of course not,' Lily looked away, pulling her eyebrows down together. Lily was the one who had just made an effort to greet him. What planet was he living on? Lily continued to look away from him, yet she could feel his gaze on her.

He was so intense, but equally so full of charm. Throwing it in her direction. What a dick. He had a wife. It was not fair. Why were all the good-looking, nice ones taken? Those smart women must get in there first and hold onto a good thing.

But if that were true, that meant she was obviously not so bright. Or maybe Lily was just unlucky? Tom's wife clearly had the sense to snap him up when she'd had the chance. Lily could see it now. She would end up an old spinster like Miss Marple. Except Miss Marple solved murders, so that was okay, unlike Lily. Maybe that was what Lily would have to do for the rest of her life, go around with her walking stick, trying to find out who took the neighbour's cat rather than find a man to share her company with.

'So, how are things?' Lily asked Tom, pushing away the apprehensive gloom. There was no escaping Tom, so she might as well start a conversation with him. Lily didn't want to come across as too rude.

'Was that a question you asked? Did you actually start a conversation with me, moi?' Tom chuckled sarcastically.

'Shut up,' Lily hit him playfully on the arm. His pecs were harder than she expected. A shiver ran down her spine. He worked out. Lily loved a man who worked out.

'Yeah, I'm okay,' Tom grinned at her, his head leaning to one side playfully, looking directly at her. His spiky brown hair stayed tactfully in place as he did. What the hell was he doing?

Lily nodded. 'Good,' she said, leaning to one side awkwardly. She didn't really know how to be around him.

Tom looked up at Lily. His pupils were huge. 'Well, if I'm being honest, things aren't too good. Feeling a bit worse for wear this morning. Had a bit of an argument with the wife and then went out drinking with my brother,' Tom straightened back up. His tone of voice changed to sound more serious.

Yeah, Lily would definitely stay well clear of him. She didn't want to get in the middle of his marriage. The reason her dad left was that he'd had an affair with another woman. That affair had ruined Lily's and her sister's lives.

'Ah, right, I see,' Lily mumbled, nibbling on her bottom lip.

'It always gets a bit messy when I go out with him,' Tom continued. 'Probably go back to bed for a bit. Sort out my head. It's banging,' Tom rubbed his head. Lily giggled at him. Such a knob!

Lily's phone started to ring inside her jeans pocket.

'Where are you?' The voice on the other end said intensely as Lily answered.

'Mum?' Why are you ringing me? I'm on the corner. I just took Meghan to school. What's wrong?' Lily said, a little distressed. Jackie was still in bed when Lily left to take Meghan to school, not more than half an hour ago. What could have possibly happened in that timescale?

'Just come home now!' Jackie gasped.

'Okay, Mum, I'm coming. I'll be right there,' Lily clicked off the phone and slid it back into her pocket.

'I've got to go,' Lily turned to face Tom. 'I'll see you,' she said abruptly.

'Is your Mum okay?' Do you want me to come with you?' Tom asked, his eyes widening like he was concerned for her mother's well-being. He was sweet. And was making his very hard not to fancy him.

'No, it's fine, she gets like this sometimes. It's fine, honestly,' Lily was walking backwards away from him and towards her apartment.

However, the truth was, she hadn't heard her Mum in this state for a long time. Since taking her medication, Jackie had actually been quite chilled. Her Mum suffered from her nerves and quite often had panic attacks, getting really worked up. At one point, she was too afraid to leave the house. At the time, Lily felt bad about vanishing off to university and leaving her sister alone with her mum. However, since being on her Prozac, she had been so much more mellow.

Lily arrived at home. Inside, Jackie was pacing up and down on the phone in the kitchen.

'Okay, so you haven't seen her then? Okay, love, thanks. Please ring me if you hear from her...yeah...okay... okay, bye love,' Jackie clicked off the phone. She looked up at Lily. Her eyes were filled with fear, distress pouring out of them. Her face was pale as if she had seen a ghost. There was something deeply wrong. What was it?

'Mum, what is it? What's wrong?' Lily asked with a shaky voice. However, Lily wasn't sure if she wanted to know the answer. But maybe it was nothing. Her mum was known for being overdramatic in the past. However, there was something about the look on her mother's face that made Lily think there was something more serious going on.

Jackie suddenly spun around, not giving Lily her answer. 'I need a Valium. My doctor said I could take a Valium if I ever felt like I needed to,' Jackie muttered, walking over to the kitchen drawer, rattling everything inside like she was trying to wake up a sleeping giant. 'I know it is in here somewhere.'

'Mum,' Lily called. There was no answer. She continued to shuffle her hand inside the kitchen drawer.

Lily took another step forward. 'Mum!' Lily shouted. Jackie spun around, still muttering to herself. Her eyes were searching the ground, moving furiously back and forth.

Lily stepped towards her Mum and touched her on both sides of her shoulders. She studied her face.

'Mum, it's okay. Take a deep breath. What's going on?' Lily needed to try to calm her down if she was going to get an answer out of her.

'It's Jasmin, I don't know where she is. I thought she had left for school, but she hadn't slept in her bed. So

I....I.... phoned the school and....they haven't seen her. I then phoned as many of her friends as I could, but nobody has seen her. Nobody Lil. Nobody has seen her.' Her Mum's eyes were wide with fear. Her Mum took a deep breath. She had been ranting so fast that she couldn't get out her words, let alone take a breath.

Lily slowly coached her mum to the kitchen chair beside her. Jackie obliged willingly and sat down. 'What if something has happened to her, Lil?' Jackie choked. She looked like a frightened little child. So fragile. Her words were barely audible. She put her hands onto her face and started to sob, bowing her head.

Lily started stroking her mum's back to try to comfort her. 'There, there, Mum, it will be okay.'

Missing? Jasmin was Lily's younger sister. She had just turned eighteen the weekend before and was doing her second year of her A-levels. Lily didn't want her mum to panic any more than she was. 'It's okay, Mum, I'm sure she's fine. She's probably at one of her friends.' Lily reassured her.

'But what if she isn't? What if something has happened to her?' Jackie continued to sob, burying her face into Lily's shoulder. Lily wrapped her arms around her and cradled her like a baby. Jackie was sensitive. She had been through a lot over the years and was not as tough as she made out.

Jasmin had become a little rebellious lately. This had put tremendous pressure on her Mum. Lily secretly knew that her Mum was grateful for Lily and Meghan to live with them. Lily guessed her Mum thought maybe she could help with Jasmin. However, Lily and Jasmin had barely spoken since she and Meghan had moved in.

'Okay, Mum, who have you phoned?' Lily asked.

'I have phoned Tara, Rhian and Eva,' Jackie lifted her head up, sniffing.

Lily passed her a tissue from the kitchen counter. 'Here you go, Mum.' Her Mum blew her nose.

The list of names her Mum had rattled off were Jasmin's childhood friends. Who knew if she still hung around with any of them? Lily walked across the kitchen and opened her laptop, which was placed on the kitchen table.

'Okay, I will go on Facebook and send out a message that we are looking for her. I'll also go onto her Facebook page and try contacting as many of her friends as possible. There might be some that we don't know.' Lily paused for a moment. Dreading the following sentence that was about to come out of her mouth.

'I think, Mum, if we don't hear anything back from her friends in the next few hours, we need to phone the police. But hopefully, it won't come to that Mum.' Her mum continued to sob. Lily turned and went through the kitchen drawer, taking out her Mum's Valium. They were actually right in front of her. Lily took a tablet out of the packet and passed it to her Mum, along with a fresh glass of water. Jackie reached for the pill and water with a shaking hand.

'Okay, Mum, go and sit down in the living room. Try to relax. I'm sure we'll find her.'

Jackie opened her mouth, but no words came out. His eyes were now red-raw from crying. Her face painted a picture of how she was feeling. Jackie shuffled herself into the living room.

Lily opened her Facebook account. She hesitated for a moment and took a deep breath. Lily hoped that this was just one of Jasmin's rebellious stunts and that she was actually at her friend's house, hungover or in bed still from whatever she had done the previous night.

Lily started to type:

"Hey guys, have you seen my sister Jasmin Knowell (tagging in her sister's name)? We have not seen her since yesterday, and she has not turned up for school. She is not in trouble. Just her Mum and I want to check if she is okay."

Lily clicked send.

Lily moved over to Jasmin's Facebook and started to scroll down through her friends list. Lily was terrible. She didn't know who any of her sister's friends were. Lily hadn't had much involvement in her sister's life. She had been too wrapped up in her own life. Lily decided that she would contact anyone who had liked or commented on any of her posts recently.

Lily went back to her post, clicked copy and pasted it into Messenger, sending it to as many people as possible. Lily got up and clicked on the kettle. A good cuppa is what she needed. Would Mum want one? Lily popped her head into the living room, but Jackie was fast asleep on the sofa. Lily smiled. At least now she was more relaxed. She walked over to her Mum and placed a blanket over her that was hanging on the back of the sofa.

Lily had just started pouring the tea when her phone began to ping frantically.

'Not seen her' 'Not seen her.'

Lots of messages began to come through from Jasmin's Facebook contacts. Lily sighed. Surely someone had heard from her. Lily sat back down at her laptop. A message pinged up.

'What is your number, Lily?'

It was a message from a girl called Chloe. Lily raised her eyebrows. Could this possibly be who she was with last night? Lily typed in her number. Within minutes, her phone was ringing.

'Hello,' Lily answered.

'Hello, is that Lily?' The girl on the line asked.

'Yes, is this Chloe? Do you know where my sister is?'

'No, sorry, Lily. But I was with her last night. We were out at a bar, but she left without me. I went home with my boyfriend then.'

'Did you not try ringing her when you saw she was gone?' Lily fumed.

'No, sorry, I just assumed she was plastered and had gone home. I'm really sorry, Lily. She's my best friend. I hope she's okay...Look, I've got to go; I need to get to class. Please keep me updated, and I'll ask in school if anyone's seen her. Maybe she went back to Dan's house to sleep.'

'Who's Dan?' Lily had not heard of any Dan in Jasmin's conversations.

'Dan's a boy in our year. He's her ex.'

'Her ex?' Lily asked, puzzled.

'Yeah, they dated for a few months, but Jasmin recently split up with him,' Chloe stated.

'Dan, Dan,' Lily mumbled as she scrolled through Jasmin's Facebook contacts. She had seen that name somewhere. 'Daniel Ford?'

'Yes, that's him. Look, I've got to go. I'll give you a ring later,' Chloe clicked off the phone. Well, she didn't seem too concerned that Jasmin was missing. Either that or Chloe was hiding something. Well, she was the one who rang Lily, so maybe not.

Lily typed into her computer.

'Dan, this is Jasmin's sister, Lily. Can you give me a ring on 07789406793? I'm looking for Jasmin. I just want to check she is okay. Thanks.'

Lily waited.

SEVEN

Lily

It was evening, and no one had heard from Jasmin. Lily and her Mum were both sitting on the edge of the sofa. She was definitely missing. There was no question about it. Jasmin was nowhere to be seen by anyone. Dan had not replied to Lily either. She had received a few more messages as the day went on, but they had all replied, saying they had not seen or heard from her.

'Don't worry, mum, she will turn up. She has to,' Lily turned to her mum. However, Lily wasn't sure who she was trying to comfort more. Herself or her mum. Something was seriously wrong. Lily could feel it in her bones. Her Mum's hand was shaking. Her anxiety was getting too much for her to bear.

A muscle in Lily's jaw twitched. She needed to say something. 'Do you want another Valium, Mum?'

'No, it's okay. I want to be with it for when the police come,' Jackie stated. She was sitting up straight, hands clasped together, waiting patiently for the arrival of the police.

'Nanny, what are we having for tea?' Meghan ran into the room. Lily's tummy rumbled, and she just realised she had barely eaten anything all day. Lily had forgotten all about dinner, and so had Jackie by the look of her.

'Pizza?' Lily asked, scuffing Meghan's head playfully.

'Oh yes, I love Pizza,' Meghan's eyes lit up.

'Okay, let's have pizza,' Lily stood up and took her daughter's hand, leading her into the kitchen. Lily removed the pizza from the freezer and shoved it in the oven.

'Why's Nanny crying?' Meghan looked up at Lily, concern exuding from her face.

'Well, she's just a bit upset about something, darling. But she's okay. Don't you worry,' Lily said, trying to reassure her daughter.

'What's she upset about? Maybe Bunny can help,' Meghan's eyes widened, focusing hard on Lily. She was deadly serious. This made Lily smile. Bunny always made Meghan feel better, so naturally, she assumed that Bunny would make Nanny feel better. That was so sweet.

'We just can't find Auntie Jasmin,' Lily said gently.

'What, you have lost her? How did you and Nanny lose her?' Meghan asked.

Lily wasn't really sure how to respond. She didn't want to say too much if she upset Meghan.

'Like I said, darling, don't worry, she's probably okay. She should be home soon. But some policemen will come to the house and help us find her, as the more people looking for Auntie Jasmin, the better.' Saying the words out loud suddenly made the realisation of Jasmin's disappearance a reality.

Lily's eyes filled up, and tears poured down her face. Her body went limp as if she had just been hit by a ton of bricks. Where the hell was she? It was Tuesday evening, and she had not been seen since last night. Lily looked out the kitchen window. The trees behind the back garden were blowing from side to side, and Lily was suddenly aware of the howling wind. Gosh, it must be freezing out there. The temperature dropped with each passing minute as it grew further into nightfall.

'Oh, where are you, Jas? Please, be okay, little sister. Please let her be okay,' Lily pleaded out loud to herself, suddenly aware she was praying to God. Not that she went to church or was even religious, for that matter. But if the big guy did exist, now would be the time to ask for his help.

Lily wiped away her tears using the back of her hand.

'Mummy, don't cry.' Meghan's eyes were distressed as they gazed into Lily's. Poor girl. She was only four. Meghan had no idea what was going on. Lily bent down and hugged Meghan. It was the only thing she could think of to comfort each other at a time like this. There was nothing like a child's hug to bring amenity to your soul.

Lily stood up. Her tummy rumbled again, and the waft of pizza from the oven set off her empty stomach. She was starving.

Suddenly, the doorbell rang. Lily jumped, even though she had been expecting it. Her Mum's footsteps paced to the door, and it creaked open. Lily peeked out from the kitchen. One male and one female police officer walked into their house. They were not wearing a uniform. Lily assumed they were detectives based on what she remembered from her crime dramas. Lily trembled at the sight of them. Blue lights flickered from outside the doorway. Wow, this was real. This was serious. Where the hell was her sister?

Another male police officer walked in after them, except he was wearing a uniform. Lily walked into the hall, leaving Meghan doing her colouring at the kitchen table. Lily stood back against the wall, letting them pass. The police officers followed Jackie into the living room. Lily's heart started to race. They had never had police in their house before. This was a first. It was so surreal to have police standing in their home. This was not like watching Sherlock. This was real. Lily tightly clasped her hands together and took a deep breath before following the officers into her living room.

'Would you like a cup of tea?' Lily mumbled. She expected her voice to be louder than it actually came out. Lily coughed in an attempt to clear her throat.

'No, we're fine, thank you. Let us start by introducing ourselves. I'm Detective Inspector Carter, and this is my colleague Detective Sergeant Millard.' DI Carter spoke calmly and professionally. 'We'll just get right to it and start taking details from you. The sooner we find Jasmin, the better,' DI Carter reassured. He was pretty young to be a detective and was quite good-looking. He had slick black hair but appeared to have overdone it with the gel. All the same, it looked good and showed off his perfect bone structure. Lily stared at him. Where did she know him from?

'Jasmin is eighteen, correct?' DI Carter said.

'Yes,' her Mum nodded. She started to sob putting her hands in her face.

'It's ok,' he said gently, putting his hand on her shoulder.

'We will start looking for her straight away,' DS Millard interjected. 'As soon as we take a statement from you, Mrs Knowell.....'

'It's Ms,' Jackie interrupted.

Sorry, I do apologise. Ms Knowell. Then the sooner we can start looking for your daughter,' DS Millard continued.

'My husband left me years ago,' Jackie looked down, scrunching up her tissue in the palm of her hand. The tissue had become completely ragged from overuse. Yet Jackie continued to use the tissue and placed it up to her eyes in a bid to try and dry them.

It was now starting to bug Lily. Where did Lily know DI Carter from?

'I know this must be a difficult time, but the more you can remember, the better, Ms Knowell,' DI Carter shifted his body posture to face Jackie. 'When was the last time you saw Jasmin?'

'Yesterday afternoon. Jasmin was going out with friends,' Jackie answered him through her bawling.

'And do you know what friends?' He spoke calmly.

'It was a girl called Chloe. I spoke with her earlier today. She said that they went to a bar together last night,' Lily interrupted.

'A bar!' Jackie bellowed. 'What the hell was she doing at a bar?!'

'Mum, please, calm down. Meghan is just in there,' Lily pointed towards the door. 'I don't know why Jasmin was there. But apparently, she was.' Shit, the pizza was still in the oven. 'Excuse me a minute, I am cooking my daughter's tea.'

Nobody responded, and Lily gladly left the living room for a moment. The tension could be cut with a knife in there. Lily dashed into the kitchen, closely followed by Meghan. As Lily took out the pizza, Meghan gripped hold of her leg like it was some sort of security blanket.

'I'm scared, Mummy,' Meghan cried. 'I don't like these people here. They're scary.'

They were a bit intimidating, especially the uniformed police officer they had with them. With his luminous coat, baton, handcuffs, and whatever else he seemed to have attached to him. In addition, his radio kept going off every few minutes. This was nerve-racking for Lily, never mind how it might sound to a four-year-old child.

Lily tightly gripped the palms of her hands before kneeling down to Meghan's height. Meghan threw her arms around Lily, holding her tightly.

'It's okay, honey. The police officers are just here to ask us some questions about Auntie Jasmin so they can help us find her. Remember? Because we want to find her, don't we?' Lily nodded as she spoke softly. Meghan nodded in agreement with Lily.

Lily got up from the floor, and as she spun around to put Meghan's pizza on the table, she noticed DS Millard was leaning by the door, watching them. Lily jumped, almost dropping the pizza on the floor. Geez! She nearly gave Lily a heart attack. What the hell was she doing sneaking up on people?

'Sorry, I didn't mean to startle you. I just didn't want to interrupt.' DS Millard said. 'They grow up so fast. Mine are teenagers now. Two girls. One fourteen and one sixteen.' DS Millard walked closer to Lily and touched her arm gently. 'Mark my word, we'll do everything possible to find your sister.' DI Carter said sternly, looking directly at Lily's gaze.

'Thank you,' Lily uttered. 'I hope so.'

'So, when was the last time you saw Jasmin?' DS Millard asked Lily.

'Same time as Mum. Yesterday afternoon. Mum, Meghan and I were here when she left to go over to her friend's house.' Lily avoided eye contact.

'And can you think of any other new friends she might be staying with or boyfriends?'

'Honestly, I'm not the best person to ask about that. Meghan and I have only just moved back home, and to be honest, we haven't really been that close. There are four years between us, but I have spent most of the day trying to find out who she might have been with from her Facebook account.' Lily cut the pizza into slices and passed it to Meghan, who was now sitting at the kitchen table.

'Good. Facebook is a great place to start and can give us a lot of clues as to where she might be. So, tell me more about this conversation with her friend Chloe,' DS Millard asked, her tone soft, as if she was trying to sound comforting.

Lily looked down at the rest of the pizza. She was dying to pick up a slice but didn't want to appear rude as she was clearly being interrogated with questions. Well, she had nothing to do with her sister's disappearance. So why was DS Millard still staring at her?

'When I spoke to her friend Chloe, she said they had gone to a bar together last night. Chloe said they normally left together when going home, but Jasmin had disappeared without her that night. Chloe said she assumed Jasmin had too much to drink and had gone home alone. Chloe went back to her boyfriends. Chloe also said Jasmin had just broken up with her boyfriend, Dan. I've never heard of him personally, but I did manage to find him on Facebook and have messaged him. However, he hasn't responded yet.'

'Okay, thanks. We will get our team to hack into Jasmin's account so we can see her messages. Maybe there is something there. Also, can we have Chloe's telephone number so we can speak to her?'

'Yeah, sure, of course,' Lily nodded, she now had a mouth full of pizza. She couldn't resist anymore.

Lily walked into the living room behind DS Millard. She didn't want to leave her Mum alone any longer. Her Mum was not coping well with the situation as it was, without all the probing questions on top. Jackie was walking down the stairs with Jasmin's toothbrush. Was it for a DNA sample? It must be. This was so surreal. It was as if she were in a dream, and Lily would wake up any minute.

'I don't have any recent photographs of her,' Jackie whimpered as she fished through all her cabinets.

'She has some recent photos on her Facebook account. You have her details,' Lily piped up, trying to be helpful.

'Okay, yes, we will use one of those. If you can think of anything else, even if it's something trivial, please let us know, as it could help more than you think. Here's my card,' DI Carter looked fixedly at Lily. 'Oh, and I think it goes without saying, but I will say it anyway. If you hear from Jasmin, please contact us immediately.'

Well, duh, Lily thought to herself.

'Of course, we will,' Lily returned his stare and took the card. Lily walked into the hall and opened the front door for them. Lily yawned and rubbed her eyes. She was exhausted. Lily knew they were here to help, but the police had, without fail, taken it out of her. Well, the whole situation had, if Lily was being honest with herself.

As the door slammed shut, Lily and her Mum immediately collapsed in each other's arms. It had been brutally painful as well as exhausting. Where the hell was her baby sister? Was she okay? These were all questions Lily would soon find answers to.

EIGHT

Katherine

It was Wednesday, and Katherine was still reeling over what she had done at the gym on Monday. Where had that anger come from? Katherine just hadn't been able to control herself. What was wrong with her? Standing in the playground at the school, Katherine watched her girls run about as they waited for the bell. The wind was smacking Katherine across her face as she stood.

What had she been thinking when she'd dropped those weights on that girl's foot at the gym? This is a question Katherine had repeatedly asked herself over the past two days. She had told Susan and the staff at the gym that it was entirely accidental. Telling them she had just overdone it on the treadmill. Then, when picking up the weights, Katherine simply became dizzy, forcing her to drop the weights accidentally, which then unexpectedly landed on the girl's foot.

'She was standing too close to me,' Katherine had interjected to the gym manager. There had been some truth in this. The girl had been standing over Katherine as she lifted weights, mocking her. What did she expect? She had provoked Katherine. However, dropping the weights had been no accident. Katherine had been certain of that. But did she care? Katherine wasn't sure. One thing Katherine was certain of was that she had a pressing weight of guilt lying on her chest. So maybe she did. But that bitch deserved it.

Katherine pushed her guilty conscience and its thoughts to the back of her mind. She had more scrumptious things to think about. A guy. A cute guy named Tom.

Katherine more or less had everything a person could wish for. Perfect friends. Perfect Husband. Perfect House. Perfect Life. Yet she consistently felt like she was drowning. Like she was trying to scramble to the surface for air, but never quite getting there. Something was missing, a hole deep inside her soul, crying out for it to be filled. But whatever she did, nothing ever filled it. Until now.

There was just something about him that gave Katherine hope. And after meeting him Monday afternoon, he was all Katherine could think about. Katherine had kept an eye out for him ever since they had met. However, she'd unfortunately not managed to bump into him again. She had been out of the game for a long time, and she wasn't sure if Tom had been flirting with her when they met. Nevertheless, Katherine had been on the prowl for him ever since. So, what if she was married? A girl can still fantasise. Right?

The stomp of stilettos were making their way across the playground. Katherine looked up. But she knew that sound anywhere. It was Alison. Strutting her sparkly pink heels as she made her way towards Katherine. Alison's long, beautiful crimson hair swayed elegantly as she wore her Louis Vuitton sunglasses. The sun wasn't even out, the sky was full of clouds, and if anything, there was a chill in the air. But Alison was the epitome of glamour among all the girls. And style was what she did best, no matter the weather. She still dressed like she was living in Hollywood.

'Hey, did you hear about that girl going missing?' Alison declared.

'Oh no, what girl?' Katherine responded.

'Yeah, some local girl has gone missing. Hang on.' Alison scrambled into her short black leather jacket.

She pulled out a folded piece of paper. IT READ: "MISSING JASMIN KNOWELL". That was the surname of that Lily, the one who was friends with Tom. Katherine had looked her up from the school database. The girl in the picture was young. Who was she? Maybe her sister?

'Hey Kath,' Susan walked over to Katherine and Alison. Katherine looked down at the ground, hoping it would swallow her up. She wasn't quite ready to see Susan so soon. She felt her face burn up with embarrassment as Susan got closer.

'Hey Susan,' Katherine looked up at her, giving her the fakest smile she could portray.

'You coming to the gym this morning?' Susan said to her. It seemed Susan was ignoring the incident that had happened two days ago. Katherine relaxed her shoulders. Thank God. But there was no way she was going back there. The gym wasn't for her.

'Ummm.....I think I am going to give it a miss,' Katherine was not ready to go back. Not yet, anyway. 'Maybe tomorrow or Friday,' she gnawed her nails nervously.

'Isn't Friday our coffee morning for Macmillan?' Susan asked Katherine.

'Oh yes, sure. Yeah, that's still on. I'll put on some nibbles for us, and we can all have a catch-up. It'll be nice,' Katherine tried to sound convincing to her friend. The truth was, she was not really in the mood to be her usual fake self.

'Okay, great,' Susan replied. 'We really need to discuss the Halloween party and also sort out the fundraising for the Macmillan coffee morning. We also need to be at the school tomorrow to discuss the details of the fair.'

'Yeah, yeah,' Katherine rolled her eyes.

'Are you not taking this seriously, Katherine?' Susan's hand was placed sternly on her hip.

'Oh God, Susan, stop behaving like a two-year-old,' Katherine spat back at her.

'Katherine, this is serious stuff. Is it not enough that you humiliated me at my gym?' Susan cried. But Katherine was the queen at pulling fake tears.

'Oh please, get over yourself. That girl bloody well deserved it!' Things were starting to get heated, and Katherine could feel her heart rate rising.

Susan gasped. Clasping her hand over her mouth. 'I knew it was no accident! I was only trying to do a favour for Bruce.'

'James, you mean,' Katherine sassed. Alison snorted, who was standing beside her. 'Look, I can sort out the Macmillan coffee for the morning. After all, it's for my dead mother. I think I can manage,' Katherine gave her a dirty look.

'Your mother would be ashamed of you,' Susan said, narrowing her eyes at Katherine.

But that was it. That was the last straw Katherine could take. It was too late. The water had boiled inside her body, and rage was thoroughly in control. Katherine simply couldn't stop herself as she charged towards her. She grabbed Susan's perfectly placed jet-black hair and yanked it down as hard as she could.

Katherine's emotions were categorically pouring their way out of her and relaying themselves onto this stupid, stuck-up cow. She was always putting her down. Flirting with her husband, acting like they were best mates. How dare she?

Susan screamed out, 'Get off me, you crazy cow!' But Katherine couldn't.

'Go on, girl,' Alison cheered.

Susan suddenly gripped hold of Katherine's long blonde hair, and that was it. They were both stuck, gripped together.

'Let go!' Susan screamed.

'You let go!' Katherine yelled. She could see the crowd out of the corner of her eye.

Sophie was looking up at her. Shit. This was silly. Katherine let go. But suddenly, a fist came flying her way, and Katherine was knocked back on the floor. Sly bitch! Susan sat on top of her.

Suddenly, someone was pulling Susan off her. Katherine peered up from the ground. A man was looking down at her. She put her hands up as the sun blinded her from seeing who it was. Although it was windy, the sun shone brightly. Katherine squinted. It was Tom. Her saviour. He reached out his hand to pull her up. Katherine gladly accepted as she rose to her feet with the help of Tom's rugged, strong arms. She was staring face to face with him. Butterflies immediately started to do star jumps in her stomach. He was so bloody gorgeous. Play it cool. Play it cool, Katherine, she told herself.

'Hey,' Tom said, giving her a lopsided grin.

Katherine fluttered her eyelashes in response. 'Hey,' Katherine responded. But then quickly realised she must look a fool, and she felt the blood pouring down her mouth.

'Oh, you're bleeding,' Tom's eyebrows suddenly raised in astonishment.

'It's okay. I only live down the road on Forest Lane,' Katherine said. 'It's just the girls. They need to get to class.'

'I'll take them,' Alison piped up, raising her hand.

Ellie tutted. 'Oh, Mum, you're such an embarrassment. I'll make my own way to class.' Ellie turned to her friends and sniggered. God, what a spoilt little bitch! She was only nine but had the attitude of a teenager. She was still Katherine's little girl, and she wasn't ready for her to grow up yet.

'Okay then, I'll just take Sophie,' Alison raised her eyebrows.

'Can I go with Sophie?' Jack asked, tugging on Tom's shirt.

Alison muffled Jack's hair. 'Of course you can, buddy. Come on, you two,' Alison said, putting her arm around Jack.

'Bye, Darling. Have a nice day,' Katherine called Sophie.

'Bye, Mum,' Sophie called back as she held Alison's hand.

Susan was nowhere to be seen. Katherine was so fed up of tolerating her for James's sake. In fact, Susan bored Katherine to death. She would have a better time watching paint dry than listening to her boring conversations.

The head teacher, Mr Turner, was making his way towards them. He was swaying his arms from side to side vigorously. Shit.

'What do you think you're playing at, Katherine!' He shouted. 'Both you and Susan are meant to be setting a good example, seeing as though you are both on the committee!' Mr Turner was a short man and nearly half the size of Katherine. But he was an awfully cross, small man.

'Sorry, Mr Turner,' Katherine pursed her lips together, trying hard to hold back her smirk. 'It won't happen again.'

'It better not!' Mr Turner waved his finger at her, and he stormed back inside.

'Do you always cause this much trouble?' Tom marvelled.

'Umm, no, not really. I'm usually such a good girl,' Katherine sniggered.

'Come on, I'll come back to yours with you. You're getting blood all over the poor children's playground,' Tom joked. 'Plus, I'm heading that way too, I live in Forest Lane as well, neighbour.' He smirked.

Katherine snorted in response as they both headed towards the gate. Almost everyone had left the school grounds now.

'Here,' Tom pulled a pack of tissues from his pocket.

'Handy thing to have on you,' Katherine said.

'Oh, I never go anywhere without my tissues. Never know when you're gonna need them,' Tom responded, grinning.

Katherine took one from him and continued to walk down Forest Lane towards her house. She looked down at the floor. She instinctively became distracted by his scent. Tom's aftershave was pouring out of him. Wow, that smells good. Katherine immediately wanted to be closer to him, touch him even. She resisted.

'Okay, this is me,' Katherine jiggled her house keys in her hand as they approached her house. She walked up the path towards her front door and turned the key in the lock. Tom followed behind her like a puppy following its master. She secretly liked it.

'Nice house,' Tom said to her, looking around the room. 'Is anyone else at home?'

'No, my husband is at work, ' Katherine replied, leaning on the kitchen counter. She bit her fingernails. But quickly realised what she was doing and shoved them behind her back in a bid to try and stop herself. Katherine couldn't quite believe her luck in finding Tom in her house.

'I'll put the kettle on,' Katherine didn't wait for an answer and just marched straight into the kitchen, filling up the kettle at the tap before clicking it on, assuming he would follow behind.

'Hang on a minute, crazy. Do you have a cloth and some ice so we can put it over that cut of yours?' Tom interjected.

'Oh yes, of course. Silly me,' Katherine had forgotten all about her dripping gash coming from her chin.

Tom walked over to her freezer and took out her tray of ice cubes. Katherine opened her kitchen drawer and reached for a clean towel.

Tom held out his hand, beckoning her to pass it to him. 'Here, let me.'

Katherine passed her tea towel to him. Her body tingled, and she felt like she was in a dream. Pinching her arm was the only thing she could do to make her realise it wasn't.

'Sit down,' Tom ordered.

Katherine did as she was told. He leant up towards her and placed the ice on her chin.

'Ouch!' Katherine flinched as he placed the ice on her wound. Her pulse was racing. Why was she so nervous? This was ridiculous. But was there something in the air? Something between them? Katherine shook the thought out of her mind. Don't be so absurd. After all, he had just caught her having a full-on girl-on-girl fight on the school grounds. Why the hell would he be interested in her? Especially one as hot as him. Surely not. Tom's just being friendly.

'Hold still. The ice will help the swelling. We don't want to ruin that beautiful face of yours, do we?' Tom gave her a captivating look. Or was he?

'I know it's early, but do you want something a bit stronger instead?' Katherine suggested to him. 'God knows I could do with one after my antics. There's vodka in that cupboard,' Katherine said, pointing her finger to show him.

'You're crazy, you know that?' Tom laughed.

He wasn't wrong. Katherine was undoubtedly far from normal.

'Why not?' Tom smiled at Katherine, making her stomach flip out with excitement. 'It's five o'clock somewhere, right? Plus, I could do with cheering up, and vodka would do the trick quite nicely.'

'Why, what's up?' Katherine looked at him with concern. Tom put the ice on the counter, moved to the cupboard, and pulled out the vodka.

'My marriage. That's what's up,' he replied, picking up two glasses from the draining board. He sat down on the bar stool at the kitchen counter opposite Katherine. Tom poured them both a glass, passed her a drink, and then necked his back.

'That bad, huh?' Katherine chuckled slightly as she watched him. But laughing made her chin hurt. 'Ouch!' she cried out, touching her chin.

'Here, put this back on,' Tom said, ignoring Katherine's comment.

'I know we don't know each other well, but do you want to talk about it?' Katherine pried. Maybe this was a bit forward. But hey, screw it.

'Not really,' Tom replied. He stared down at his drink as he swirled it around. 'Well.....it's just not the same as it used to be,' Tom paused. 'Actually, you don't really want to hear about this. I came here to comfort you in your hour of need, not the other way round.'

'No, it's okay,' Katherine poured another drink for them. She really did want to know about it. She loved a bit of gossip, and hearing about it first-hand was her favourite kind.

'The truth is, I haven't spoken to my wife for three nights after I stormed out of the house and went for a drink with my brother. But when I woke up the next morning, she was gone, with a note saying she had gone to stay with a friend for a couple of nights. She said she needed time to think.' Tom used the pause in conversation to swig back some of his vodka. 'I mean....what did she have time to think about?' Tom raised his voice slightly and slammed the glass back down on the counter.

Katherine jumped back. *Wow*! And she thought she had problems. Katherine put her arms around him. 'I mean, I am the only one left trying to hold the house together and look after our son while she swans off, doing God knows what,' Tom continued angrily.

'No, you're completely right,' she agreed. 'God, I'd kill to have a husband like you.'

'Sorry, I shouldn't be talking about this with you,' Tom said, taking a deep breath. 'Such a mood killer. Tell me about yourself. You have an older girl, too, right?' Tom tried to sound more enthusiastic. Katherine dropped her arm. It was getting a bit awkward, hanging it around his arm.

'Yeah, Ellie. She's Nine. Then Sophie, who has just turned four and is in Jack's class.'

'So, what do you do for work?' he downed the rest of his drink before looking back up at her.

'Nothing, stay at home mum.'

'Snap,' Tom raised his glass to her. She giggled and met her glass with his, even though Tom's was now empty.

'Well, stay at home dad, obviously,' Tom gave Katherine a lopsided smile.

'I was a solicitor, but I gave up work about ten years ago,' Katherine revealed. She glanced up at the ceiling. This was not something Katherine liked to really talk about. Being as it was one of her biggest regrets.

'Oh really?' Tom sounded intrigued. 'Do you ever think about going back?'

'Yeah, maybe. Now that Sophie is in school full-time. I would like to,' Katherine enthused.

'And fun. What do you do for fun?' Tom asked.

'Well, I don't do much for fun. We have dinner parties and that sort of stuff. But it's mostly James's friends who end up coming over. James, that's my husband,' she paused to introduce him. 'I usually meet up with the other mums from the school to organise PTA stuff.' Katherine avoided his intense eye contact by looking into her glass. 'I have also just started going to the gym. Can you call that fun?' Katherine half chuckled to herself.

'Why does a good-looking woman like you, with a slim figure, need to get into shape? You are a great size. You don't need to lose weight. Anyway, going to the gym isn't classed as fun.' Tom spun to the side, facing Katherine directly. She couldn't see it, but she knew her cheeks were now a flaming red.

She looked up, matching his gaze. She bit her bottom lip awkwardly. Tom's scorching green eyes burned their way into hers, not removing his focus on her for even a second. Katherine stared back. She could get lost in them for an eternity. Tom's intensity kicked-started Katherine's heart rate once more as if it had been shocked by a defibrillator.

She smiled coyly as she looked back at him, their faces just inches away from each other. A sudden uncontrollable outburst of feeling absorbed her. Her knees touched his. His aftershave overpowering her. Katherine was entranced by him. Her body relaxed, and she imagined him and her as the only people in the world. Tom swigged the rest of his drink, returning his gaze to hers, smirking as if he had a secret he didn't want to share. His breath was so close to hers that she could smell the vodka. Tom had a hot, intangible charm she was failing miserably to resist.

As their eyes locked, a rage of electrifying tension shot up Katherine's spine. Her pulse was racing, and her breathing changed from its normal rhythm to panting. Did he feel the same? Her mouth filled up with elevated saliva. Katherine swallowed. She knew what was about to happen next.

Katherine slowly put down her glass on the counter beside her, not taking her eyes off his gaze. She wanted to touch him, caress him, and have all of him—and more. His scent seduced her, pulling her forward. Katherine leaned in towards him. She hoped she had got this right.

She had. Katherine brushed his soft, smouldering lips with hers. He tasted so sweet. So edible. They locked lips and started to kiss. Soft at first. There was a sense of doubt rattling around her mind. Should she be doing this? Absolutely not! Katherine had not cheated on her husband before. Even when James thought she was, which he had done on many occasions, she had never touched another man until now. The faint scent from his aftershave lured out of him. She could smell the sex and desire oozing its way towards her, which only drew Katherine in further and no matter how hard she tried to stop, it was too late. His touch was too good for her to stop. This was going to happen whether she liked it or not.

Tom stopped briefly for a moment. He gazed closely at her, clutching her face with his hand. Suddenly, Tom let go of her face and stood up abruptly, lifting Katherine up by her hips and landing her on the kitchen counter beneath her. As Tom pushed up against her, she could feel his penis harden beneath his trousers. Katherine slowly brushed her hand over it. Her mouth curled upwards. It was big.

Tom stroked Katherine's silky blonde hair as he started to kiss her again, this time harder. Katherine could feel her juices flowing already as he gripped the back of her head firmly, kissing her dominantly. Tom stopped once again, leaving Katherine craving more.

Tom ran his fingers over her hair and leaned in towards her face. 'Do you want this?' Tom whispered in Katherine's ear.

Katherine's breathing was heavy as she gasped for breath in between their passion for tonsil tennis. Tom pushed his lips onto hers. Hard. Katherine leant back slightly, her sweaty hands firmly placed on the kitchen counter behind her, letting him consume her. There was certainly no way she was stopping this. Not for anything.

'Yes,' Katherine replied, her voice hoarse. 'I really do.
'

Tom ran his hand slowly up her leg towards her thigh, and Katherine quivered. 'How badly?'

A tingling sensation ran up her leg and into her vagina. Tom unbuttoned Katherine's top button of her jeans before tugging at her knickers. He slipped his hand inside them, and it was met with her vagina. He stroked his hand over her and softly ran his finger inside her. Tom faintly started to massage Katherine's clit with his thumb as if he was barely touching it. Yet surprisingly, hitting just the right spot. Katherine couldn't remember the last time a man touched her there, but it was so good. Too good. From that one touch, her body was now a slave to him. He had her full attention.

'Fucking badly,' Katherine whispered, tossing her head back. She closed her eyes and let out a joyful pleasure. Suddenly, Tom took out his thumb from her knickers. What! No! Come back!

Tom stopped kissing her for a moment and slowly started to pull down her jeans. Katherine lifted up her bum slightly, helping him to whip them off. He tossed them on the floor. Her breathing was heavy, desire in full swing. Tom grabbed hold of her knickers, shoving his fingers deep inside her vagina, pumping them vigorously this time. Back and forth. Back and forth. She was wet. Very wet.

'Oh wow,' Katherine cried out. Tom grabbed hold of her back, pulling her closer to him. Kissing her hard. Katherine gasped as she tried to get in short breaths in between kisses. *Wow*! He was really picking up the pace here. Tom slipped his other hand up her top. Then suddenly, it seemed like he ran out of patience as he ripped open her shirt. Katherine's buttons bounced about the place across the kitchen floor. Tom placed his hand around Katherine's back, and her bra was unhooked in no time. He tossed it to the side. Then took a moment to stare at her breasts, and still rubbing her clit with his one hand, he dove his face straight into them. Tom kissed her nipples and then started to suck on them slowly. It was that good. She almost came but managed to resist just in time. Katherine decided to focus on him. She sat forward. Tom took his hand out, away from her vagina. Katherine tugged at his jeans until she managed to pull them down. His hard throbbing penis was on show beneath his boxers, waiting to be met by her hot dripping vagina. Katherine yanked his boxers down and grabbed hold of his penis. His wide girth was even more enormous than she expected. Katherine smirked. She had not had the pleasure of dealing with a penis of this size before. Katherine tightened her fingers around his cock and started to stroke it up and down. Tom arched his back and moved his pelvis to the rhythm. But all of a sudden, Tom pushed her hands away from him. Had she done something wrong?

Tom leaned into her face once more. 'I'm going to have you begging me to cum,' Tom whispered as he sucked on her earlobe. Katherine had no idea he would be capable of this. Suddenly, it dawned on her that she may have been waiting for this sex her whole life.

Tom spread Katherine's legs wide apart. He teased his fingers up her legs. Katherine shuddered as the wetness from her vagina was now dripping firmly out of her and onto the end of the counter beneath her. Her body ached for him.

Tom reached her pussy lips once more and parted them skilfully like a pro, two fingers entering inside her as he thrusted. She was so wet for him. Teasing her, she was close to erupting. Not enough to send her to an orgasm, but enough to send her wild. She just wanted more.

Finally, Tom gave her what she wanted, and he ploughed his cock deep inside her, then he pulled it out just to ram it back inside her, harder each time. Tom kissed her firmly. Impatiently. Urgently. Like he wanted her as much as Katherine wanted him. She dug her false nails into his bum cheeks hard, forcing him deeper inside her. Katherine screamed out. This was nothing like she had ever experienced before. Small orgasms exploded inside her, cum running down her leg as he continued to penetrate her hard.

Tom stopped, pulling out his cock. Katherine gasped. Her pussy pulsating.

'What do you want, Katherine?' Tom spoke so confidently. He was driving her crazy. Katherine gripped her hair firmly as if trying to rip large chunks out of it.

'I want to cum,' she mumbled.

'I can't hear you, Katherine.'

Tom thrusted his cock back inside her.

'I want to cum,' she screamed as he penetrated her vigorously. Wow, this guy really knew his way around a biology class. Katherine picked up her bum, moving her hips in sync with his movements. Then Tom picked up the pace, going faster and faster. She became powerless, and all she could succumb to was the pleasurable pounding she was receiving. She moaned loudly.

Katherine felt Tom's cock spasm as cum exploded into her insides, quivering streams of cum filling inside her pussy. Euphoria shivered down her spine. Immense wetness dripped further down her legs. Katherine's thighs wrapped tightly around his waist, her toes curled as she let go of so much built-up tension. The orgasm set her free. Tom smirked, knowing what he had just done to her. Pleased with this performance.

Collapsing back onto the counter, she sighed an enormous sigh of contentment. That was the best sex she had ever had. Tom was her new drug. And she wanted more.

NINE

Tom

Tom zipped up his chinos and buttoned up his shirt. He gazed down at Katherine. What they did was so wrong, but it was totally what he needed. Tom rubbed his nose. The cocaine was irritating it. He could do with another line right about now. Tom sniffed hard to see if it gave him a bonus buzz. Nothing. After passing out on the sofa the previous night, he had been woken up by Jack tugging at him that morning. His head had been banging. But as he began to wake up, the pounding of his head increased. He wasn't sure if he would be able to do the school run with Jack. His mouth had tasted like copper, as if he had been sucking on a dozen pennies.

As Tom dragged himself to a sitting position that morning, the living room looked like the aftermath of one hard-core session. He'd had the urge to vomit and had been in one hell of a state to take Jack to school. But he had to. No one else would.

But after reaching into his pocket, he had been pleasantly surprised to find the last of his cocaine. Tom had decided to use the last of his stash to get himself going that morning. Little did he know that he would also end up banging one of the mums on the way home from school like a god damn stud. What the fuck had he been thinking? Now that the effects of the cocaine had clearly worn off, the realisation of what he had done was dawning on him. He could do with more to stop reality from setting in.

Katherine was still naked when she sat up on the kitchen counter. She leaned over and grabbed an apple.

Before biting into it, she said, 'I'm not sure if it's true, but one of the mums this morning said that Lily's sister was missing.'

'Oh my god! You're kidding. Poor Lily, I hope she's okay.' Tom looked to the floor, his eyes pacing back and forth as if searching for something. 'I should go over there and see if she's okay.'

'What, no. I don't think that's a good idea. She'll have her whole family around her. I don't think they'll want you there,' Katherine raised her voice alarmingly.

'I can't believe you're only telling me about this now!' Tom raged suddenly at Katherine. She jumped back, grabbing her top to cover her chest. What the fuck was she doing? He had just been sucking on her nipples and had seen everything. It was a bit late for her to be shy and pretend like she was some sort of nun.

Holy Cow! He had to get out of there. 'Okay, I've got to go. I'll see you around,' Tom rushed towards the door, awkwardly chucking his shoes back on. He couldn't get out of there quick enough.

'Yeah ... okay, bye then, ' Katherine waved nonchalantly as Tom walked out the door.

Outside, Tom walked down the street towards his house. The air was chillier than he remembered it to be from earlier that morning. The wind pushed against him as he marched. Tom wrapped his arms across his chest and cuddled his hands as deep as he could into his pits. It was all he could do to acquire some warmth from the harsh weather that was building up around him. His legs were heavy as he walked. Teleporting would have been a great trick to have right now.

Maybe he was being punished? He had been a bad man. But Tom had not had sex in the last six months.

Now, he'd managed to bed two different women over the past few days, and neither of them were his wife. What was he thinking? Stupid twat! Tom whacked his head with his hands. There was something seriously wrong with him.

However, if Tom wanted to have sex with his wife, he would have to find her first. Scrap that. He would do anything just to see her, so he could talk to her. Carol does actually pay for everything around the house. What if she didn't come back? Tom wouldn't be able to pay for anything without her. How was he going to cope without her? Carol had literally done a Houdini vanishing act on him and Jack. It had been a successful one, too, as he really didn't know where the hell she was!

Finally, he was home. Even though Tom had only walked a half a street, it felt like he had climbed a mountain to get home. As he strolled inside, his mind was on Carol. Their whole house was filled with her. Her flowers. Her decoration. Her fucking Potpourri. Even though Carol had not been in the house for the past two days, her scent still clung to everything inside, reminding him of her every time he sat on the sofa or went into the toilet to have a shit.

Tom strolled upstairs. He needed a shower so he could get that woman's juices off him. He stunk of cum. Tom couldn't stand the smell. He needed to get it off him and pronto. In the shower, Tom could see his life unravelling around him. Was his addiction back? Was he ever going to see his wife anytime soon? Tom exhaled deeply. A tear ran down his face as the hot water washed over him. Tom didn't really want to think about any of it. He didn't want to admit anything to himself. He would be fine. Just don't buy anymore. That was the last time.

Tom climbed out of the shower and got dressed to see Lily. He wanted to make sure she was okay.

In the kitchen, he grabbed a cold can of Pepsi. His mouth was like sandpaper. He stopped in the hallway. He pressed the house phone for messages as he sipped his drink. But there were no new messages. Where the hell was she? Tom contemplated for a moment. Should he ring her? No. She obviously did not want to talk to him.

Tom scrolled down the numbers on his phone until he got to his dealer, Kilo. Tom hesitated over his number momentarily before shoving his phone back into his pocket. No, let's go and see Lily. She would give him more comfort. Plus, it was a good distraction.

Tom looked up into the hallway mirror before leaving, brushing back his brown hair using his fingers as a comb. He immediately looked less like Shaun of the Dead. Okay, that will do. Now, he was ready.

***

Tom walked up to Lily's house. He didn't know which apartment was hers, although the army of reporters outside the ground-floor apartment on the corner kind of gave it away. Tom paced back and forth. Should he really go and see her? Maybe Katherine was right. Maybe Lily wouldn't want to see him.

Fuck it, let's just do this, he thought.

Her sister was missing, and Lily probably needed all the friends she could get right now. At least, that's what Tom had convinced himself to believe. Yes, that's right, Lily needed a friend. Plus, there was something uniquely gorgeous about her. Lily wasn't like other girls. She was stunning, yet she didn't even know it. Lily didn't need to plaster herself in makeup. She was naturally flawless. In addition, Lily wasn't superficial like other women. Unlike that Katherine, who clearly thought she was the bee's knees. If only Tom did more thinking with his head and less with his dick, then he probably wouldn't have fucked her.

Tom could be himself with Lily and felt no pressure to please her. This was most likely because Lily didn't like him that much, but Tom wanted a challenge, and it was better than his wife's pressure.

Tom picked his way around the army of reporters and walked up to Lily's door. Well, here goes nothing. Tom knocked loudly on Lily's front door. Lily answered the door. Her eyebrows rose, and her mouth gaped open. She beckoned him inside the house, looked around outside warily, and slammed the door shut behind him. It made Tom jump. Shit. Lily was more paranoid than he was. She walked into her living room, and he followed her.

'What are you doing here?' Lily demanded, folding her arms.

'I just heard the news about your sister going missing. Have you heard anything?' Tom stuttered. His pulse quickened. He was frozen to the spot as he stared at her. This was probably a mistake. Lily clearly didn't want him here. He was such a fool.

'Why? So you can go gossip to all the PTA mums down the school!' Lily shouted.

'What? ... no. I came over here to see if you were okay,' Tom was ready to walk away. She clearly didn't want to be disturbed.

'Really? Are you sure you weren't sent over here?' Lily exclaimed.

She was shouting too loudly for him. Tom leaned the palms of his hands on his head for comfort. 'No! Do you want me to go? I'm sorry, Lily. I was just coming over to see if you were okay and if there was anything I could do. Maybe I could get Meghan for you or something. I'm just concerned.' The words were tumbling out of his mouth before Tom could stop himself. He didn't really want to get Meghan from school. Picking up one kid was bad enough. But now he had offered.

Lily stared at him for a moment, not saying anything.

'Okay,' Tom got ready to turn around, ready to leave. Just as he was about to leave, Lily's lips started to quiver, and an abundance of tears broke out, streaming down her face.

Tom shuffled forward and grabbed hold of her. Lily continued to sob into his chest.

'I'm ... sorry,' Lily wailed.

'It's okay,' Tom stroked her long brunette hair. He briefly sniffed it. Oh, wow, his body tingled. It was so sweet, like fresh rose petals, and it matched her personality.

Lily looked up at him. Tom gently wiped away her tears as he gazed at her. She was so precious, like a little porcelain doll. Her skin was made to perfection. God, she had no idea how beautiful she was. Tom gazed at her. He couldn't help but smile. Fuck it! Tom leaned in towards her lips, but Lily backed off from his kiss as they locked eyes. Had he got that wrong? It seemed so right.

'I can't,' Lily said, pushing Tom away and stepping back.

'I'm sorry, I didn't mean to do that. I just thought ... never mind ...' he uttered.

'No, it's not that I don't want to. And believe me, I could do with the comfort right now. But you're married. It's not right,' Lily looked down and shook her head.

'Yeah, I know. But it's not really a marriage right now. I mean, I don't even know where my wife is. All I know is that we could be split up. And you ...' Tom paused, 'You are so beautiful and just so lovely. I ... I ...' he didn't know what else to say to her. Shit.

Lily blushed before smiling back at Tom.

'Thanks for giving me the compliment. It's always nice to hear you are beautiful from someone other than your daughter or mother. But you're still married,' Lily waved her finger at him. Tom nodded. This girl was going to be harder for him to crack than he thought.

'Do you want to have a cup of tea?' Lily offered. 'You can help keep me company if you like? I am going crazy in this house. I was out all day yesterday handing out leaflets. Mum's out now with her friend to give me a rest,' Lily revealed.

'Yeah, okay. Do you have coffee?' Tom asked.

'Yeah, sure,' Lily walked into the kitchen, and he followed.' When was the last time someone saw her?' Tom asked intriguingly.

'Monday night. Apparently, she was out with her friend Chloe at some bar,' Lily replied. Chloe? That name sounded familiar to Tom, probably from a recent film or programme he watched. He didn't know any Chloe.

'God!' Tom said as he gulped down his coffee. It was helping his hangover. 'How old is she?'

'Eighteen,' Lily replied.

'Oh bloody hell, Lil!'

'I know. Here's a copy of one of the fliers I've been handing out. I used a recent picture of her from her Facebook account.'

Tom grabbed the flyer and sipped some more coffee. He coughed, choking on his coffee. He froze as he stared at the picture. Blood drained from his face. Without warning, his hand had let go of his coffee. The cup smacked hard on the tiled floor beneath him, smashing into tiny pieces. Tom continued to gaze at the picture; his jaw dropped, and his mouth gaped wide open. His heart pounded hard, and his breathing was rapid as if a personal hurricane was swarming around him.

'Shit, sorry,' Tom eventually said as he looked down at the broken pieces. Lily jumped up and ran over to the sink. She returned with a dustpan and brush, along with some cleaning spray. Kneeling down, Lily started brushing up all the broken cup pieces. 'I'm so sorry, the cup just slipped out of my hand. Here, let me help you.'

'It's okay, it was an accident. I'll clean it up,' Lily said as she sprayed the floor and wiped up the coffee with a cloth.

Tom was still looking at the flyer, entranced by the image.

He needed to get out of there. It was just wrong for him to be there. 'I just remembered. I need to go. I ... forgot about something. Do you want me to take some of them and hand them out?' Tom offered. Shit. Please say no. Why did he say that? He didn't really want to do that. Tom was just trying to be polite.

'Oh yeah, that would be helpful,' Lily grabbed a bunch lying next to her printer. Lily looked up at him. 'Are you okay, Tom? You look like you've seen a ghost.'

'Yeah, I'm good. I'll see you on the school run. Let me know if you need anything,' Tom didn't look up as he rushed out the door, forgetting to take the bunch of flyers he had offered to hand out.

Oh, my Christ! Oh! What the fuck! There were no words. Tom's mind was spinning. His heart hammered away so loudly that it was setting off his headache once more. Tom grabbed hold of his chest as he ran around the corner. Tom struggled to take in breaths. He bent over and vomited into the curb. Tom's body shook uncontrollably from the sudden agonising catastrophe he had just witnessed. That was J! J is Jasmin. Jasmin is Lily's sister. Jasmin was missing. Tom was probably one of the last ones to see her alive. What's more, he couldn't remember what happened after he fucked Jasmin in the bathroom toilet. Did he leave with her? Did he know where she was? One thing Tom knew for sure was that he was in a whole heap of fucking trouble.

TEN

Katherine

Katherine wrapped her beige trench coat around herself as she stepped into her white Mercedes SUV parked in the driveway. She knew she should just go and do some retail therapy to take her mind off what she had just done. But on second thought, she wanted to see if Tom had gone to see Lily.

Tom couldn't be too far down the road. She knew Lily was meant to be living in the small apartments at the bottom of the street. Katherine had been trailing behind them after she had met Tom on Monday afternoon. She had been intrigued by this girl with whom Tom was so intent on finding. Katherine had not seen her before and was keen to find out who she was.

Now, in the car, Katherine hesitated. Should she follow Tom? But the devil inside her needed to know if Tom was going to see Lily straight after he had just bedded her. Yeah, okay, Lily's sister was missing. But what did Tom have to do with that? Absolutely nothing. So why did he want to go over there and see her? Why did he need to be the one to comfort her?

Katherine put on her sunglasses in a bid to disguise herself. Hopefully, Tom wouldn't recognise the car. She pushed the ignition button and slowly pulled out of the drive, crawling the vehicle down the street. There. Katherine spotted Tom at the bottom of her street just as he turned the corner. The car behind pressed the horn once as it drove right up her arse. 'Yeah, okay, idiot,' she muttered under her breath. Katherine pulled in and let the car overtake her before he could honk again and blow her cover.

She pulled back out and continued to drive down the road once he had passed. God, it was bloody freezing! Katherine switched on the heaters and turned the corner. Tom walked down the street and stopped. Katherine let out a sigh of relief. He was just going home. Katherine was a bit of distance away, pulled in on the other side of the road. But it looked like it was Tom's house. She could see him fiddling around with the front door as if he were unlocking it. Tom went inside. So that's where he lived. Interesting.

Katherine suddenly became aware that she was acting like a crazy person, following Tom home. She wasn't his wife, spying on him to see if he was having an affair. Tom wasn't even hers in the first place. But she was hooked. She didn't want anyone else to have him.

Katherine sighed. She was being a total cow. Lily must be going out of her mind with worry. She couldn't imagine what she would do if it happened to her. What if that was Ellie who had gone missing? Katherine would be frantic with worry. She would do everything to find her. Maybe she should get some flowers and bring them around for Lily.

Katherine also made a mental note of Lily's apartment. Katherine had a friend who lived in that apartment block when she was younger.

Yes, flowers were a good idea, Katherine convinced herself. Let Lily know that some of the mums at school were thinking of her. Sometimes she had this darker side that allowed her to get carried away. But Lily must be feeling lonely. That was something Katherine learned a lot about. It wasn't a nice feeling.

Mary's will be the best place to go. She always does excellent flowers. Katherine drove down to Mary's, which was only about a five-minute drive away.

When she got there, she ordered a bunch of lilies. Lily should like them. After all, she was named after them. Plus, Katherine enjoyed a good bunch of lilies. It took Katherine back to her youth. Her mum always had lilies placed in the kitchen, inside her purple varnished vase, each week without fail. It would boast a fragrance that would fill the room. Katherine smiled. But her expression quickly changed as she stared down at the flowers, pulling her back to the last time she'd seen these flowers. Oh, mum, life is so empty without you in it, she thought. Katherine wished more than anything she were still here, giving her some advice. What would she make of everything going on? Would she like Tom? Her mum never really thought much of James, except that she had not listened to her mum at the time. Now, twelve years on, maybe her mum had been right.

'Would you like a name on the card, Katherine?' Mary asked.

'No, that's okay, Mary. I will hand-deliver them and say they are from a few mums at the school. Lily doesn't know me that well, so it will be a good time to introduce myself.'

'That is a lovely idea. Poor family. They must both be worried out of their minds.'

'I know,' Katherine agreed.

As Katherine took the lilies, she walked outside and placed them in the boot of her car; the smell of the flowers flooded its way out, reminding her of her mother once more. Katherine had sunk into a deep depression when she had died. Her mother had been her world, and she had been completely lost when she died. Katherine sniffled and wiped away a small tear that was brewing behind her eyelids. James had been the one who had saved her from the deep depression. And for that, she was forever grateful.

Katherine drove back down to Forest Lane until she reached Lily's apartment. A mountain of reporters were still queued up outside.

Katherine pulled up further from her house and across the street towards her own home, away from the reporters. Katherine walked up the steps of Lily's front door, but as she was about to knock, she noticed two people inside Lily's front window talking. Katherine looked harder, and she watched Tom and Lily talk. *Great*! He did come to see her. Why had he been so eager to go and see her? That whore.

Katherine clenched her fist in fury and decided she wouldn't knock. What would she achieve by disturbing them? Katherine threw the flowers on the floor and spun around like a moody teenager, stamping her feet down the steps outside Lily's home.

That bitch! Really, what was so special about her? She was a drip! Missing sister or not! Katherine's head was pounding as the hatred suffused through her cursed veins. Her heart ached like it was being crushed into a million pieces. Tom wasn't so perfect after all. But who was? She couldn't forget what Tom had done to her body. He had given her the thrill of the century. Despite him chasing after Lily, Katherine still wanted more of him. And one way or another, she was going to get him.

ELEVEN

Katherine

'Yes, tell him it's Katherine,' Katherine started pacing up and down the kitchen on her mobile. It was later that afternoon, and Katherine was on the phone with Cunningham and their sons. Whether or not it was because of her recent orgasm, she had plucked up the courage to phone her old boss, Richard. Katherine tapped her foot nervously as she waited on hold for his secretary, Rebecca.

'He's on the other line a moment, but he said stay on the line, and he will be with you in a minute. Is that okay?' Rebecca asked.

'Okay, yes, I'll wait a moment,' Katherine replied. Her heart was racing, and she was flapping her hands as she started to pace instead. What was he going to say? Maybe he was going to just say get lost. Come on. Come on, Richard.

'Hello, Katherine,' Richard said on the other end of the line.

'Hey, Richard,' Katherine was biting her nails. She hadn't been this nervous since her wedding day.

'So, what's up, Katherine? What's it been like, ...eight...nine years?'

'Yeah, nine years .... almost 10 years,' Katherine paused. 'So I know it has been a long time .... but I was thinking about returning to work. I wasn't sure where to start. But I wanted to call you, and maybe you could help.'

'Really? What made you think of going back to work?' Richard questioned.

'Well, my youngest has just started school full-time, and I thought now would be a good time.' Was that a good enough reason? She should probably have said something more educated than that. Like she was ready to get her career back on track, she wanted this and was determined to reach the top.

'Okay, do you want to come in and see me early next week, Katherine? We might be able to help.'

'Oh yes, please, that would be perfect!' Katherine exclaimed. It came out more excited than she had anticipated.

'Okay, I'll pass you back to my secretary, and she can set up an appointment with you,' Richard said.

'Okay, great. Thank you, Richard.' Katherine was doing her best to keep a lid on her excitement, but it was unravelling out of her like a can of worms being opened.

'You're quite welcome...Oh, and Katherine?' Richard began.

'Yes?' Katherine replied through gritted teeth.

'I look forward to seeing you,' Katherine giggled, wrapping her finger around her Goldilocks hair, legs crossed over like a goofy teenager.

'Me too. Thanks again,' the phone clicked onto his secretary.

'Katherine, is 10 o'clock on Monday okay? ' his secretary asked. It was now Wednesday afternoon. She could not think of anything she was doing on Monday, and even if she did, it was now cancelled.

'Yes, that's perfect,' Katherine paused momentarily, trying to think of her name again. Thank you ... ummm .... Rebecca, right?

'Yes, Rebecca, see you Monday, Katherine,' she clicked off her phone, taking a huge breath. Thank God she was off the phone. That was so nerve-racking. What was she going to be like on Monday? Oh well, she would think about that then.

Katherine looked out her kitchen window. She had a good feeling about the future. New beginnings. It would be so lovely to be back at work. Fighting crime. Well, not literally fighting crime, but near enough. Katherine bit her nails. But what if she was no good? A laughing stock amongst everyone else? That would be embarrassing. Katherine shook her head. It will be fine. It's just an informal chat, after all. She started to do a victory dance, waving her arms frantically and punching her fists in the air.

Flashbacks of Tom kissing her neck and caressing her body crept into her mind. She couldn't get the images out of her head. Katherine travelled back to that moment. She closed her eyes, reliving the moment again in her head. When she opened her eyes, that feeling was quickly ripped away from her.

The pile of washing was lying in the corner of the room. Katherine rolled her eyes, Eugh! More washing. If she returned to work, they would have to get a cleaner to do all this God-forsaken housework. Who liked doing housework? Absolutely not her! It wasn't like they couldn't afford a cleaner. However, James had insisted that as she was at home, she was around to do it. What mug would agree to that? Clearly, she would.

Yes, a change of scenery would be lovely. In fact, it would be God dam amazing! Katherine would feel like she had a purpose in life, something she had not acquired in a long time. Other than being a mother, of course. But she didn't want that to be all she ever did with her life. Katherine didn't just want her gravestone to read

"Beloved mother and housewife". She wanted it to read "Beloved mother and kickass lawyer." Being a lawyer was the only time in Katherine's life when she was in control, where she mattered and could make a difference.

Most importantly, being a lawyer gave her power. She liked being powerful instead of a weak victim.

***

Later that evening, Katherine was cooking in the kitchen. The waft of chicken circled around the kitchen as it sizzled in the frying pan. Wednesday night was curry night. She didn't feel like chicken curry tonight, but she wouldn't dare change it to another night. There was a schedule. And all hell would break loose if the schedule changed. James was one for routine. Katherine had a set menu for each dinner they had every night, like some sort of school dinner lady. But it was so dull, knowing every day what you would have. What if she wanted to go wild tonight and mix it with Pizza? What then? Oh no, that would be too much.

James walked into the room, sniffing the air as if he was Gordon Ramsey about to give her a bollocking about her food. She held her breath for a moment, waiting for his reaction. Then she felt a surge of rage. If he even dared say something to her, she was going to stick her spatula so far up his arse he would need nappies in the perceivable future. Katherine squeezed her spatula tightly. She waited. He said nothing. James grabbed a cup of coffee from the coffee machine and sat down at the table behind. Oooooh, so lucky.

'So, how was your day, dear?' James inquired.

Yeah, good, you know, I had the best sex of my life over this kitchen counter and got an interview for a job, Katherine thought gleefully to herself.

'Yeah, good. I cleaned the house, did the washing, and did the ironing. So everything is spick and span,' Katherine poured her homemade curry sauce into the chicken. It sizzled.

'How come there's a brand new bottle of Vodka in the cupboard? Wasn't it half full?' James's brows snapped together as he asked the question. God, he didn't miss a trick. He should be a bloody detective with his skills instead of a boring architect.

'Oh yeah, I accidentally smashed it when I was cleaning earlier. I was doing the inside of the cupboard when I knocked my arm into it. So I replaced it with a new one, in case you wanted a drink,' Katherine lied. She had already made up the story earlier in the day. In case James noticed the bottle had gone. He always noticed.

'Oh right, thanks, Dear. Having a clumsy moment, were you?' James mocked, tilting his head to the side. But Katherine didn't care. More fool him. The lie had worked. Katherine had managed to cover her tracks without sounding suspicious.

'Something like that. You know me, silly dipsy thing,' Katherine replied. James nodded in agreement.

'How is dinner coming along?' James peered over at the pan.

'Nearly ready,' Katherine answered and continued to stir the food.

'Good. I feel like my wife is starving me,' James cackled.

'Girls, dinner is ready,' Katherine called, ignoring James's stupid comment. He was welcome to cook his own dinner, but didn't want to.

Ellie and Sophie came and sat down as Katherine served up their meal. She sat down, shuffling in her chair. She was trying to find the words to discuss going back to work. Maybe start with a compliment? Yes, a compliment. Katherine picked up her fork and took a bite. Mmmm, nice. Not to be a big head, but she was a good cook and was something Katherine had inherited from her Mother. Katherine used to cook with her mother when she was young and learnt all her recipes from her.

'So, you're looking handsome this evening, James. Swimming is making you look younger or something. Plus, more athletic. How are you getting on?'

'Yes, good. Speaking of. How's the gym going?' Oh shit, how was she going to get out of this one? Katherine didn't want to put him in a bad mood.

'Yeah, good, I might go again tomorrow.' Except she had no intention of going tomorrow. Or ever, for that matter.

'That's the spirit, don't give up,' James enthused.

'No, I won't.'

'So....' Katherine started.

But it was cut off by James. 'How about you girls? How was your day?'

'I got a gold star!' Sophie blurted out.

'Oh, good for you,' Ellie sneered. 'I got homework'

'Ouch!' Sophie cried out.

'Ellie, don't be so nasty to your sister. Just eat your dinner.' Katherine spoke forcefully, locking eyes with Ellie's. Ellie bowed down and continued to eat her food.

Ellie knew that if she tested Katherine, she would have her laptop taken from her - Ellie's pride and joy.

'So, I spoke to my old boss today, honey,' Katherine glanced up at James, trying to sound as breezy as possible.

'What at Cunningham and Sons? Whatever for?' James raised his eyebrows, leaning back in his chair.

'Yes. Well, I was thinking of returning to work, but now Sophie is in school.'

James pressed the heels of his hands into his eyes. And by the looks of things, he was doing it hard. That is not a good sign. He was quiet. What was he thinking? She couldn't tell what his next reaction was going to be. Was he mad with her? What?

'I don't understand,' James stated, his tone cold. I thought you liked being there for your kids, being a mother. Why would you want to abandon them?' He lowered his eyes, scrutinising Katherine.

'Yes, of course, I like being a mother, but I'm not abandoning them. I would return to work, not leaving them to fend for themselves.' Katherine stated. 'I just thought with Sophie now in full-time school, now would be a good time.'

'What, so that gives you the excuse to do it?' A tremor of rage was becoming apparent in his voice. 'The girls still need you around, whether they are in full-time school or not. Plus, the house needs sorting daily. Or it would be a state.

'Well, I thought we could get a cleaner, with our wage.....' Katherine began.

'A cleaner! Are you insane? And have someone else going through all our stuff? 'James stopped briefly, raising his hand as if to prevent her from talking. 'No, I don't think it's a good idea, Katherine. Especially with your condition as well. Being a solicitor is an exceedingly demanding job, and I don't know if you can cope.' James was, of course, referring to her depression. Katherine looked at the girls. The fright was oozing out of their little faces. Maybe this was a good time to stop the discussion. James was clearly not taking this news well.

'But it is up to you,' James continued. 'If you think it's a good idea to be around less for our girls, then go for it. Let's just finish the rest of our dinner before the atmosphere gets sour with your absurd ideas.'

Katherine kept her mouth shut. She picked up her fork and imagined throwing it at him, landing straight in his eyeball. Stupid smug prick! Instead, she clenched her fork with an all-mighty grip, looked down and finished the rest of her dinner.

James was a man of impetuous will. But Katherine's will was going to be stronger. Screw him! He wasn't going to tell her what to do. If she wanted to go back to work, that was what she would do. One way or another! Little did Katherine know that her decision to return to work would have some awful consequences, such as James losing control and doing something incredibly foolish.

TWELVE

Tom

As he plodded down the street, Tom had his hands rooted inside his pockets. He had decided to take his headphones to school that morning so he could listen to music on the way back. He was grateful that he had, as it helped him dodge Katherine by plugging them in and pretending he couldn't hear her, despite Katherine's best efforts to get Tom to stop. On his way out, he was quite a distance away from her at the other end of the playground, so he had managed to dart out of the way of her. Pretending he couldn't hear her calling his name.

The last thing Tom wanted to do was to talk to Katherine right now. Tom had more on his mind than her. Jasmin. J from the bar the other night was Jasmin. How could that be? She was only eighteen. Fucking eighteen. Barely an adult. Still really a child. She was still at school for God's sake. What was he going to do? He couldn't go to the police. Tom was probably the last known person to see Jasmin alive. Even if he did, what would he say? 'I shagged her, and then I woke up the next morning not knowing what happened.' The police would lock him up and throw away the key. Undoubtedly. Not best to keep quiet. Maybe play dumb if they came knocking? Mind you, he didn't know how he would pull that one off. Tom threw his palms into his face and rubbed his fingers on his temples. "Are we human, or are we dancer?" The Killer's song blasted into his ears, piercing his eardrums. The truth was, Tom didn't know what to do. Tom wasn't good with dilemmas. He would rather run away from conflict. Even though he generally started them.

His wrongdoing was the reason Tom was fired from work. On reflection, sleeping with the boss's wife was not the best move. When his boss caught them shagging on his desk in his office, that had made it so much worse. Not Tom's finest hour. His boss had immediately fired him, and he had not seen his boss's wife since. That had been six months ago, and now he was doing it again. Shit, what was wrong with him. A drink would be great right about now. It would take the edge off everything that was going on. Or even a bag of coke.

Tom reached his driveway. He halted. Carol's silver Mercedes was parked in the driveway. What the fuck was she doing here? Was she moving her stuff out? His legs were powerless to move as if his feet had been stuck to the ground. Tom was too nervous to find out. He stood grounded on the spot for what seemed like forever. Eventually, Tom managed to move his limbs and approach the front door. Just rip the bandage off. Tom opened the front door. Inside, the stillness was eerie. Where was she? Tom trod lightly as he walked down the hallway. Tom reached the living room. Carol was sitting on the sofa, looking through their old family album.

'Hi,' Carol smiled gently as she looked up at him.

'Hi,' a fortuitous sensation of disbelief imploded through Tom when he saw her. He had missed her so much. It was only when he saw her that the realisation came flooding in. Tom had thought he was never going to see her again. Now, seeing her in the flesh, Tom was so relieved to see her back in the house—their house. But what was she going to say?

Carol stood up and poised herself in front of him. 'I'm so sorry for leaving Tom. I think that is literally the worst thing I have ever done. Being without you and Jack for the past few days has undoubtedly been unbearable. Work is nothing compared to not having my family. I'm so sorry about our fight, Tom. Please say you forgive me?' Carol pleaded.

Tears streamed down her face. It was not often that Tom saw her cry. He stared at her. Tom didn't know what to say. How could he start over with her? Although Tom was angry and hurt that Carol had left him and Jack. He had done things so much worse than that.

But Tom wanted to desperately forget about that so they could be together again as a family. In fact, Tom was glad that Carol had returned. He would be screwed without her. Tom needed her.

Plus, Carol always stood by him. Despite his mistakes, she was always there for him when he needed her. However, Tom wasn't sure if she would forgive him if she ever found out what he had been up to over the last few days.

'Are you kidding? Of course, I do. I'm sorry too, Carol. I've missed you so much. I didn't know if you were coming back. Jack has been asking continuously about you. I didn't know what to say. I've been in pieces since you left.' It was true. The anguish Tom had experienced since Carol had disappeared had left Tom an emotional wreck. So much so that it had led him to do some crazy things. Maybe he just needed to get it out of his system. Yes, he just needed to get it out of his system. It had just been stupid, meaningless sex. Nothing compared to the love he had for his wife. His sweetheart. His soulmate.

Tom grabbed hold of Carol and squeezed her tightly as if never wanting to let her go. Tom needed her security more than ever. Her sweet-smelling perfume gave him great comfort. A comfort he knew well. Tom let go of their hug and looked at her instead. Tom brushed away Carol's tears and pulled her wavy, polished black hair behind her ear. It always sat so perfectly when her hair was down. This woman was amazing. How could he have cheated on her? The guilt lay like a rock in his heart. He had made a terrible mistake. Many terrible mistakes.

'What did you say to Jack?' Carol asked Tom, interrupting his anticipation.

'I told him you had to go away for a few days for work,' Tom said, pausing briefly. 'Where have you been?' He had no idea where she had been for the past few days. Despite her leaving a note, Tom had not heard from Carol. She had not rung him or rung Jack.

'I'm sorry I haven't rung you and Jack,' Carol whimpered as if reading Tom's thoughts. 'I just needed time to think.'

'I get that, but we didn't know where you were. I had to pick up the slack at home and not too well, I might add,' Tom hesitated. 'I've been a complete mess! I didn't know if you had left us for good or what!' A sudden rush of anger rose up in Tom. He had desperately missed Carol. But was equally angry with her. She had been the reason Tom had gone and done what he had done. He didn't even know the full extent of his repercussions. If only they had not had that argument and he had not stormed out, then none of this would have happened.

'I know it's all my fault,' Carol chewed her bottom lip. 'I went to stay with a friend at work. She made me see sense. I'm going to be home a lot more from now on. Work is work, but I don't want to miss out on my family. That is just as important, too.' Her eyes were wide with sincerity as if she really believed what she was saying.

But Tom was yet to be convinced. Her work had come first for years. What made now any different?

'Can we agree to start again?' she pleaded.

Tom wanted the same. He desperately wanted to make things right between them.

Tom grabbed hold of her again, pulling her in tightly. Carol rested her head back down on Tom's shoulder. This was the most physical contact they'd had in several months. Tom was hopeful, more than he had been in a long time.

'What happened to you Monday night anyway?' Carol asked.

'I don't know what happened. It's all a bit of a blur,' it was the truth. Tom didn't know what had happened. 'I only remember waking up the next morning.'

'Well, you must have struggled to get home or something because there was mud all over your clothes. Plus, were you in a fight, too? There were splashes of blood down your shirt. It didn't look like your own either, as when I lifted up your top, I couldn't see any cuts on you. I had to strip you off.'

'What?' Tom's face dropped. His heart was pounding as if it was banging against his soul.

'Yes,' Carol repeated. 'Can't you remember me doing that?'

'Umm... no!' A gloom of horror came over Tom's face. Sweat eased its way into his palms, and he clenched his fists firmly.

'Did you get into that much of a state that you had a blackout? God, Tom, you haven't had a blackout in years.'

'Why are you just telling me this now?!' Tom yelled.

'Well, I thought you knew. Calm down, Tom. You probably just got into a fight with someone. Especially if you had taken that stuff. Had you taken anything?' Carol spoke calmly towards him. Tom knew she was trying to diffuse the situation so he wouldn't lose his temper and start smashing up the place like he had done in the past.

'Please don't talk down to me. You used to do cocaine all the time and drink like a fish,' Tom retaliated.

'Yes, but I didn't have a problem, Thomas.' Tom hated it when Carol used his full name like that. This was a great start. They were fighting already. Maybe he should tell Carol the truth of that night, well, of what he could remember anyway.

'Okay, yeah, I did a little bit at the start of the night. I remember being in the bar with Damian. He kept ordering shot after shot. Then blank. I can't remember anything. Not leaving or anything. Fuck.'

'Have you spoken to him?' Carol asked.

'No, I was planning on ringing him, though,' it was true. If he was going to find out what happened, then he would need to speak to Damian. Up until now, he had been trying to forget about it and just assumed Jasmin's disappearance had nothing to do with him. But what if it was? Maybe Tom had said something. Or even... Tom gulped. He did something.

'Aww, I'm sure if something happened between you guys, you can sort it. You're brothers, after all,' Carol said. Oh, good, she thinks the fight was between him and Damian. Maybe Carol was right. Tom and Damian were known to get in the odd tiff when alcohol was involved.

However, Tom had a feeling that if he had been in a fight, it wouldn't have been with Damian. He always looked out for him. Tom remembered starting a fight with him a few years back, but Damian refused to fight him. Instead, he helped him get into a taxi and took him home. So, if Tom had been in a fight on Monday night, Tom was almost sure it wasn't Damian. But who?

'What did you do with my clothes?' Tom asked, concerned. Shit, there might have actually been evidence on them if he had done something.

'Oh, I think I chucked it in the wash before leaving for work. I didn't want them to stain. They didn't even look like they were your style of clothing. I assumed they were Damian's. And you weren't wearing them when you went out. So I thought he might be a bit mad if you gave them back to him in that state. Haven't you done any washing? They should have been in the washing machine.'

'No, I haven't done much around the house, not been up to it,' Tom admitted. 'I had wondered why I was only in my boxers when I woke up. I wasn't even sure what I had done with my clothes. So I guess at least I know I was dressed when I came home.' Tom walked over to the washing machine in the kitchen. Tom pulled out all the clothes; sure enough, his outfit from Monday night fell out. The shirt was spotless. Thank God for that.

'Hey, do you want a cup of coffee?' Carol had followed him into the kitchen.

'Ummm yeah, sure....please,' still holding the shirt. Tom stared evasively at the ground. He was trying hard to process everything that was going on.

Carol switched on the kettle. 'I've taken some holiday leave off, so I can be around the next few weeks and spend some quality time with you and Jack. I'm looking forward to it.'

'Oh my God, are you feeling okay? Taken leave? You're not dying, are you?' Tom took a gander up at her.

'No, I thought it would be nice. A fresh start for all of us,' irritation permeated through her tone.

'Sorry, yes, I agree. A fresh start for all of us will be good,' Tom agreed. It will be nice to spend some time with you, for me as well as Jack.' Tom smiled.

A song started to play on the radio in the kitchen. It caught Tom's attention. "I'm on the highway to hell...I'm on the highway to hell," sang out AC/DC.

A fresh start for him and Carol? Yeah right. The nightmare had barely begun, and it was about to get a whole lot worse. Tom was on the highway to hell.

THIRTEEN

Lily

Lily hadn't taken Meghan to school for the last few days. The neighbour had taken her. But today was different. Lily needed to get out of the house. The house was driving her stir-crazy, and she started to think the walls were shrinking and beginning to cave in on her. Plus, Lily needed to get away from her mother before she strangled her. She couldn't take much more of her crying.

So Lily looked forward to getting out of the house as she inspected herself in the mirror. Her eyes were droopy, and huge bags were underneath them due to the lack of sleep she had endured. Lily was not in the mood to compete with the Barbie queens today, but a bit of concealer would stop her from looking like the Walking Dead.

Lily chucked on her favourite jeans as usual, along with a maroon top and her denim jacket. Downstairs, Meghan was eating her Weetabix like the good girl she was. This must be so distressing for her. Meghan had become a lot quieter over the past few days since the police had completed their visit. Meghan and Lily had only been moved in for a couple of weeks before Jasmin had disappeared. Still, unlike her and Jasmin, Meghan and Jasmin had really hit it off. Doing each other's hair and nails when Jasmin had been in the house.

'Okay, Mummy, I'm nearly ready. I just need to brush my teeth. Will you put my toothpaste on for me?'

'Yeah, of course, Meg,' Meghan followed Lily to the bathroom, where they bumped into her Mum.

'Hey, Lil,' Jackie greeted her. 'Hey, pumpkin,' she said, smoothing Meghan's pigtails. Her mother was not looking great. If her eyes were not open, Lily might be concerned that she was dead.

'Hey Mum, how are you doing this morning? I thought I would take Meghan to school today. Get a bit of fresh air. Did you want to come?' Lily asked politely, even though she was sure of the answer.

'No, you go, love. I'm just going to stay here. In case Jasmin comes home,' Jackie stood firmly on the ground, her body language disengaging as she spoke.

'Okay...Mum. I'll be back soon,' Lily focused on her Mum. But she continued to look into thin air. Not moving. Shit, she was not coping well. Not at all. Maybe Lily should ring her doctor to come out and see her. Yes, that definitely seemed like a good idea. As soon as she got back, that was what she would do. It was all too much for her mother to cope with. And Lily was already feeling the pressure of dealing with it by herself.

'Ready, Meg? Let's get your shoes and coat on,' Lily called over to Meghan from the landing hall.

Meghan wiped her mouth and ran towards her, 'Yup!' she answered.

Outside, the weather was milder than it had been the previous day. The clouds had swarmed and were dark.

'Looks like a storm is brewing in the air today,' Lily said aloud. Not really expecting an answer from Meghan. The sky looked like it was biding its time until it exploded. But the wind was still, a lot stiller than the previous day. Yes, something was undoubtedly fermenting in the sky. Lily stepped outside. The reporters had seemed to have almost disappeared compared to earlier in the week. Only two were left hanging around outside her apartment now. Maybe they were getting a bit more bored with a lack of a story. She walked down the street towards Kitterton Academy. Hand in hand with Meghan.

She was definitely a lot quieter since Jasmin's disappearance. Usually, Meghan would be singing her heart out to the latest Taylor Swift song or her favourite nursery rhyme. Yet there was a nonexistence from her. But it was no wonder, really. Meghan didn't have the mind to cope with this kind of trauma. Adults didn't, so God knows how a four-year-old is coping.

Soon enough, they both reached the school's gates. The mountain of SUVS, Range Rovers, and Mercedes piled in one after the other as they all attempted to show off their dominance, pushing their way to find "the" spot they could park in. There was clearly a shortage of spaces due to the number of overpowering vehicles forcing their way into them. God help the poor mites that were driving around in their banged-out Ford Fiestas. They had no chance. Lily chuckled. Wait a minute, she knew him, spotting a man in a black Range Rover. That was DI Carter. What was he doing here? At Kitterton Academy? Lily slowed down so she could wait for him. Lily focused on his car, intent on not letting him out of her sight. He found a spot up ahead of the school gates.

'Mummy, what are you doing? Why have you slowed down? Come on....' Meghan tugged at Lily's hand in pursuit of dragging her up towards the school gates.

'Okay, Meghan, wait a minute. I want to speak to the policeman. You know...the man looking for Auntie Jasmin,' Lily daren't take her eyes off him. DI Carter got out of his car and helped out a girl. She looked around nine or ten, maybe?

'Detective!' Lily ran across the road, frantically waving her arms like some lunatic. DI Carter suddenly went as red as a beetroot. He was clearly embarrassed, but Lily didn't care. She wanted an update. In fact, she needed an update. Any new leads he had would hopefully give her some rest from what was going through her tortured mind. What in God's name were they doing to find her sister? She knew police resources were stretched, but still, pull your bloody finger out, or she would do the investigating herself. Which is what Lily had started to do anyway.

'Hi, Ms Knowell,' DI Carter greeted reluctantly. 'What are you doing here?'

'Taking my daughter to school. What are you doing here?' Lily repeated the question back at him.

'The same,' DI Carter responded. 'I take my daughter to school when my ex-wife can't,' he said, helping to put his daughter's backpack on.

'Right, I see,' Lily answered. She wasn't surprised he was divorced. Statistically, the divorce rate among police officers was higher. Lily had seen that in one of her crime dramas. Not really surprising, though. Their job had to be stressful. The things they must see. 'So, is there any update on my sister?'

'Yes, we're doing everything we can to find her. We have officers out everywhere looking for her. Plus, we have a few leads on the people who might have been the last ones to see her. But please, we can't talk about this here. DS Millard and I were going to come to your house shortly to ask you more questions.'

'Oh really? Were you? Yes, okay, I understand,' Lily nodded at him. It suddenly dawned on her that it was probably inappropriate of her to stop him outside the primary school where he was taking his daughter.

'Come on, Isabelle,' DI Carter called to his daughter. 'I'll speak to you later, Lily,' he whispered as he walked past Lily and stepped inside the school gates.

Lily waited until he was far enough ahead and then trailed behind as if she was back in school being told off by her teacher. She dropped Meghan off at her classroom, giving her the usual kiss and cuddle goodbye. However, Meghan squeezed Lily much tighter than usual.

'You're not going to go missing, are you, Mummy? Please don't go missing like Aunty Jasmin. Then I won't see you anymore,' tears bubbled up in Lily's eyes. That poor girl. 'Because Daddy has gone missing, and that just leaves Nanny, but she is sad all the time.' Her eyes shifted from side to side. They looked glassy, as if she were a million miles away.

Lily crouched down to reach her daughter's height. She gently grabbed hold of her face and tilted it upwards, 'Mummy loves you. Mummy is right here, and I will never ever leave you. I promise. Okay?'

Meghan nodded in agreement with her mother. But her eyes were still wide with fear. Lily wished she could wrap her up in a huge blanket, keeping her safe forever.

Lily was worried this was having a real effect on Meghan. Maybe going to school was not a good idea. But then, what would she do at home? Sit around the misery of her mother all day? No, school was probably the best place for her at a time like this. Her teachers were aware of the situation and would look after her. Lily had to let her walk away. As much as she didn't want to. This is what Meghan needed. It was the right choice. She had to learn to be around other people and children. Learning the wonders of the world despite the dangers lurking around each corner. Maybe she could just have a quick word anyway. Just to check.

'Miss Norton?' she spun around at the classroom doorway to meet Lily's gaze, 'Can I have a word?'

'Yes, of course, Lily. Is everything okay? Is there any news on your sister?'

'Unfortunately, not yet. I'm worried about Meghan. I think it may be affecting her more than we initially thought. Please keep an extra eye on her.

'Yes, of course. We have been monitoring her closely. She's been a bit quieter in the larger groups, but gets involved when she plays with the smaller groups in the class. She feels more comfortable with children, especially. She and Sophie seem to be getting on well. So we have been pairing them up a lot. If you have any concerns at all, Lily, please don't hesitate to come and see me. I'll let you know if she does something drastically out of the ordinary. You can always look at counselling?'

'Oh, thank you so much, Miss Norton. Maybe I will. I feel so much better knowing that you are watching out for her. Thanks again,' Lily walked off towards the school gates. Sophie and Meghan are friends? Sophie. Katherine's daughter Sophie. Strange that they were friends, seeing as though Lily and Katherine were completely different.

Oh God, there she is, too. Katherine was chatting to one of the other mums as Lily walked out of the school gates. Lily put her head down as she walked past her. Katherine wouldn't want to talk to her. But she glanced up at her as she chatted.

'Hey, I've got to go,' Katherine said to the woman.

'Hey, wait up, Lily,' she called, racing towards Lily in her high-heeled black boots. Shit, they were lovely boots. Katherine effortlessly put Lily to shame every time she saw her. With her gorgeous skinny jeans, black leather jacket and gorgeous bright red lipstick. Lily didn't have a clue which designer she was wearing. Still, it looked like some poor beggar had really taken the time to slave away, making them with expensive material. A huddle of underpaid kids somewhere had worked hard to make her look that good, no doubt.

To have that figure again would be amazing. Maybe it was time Lily dug out her old trainers and went running again. If they hadn't decayed away, that is. Where were they anyway? Probably still in one of the boxes from when she moved back home. Lily would have to dig them out when she got home. Maybe a run would help clear her mind.

'Hey Katherine,' Lily smiled. Oh no, she was starting to learn the fake, in-genuine smile. Was she becoming one of them?

'Hey, it's Lily, isn't it?' Katherine asked.

'Ummm, yes. Can I help you?' Lily raised her eyebrows. She didn't really know where Katherine was going with this conversation. Was this about to be a mean-girl situation?

'You're Tom's friend, right?'

'Well...I don't know if you would call us friends. We have not long met. But yes, I know him.' Again, Lily was suspicious of where Katherine was going with this scenario.

'Look, some of the girls and I are having a Macmillan coffee morning to raise money for cancer. I wondered if you would like to join us? Buy a couple of cakes, that sort of thing. It would be nice for you to join us. We can all get to know one another a bit better,' Katherine suggested.

'Ummm....when is this?' Lily mumbled.

'Now,' Katherine responded.

But Lily wasn't sure. Things were really complicated at home. 'Oh...I...er...really should get back home,' Lily stuttered.

'Oh yes, I understand. I just thought you might like to be out of the house for an hour or so,' Katherine paused. She looked away at the trees to the side of her as if something in them had caught her eye. 'I...err...heard about your sister going missing, Lily. Might take your mind off things,' Katherine said, looking back at Lily.

Lily was curious to find out more about Katherine. In fact, she was in complete worship of Katherine. After all, she was impeccably flawless. How did she pull it off? And all the time.

'I guess you're right. Maybe I could come in for a bit,' Lily agreed.

'Oh goody!' Katherine exclaimed. Clapping her hands. Lily was already slightly regretting this decision. She twiddled her fingers, entwining them with each other as she cautiously walked next to Katherine down the side of the street.

Lily didn't say too much to Katherine. That's not to say there wasn't a lot of conversation. She bragged about all the things she was doing at the school. She was so stupidly brilliant. These women were able to accomplish more in one year than Lily had managed to achieve her whole life. An affluent lifestyle with a gorgeous husband. It would be amazing to have her life, even just for one day.

'Okay, here we are,' Katherine walked up her drive and towards her front door.

Oh my God, this was actually happening. Lily was actually going to go inside this perfect doll's house.

'The girls should be here soon. They've popped into the shop to get a few more supplies as a few more mums from the school said they would join us. They should be here around 9:30,' Katherine explained.

'Yeah, okay, sounds great,' Lily stepped into Katherine's house behind her. Blimey, her house was more perfect on the inside than it looked on the outside. It was like walking into a NEXT store. Everything was carefully positioned. Lily had gone to five-star hotels that didn't look this good. She would kill to have this house.

Her dog waddled over to her. Lily gave him the affection he wanted and stroked him on the back.

'That's Sam,' Katherine informed. 'He doesn't normally get up for strangers much. He's old.'

Lily smiled. Still stroking him. She liked animals. Especially dogs. There were no pretences with them. They were just loyal to you.

'So, do you want coffee? Or can I pour us a cocktail?' Katherine beamed.

Cocktail? Was she crazy? It was 9 am! Plus, wasn't this supposed to be a Macmillan Coffee morning? Meaning you drank coffee. What a wacko. Although Lily strangely quite liked Katherine, there was an excitement about her.

'Ummm... no... I think I'll have a coffee, please,' Lily requested.

'Okay, suit yourself,' Katherine smirked.

'Hello? Kath?' A voice appeared from the hallway. 'I have supplies.'

A woman appeared wearing a pink and maroon V-neck dress covered in glitz on the top half, along with knee-high boots. Lily's heart rate picked up, and she twiddled her fingers again. She was nothing like these people. She was so far away from these women that it was as if they were living in two separate dimensions.

Sam ran off at the sight of her and buried himself in his bed.

'Hey, I'm Lily,' Lily mumbled, avoiding eye contact by looking down at the floor. Oh God, this was so awkward.

'So, have you finally decided to get a maid in Kath? Smart move,' the woman proclaimed to Katherine. More shame poured over Lily as she spoke those words.

'No, Alison, this is Lily, I asked her to join us for the coffee morning,' Katherine corrected.

'She isn't a mum, is she? A little young, aren't you? No offence,' Alison gave her mirthless laugh. A vulgar feeling rose up inside Lily. No offence? Why did she say it then if she didn't want to offend her? What a bitch.

'Oh great, you're making cocktails. I'm so glad it wasn't just coffee. Yuck!' Alison gleamed as she chucked the shopping onto Katherine's kitchen counter. 'So, I hear they are still looking for that girl. Who wants to bet a body will turn up? I'll put down a 100, no wait, make it 200. I have the money.'

'Alison,' Katherine asserted.

'What?' Alison said astoundingly.

'The girl who's missing is Lily's sister,' Katherine uttered.

'Oh shit. Sorry, honey,' Alison blurted whilst scoffing a cracker from her shopping bag. Oh my god! She was literally the most insensitive cow Lily had ever met in her life. Maybe Lily should go.

The doorbell rang.

'I'll get it,' Alison insisted, running out of the kitchen before anyone could say anything. Looks like she was staying then.

***

Lily had endured all she could take at Katherine's pretentious so-called "Coffee Morning". If you could call it that. Lily had only been there for half an hour or so, and Katherine's friends were not what she thought they would be like. She had literally nothing in common with them. So Lily decided to go to the bathroom and then make her exit.

'Hey Katherine, can I use the loo?' Lily turned to face Katherine, who was standing in the kitchen, fussing over the nibbles.

'Yeah, sure, there's one out there,' Katherine pointed out as she continued to unravel the pre-prepared sausage rolls she had clearly made before everyone's arrival.

'Okay, great, thanks,' Lily replied, walking away from her and into the bathroom. Inside, there was a gorgeous smell of lavender spraying out from the toilet air freshener. In addition, there were individual hand towels neatly stacked. The bathroom bin had discarded hand towels inside it. So she used the hand towel once? Then what...it was washed after just one use? That was preposterous. It must create so much washing. There was no way Lily would keep that up in their house.

After Lily had finished, she walked out of the bathroom and found Katherine blocking her path. She stumbled, falling slightly into the bridge of the door. Lily was not expecting to see Katherine staring at her.

'So, what do you think of Tom?' Katherine demanded, her eyes narrowing at Lily. Katherine was leaning on the wall opposite Lily with her cocktail in her hand. She took a sip. Waiting for Lily's response. But Lily wasn't sure what Katherine was getting at.

'Yeah, he's okay. He has been really supportive since Jasmin's been missing,' Lily mumbled. Why was she being interrogated?

'I bet he has,' Katherine replied coldly.

'What?' Lily responded, clasping her hands together nervously. She could feel the heated sweat on them. What was her problem? What was going on?

'Nothing. You know he's married, right?' Katherine sneered.

'Yeah, of course,' Lily replied.

Katherine had literally done a complete turnaround in personality. Why was she behaving like this? First, she dragged her to this tortured coffee morning, and now she was interrogating her about a man Lily had only met a few times. Whom she had only briefly talked to. Is this why Katherine had invited her over? To grill her? But why? What was Tom to Katherine? There was something fishy going on here.

'Isn't something going on between him and his wife, though?' Lily continued. 'Well, I don't really know. I don't really want to get involved. It's none of my business. Plus, I don't really know him that well. I only met him this week and have only spoken to him a few times. And that was briefly,' Lily wanted to make sure she got that bit in. But lord knows why she felt like she needed a reason to defend herself.

'Ah, right, I see,' Katherine said, eyeing her up as if she were some sort of headmistress. 'He's hot, though.' Katherine abruptly changed her tone to become a lot softer. Was she bipolar?

'Oh yeah,' Lily blurted out before she could stop herself. It was true. She was attracted to Tom. There was something extraordinarily charming about him. But he was so full of problems. So, it was a complete no-no as far as Lily was concerned.

'And the things he can do to you,' Katherine coaxed.

'Yeah.....what?' Lily stopped. 'Ummm, no. What do you mean?' Lily quizzed.

But Lily's phone started to vibrate, interrupting them. It was her Mum. Shit. Her Mum. Was she okay?

'Sorry, Katherine, I need to take this.' Lily turned around so that she could face away from Katherine as she answered the phone.

'Lily, where are you? Get home now!' her Mum screamed down the phone.

'Mum, what is it?' Lily put her finger in her ear to hear what her Mum was saying in the other ear, up against the phone.

'Lily, just get home now!' her Mum bellowed down the phone.

'Mum, you're scaring me. What's going on? Just tell me? Is it Jasmin?'

Jackie started to sob on the phone. 'They found her, Lily.'

'That's good, right! Thank God they found her!' Lily gave out a massive sigh of relief. Lily spun back around and barged past Katherine, heading for the front door. Finally, good news. She could get out of this party, and her sister was safe.

But was it? Jackie paused on the phone, and she could hear her take a deep breath.

'No, Lil....,' Lily could hear the shaking in her Mum's voice. 'They've found her body. Jasmin's dead, Lil. My baby is dead!' Jackie wailed down the phone.

Lily stopped walking. She had reached Katherine's front door. As the words hit her ear, she almost immediately dropped her phone, which slammed to the floor. Her limbs became weak; they wanted to move, but instead, they gave way, and Lily fell to her knees, collapsing on the ground. Dead? She couldn't be dead. They had to find her. It was a mistake. It had to be someone else. It had to be a mistake. Lily clasped her face in the palm of her hands and bent forward.

'No!' Lily screamed out. Her heart ached from the pain as her brain started to comprehend the reality of what was going on.

Lily couldn't quite grasp what her Mum had just said, as if her brain had become short-circuited and needed to be rebooted. No, not her baby sister. How could this have happened? Not to her. Deep down, Lily hoped Jasmin had been testing the boundaries with their mother and was secretly staying with her ex-boyfriend, Dan. Seeing that he wasn't replying to any of her messages.

What kind of monster had done this to her? One way or another, Lily would find out, even if it was the last thing she would ever do. She had to find out what happened to her poor baby sister.

FOURTEEN

Katherine

Lily brushed past Katherine, almost knocking her to the floor, as Lily answered her phone. Katherine still had questions to ask her. She was not done with her yet. Yet Lily looked serious on the phone out in the hallway next to the front door.

Who was she on the phone to? It better not be Tom. Keep your friends close and your enemies closer; that is what her father would always say to Katherine. So that's exactly what she was doing. What was so intriguing about this girl? Why was Tom so interested in talking to her whenever they went to school? And what's more, what was going on between them? Was he attempting to make his way around all the mums at school? What was his deal? The endless number of questions rattled around in Katherine's head. It was too much for her to bear. *Men*! They were all idiots. Yet he was an idiot, Katherine couldn't get out of her head. An idiot who made her feel things she could only assume were dead before now. She lost herself for a moment as she had a flashback of Tom spreading her legs open and pushing himself inside her. Katherine closed her eyes momentarily, reliving the memory of Tom's touch. Oh God, her heart ached for him so much.

She opened her eyes and saw Lily collapsed to the ground, sobbing her heart out. Shit. What was going on?

Katherine walked over to Lily, but as she saw her coming, Lily almost immediately scrambled to her feet, giving her a dismissive wave.

'Lily, what's wrong?' Katherine asked. Lily turned to face her. God, she looked like shit. But she didn't answer. Instead, Lily clambered to the front door.

'I've got to go,' Lily finally said, yanking open the front door.

'Where are you going?' Katherine called after Lily.

'I've got to go. It's my sister.' Lily ran off down Katherine's drive.

But she wanted to find out what was going on. Had they found Lily's sister? Was she dead or alive?

'Wait!' Katherine cried out, grabbing Lily's arm hard and stopping her in her tracks.

'My sister is dead, Katherine!' Lily shrieked, spinning around to face her. 'Is that the goss you want to hear from me?' Tears shimmered in Lily's eyes, and in that moment, she forgot about her obsession with Tom. Instead, she just felt pure sadness for her.

Katherine wasn't quite sure what to say to her. Finally, she said, 'Oh, Lily, I'm really sorry.'

'Please, Katherine, not now. Just leave me alone,' Lily shrugged her arm out of her grip.

Katherine willingly released her grip and watched as Lily ran off down the road. What the hell? Was her sister actually dead? Dead and murdered. Katherine thought she was probably just a silly little teenager who had run away from home. Who could blame her? Katherine had thought. She had heard the whispers about Lily's mother being an unstable mess. But murdered? In this quiet suburb. Who would want to harm her?

Katherine returned to her house, and Alison was barely standing. Swaying back and forth to the music. Most of the other mums were now scoffing down their cakes, sausage rolls and whatever else they could eat. It was time for coffee and to sober some of these mums up. Most of them had to drive home.

Wow, some coffee morning. Her mother would be turning in her grave if she could see this now. A bunch of drunken girls at 10 o'clock in the morning. Well, at least her guests had dug deep into their pockets because of the cocktails. So, win-win.

Except James wouldn't be too happy if he came home right now. Although Katherine would see to it that James would not find out. The only problem she had was Susan. She was a bit of a teacher's pet when it came to James. Plus, Katherine was sure Susan had a crush on him, which is why Katherine had not invited her. That and the fact that they had not spoken since their big fight on the school grounds not two days before, like some squabbling teenage girls. But she deserved it. Stupid smug cow. Since then, Val had gone off with Susan, and Alison had gone off with Katherine, along with all the other mums siding with her.

But it seemed Susan had, for some reason, kept quiet about their fight. If she had told James, then Katherine would have known all about it. But why? Not that she was complaining, as she didn't want to deal with the shit she would get off James for it. But Katherine would have thought this would have given Susan ample opportunity to score points with James.

Soon enough, the coffee morning was over, and everybody had left. Everybody except Alison. She had passed out on Katherine's living room sofa. Katherine had given her a blanket to cover her up, a cup of water and two paracetamol tablets for when she came round.

She sighed at the mess the girls had left behind. Better get my little cleaning apron on then, she thought to herself.

But as Katherine started to clean, she couldn't get Tom out of her mind. After going back and forth, she eventually decided to give in and text him.

Katherine typed in, 'Hey Tom, it's me again. The girls just left. What are you up to?' She put her phone on her kitchen counter and scrubbed the dishes with her kitchen gloves.

Within a few minutes, the doorbell rang. Katherine skipped over to the door, hoping it would be the one person she expected it to be. It was. Katherine opened the door to find Tom standing on the other side. Sexual excitement sprang into her like a dog on heat. She wanted to grab him and touch him, doing everything possible to him.

'Now, don't get any ideas,' Tom said sternly. 'I've only come around to say for you to leave me alone.'

Katherine stepped back, shocked by his words. She thought Tom had been into her as much as she was into him. He was, Katherine decided. His eyes were staring intently into hers. Tom did want her.

'Are you sure about that?' Katherine took a step towards him. Tom did nothing. Katherine leaned over him and gently pushed the front door shut behind him.

'I can't,' Tom said. 'The other day, it was a one-off. It can't happen again,' Tom mumbled. But his eyes were still fixed on hers.

She carried on. Using her body to gently push him against the closed front door. 'So why did you come over then if you didn't want me?' Katherine spoke slowly and seductively.

She pushed her lips onto his and gingerly touched his penis above his trousers. It was aroused. Katherine curled her lip upwards. She was pleased. Tom reacted by passionately kissing her back, spinning her around so Katherine was now pushed against the front door. He lifted his hand up her top and started to grope her breasts firmly. She let out a moan.

Alison snored loudly on the sofa in the living room, startling them both.

'Who's that?' Tom stopped, backing away from her.

'Oh, that's Alison. Don't worry, she's passed out. A few too many cocktails this morning,' Katherine grinned at him.

'What! I thought you said there was no one here.' Tom ran his hand through his hair backwards.

'Well, no one's really here. She's passed out, Tom. She's not going to hear,' Katherine insisted, pulling Tom back towards herself.

'Sorry, Katherine, I can't do this.' Tom pushed Katherine to the side and walked out her front door, slamming it behind him. She leaned her head on the back of the front door. Great. Thanks a lot, Alison.

Katherine thought about Lily for a moment. She had briefly thought about telling Tom about Lily and her sister, who had now been found. But Katherine wanted Tom's full attention, and there was no way that was going to take Tom away from that stupid girl Lily.

Katherine knew that as soon as Tom found out, he would be gone. Straight around to her house. The same way he did when he found out she had gone missing.

But then the door knocked again. Katherine smiled. Yes. He's come back. Katherine turned around and swung open the front door.

She huffed, rolling her eyes when she saw who it was. It wasn't Tom. It was Susan standing in front of her. Oh, what did she want?

'Hi Katherine, can I have a word?' Susan asked.

'If you must,' Katherine answered coldly, moving to the side to let Susan inside the house.

'I'm sorry for how I acted the other day,' Susan said sincerely. Well, this was odd. Susan apologising. That was the last thing Katherine expected Susan to do.

'Oh, okay,' Katherine grumbled.

'Is that all you've got to say!' Susan suddenly spat.

'What!' Katherine yelled back at her. What kind of an apology was this?

But instead of shouting back, Susan straightened up her white Ralph Lauren shirt and took a deep breath as if she was trying to compose herself.

'I'm sorry, Katherine,' Susan reiterated. 'Can we be friends again? I miss us all hanging out together.'

'So, I assume you haven't told James about our fight?' Katherine put her hand on her hip, shifting her body to one side.

Susan shook her head. 'Of course not. You're my friend.'

Katherine could sense that there was something not quite right about this scenario. However, she must be telling the truth, as there is not a chance in hell James would have let their fight slide.

'Okay, I forgive you,' Katherine said, leaning forward and hugging Susan awkwardly.

But it was a lie because there was no way Susan was any friend of hers. Keeping to her motto, Katherine would keep Susan close, purely so she could keep an eye on her. Katherine was sure there was an ulterior motive for Susan coming around and apologising to Katherine. She didn't trust Susan's apology one bit. She was up to something for sure, but for the love of all reasons, Katherine could not think what it was.

FIFTEEN

Lily

The flashing blue lights dazzled Lily's eyes as she approached the front of her house. The grey, dull sky outside had darkened, making it look like it was nighttime even though it was late morning. There were reporters everywhere, swarming her house and covering half the street like vultures trying to attack it. Neighbours were out on their doorstep, nosing at the situation surrounding them.

'What's going on, dear?' Mrs Pattison (Lily's next-door neighbour) asked her as Lily walked past to her house.

Lily spun around, facing her, 'What?' she answered, puzzled.

Mrs Pattison was mumbling something else, but Lily couldn't hear what she was saying over the sound of her thumping heart. Lily ignored her and walked into her house.

As she stepped inside, her heart felt like it was crumbling into a million pieces. Jackie took her hand, but she couldn't feel her touch; it was numb, as if it had evaporated through her skin. Everything was in slow motion, and Lily felt like she was seeing what was happening through another person's eyes. Not her. Not her. The words circled around in Lily's head, like on a loop from a broken record player. Lily spun around the living room. There was talk going on around her. Lights. Chatter. Yet Lily heard nothing. Not her. Not her baby sister. Not Jasmin. It wasn't true. It couldn't be.

'Lily...Lily. Did you hear what I said?' DI Carter was facing her. Her knees were weak, and before she could stop herself, she started to collapse towards the floor. Arms grabbed her before she hit the ground. Lily looked up. DI Carter had caught hold of her. She began to sob in his arms. Lily hadn't been there for Jasmin. She had not protected her. If Lily had been a proper sister to Jasmin and had been there for her like she should have been, then maybe Lily would have known where Jasmin had been going that night and stopped this from happening. She could have saved her. But it was too late. And now they said Jasmin was dead. The tears continued to surge down her face. Lily was still finding it hard to take in and digest.

Oh no, poor Mum too. How was she going to cope? Lily's chest was tight as if it was being squeezed together, suffocating her. She struggled to get in a breath with each thought. DI Carter stroked her hair. It was nice amongst the pain and anguish that was screaming out inside her.

DI Carter let go, gently placing Lily onto the ground. He crouched down in front of her and lifted up her chin. 'I'm so sorry, Lily. You must have been close,' DI Carter said gently. Lily continued to sob, not saying anything back to him.

'This is now a murder investigation. We will do everything in our power to find out who killed Jasmin,' DI Carter continued. Lily nodded in agreement. It was all she could get her body to do. 'We'll be back soon with an update. Please ring me if you need anything or if you can think of anything in the meantime. You have my card with my number on it.'

Lily grabbed his arm before he got back up. 'Are you sure?' She sniffed. 'Are you sure it's her?'

'We'll need you to identify the body, but yes, we're pretty sure it's her,' DI Carter replied softly.

Lily nodded again and let more tears swim down her face.

The police left.

***

Eventually, Lily scrambled to her feet after some time and walked over to her Mum, who was wailing on the sofa.

'Mum? Mum, are you okay?' Lily shook her Mum. She didn't reply.

'My baby. My baby,' Jackie screamed out. She was curled into a foetal position. There was no way she was going to handle this. Lily grabbed her phone from her pocket and dialled.

'Hello? I need a doctor from the practice to come out and see my mother, Barbara Knowell. Preferably Doctor Wilson, as he is her doctor and familiar with her,' Lily spoke frantically.

'Is it an emergency?' the receptionist on the other end muttered.

'Yes, it's an emergency,' Lily continued frantically.

'And what seems to be the problem?' the receptionist commanded rudely. Oh my god, what was her problem?

'She's spaced out. She needs something to calm her down,' Lily stated. Lily had lost her patience with this God-forsaken woman.

'Okay, I need something more than that?' the receptionist asked abruptly.

Steam was now imploding its way out of Lily's ears. 'Well, she just found out her eighteen-year-old daughter has been bloody murdered; she suffers with her nerves as it is and has already had two nervous breakdowns before this, for far less trauma in her life. So, God knows what this is going to do to her. She needs a doctor. Preferably, Doctor Wilson. Is that enough information for you?' Lily yelled down the phone at her. Lily was panting hard in between tears that were streaming down her face. She was clenching her fist. Shit, that was a bit harsh. She'd scared herself, never mind the secretary.

'Oh God, I'm sorry. Yes, I will get a doctor out to you as soon as possible. Stay by the phone. Doctor Wilson is in today, so I will let him know the situation and see if he can come out personally.'

'Thank you!' Lily said sternly. She clicked off the phone. The rage inside Lily was too much for her to control. Blood was pumping vigorously around her body. Lily paced back and forth, desperate to try to calm her nerves. It wasn't working. The anger and pain were merging together, and she couldn't tell which was which.

How could someone kill her gorgeous baby sister? What murdering bastard would do that to her? There was so much cruelty in this world. How could she even tell Meghan? Oh God, Meghan. More tears spilt down Lily's face, and she dropped to her knees. Falling to the ground once more. Lily needed to be strong, but didn't know how. Oh, Jasmin. Had she suffered? She must have been so scared. She was only eighteen. The tears continued to pour, as her chest was painfully torn away from her soul. The overwhelming pain of sadness was too much to carry. Lily couldn't breathe, and the world started to spin out of control. Then blackness.

The next thing Lily knew, she awoke to the doorbell ringing. Lily wasn't sure how long she had been crumpled on the floor of her living room. She got up and peeked over at her mother, who was still lying on the sofa in the same foetal position as she had been in before Lily had passed out. Jackie's eyes were wide open, but they were also glazed over.

'Mum? Mum?' Lily waved a hand in front of her Mum's face. Nothing. 'Mum? Mum?' She shook her, but there was no response from her. It was as if the lights were on, but no one was home. Jackie looked shell-shocked from the news or something. Oh shit. This was not good. The doorbell rang again. Lily ran to the front door.

She opened the door and was face to face with Doctor Wilson. 'Thank heavens you're here, Doctor Wilson. Come in. Come in,' Lily waved him in.

Doctor Wilson was an older, tall man with round, oval glasses.

'Thank you,' Doctor Wilson replied, looking sombre as he stepped inside.

'She's in here,' Lily said, walking towards the living room. Doctor Wilson followed behind her.

'Ms Knowell? Can you hear me?' Doctor Wilson bent over her, touching her shoulder. 'Barbara?' Her mum didn't respond.

'How long has she been like this?' Doctor Wilson asked, turning to face Lily.

'Ummmm.....I don't know. A while,' the truth was she was equally not in a good place either, but her Mum was, by far, worse off.

'Okay, maybe we should get her checked out.'

'For what, exactly? Are you sending her back to Kitterton's mental health hospital?'

'No, not now. I think your mum is having an extreme shock reaction, which could affect her heart. So, I think it's best to get it checked out.'

Doctor Wilson must have seen the look of horror on Lily's face. 'Don't worry,' he said, touching her arm. 'This is a lot for her to take, and with her age, she could be more at risk of a heart attack. But it's unlikely. However, you can never be too careful. I can also arrange for a mental health specialist to come and have a chat with her.'

Lily nodded. She didn't really feel like talking. Doctor Wilson left the room as he spoke to someone on his phone. She stood over her mother, waiting for the moment she woke up from this awful nightmare. Like she would wake up, and everything would be as they were last weekend. All of them sitting down for breakfast together about to celebrate Jasmin's birthday. Jasmin and Meghan giggling with each other, not a care in the world. It didn't seem real that she was dead. How could Lily accept that she was? Not when Jasmin had her whole life ahead of her. A career, a husband, children. All that was taken away from her.

Doctor Wilson returned. 'Okay, an ambulance is on its way.'

'An ambulance?' Lily said, puzzled. 'Is that necessary?'

'Don't worry, Lily. It's protocol. They will take her in and get her settled. You can go and visit her later if you like.' He pushed up his glasses and stared at her intently. 'How are you coping, Lily?' he spoke softly.

'Yes, okay,' Lily lied. 'Tough as old boots, me.'

'Well, make sure you take care of yourself and that daughter of yours.'

'Okay, thank you, I will, Doctor Wilson,' Lily said, chewing her fingernails. Maybe they had made a mistake? It was another missing teenage girl they found. But Lily immediately felt guilty for thinking that, as it meant some other poor family would be going through what they are going through now.

'No problem. Have the police suggested a bereavement officer?'

'Ummmm...I think so', but the conversation with the police earlier that day had been a blur to Lily. There wasn't much Lily took in other than "Your sister's body has been found." Those words just echoed over and over in Lily's head.

Lily caught a glimpse of the clock, and her thoughts were sharply interrupted. Shit Meghan. Lily had forgotten entirely about her. 'Sorry, Doctor Wilson, please give me a minute,' Lily took out her phone and dialled Mrs Pattison's number.

As well as being their next-door neighbour, Mrs Pattison had been a family friend for years and had been especially good at helping Lily with Meghan since Jasmin's disappearance.

'I am already on my way, dear,' Mrs Pattison answered before Lily had a chance to open her mouth.

'Thank you so much, Mrs Pattison. I will see you shortly,' Lily sighed.

'Okay, dear, I won't be long,' she said, then hung up.

It wasn't long before the ambulance arrived.

Lily hugged her Mum tightly, but there was no reaction from her. 'Bye, Mum,' she called as her Mum entered the ambulance with the help of paramedics.

'Thank you, Doctor Wilson, I'm so glad you came.' Lily could feel herself welling up again. She had briefly put the situation out of her mind whilst she focused on her Mum. How was she going to manage to cope with this? And all by herself? The weight of the world was truly on Lily's shoulders, and all she wanted to do was run. She wanted to run as fast as she could for the hills and not turn back. Except she had to be brave and let her little girl know that her favourite person was never coming back. With his thought, Lily collapsed to the ground and sobbed her heart out.

SIXTEEN

Tom

'Are you sure you don't want me to come? I can always go and pick him up,' Carol said to Tom.

'No, it's okay. I don't mind. You stay here. I'll be back in a minute,' Tom replied to her, opening the front door and abruptly shutting it behind him before Carol could follow him. Tom didn't want Carol to come with him and pick Jack up from school. He didn't want to risk them bumping into Katherine.

Not today anyway. Tom wasn't sure what he would say. That Katherine was one firecracker, and fuck knows what her big mouth would say. Tom was going to have a fresh start with his wife. Even the sun was on his side this fine Friday afternoon as he stepped out of the house and up the street towards Kitterton Academy. The air outside was warm, it made a change from the miserable weather they had tolerated the past few days and even earlier that morning. After Carol had returned earlier that day, Tom had chosen to see it as a sign. So that meant he would put all these other women behind him and piece his marriage back together, even if they threw themselves at him. Tom nodded to himself. Yes, that would be his focus now.

As he approached the school grounds, Katherine was picking up Sophie outside Miss Norton's classroom. Oh crap! He really didn't want to see her. How could Tom avoid her? He tried to hide behind a crowd of mums as he approached the door. Praying Katherine would be gone by the time he got there.

However, Miss Norton must have spotted him. As she called out, 'JACK.'

'Daddy!' Jack ran out, leaping towards him. Katherine looked up as she stood outside the classroom, talking with other mums. Shit, she had seen him.

Tom glanced up at her and put his arm around Jack's shoulder.

'Hey,' Katherine called over to Tom, waving. He briefly ignored her and looked down at Jack. God, when was she going to get the message?

'Hey Buddy, how was school today?' Tom asked.

'Yeah, good, Dad. Sophie is my new best friend,' Jack replied.

'Ah, right. That's nice, Jack,' Tom said, pretending to care. He hoped things wouldn't get too awkward between him and Katherine. Maybe she would lose interest soon. Maybe if Tom ignored her, she would move on to another poor guy to sink her claws into. Tom only wished he didn't have to see her every day.

Tom looked over his shoulder. Katherine was still talking to her friends. He grabbed Jack's hand and led him out of the playground as fast as he could. 'Hey buddy, so there's a surprise for you at home?'

'A surprise, really? Is it a new game for my tablet?' Jack squealed excitedly.

'Better than that,' Tom replied, cracking a cheeky smile at him.

'What's better than that, Dad?' Jack's voice went higher with excitement. His face was full of anticipation, waiting for Tom to reply.

'Mum's home,' Tom revealed, his voice high with excitement to match Jack's enthusiasm.

'She is!' Jack started running down the road before Tom could stop him. Aww, bless him. Tom was so happy that Jack was happy. This fresh start was going to be good.

However, as they reached home, things would not seem as simple as Tom would like to think. His mistakes would be catching up with him really soon.

***

'Mummy!' Jack screamed as he ran into the house.

'Aww baby,' Carol flung her arms out, ready to embrace him in a hug. But Jack charged at her like an elephant. 'Mummy, I missed you so much.'

'Mummy, I like my new school so much...I have a new best friend, her name is Sophie....she is so lovely...I shared my biscuit with her today,' Jack rambled at her. Trying to tell his mum as many things as he could. Tom's soul filled with warmth. He had made so many terrible mistakes this past week. He had failed himself miserably. As a husband. And as a father.

'Mummy, I don't like you working so much,' Jack sobbed and continued to hug Carol.

'I know, baby. Well, Mummy will be staying at home for a little while. I have taken a break from work. Does that sound good?' Jack nodded intently at her. Carol smiled and started tickling him under the arms. Jack giggled before running off to go and watch TV in the living room. Tom smiled as Jack ran off. He looked so happy. Tom looked up at Carol. Her face dropped, and she gave him a cold look. Tom's palms instantly became sweaty as panic spiralled through him. Oh shit, what was wrong? What had she found out?

'Don't give me that look,' Carol frowned at him.

'What? What is it?' Tom's voice trembled. He couldn't hold it back.

'You know what! Carol scolded. 'Cocaine. That's what.'

'Oh!' Tom sighed, relaxing his shoulders. He was suddenly aware he had tensed up, expecting a different outcome.

'Oh? That's all you have to say. Tom, you promised! You remember what happened the last time you took cocaine?!' Carol started to yell but quickly lowered her voice. 'How long have you been doing this?'

'Where did you find that?' Tom quizzed.

Carol huffed. 'In your trouser pocket. 'But that is beside the point,'

'What were you doing going through my trouser pockets?' Tom demanded.

'I was trying to clean up a bit. Do some washing while you were picking up Jack. It's always you doing the housework around here, so I wanted to help,' Carol said.

A distasteful feeling sat in his heart. Carol was only trying to help, and he had more or less accused her of spying on him.

'How long, Tom?' Carol repeated.

'The past week...It started the night I left to go out with Damian. I've stopped. I promise. I realised it was stupid as soon as you turned up today, I've not had any since,' Tom admitted.

'Okay, I get it, Tom; it was a slip-up, and I know this week must have been hard. I'm at fault, too, so I'm sorry for putting you through all this. I know you must have been all over the place, but....' Carol hesitated. 'But Tom, you were looking after Jack. I left you with him because you're a good Dad, and I trusted you,' Tom cowered like a puppy being told off by his master.

She was right. He had meant to be looking after Jack, but the need to do the drug had overcome his sense of responsibility. Tom had reasoned with himself that he could do both without any issues. On reflection, that was probably not true. An unwavering gloom hit him. Tom was worried he was at the start of a comedown. There were already ulcers appearing in his mouth, and Tom was doing his best to feel high-spirited despite having gloomy thoughts surrounding him. However, Tom couldn't tell if that was the drugs or a guilty conscience.

'This can't happen again; do you understand me?' Carol said firmly.

'Yes, I know,' Tom knew she was right, but he didn't like being put in his place, especially by his wife. Who did she think she was? She wasn't the boss of him.

'Tom, something bad could have seriously happened, you get that, don't you?' Carol continued, stabbing the knife in further. The more Carol talked, the more Tom's legs started twitching, and his hands became sweaty. He didn't feel too good.

'Okay, well, we both have done and said things. So, let's just draw a line over it,' Carol finished.

Tom's heart was beating rapidly as palpitations threw themselves at his chest. Please stop. Please just stop. Tom was losing control of his breathing as his heart pounded faster and faster until he wasn't sure if there was any air reaching his lungs. He was going to be sick; it rose up through his throat. Sweat was dripping down his face, and Carol became blurry.

'Tom, Tom,' she shouted at him. 'Are you okay?' He could briefly feel her touch as she shook him.

'I don't feel so good. I feel like I am dying, Carol,' Tom mumbled. 'Please help me.'

'I'll get you some water,' but it was too late. Tom blacked out.

***

Tom woke up. He was in his bed. He looked at the clock. He had been asleep for hours, and it had gone dark outside. Carol was not in bed. He got up and walked downstairs wearing just his boxers and a fitted white vest. Carol was watching TV on the sofa.

'Hey,' Tom said to her.

'Oh hey, how are you feeling?' Carol asked, touching the back of her hand to Tom's forehead. It had gone from red hot to cold and clammy.

'Yeah, much better. I think I just needed some rest. I hadn't been sleeping much,' Tom paused. He looked down, 'Especially when doing that stuff. The last week has been a bit of a roller coaster,' Tom sat next to Carol. He was feeling much more relaxed now.

'Oh, I'm glad,' Carol responded.

'Thanks,' Tom stared at her, grinning.

'Don't be silly. Of course.' Carol stared back at him, returning his gaze. Tom needed closeness. He didn't want to be alone. Tom's chest was fluttering as they both looked at each other. Should he lean in and kiss her? It had been so long. But before he could act, Carol leaned in towards him, kissing him on the lips lightly. He glowed with haste and happiness. They continued to press their lips perfectly. Shivers ran down his shoulders and through his arms. Carol wrapped her arms around Tom heartily. Oh, that feels so nice.

'Come on,' Carol whispered to Tom. She took his hand gently, turning off the TV with the other. It had been a long time since they had been together. This was weird. Did he still have sexual feelings for her? She definitely gave him comfort. He must have some sort of feelings for her, or he wouldn't be kissing her. Tom was getting a hard-on, so yes, it seemed he was still attracted to her.

Upstairs, Carol pushed him onto the bed and started to get undressed. First, she slowly undid the buttons on her olive-green dress. It fell to the ground. This was actually quite sexy. Tom sat up on the edge of the bed facing her. He ran his hands over her perfect, slender body, kissing her stomach tenderly. Carol let out a soft moan.

She gripped hold of Tom's shoulders, and he used his elbows to crawl up the bed. He slipped off his boxers as Carol climbed on top of him. He fell back onto the bed, resting his hands underneath his head. As Carol climbed on top of him, he slipped himself inside her. The sensational pleasure sparked off his penis, giving him full-blown delight as Carol continued to ride him, pulling out slightly and then taking him all the way in. She moaned lightly.

Is that all she had? He wanted more. His dick was being teased. Tom flipped Carol around, so she was now lying on her back, and he was on top of her. Tom grabbed hold of her arms sharply and pulled them back over her head. Gripping them so she couldn't move. He slipped his penis back inside her and restrained her hands tightly. Each time she tried to move them, he held them tighter. Tom continued to pound her harder and harder. Carol let out another moan. This time, it was more of a loud scream.

'That's more like it, darling,' he mumbled. Yes, that's right. Stay there. Right there. This gave Tom great excitement as he thrashed himself deep inside her. Carol screamed out again with pleasure. Tom smiled cunningly as his wife took the beating of his cock. It was right there that he couldn't hold back anymore. He let out an almighty growl as his orgasm exploded, his penis quivering inside Carol. Tom didn't feel Carol shudder, though. Well, that wasn't good enough. She needed to finish, too. What kind of man would he be if he couldn't get a woman to cum for him? Tom pulled out of her and slipped his fingers into her clit. She was wet. Very wet. This wouldn't take long. Carol had her eyes shut as his fingers pulled out of her clit. All of a sudden, he could feel her vibrating onto his fingers, with her orgasm shortly following. Carol let out a massive groan at his action.

'Wow, where did that come from, Tom?' Carol turned and kissed him.

Tom laughed. Oh yeah. That's how it's done.

SEVENTEEN

Lily

Lily opened her eyes. They were so sore. Sore from so much crying, she had endured the day before. It had been one of the most emotional days of her life. Being told her sister was dead. Even now, the day after, Lily was expecting it all to be a bad dream, like she would wake up today and hear Jasmin's music coming from her bedroom, as it had been every Saturday morning since Lily and Meghan had returned home. Instead, there was just silence.

Lily walked out of her bedroom and down the landing. She peeked inside Meghan's bedroom. Her breathing was deep between her snores. Wow, she was still flat out. Meghan was generally up at 6 am, but today it was Saturday, and she was sleeping in. Lily wasn't surprised. They had both encountered a long week. She walked past Jasmin's room. She couldn't face going into her room just yet.

Lily shuffled down the stairs. The house was filled with an eerie stillness. In the kitchen, she walked over and put the kettle on. She needed a cup of tea. She couldn't do anything in the morning without a cup of tea in her hand.

The house phone rang. Oh great, who the hell was that? It was so early, way too early to deal with any more crap that was likely to be thrown her way. Lily casually strolled over to the mobile house phone that lay in its holder.

'Hello?' she yawned.

'Hello, Lily Knowell? It's the police. DI Carter.'

'Oh, hello. What's going on?' Lily replied distressingly. Suddenly, she felt fully awake. What was it now?

'I wondered if you or your mother could come down to the police station this morning and formally identify your sister's body?'

'Why?' Lily asked, hopeful. There was a chance this might not be Jasmin.

'Remember, I mentioned this to you yesterday. Even though the DNA evidence suggests that the body we recovered is your sister, we still would like someone to come down and formally identify the body,' DI Carter spoke softly and calmly.

'Ummm.....right. Okay, I'll come down,' Lily volunteered. 'My Mum has been admitted to the hospital. I need someone to watch Meghan. I'll be down later on. Is that okay?' Hopefully, Mrs. Pattison will watch Meghan for an hour or so.

'Yes, of course. Take your time. Do you want me to pick you up and bring you down to the station?' DI Carter offered.

'Umm... no... that's okay. I'll take Mum's car.'

Lily's tears started to surface, and she could feel her voice starting to choke up. She needed to get off the phone. 'Okay, bye then,' she said, then clicked off the phone. But as she did, tears flowed their way down her cheeks. She slid down onto the floor and began to bawl her eyes out. The phone dropped to her side.

Lily thought of her Mum. She hadn't been up to attending the hospital yesterday to visit her Mum. Still, she had phoned the hospital last night, where her Mum's nurse had advised her that she was doing well and they were keeping her in for observation and should be home later today.

The kettle had boiled, and Lily didn't really feel like it anymore. Steam circled above her head. She didn't feel like anything. She felt stuck as if she didn't know what to do with herself.

Lily picked up the phone and dialled Mrs Pattison's number.

'Hello, Mrs Pattison speaking,' she answered after several rings, slightly out of breath.

'Hi, Mrs Pattison,' she said through sobs.

'Oh hello, dear. Are you okay?'

'I need to identify Jasmine's body; would you be able to watch Meghan for me?'

'Oh, you poor dear. Yes, of course I will. Just drop her off when you leave. I'll be here.'

'Thanks,' Lily choked, and clicked off the phone.

Lily reached up and leant on the kitchen counter, gripping it hard. Her legs wobbled as she stood back up. You can do this, Lily, she told herself. You have to do this. But going to the morgue alone gave Lily a fathomless depth of fear. She wished her Mum could do it. Lily wasn't sure if she was strong enough. What would it be like there? It wouldn't be a nice place, she imagined. Probably even haunted. Maybe Tom would go with her? Or was that too much to ask? Perhaps. Nonetheless, he had been a good friend and had been really supportive towards her. Well, he was her only friend despite trying to kiss her. She had nothing to lose. Lily picked up her phone and dialled Tom's number.

'Hey,' Tom answered after a few short rings. 'Are you okay?' he was whispering.

'No, she's dead, Tom. Dead,' the words just spluttered out, then more tears ran down her face, and she sobbed down the phone. Get a grip. You can't just keep crying all the time, she told herself.

Lily cleared her throat and brushed away her tears. 'Anyway, the police want me to go down and formally identify the body of my sister. And...' Lily suddenly realised that Tom had not responded. 'Tom, are you still there?' He made noises as if he were clearing his throat.

'Yes, I'm still here,' Tom made the same noises again. 'Oh my God, Lily. I'm so sorry. That's absolutely terrible. I can't believe she's dead. I'm really, really sorry.' Wow, he sounded more cut up about it than Lily had expected.

'Look, I know it's a lot to ask, but I wondered if you would come with me...you know, to identify her body?' Lily pleaded.

'Ummmm,' Tom hesitated. He didn't sound convinced.

'You don't have to go inside or anything. It's just my Mum has gone to hospital and I.....I really don't want to go on my own. I have never had to do anything like this before....and...I'm sorry. I shouldn't have called or asked you...it's just....' More tears crashed down Lily's face like a storm. For God's sake!

'Lily, stop, it's okay. I'll sort something out and come with you,' Tom reassured. Lily sighed. Immense gratitude washed over her. Thank heavens she would not be doing this alone.

'Okay, can you meet me at mine in an hour? I'll take my Mum's car.'

'Ummm...can we do a bit later?' Tom asked.

'Yeah, I guess so. I suppose she's not going anywhere,' Lily said, using dark humour to keep the conversation light and to control her emotions. 'Come here for one o'clock?' Lily asked.

'Yeah, okay, I'll be there,' Tom rushed quietly. 'Sorry, Lily, I've got to go. See you at yours at one,' Tom clicked off the phone.

'Bye then,' she said out loud to herself.

EIGHTEEN

Katherine

'Okay, love. I'm off. The boys and I will be back tomorrow,' James kissed Katherine on her cheek the same way he did to his daughters.

'Yeah, bye,' Katherine was clutching her coffee in the kitchen, looking out the window. She didn't even turn to face James as he walked out the door. Her mind was on other things.

It was the weekend. Thank God it was finally the weekend. It seemed to be the most fulfilling week ever. Katherine was used to the first week of term being so hectic. It was always hard to get back into the swing of things, organising the never-ending list of school events. This was usually the highlight of her week, something she looked forward to all summer. But this week had been remarkably different. A murder. What had happened to that poor girl? Katherine couldn't get the thought out of her mind.

There was a murderer in the area. But who? Who would want to kill a young, innocent girl? Katherine took another sip of her coffee. She shuddered at the thought. But it equally somewhat intrigued her, too. Was it a man? A girl? Did they know her? Or was it a stranger? How would it feel to take a life?

Katherine turned her thoughts back to James. Katherine yawned. Thank God James had gone hunting this weekend. She needed peace and quiet instead of her husband breathing down her neck. Katherine always had to conform to a certain way when he was around, which was exhausting. Ellie had gone to dance and was then going to a sleepover at her friend Isabelle's house. So, it was just her and Sophie. Maybe they could cuddle in and watch a movie today after Katherine had cleaned the house. Drama free.

Katherine's mobile suddenly rang. It was Alison.

'Hello,' Katherine answered.

'Hey Girl, what are you doing?' Alison beamed.

'Nothing much. Just about to get on with the housework,' Katherine replied.

'Are you kidding? Bugger that. Fancy going for a run with me instead?' Alison asked.

Katherine paused. She had to clean the house, so it was back to its spotless state. But then again, James wasn't here to see it. Today, she was giving herself the day off. Although she still had to watch Sophie.

'I have Sophie. James is out hunting for the weekend with the boys,' Katherine replied.

'Don't worry, I'll bring Jean over with me. She is watching Amy anyway,' Alison asserted. Jean was Alison's trusty nanny. Although Alison was at home, Jean would watch Amy and do all the housework. Then Alison would get involved whenever she felt like it.

'Oh, okay. Yeah, go on then.' A run was just what Katherine needed to clear her head.

'Okay, we'll be round in the next hour or so,' Alison clicked off the phone.

'Hey, guess who's coming over?' She turned to face Sophie, who was sitting watching TV in the living room.

'Who, Mummy?' Sophie anticipated, turning around to face Katherine.

'Auntie Alison and Amy,' Katherine beamed.

'Yay!' Sophie exclaimed, jumping up and down on the sofa.

'Yes, they'll be here soon,' Katherine replied.

***

It was gone midday by the time the doorbell rang. Katherine had gotten dressed and put on her running gear. She was ready to exercise those demons before she met with her old boss, Richard, on Monday.

She was just making her way when the front door opened.

'Hey, it's only me,' Alison called, walking into Katherine's house along with Jean and Amy, closing the door behind her.

Without saying anything, Jean scurried over to Katherine's kitchen with a big shopping bag in her hand. Katherine could only assume she was doing some cooking.

Amy ran straight over to Sophie, who was sitting playing in the living room area.

'Hi Sophie, this is my new dolly, Susie,' Amy said to Sophie.

'Oh, nice. Do you want to play in my room? We can play with my dolls, too.' Sophie asked.

'Yeah, sure,' Amy replied.

'Be good, Sophie,' Katherine called as they both ran upstairs to Sophie's room.

'Yes, Mum,' she shouted from the top of the stairs.

Katherine rolled her eyes. 'She has been whining all fucking day! So, we stopped to get her that new stupid Suzie doll she wanted. Anything to shut her up!' Alison moaned to Katherine.

Katherine gave out a small chuckle. Alison was not immensely tolerant of Amy, even though she was the sweetest kid.

'Ready?' Alison said.

'Yes,' Katherine nodded. 'Are you sure Jean is okay with this?'

'Of course she is,' Alison waved her hand up as if this was no problem at all. 'She's cooking a chicken salad for lunch too.'

Katherine turned back to the kitchen. Jean, who barely said anything, was already making herself at home and rummaging around her cupboards.

Katherine, satisfied that the girls would be fine with Jean, turned and opened the front door.

Outside, the air was crisp, and the sun beamed down. It seemed like summer was still not quite over yet. However, there was a slight breeze in the air. Katherine's hair flickered in the wind, and she brushed it behind her ear. It was a good day to go running. Not too hot.

'The gym is so overrated. All those sweating losers. There is nothing like a good run with some good old-fashioned fresh air,' Alison said, sniffing the air. She raised her hands and exhaled deeply.

'I totally agree,' Katherine replied, as she did a few basic stretches before they started.

'So, do you want to do a loop around the woods and back up to yours?' Alison asked.

'The woods? Where that girl was murdered?' Katherine replied.

'Yeah, there's a lot of police down there. I saw them on my way to yours. Come on, girl, don't be a sap. It's not as if we are going to get murdered,' Alison implied.

'Yeah, okay, whatever. Let's just do it,' Katherine replied as she started jogging on the spot, eager to get going. Plus, she could nose at the crime scene as they jogged past.

Katherine and Alison started to run down the street together, side by side. Alison was used to running daily. She did everything she could to keep her figure intact.

Katherine, on the other side, was not so strict. However, she didn't have a problem with her figure and was always happy with it. James seemed to have more of a problem than she did. But she did enjoy running. There was something about running that made her feel free. Especially when running outside, she was so glad not to be on a sweaty treadmill at the gym. But outside, experiencing proper freedom for all that it was worth. Maybe it reminded her of when she was a child, when she used to run around the field behind their garden. It was probably the happiest time of her life. No stress. No worries. Just freedom. Katherine was in such a hurry to grow up, but now she would give anything to be that carefree child. Her body tingled with delight as the wind brushed against her face.

Although Katherine was already out of breath as they reached the woods, less than a mile from her house. Alison was also sweating but keeping up the pace quite nicely.

The echoing sounds of their trainers walloped against the ground. It was grinding on Katherine's ears. Her breathing was loud, but she tried to control it by using the labour technique, as if she were back giving birth. In through the nose, out through the mouth. Shit, it wasn't working. Enough was enough. She had to stop.

'Keep going, Ali, I'll catch up to you; I need a breather.' Katherine bent forward, leaning her hands on her thighs in an effort to catch her breath.

'Okay, meet you back at your place,' Alison waved as she continued to run.

Katherine continued to exhale deeply as she attempted to catch her breath, in an attempt to get her body moving again. She started to stroll, preparing herself before she would start running again. As Katherine turned the corner, she bumped straight into something. Someone. Katherine looked up. It was Tom. What a brilliant time to see him, just when she was a sweaty mess. She was not prepared for this. But an unwavering sense of alleviation spilt over her as she looked at him. He was there, standing in front of her. Katherine's face lit up with pleased bewilderment.

'Hey,' she stopped to look at him.

Tom stared up at her, not saying anything.

'Hey,' Tom said eventually to Katherine. He completely avoided her eye contact and stepped out of her way to keep walking, completely ignoring her presence.

'Hang on a minute,' Katherine grabbed Tom by the arm. 'Is that it?'

'What else do you want me to say?' he said sheepishly.

'Don't you want to talk?' Katherine asked.

'About what?' Tom replied coldly.

'About us? The other day, that was pretty intense. Then again in the hallway.'

She searched his face, but he still avoided her gaze. He was silent. Tom had stepped back, standing away from her as if she were the plague, and he needed to be as far away from her as possible.

'Why are you avoiding me?'

'Why do you think, Katherine?' Tom looked up at her. His eyes were wide and serious. 'You're gorgeous. You know that you are. But I can't. I'm married, and you're married. We just can't.'

'We already did, though. Again, it didn't stop you before,' Katherine corrected. What the hell? How could he do a complete one-eighty on her?

'Yes, I know, but it was a huge mistake,' Tom retorted.

'Plus, your marriage is dead in the water. You said it yourself.' Katherine was not giving up without a fight.

'Not anymore, she's back. We are giving it another go. I really want it to work,' Tom informed.

'Didn't you feel something between us?' Katherine exclaimed. 'That wasn't just me?'

Tom looked up at Katherine to match her gaze. 'It was a momentary lapse of judgement. I was attracted to you. You were there. My wife wasn't. It was a huge mistake.

But Katherine knew he was lying. The look he was giving her spoke the real truth. 'I don't believe you. You want me as much as I want you. Wife or no wife. You can't help what you want.'

I'm really sorry, Katherine, I have to go. I'll see you around at school, okay?' Tom started to walk off.

She grabbed his arm before he could go. 'You're not just going to use me and toss me to the side like I don't matter to you. You've really got inside my head. You're driving me crazy. I can't stop thinking about you!'

'Katherine.....' Tom started. But she stopped him from talking by putting her finger over his lips.

She moved closer to him, her lips almost touching his. 'This is going to happen again, Tom, or I'm going to tell your wife,' she whispered.

Tom grabbed her arm and kissed her passionately before pushing her back away from him. 'Fine if that's the way you want to play it. Not now. I'll ring you.'

Tom successfully dodged past her and walked down the path out of sight. Katherine stood pegged to the ground. Her heart exploded in her chest.

Her legs wobbled. They were like jelly. Katherine couldn't keep them up. She collapsed onto the ground.

'Are you okay, love?' Katherine jumped as a hand gently touched her shoulder. She sat on her knees, whimpering. How could a man she barely knew make her weak like this? She lifted her head to find a man in his 60s looking down at her, eyes wide with concern.

'Yes, I'm fine, thank you. Just overdid it a bit,' Katherine replied to him.

'Oh yes, well, don't over-exert yourself too much, love. It's not the end of the world. You can always pick yourself up,' the man continued to walk up the path with his black and white collie. Then disappeared from sight.

Shit! What had she just done? Had she just blackmailed Tom into sleeping with her? That's not how she wanted it to be. But Katherine couldn't help it. She wanted to have him again, and nothing would get in her way.

NINETEEN

Tom

Tom's hand was still shaking as he clicked off the phone to Lily. He swallowed hard. He felt like he'd swallowed a golf ball. He just stared at the pictures on the wall in his and Carol's bedroom for a moment as if they might have the answers to his problems. Dead. Lily had said. They found her dead body. Fuck. What was he going to do? This couldn't be happening. Oh fuck! Tom's breathing became more rapid. Breathing excessively, he slouched off the bed and tried to take in deep breaths.

Come on, Tom, he said to himself. Pull yourself together. Maybe it's not her. Perhaps the police made a mistake. But how often were the police wrong?

Oh God, he was meant to be going to the fucking zoo too. Tom needed to get out of this so he could go to the morgue with Lily. Even though it was one fucked up situation, she had no one to go with, and Lily needed him.

He looked around the room and grabbed his dressing gown that was hanging on the back of the bedroom door. Then, he wrapped it around himself. He darted to the bathroom and grabbed some tissue. Scrunching it up in his hand.

'Tom, are you nearly ready?' Carol called from downstairs.

He took a deep breath and walked down the stairs. Carol was packing their picnic into her big mummy bag on the kitchen counter.

'What's wrong with you?' Carol stopped what she was doing when she saw him.

'Sorry, love, but I feel under the weather. I think I've picked up a chill from all this change in weather we have been having lately. I don't think I'm up for the zoo today.' Tom forced out a fake cough and swiped his forehead with the back of his hand as if it were sweating. Carol didn't say anything. Was she buying it?

'Oh no, Jack was really looking forward to going. I was really looking forward to going,' Carol sighed.

'No, you guys go. Have fun. Spend some good quality mother-and-son time together. I'll probably go back to bed anyway.'

'If you're sure, love?' Carol stroked his arm.

He nodded. 'Yeah, of course. There's no reason why you should both miss out because I'm feeling poorly.' Ah, good, it seemed like she was buying this.

Tom leaned in towards her, giving her a kiss on the cheek. Was he doing the right thing? Lying so he could go to the morgue with Lily to identify her dead sister, whom Tom slept with, whom he may or may not have killed. This was certainly not a good idea by any means. But what choice did he have? He couldn't let Lily identify her dead sister's body alone. He had to go.

***

Tom pushed Katherine to the side. Stupid blackmailing bitch. He could do without this right now. Who did she think she was? Demanding that he have sex with her? Like he was a piece of meat, she could shag whenever she wanted. He was a married man and meant what he said. Why couldn't Katherine get that into her thick skull?

It wasn't difficult. People hook up all the time, have sex with one person and then move on. Tom was out of his mind when he thought it would be a good idea to sleep with her. At the time, he was high as a kite, and his dick was doing all the talking.

Still, Katherine had another thing coming if she thought he and she would hook up again. Like fuck were they! He just had to tell her what she wanted to hear to get him off her back. Kissing her was all he could think of to do just that. Just until he figured out what he was going to do with her. Tom huffed to himself as he continued to walk out of the woods and towards Lily's apartment.

His mind instinctively went back to his phone call with Lily. 'She's dead, Tom,' the words were still ringing in his ears. Tom still couldn't believe Jasmin was dead.

Part of him wanted to go with Lily to the morgue and see for himself that it was Jasmin. He had almost hoped that she had been around one of her mates or a boyfriend, even. Anywhere, as long as she was alive and well, Tom could stop quivering every time he heard a loud noise. This happened earlier when the postman rang the doorbell to deliver a package. There was a huge part of him that was screaming out at him to run and hide under his duvet like a small, frightened child.

But as Tom reached Lily's doorstep, it dawned on him that this was really happening. He could only hope the police had made a mistake because if the girl's body at the morgue really was Jasmin, as the police suspected, then Tom wasn't sure how much more of this his nerves could take.

TWENTY

Lily

Lily walked down the creepy corridor along with Tom and DI Carter by her side. Lily gulped. Her heart was in her mouth. Her hands were shaking, and her body was unsteady. It was as if she were on the set of a crime drama, and the events in front of her were not really happening. Everybody here was just acting their part.

As they reached the end of the corridor, a dull white door stood before them. Its original painted white colour was long gone, and it was now left with a faded, dull, off-white version. It had numerous scratches on it, unquestionably from all the dead bodies that had banged their way through the door on a trolley, being transported to the gloomy morgue.

'I'll wait here,' Tom pointed to the seats opposite.

'Ummmm...yeah, okay,' Lily was only now aware that she had been gripping tightly onto Tom's arm, but it seemed he was too polite to say anything. 'Oh, sorry. Here, have your arm back,' Lily said as she let go.

'Ready?' DI Carter turned to Lily.

'No,' Lily blew a colossal breath out. She was certainly not ready to see her beautiful baby sister lying cold and dead in a mortuary. Up until now, Lily had convinced herself this was not real, and it was just pretend. She was living miles away from reality at the moment. But Lily had to pinch herself now. This was real. And it was like nothing she would have ever imagined.

Lily just had to walk in and say yes; it was Jasmin. Like ripping off a bandage. However, Lily felt that would not quite be the case. Okay, here goes nothing, she told herself. With her heart beating double its normal pace, she walked inside.

'First time seeing a dead body?' DI Carter said. Lily nodded at him.

'Okay, you'll be fine,' DI Carter held Lily's hand. Her eyebrows raised. This was unexpected. However, his warm touch gave Lily a small sense of comfort.

Lily instantly held her nose as she was escorted in. Lily's stomach quivered, and she had the overpowering feeling of vomiting. But managed to resist just in time and swallowed it down. Yuck! What was that smell? It didn't even smell like death. Not what she imagined death to smell like anyway. It was like someone had left an uncooked chicken out to defrost in the window and accidentally forgotten about it while the warm sun had burned down on it.

Lily and DI Carter followed the pathologist, who led them to another room. Therein the middle was the outline of a body with a white sheet covering it. Lily stepped closer, and the pathologist lifted the sheet back. She braced. He rolled the sheet to her collarbone, uncovering just her head.

It looked so strange. It wasn't what Lily was expecting at all. Her face looked more like a rubber doll than anything. But with bruises all over her face. It was so strange to look at; the young, vibrant soul that had once been there had now been ripped away, and all that was left was this meaningless body. This was not what Lily remembered her sister looking like. But despite no life living inside her, there was no doubt about it. It was her sister. It was Jasmin.

Lily clasped her hand over her mouth. 'That's her,' Lily sobbed. Her heart tightened, and it was as if the air had evaporated from the room for a moment.

She couldn't bear to look at her dead sister's face anymore. Her hands were now gripped tightly over her eyes. Even though she was no longer looking, she was trying desperately to erase the vision from her mind. It wasn't working. She couldn't do it. Lily could no longer be in the room. The shadowing echo of death was swarming around her. The smell. That awful smell was too much to withstand any longer. Her legs started to run. She needed to get out. Lily was out of the morgue and down the corridor before she knew it. The sound of voices echoed behind her. Calling her name, but she couldn't stop. A sign for the ladies' toilet was suddenly in front of her, and she ran inside. Straight to the bathroom, the overwhelming surge of vomit began to projectile out of her stomach. Streams of tears were streaming down her face. Lily started hyperventilating, desperately trying to get in gasps of air that weren't coming. It was too much. Everything was just too much. How could she carry on? Her sister's death. Her mother's illness. She couldn't do it. She wasn't strong enough to do it. The sound of knocking on the door interrupted her thoughts, and she stumbled back.

'Lily? Are you okay?' DI Carter's voice whispered from behind the door. 'Can I come in?' he continued. But Lily couldn't answer him. She was too busy attempting to take in breaths. The toilet door creaked open, and DI Carter abruptly appeared.

'It's okay, breathe, Lily, breathe,' DI Carter coached her as he stroked her back gently. It was helping, and her breathing started to come back under control. Lily touched her chin. Christ, there was vomit all over her. Lily grabbed some toilet paper and wiped away the leftover vomit from her chin. Then walked out of the toilet cubicle to face DI Carter.

'Thank you,' Lily stuttered.

'Are you okay?' DI Carter repeated.

She nodded at him. But she was not okay, far from okay, in fact. Lily walked up to him and hugged him out of nowhere. She needed a hug from someone, and he was there. DI Carter responded by wrapping his arms around her. She was glad. His touch gave her a sensation of security. It was so lovely amid the bleakness that surrounded her. It was what she needed.

'Sorry,' Lily finally let go of DI Carter. She was sure she was overstepping some sort of boundary.

'It's okay, it's a lot to deal with. Plus, I know your Mum is not doing so well and must be tough to cope with, especially on your own with a four-year-old daughter,' DI Carter was soft and wistful.

Hearing the words out loud from DI Carter made her immediately start to sob again.

'Sorry,' Lily repeated. She couldn't bear to look at him. She was never one for crying in someone's company and much preferred to cry by herself where nobody was looking. But that had gone out the window the past few days.

Lily took a deep breath. She needed to pull herself together. Now was not the time to be crumbling. Lily was unaware she had been holding DI Carter's hand. She swiftly let go of it and walked out of the ladies' toilet and back into the corridor. Tom was outside looking up at her.

DI Carter scratched the back of his neck awkwardly. 'There's something else, Lily, that I think you should know. The autopsy shows that Jasmin was approximately seven weeks pregnant. Did she tell you?' DI Carter asked.

Lily's heart sank like a bottomless pit. What was he talking about? 'Ummm... no! I didn't know she was pregnant,' she exclaimed, unable to keep the surprise in her voice back.

'Well, we can't figure out if your sister knew or not yet. It may have had something to do with her murder,' DI Carter continued.

Lily turned to Tom, almost forgetting he had been there. His face was as white as a sheet. This was obviously a bit too much for him, too. Maybe she shouldn't have pushed him into coming with her. It was time to leave. She had seen and heard enough for one day. All she wanted to do now was go home and pull the blanket over her head, then stay there for the rest of the day.

'Thank you for today, DI Carter,' Lily sobbed.

'I'm really sorry to have put you through everything today,' he looked at her with his big, brown, gentle eyes.

'Please keep me updated. I want to know everything that is going on in my sister's case,' Lily said, with more assertiveness.

'Yes, of course. I'll be in touch soon. Please call me if you need anything Lily,' DI Carter continued to stare at her with concern.

'Yes okay, bye,' she said, turning to face the exit. She couldn't say anything more. Lily was grateful that Tom was being so quiet. As talking would most likely set her off again. She was on an emotional rollercoaster and desperately wanted to get off, but she couldn't.

'Come on, let's go,' she said to Tom. He got up from his seat, his head down and fixed to the floor. God, he was really taking this hard. She suddenly felt terrible for asking him to come. This was not a nice thing to witness. Not when you didn't have to, as well.

As Lily left the morgue with Tom and sat back in her Mum's car, she couldn't get the words out of her head. Pregnant? How could she be pregnant and Lily not know? Aww, Jasmin, what did you get yourself into?

TWENTY-ONE

Tom

Pregnant? How the fuck could she be pregnant? Surely, she was already pregnant when Tom and she had sex? Seven weeks, the pathologist said. It had barely been a week. So yes, Jasmin must have already been pregnant when Tom had slept with her.

'I'm sure this Dan fella had something to do with it,' Lily ranted in the car.

'Who's Dan?' Tom asked her.

'Dan was her so-called recent ex-boyfriend! There was so much I didn't know about her life. How could I not have known all this was going on?' Lily fumed.

That made two of them. Lily was not the only one in the dark. Tom had no idea this one-night stand had so much baggage. Or had he known about the baby? For all he knew, this girl could have told him, but he couldn't remember. Tom had never wanted to remember what had happened in one night as much as the night Jasmin was murdered in all his life. He would happily trade in one year's worth of memories just to have that one night of full recollection.

Tom's thoughts were hindered as he unexpectedly jolted forward in the car. Lily had run the car off the road, almost hitting an oncoming vehicle on the opposite side of the lane. She stopped, parking it on the side of the old reservoir turning. Her head fell forward onto the steering wheel, and she started wailing.

Tom attempted to clear his throat. He wasn't really sure what to do. His heart was in his mouth from the sheer shock of her actions. He gently put his arm around her in an attempt to try and comfort her.

'I'm so sorry, I hate crying in front of people,' Lily sobbed at him. 'I just can't help it. It won't stop coming out.'

'There, there, it's okay,' Tom pulled Lily towards him so her head rested on his shoulder. Lily's fragrance was so sweet, like cotton candy. It was so inviting.

Lily started to kiss his neck. Shivers grew through his body. It was wrong, so wrong. He had to stop her. But then Lily started to touch his penis. Oh, dear God. This was wrong. Very wrong. Tom turned to face Lily. She was exquisite. But she was vulnerable. He would be taking advantage, plus Tom promised himself he was having a fresh start with Carol, and he didn't want to disappoint her. He already had one psychotic woman on his case.

'Lily, I can't,' the words were pouring out of his mouth before he could stop himself. But he was glad they came out. Otherwise, he probably wouldn't have stopped her.

'I thought you wanted this?' Her eyes flickered in confusion.

Shit! He had upset her more. 'I do, I really do! And I would, it's just....' Tom paused. 'It's just my wife came back yesterday, and well, I really want to make it work. You know it's Jack as well, and he's so happy when we are a family.'

'Oh, I see. Do you love her?' Lily asked.

Tom wavered for a second. He wanted to be in love with Carol. 'Well, I missed her so much when she wasn't there. I really want it to work. Plus, I don't really think you want this. You're just really upset about what happened with your sister.'

'Oh, I'm such an idiot,' she sobbed. She stopped crying and turned to look at him. Even with her eyes red raw from crying, she was still so beautiful. 'But maybe you are right, Tom. My head is all over the place right now. I'm devastated about my sister, and I'm not thinking straight at all. But I do want you. I wanted you the day I met you. You are gorgeous, good-looking, and funny. I'm just gutted I didn't do it with you the other day. I was trying to do the right thing. Now, here you are, trying to do the same thing. Our timing is completely off,' Lily admitted.

Fucking hell! Lily was really doing her best to make this as difficult as possible for him when all he wanted to do was rip off her clothes. But he couldn't. Over the past week, he had done enough damage to last him a lifetime. This was his chance to start doing the right thing. But yet here he was being tested once again. It was fucking torture.

'Come on, let's get you home. Do you want me to drive?' Tom wanted to get Lily home before he did something he would regret.

'Oh yeah, okay then. I don't think I'm up for driving,' Lily replied.' Thank you.'

Tom jumped out of the car, and Lily scooted over.

He drove Lily back to her house. There wasn't much conversation between them the rest of the way home.

'Thanks for coming with me, Tom,' Lily turned to him as he pulled up outside her house. Tom handed Lily back her keys.

'Listen, anything you need. Just let me know, okay?' He leaned in and hugged Lily.

'Thanks, I will,' Lily replied.

Tom jumped out of the car. Then, once he was happy Lily had walked into her house, he spun around and returned to his own house. Tom prayed he would not see Katherine on the street as he walked towards his house. She was too much shit for him to deal with. In his face all the time. Tom wanted her to leave him alone, yet she seemed to be everywhere he bloody turned.

His mind travelled back to the night he went out with Damian, and that moment he had been with see Katherine on the street as

Jasmin. Where was Damian? He hadn't heard from him, and despite Tom ringing him consistently over the past couple of days, he hadn't been able to get in touch with him.

Tom decided to call him again. He took out his phone and dialled Damian's number.

'Hello,' Damian answered. Tom let out a sigh of relief. Finally.

'Where the fuck have you been?' he scolded down the phone.

'What do you mean, man? Ah, sorry, I forgot to call you back. Work has been slammed this week. What's up?'

'Have you been watching the news?' Tom questioned.

'No, not really,' Damian muttered.

'Oh My God, please don't tell me you don't know that girl at the bar had gone fucking missing!'

'Oh yeah, I did hear some teenage girl had gone missing. She wasn't at the bar, though, was she?' Damian replied, calm and collected.

How did he not know it was the girl at the bar who had gone missing? And more importantly, how could Damian be so calm at a time like this?

'Damn, she's dead! Like cold fucking body dead!' Tom exclaimed.

'What? Who's dead? Start again, Tom. Calmer,' Damian ordered.

'That girl you were dancing with at the bar was actually an eighteen-year-old girl. She was the sister of one of the mums at the school who lives in the street behind me,' Tom stopped to take a breath. 'Oh yeah, and I fucked her, and I was probably the last person to see her alive!' Tom bellowed. He let out a deep breath.

Damian said nothing for a moment. Finally, he exhaled deeply down the phone, 'Wow, Tom, you get yourself into some pickles.'

'The worst part is I can't remember a thing,' Tom continued to rant.

'Well, you remember shagging her, obviously,' Damian concluded.

'Yeah, I remember that bit, but nothing after that!' Tom was still shouting down the phone. 'What do you remember? Did we leave together?' Tom hoped his brother could shed some light.

'Ummm no.... I remember you giving me back my coke and heading to the bar. I came to find you after going to the toilets shortly after, but I couldn't find you. I tried ringing you, but when you didn't pick up, I assumed you had buggered off home,' Damian stated.

'Oh fuck, this is bad. I was really hoping you were gonna say you saw me leaving or we caught a cab home together,' Tom sighed, his voice now quieter, but reeked of disappointment instead.

'Don't worry, mate, maybe you should go and tell the police what happened,' Damian suggested.

'They will never believe me. Plus, what am I going to say? I don't think I killed her, but I can't remember. I'd be giving them a killer on a plate. They would lock me up and throw away the key,' Tom's voice was shrill.

'Okay, don't say anything, mate. Hopefully, they will have other leads and suspects. They won't be looking for you,' Damian assured. 'And if they do, just tell them the truth.'

'There's another thing too,' Tom scratched his nose. 'I...ummm...have just been at the morgue to identify her body with the lead detective on the case,' Tom revealed.

'You did what?!' Damian bellowed. 'Why in God's name would you do that?' It was Damian's turn to shout. In hindsight, it was probably a foolish thing to do. Maybe he was just hiding in plain sight. For now.

'Well, I am friends with Jasmin's sister, Lily, you know, one of the mums up the....'

'Wait a minute.....the other woman you have got yourself involved with is the sister of the dead girl you fucked at that bar. Are you serious, Tom? You do realise you have a wife as well, right? Along with a fucking kid! How many other women are you banging?' Damian demanded.

Tom ignored the latter. Who put him on his high horse? Damian wasn't perfect himself. 'Lily is just a friend. I was supporting her. I didn't know it was her sister, did I?'

'Well, I wouldn't put it past you,' Damian exclaimed.

'What do you take me for? I admit I've made a few mistakes this past week. But so have you. Plus, this never would have happened if you hadn't taken me out,' Tom proclaimed.

'Oh no, Tom, don't blame me for this. Listen, go home, and keep yourself under the radar. No more fucking trips to the morgue, and hopefully, they will find out who did it in the meantime,' Damian ordered.

'Okay,' Tom replied. 'Speak to you soon?'

'Yeah, speak to you soon, bro. Just stay out of trouble. And definitely stay away from that girl, Lily.'

'Okay, I will, bye,' Tom clicked off the phone.

The words played over in his head, "Go home", "hopefully they will find out who did it in the meantime". But what if they couldn't find who it was? Tom's chest was beating so hard he was worried it might explode. But what if it was he who killed Jasmin? This thought scared Tom more than anything.

TWENTY-TWO

Lily

It was Monday morning, and Lily had been crying for the past two days. Ever since she visited Jasmin at the morgue on Saturday. But Lily decided that today she would stop wallowing around in self-pity and get her arse off the sofa. She needed to do something about her sister's murder. She had to find out what happened to her, and she was sure this Dan fella had something to do with it. No one could get in touch with him. He wasn't returning her messages, and the police didn't have much to say about the matter either.

However, she had managed to find his address on Facebook and had planned to go straight over there after dropping Meghan off at school. As Lily drew nearer to Dan's house, she was slightly regretting the decision. She wasn't even sure what she would say once she got there. There were several possibilities. Should she start by asking: "Why haven't you been answering my messages?" or just come straight out and say, "did you kill my sister?" Lily shivered as she walked. She wrapped her favourite black and white cardigan around herself. Lily swept the wind out of her face and tucked it behind her ears. She should have wrapped up a little more today. Although it looked sunny out the window this morning, it was chillier than it looked.

Lily looked down at her phone. '51 Decklan Drive,' she said out loud. Lily walked up to Decklan Drive and counted the numbers. 45, 47, 49 and then 51. This was the place. Lily's hands suddenly started to tremble, and she clasped them together. The same way she always did when she was nervous. Lily's heart started to beat faster, and she swallowed hard. She slowly crept towards the front door and tapped on the door with a shaking hand. Moments passed, and nobody came to the door. Perhaps they're not in? Or should she knock again? Maybe they didn't hear. But as she went to knock again, the door swung open, and a woman in her 50s stood before Lily. She blinked. What was she going to say again? Her mind had suddenly gone blank.

'Hello, may I help you?' the woman asked. She was well-spoken and had a pleasant mannerism about her. Her smile was so warm and gentle. Lily instantly liked her.

'Hello,' she croaked. 'My name is Lily. I...ummmm...I'm looking for Dan.'

'Daniel, yes, of course. He's here,' the woman turned to look up the stairs. 'Daniel!' she called.

'Would you like to come in, dear?' The woman asked. Lily assumed she must be Dan's mother.

'Ummm....yes, okay,' Lily stepped into their wide hallway. A boy came down the stairs and looked up at her.

'Who are you?' the boy asked, cautiously narrowing his eyebrows at her.

'My name is Lily; my sister is Jasmin.'

'Oh my Gosh!' he said, stopping dead before her. 'What in heaven's name are you doing here? How did you find out where I lived? Has Jasmin sent you here to get some of her things? There's not much but....'

'No, she hasn't sent me.' It had become apparent quite quickly to Lily that Dan didn't even know Jasmin was dead or even missing. 'You are Dan? Her ex-boyfriend, right?' she asked.

Dan continued to babble. 'Yes, she broke up with me just before we went on holiday. It was nice to get away, to be honest. I don't know what has been going on with her lately. Even before we broke up, she had been acting strange for the past couple of months. So, to be honest, I wasn't surprised. That's not to say I wasn't hurt, but certainly not surprised.'

Lily stared at him intently. 'On holiday?' She raised her eyebrows.

'Yes, we've been on holiday in the States. We only came back this morning.'

'How long have you been gone for?'

'Three weeks, why? Is there something going on?' Dan spluttered.

Lily had surprisingly only just noticed that suitcases were lying in the hallway with airport labels on them. Oh shit. If Dan didn't know what had happened to Jasmin, she would have to tell him. She shouldn't have come. This was not good. Sweat started to pour from Lily's palms.

Lily opened her mouth reluctantly, 'Ummm...Jasmin....ummm,' she couldn't get the words out. She couldn't tell him. 'I have to go,' she tugged at the door, trying to open it, but struggled to undo the latch. Stupid door. Just open. Dan touched her hand.

'What is it? What's going on? Please tell me. Is Jasmin okay?' his voice was shaky.

'She's dead,' Lily mumbled, looking down as she spoke. Suddenly, the latch clicked open, and she ran out of the house. She couldn't stay there a moment longer. It had been a huge mistake going there. On holiday! Lily couldn't believe he had been on holiday, and her poor ex, Dan, had no idea Jasmin was dead or that she had been pregnant either. This was driving Lily cuckoo. Who killed her sister?

Lily took a deep breath. She needed to find out more. Someone was bound to know more about where she was and what happened to her. Surely?

Lily decided that she was going to ring DI Carter. Find out what was going on. She took out her phone from her pocket and dialled DI Carter's number. Lily held the phone to her ear as she returned to her house. There was no answer. She clicked off the phone and decided that if he was too busy to answer, she would go down to the station and see him in person. Lily needed an update. And she needed one now. Someone had taken her baby sister away from her, and she needed to find out what the hell the police were doing in their so-called investigation.

***

Lily pulled up to the station after borrowing her mother's car again. She looked into the rear window and checked her mascara. Lily had put on some makeup before going down to the police station to try to make herself look a little better than she had. However, Lily hadn't been getting much sleep the past few days since she had been informed of her sister's death. Her eyes were now starting to twitch, and as a result, she was consistently rubbing them. Lily was worried her make-up effort earlier that morning had been pointless. However, as she looked into the mirror, there was no evidence of it being tarnished. Okay, she was ready.

Lily got out of the car and strode into the police station. She had decided to wear something other than her favourite jeans and opted for black leggings with a black high-waist ruffled skirt. But Lily still had on her black and white cardigan. Admittedly, it was more like a security blanket.

DI Carter had said to let him know if she needed anything, so here she was. She wanted something. Answers! Like what had he found?

But, maybe coming to hunt him down at the station wasn't such a good idea. Was she just going to annoy him? Except, she needed these answers. She couldn't simply mope around the house, twiddling her thumbs while there was a killer on the loose. What if he did it to someone else? What if he were planning his next murder right now on some other poor eighteen-year-old girl?

'Hi,' Lily said to the policeman behind the desk. 'I'm here to see DI Carter,' she stated clearly.

'Okay, love, does he know you're coming?' the policeman asked.

'No, but he said if I need anything, get in touch.'

'Right, wait here a minute, and I will see if he's free. What's your name?'

'It's Lily,' she replied. The policeman nodded and disappeared out of sight.

Almost immediately, the policeman appeared again as if by magic. Lily jumped back, holding her hand up to her chest. She was not expecting him to emerge so quickly.

'He will be with you in a minute,' the policeman at the desk told her.

'Okay,' Lily sat down on the chair. She touched her face, still conscious of what it looked like.

After about ten minutes of waiting and reading all the flyers on the wall twice, DI Carter entered.

'Hello Lily. What are you doing here?' DI Carter's voice was stern, and he ran his fingers through his head as if trying to shake away some sort of stress. He didn't seem all that happy to see her.

'Ummm...Sorry, I tried ringing, but you didn't answer,' Lily spluttered.

'Yes, because I'm busy working, trying to solve a murder,' DI Carter barked. He was undeniably stressed. Lily could sense the tension in his voice.

'I went to see Jasmin's ex-boyfriend Dan. It turns out he was on holiday and...'

'You did what?' DI Carter interrupted, 'Lily, this is a murder investigation. You can't just swan off doing what you please. You need to let the police do their job,' he ordered.

Lily could feel the rage building up inside her. How dare he speak to her like that! It was her sister who had been murdered, after all, and she had a right to know what he was doing to try to find out who did it.

Lily clenched her fist but quickly placed it behind her back so he couldn't see how angry he was making her. 'I just want to know what is going on DI Carter,' Lily's tone was sharp and angry. 'I think I have that right, don't you?' She raised her eyebrows at him, unclenching her fist and placing her hand carefully on her hip instead, waiting for his response.

'I'm sorry, you're right, you do. Things are just a little hectic around here at the minute,' DI Carter touched her arm gently. 'Why don't you go home? I'll come by later to give you a full update.'

Lily relaxed her shoulders. Maybe he was right. Perhaps she should let him do his job and speak to him later when he is less busy. As much as it pained her to wait, DI Carter clearly didn't want her to be there.

'Okay,' Lily said. 'But I want answers,' Lily narrowed her eyes at him to tell him she was deadly serious.

Lily walked towards the door. Could life possibly get any worse? But the next thing she knew, Tom came barging through the doors in handcuffs, escorted by DS Millard and two other police officers dressed in uniform.

Lily could feel her face drop. What the hell? Tom? Arrested? Lily's body hardened, and suddenly, she couldn't move, as if glue had been plastered to her feet. Surely, this had nothing to do with Jasmin. What had Tom done?

'What are you arresting him for?' Lily demanded. Her hand gripped her hip as she narrowed her eyes at DI Carter.

'Go home, Lily. You shouldn't be here!'

'Tell me!' Lily barked at him. 'Is he a suspect in my sister's murder?'

DI Carter grabbed her by the arm and led her outside the station.

'Yes, what you are thinking is correct. He's a suspect. Now, please, Lily, go home. Let us do our job,' he repeated his order to her.

Lily pondered for a moment. She wanted to know more, but was equally exhausted and didn't have the strength to argue. 'Okay, DI Carter. I'm going.'

'Oh, and Lily?' he added.

'Yes?' Lily spun back around to face him.

'Please don't do any more investigation work,' He added.

Lily nodded before turning around and walking to her car. She was riddled with disbelief. How could this be? How could they think Tom would have anything to do with Jasmin's death? Did this mean he knew her? All the time she and Tom spoke, he never once mentioned he knew her. What was he hiding? Had he slept with Jasmin?

'Oh God,' Lily said aloud as she got to her car. Was Tom the one who got her pregnant? Is that why she's dead? Because she got pregnant? Lily's mind was going into overdrive. She didn't know what to think.

But the police seemed to know something. Otherwise, they wouldn't have arrested him. They don't arrest people on hearsay. They must have some sort of evidence to suspect Tom. Lily dragged her fingers down her face in frustration. What the hell was going on?

Surely, they must be mistaken. Tom couldn't have done it, could he? How well did Lily really know Tom?

TWENTY-THREE

Katherine

Katherine was on her way to Cunningham and Sons that afternoon; Richard's secretary, Rebecca, had rung and changed the appointment. Katherine didn't want to miss it, so she asked Alison's nanny, Jean, if she would mind picking up the girls from school and watching them until she returned. Thankfully, Jean had agreed. Sophie and Amy got on well together. She hoped Ellie would behave herself. Anyway, she wouldn't be long. It was only an informal chat, and she'd need to be back before James returned home, too.

Katherine tugged at her black pencil skirt as she walked through the door at Cunningham and Sons. She looked at the clock as she walked in. She wasn't as late as she thought. 4 pm, Rebecca had said. Katherine had a few minutes to spare.

Katherine thought about what it would be like to work for her. It had changed a lot since she was last here. The outside was now much more modern-looking. She smiled. If she did go back to work, James would just have to get over it. Grow a pair.

Although she didn't really expect anything to happen. She was just enquiring. Katherine bit her nails as she walked into the building. It smelled the same, and she remembered that scent well. It had a distinct fresh smell about the place. Like the smell of success. However, like the outside, the interior had changed a lot since then. It was now so minimalistic. It was nice. Much better than it used to look.

The last time Katherine was here, she was a young, hopeful thirty-year-old with no ties and had the world in front of her. Ready to take on any challenge that lies in front of her. Now, nine years on, could she do it again? Katherine sighed profoundly and walked up to the desk.

'Hello, I am here to see Richard Morris,' she projected as confidently as possible.

'Yes, please take a seat, and I will call him,' the young, pretty brunette receptionist replied to Katherine as she picked up her reception phone. 'Katherine Lippet, I believe?' the receptionist looked up, placing her hand over the phone. Katherine nodded.

The receptionist was perfectly dressed; it reminded Katherine of Virgin Airlines, with the plush red lipstick and tight red dress. Katherine have her a fake smile and turned around to take a seat. She may be pretty, but she was probably stupid, especially considering she was just a receptionist. Any old dimwit could answer the phones, not like being a solicitor. That took real brains.

Katherine sat down and started to gnaw at her nails again. Oh shit. Her elegant pink nail varnish was starting to flake off her nails. As soon as she knew of her nail biting, she shoved her fingers to the side. That was one bad habit she somehow couldn't get rid of when she was nervous.

Katherine looked around at the solicitors coming in and out of the foyer, busy on their phones. Speaking to clients, dashing out to court. Katherine smiled. She had missed this life so much. It was so exciting. So mesmerising. It was the reason she got into law in the first place.

'Katherine,' Richard was walking towards her. Katherine stood up to greet him. Richard had gone a little grey from the last time she had seen him, and a few wrinkles were now starting to appear. But it looked good. He had a Richard Gere thing going on.

'Oh my God, you look fabulous. Look at you. You look like one of the real housewives of Orange County,' Richard said, leaning in to hug her.

Katherine gave him a disarming smile. Was that a compliment? She decided she would take it as a compliment and embraced Richard's hug. 'Yeah, well, you know me. You have to keep up appearances, or everything falls apart.'

Richard laughed. 'Same old Katherine. Come. Come.' Richard gestured with his hand for her to follow him. She did so gladly. Katherine walked across the marble floor and over to the lift. They both giggled like two schoolchildren as they went inside.

'Remember when we......' Richard blushed.

'Yup!' she smirked at him and rolled her eyes to look in the other direction. She could feel her face heat up. No doubt it was now a rosy, red colour. 'That was after the Dutson v Watson case, right?'

'Yeah, I think it was,' Richard replied.

'That was a long time ago,' Katherine stated.

'It was. Before you became a bore and settled down.' Richard joked.

'Shut up, I'm still fun,' Katherine smirked back at him.

She thought back to that time when she and Richard used to have hot, heated sex after they won a case. That thrill. That excitement after winning a case. It was probably the best time of her life. Now, being back here and in Richard's company, it confirmed that she wanted to return here more than ever. Minus the sex, of course.

Katherine followed Richard into his office. He was now a partner and running his own division. Wow, a lot has changed in nine years. When Katherine left, they were both associates. Now, he was a partner! He had reached the top, whereas she had been at home raising a family. Not really moving forward. Just the same mundane tasks of cleaning, washing, ironing, etc, etc, like she was Lynette Scavo. Richard was right. She was a bore.

Katherine wished more than ever she had said no to James all those years ago and continued working whilst raising their children. But she was so helplessly in love with him at the time and just wanted to make him happy. Nonetheless, she couldn't turn back the clock. Katherine was here now. And so was Richard—someone who knew her and appreciated what a damn good lawyer she was.

'So, I am not going to beat around the bush,' Richard said. 'There is a job for you here if you want it. I can give you the position of associate solicitor. You will need to do some back-to-work training, but we can work around that.'

'It's perfect,' Katherine exclaimed. 'Thank you, Richard. Thank you so much!'

Richard smiled. 'Of course. I would do anything for you Katherine. I know you will be amazing. Plus, I was going to say I am happy to give you a promotion in the coming months, depending on how well you get back into the swing of things. Also, do you still want to become a barrister?'

'I haven't really thought about it. Yeah, I guess so. It's still an option.' Katherine declared. 'Richard, you honestly don't know what this means to me.'

'Come on, we can celebrate with a drink,' Richard said.

'Actually, I.....' Katherine started, but she was interrupted by the sound of his phone ringing.

Richard answered it. 'Richard here.......Yes...Ah, ha, I see. Umm....yes, I can come. Anything for Ann. You say he has been arrested and is at Kitterton Police Station?..... Okay, I will make my way down there. I am in the centre, so I am unsure how long it will take me to get there. But I will be as quick as I can. Okay...It's no problem. I'll meet you there. Yes okay...Bu-bye.'

Richard put the phone down, looking up at Katherine. 'It looks as though I have a new client. An important friend recommended me, too, so I need to go. It's a serious case, too.'

'Whose Ann?' Katherine blurted out.

'Oh, Ann is a dear friend of mine. She passed on my details to a friend of hers, Carol,' Richard informed.

'Oh right, I see,' Katherine nodded. Surely, that wasn't the same Carol she knew. 'What have they been arrested for? If you don't mind me asking?' Katherine asked, curiosity getting the better of her.

'Murder,' he answered bluntly, 'Her husband has been arrested for the murder of that young girl. Ummm, what was her name?'

Katherine was plagued with dazzlement. 'Not Jasmin Knowell?'

'Yes, that's correct. Jasmin Knowell. You heard about that?' Richard asked.

'Her sister is actually a friend, a fellow mum at my kids' school and lives on the same street as me.' Katherine sat down in one of Richard's leather office chairs.

'What was the name of the husband who got arrested?' Katherine knew she was overstepping slightly, but couldn't help it.

'Well, I really shouldn't be telling you, but the client's name is Tom Dwelling.'

Katherine's heart literally stopped beating for a few moments as if a boulder had struck it. Were her ears deceiving her? Tom. Been arrested? Surely not! This was madness!

Richard must have noticed the colour leave Katherine's face. 'You know him?' Richard asked.

Katherine closed her mouth and gulped down the shock. 'Uh, yes. He is one of the dads at the school and lives on my street too.'

Richard chuckled. 'You have more drama going on than a group of hens on a night out,' Richard grabbed his jacket hanging on the back of the chair. 'Sorry to love and leave you, Katherine.'

'No, that's okay, it's fine,' Katherine reassured. 'I need to get back anyway.'

'If you see Rebecca on your way out, she will sort all the details out. Let her know when you want to start, and she'll let me know. Also, here is my card. If you need to ring directly for anything. My mobile number is on here. Welcome back,' Richard cheered.

'Okay, great, thanks,' she grabbed his card. Katherine was left standing in Richard's office as he disappeared from sight. Katherine let out an uncontrollable sigh. Whew! What an afternoon! Tom, a murderer? Surely not.

But she couldn't think about that right now. She had a job. What's more, it was her old job, back working with her old amazing boss. Now, how would she break the news to her husband? Crap.

TWENTY-FOUR

Tom

Tom wriggled uncomfortably as the cuffs tugged against his wrists. They were tight. Very tight. Yet his hands were shaking uncontrollably behind his back. Tom was quaking on the brink of terror. It instantly brought him back ten years prior, when he had previously been arrested. He had tried to block the bleak memory out of his mind. His brain could not comprehend what was happening. Surely this wasn't real. Not again. For fuck sake. Please, not again.

Tom turned around, and Lily had disappeared outside. Shit, what must she be thinking? Well, she is probably gobsmacked, to say the least. His chest was fluttering like a captured bird. Tom tried to take in deep breaths, but it was useless; it was rapidly out of control, breathing deeper and deeper. Come on Tom, get a grip. If he had survived this once before, he could survive it again.

'You can put all your possessions in here,' the policeman instructed Tom. He did as the policeman asked, pulling out his keys, phone, wallet and some gum. He chucked it into the tray in front of him. A female detective police officer guided him down the gloomy corridor, and they stopped halfway outside one of the cells. She took off his cuffs and gestured for him to go inside. Tom clenched each wrist in an attempt to soothe them from the tight grip they had been placed in. He looked inside the cold, tiny cell before him and shuffled in. Tom jumped as the door slammed shut behind him. This was his worst nightmare come true.

'We'll be interviewing you shortly,' the female detective said from behind the door. Shortly followed by her footsteps clicking down the corridor. She was gone. Tom was alone. Alone with his thoughts. He lay down on what he assumed was meant to be a bed. However, the floor looked more appealing than what was placed in front of him. He turned his head. A revolting smell came from the corner. There stood a manky toilet you wouldn't want your worst enemy to pee into. It looked as though it had been there since the Stone Age. He'd hold it in. Maybe not drink much. Not that there was anything to drink. Would they provide a drink? He couldn't remember. He was in his late teens the last time he was here. And Tom had done his best to block the trauma from his mind.

Tom's stomach rumbled. He hadn't eaten anything since breakfast. It was now late afternoon, although food was the last thing on his mind. His thoughts travelled back to when the police had come for him earlier that afternoon. What was going on inside Carol's mind? Oh God, Jack. He must have been so scared when the police came and took away his Daddy. Thank God Carol had come back when she did. Who knows what would have happened to Jack otherwise.

Tom yelled out. There was too much going on in his head. He didn't like being alone with his thoughts. Usually, the TV, music, or something else could distract him. But not here. There was no escaping his demons here. There was nothing to do but think. He desperately tried to remember what happened that night. He was at that bar and had met Jasmin. Eighteen. Although he wouldn't have guessed she was so young and still at school. She looked at least twenty-two.

'Thomas Dwelling,' a deep, manly voice shouted through the door.

'Yes,' Tom jumped up almost immediately. What was going on? A key turned in the cell door, and it swung open. On the other side was a large, tall, uniformed police officer standing like a robot, staring at Tom.

'Come with me,' the police officer grunted.

'Where are we going?' Tom chipped. There was no reply. The policeman turned his head and escorted Tom down the corridor to a room. Tom instantly recognised the door. It was an interview room. The police officer gestured for Tom to go inside, and he did as he was told. Wow, friendly bunch of twats they have working here. The room was empty. Now Tom knew something was up. There was no solicitor. In fact, there was nobody. Not even the detectives. What was going on? Carol had promised she would phone someone to come to the station. Either she had broken her promise, in which case he didn't blame her. Or they just hadn't arrived yet. Tom hadn't even been given a phone call. Which he knew he was entitled to.

Tom sat on the chair; a camera stood high up in the corner with a flashing red light attached to it. They must be watching, trying to figure him out, no doubt. Tom didn't even know whether he was guilty. Or Tom wouldn't be in this situation now. He chuckled. Really, how the fuck had he got into this situation? Tom crossed his arms on the desk before him and planted his face into it. The way he used to when he was bored at school, waiting for a lesson to end. But as soon as he did, the door to the interview room whirled open. In came DI Carter and another female detective, who presumably was on the case too.

'I am Detective Sergeant Millard,' the female detective said. 'And this is my colleague Detective Inspector Carter,' Tom already knew who he was. DI Carter stared at Tom with daggers as if he wanted to kill him. Tom glared back at him. What happened to innocent until proven guilty? Jesus Man. How was this man so certain it was Tom who'd killed that poor girl?

'Are you happy for us to start? While we wait for your solicitor to arrive?' DS Millard asked calmly. She had a pleasant mannerism about her, which was more than could be said about DI Carter.

'Yes, of course, because I didn't do anything!' Tom directed his eyes to DI Carter.

'Interview commenced at 4.50 pm,' DS Millard stated.

'So, Mr Dwelling, can you tell us where you were the night Jasmin Knowell went missing?' DI Carter challenged.

'Ummm.....well, yes, I did go out for a drink with my brother, and yes, I did meet her at that bar.....what was it called? Oh yes....the Smoking Gun. But I swear I don't remember anything after that. But I'm pretty certain that I did not kill her, though,' he contested.

DI Carter sized Tom up. 'I didn't ask if you killed her. I asked where you were. What's the matter, Mr Dwelling? Guilty conscience?' DI Carter slammed his hands down on the desk. As that was going to give him some ultimate revelation to confess or something.

'Ummm....yes, I know, but you arrested me on suspicion of Jasmin's murder, so I'm telling you I didn't kill her,' Tom protested.

'Are you trying to be funny, Mr Dwelling?' DI Carter spoke through gritted teeth.

'No, I'm just stating a fact. What's your problem? I'm telling you what I know,' Tom was losing his patience with this guy.

'I think maybe I will just wait for my lawyer to arrive.'

DI Carter ignored the latter. 'So what were you doing with this sixteen-year-old girl when you met her? Just chatting, were you? Or doing more than that? Grooming? Sexual activity?' DI Carter's voice grew louder with each word, angrier. Fucking hell. Talk about interrogation. He should be working for MI5.

'What are you talking about?' Tom retaliated.

DI Carter opened his mouth, but DS Millard touched his arm, shaking her head to stop him from talking.

He ignored her. 'We have a witness who says they saw you and Jasmin Knowell leave the toilet and bar together.' DSI Carter was almost shouting at Tom now. DI Carter's body was now shaking with anger.

'DI Carter!' DS Millard shouted sternly, narrowing her eyes at him.

Oh shit. *A witness*? Should he tell the truth or lie? Lie and say what? Tom clenched his hands together. They were so sweaty. They always got sweaty when he was nervous. Although this time, he had John McClane and his comrade watching his every move to see if he was the murderer.

'Okay, so I.....' Tom started.

The interview door burst open. 'Don't say another word!' A voice shouted.

It was Tom's solicitor. 'Hi Tom, my name is Richard. I'm your solicitor. Don't say anything else. I have spoken with your wife,' Richard whispered into Tom's ear as he sat in the seat beside him.

The door opened again, and another police officer beckoned DI Carter. DI Carter got up and left the room.

'Interview suspended at 5.10 pm. DI Carter has left the room,' DS Millard said as she clicked off the tape.

DI Carter returned minutes later. He sighed and then threw his chair against the wall. 'Okay, you're free to go. For now.' He narrowed his eyes at him.

Thank god for that. What was going on? What had they found? Well, he wouldn't be told twice, so Tom rose up and headed straight out the door. He didn't want to be in there a minute longer than he had to be.

Out in the police station reception area, Carol stood with her arms folded in front of her chest. Tom approached her with caution. Even though she was here, he was unsure how she would react. Carol wrapped her arms around him as he drew close enough and squeezed him tightly. Tom gently responded with the same squeeze.

'Carol has given you an alibi for that night,' Richard informed Tom. 'She has said you were home by midnight. Jasmin had an altercation with her attacker. She was wearing a Fitbit watch at the time. The screen cracked and froze at 1.34 am. So the police know it was roughly this time. Therefore, it is unlikely that you would have killed her, being home way before the incident occurred.'

'Also, we're not meant to know this,' Richard suddenly lowered his voice and waited until they were outside the police station to talk again. 'I have friends in the police, and apparently, the CCTV at the bar wasn't working that night, so they don't really have anything else to go on,' Richard tapped his nose. 'Apart from one witness identifying you went inside the toilet with her; there was really nobody else that remembers seeing you.

And although your fingerprints were found on her clothes, this could have easily got there when she was still alive at the bar. So they really don't have anything to tie you to her murder.'

Tom clasped his hands on his chest. 'Oh, thank God, that was some scary shit,' he turned to Carol. 'Thank you.'

But her face was wooden. She was not giving anything away. 'Let's just go home.'

TWENTY-FIVE

Tom

Carol slammed the door hard behind her. Her eyes were blazing like a fire had broken out in them. Tom stepped back. He could see that everything was not alright. She had not said one word to him in the car. She had waited—waited until they got home.

'I know, I know. I'm sorry,' Tom apologised.

'SORRY....SORRY!' Carol stepped forward, staring at him; her eyes didn't blink. The storm was positively blazing through her rich brown eyes. Tom had most certainly angered the beast. The vein in her head was pulsating so hard it was almost leaving her forehead.

'Surely you have a bit more than "I'm sorry!" The curve in her face was a harsh truculence. She was well and truly furious, although she had a right to be. Tom didn't even know what to say to Carol. Where would he start?

'I can explain,' Tom started. But he didn't have the words to explain.

Carol folded her arms across her chest. 'Okay, I'm listening. Go for it. Explain! I really can't wait for this one.'

'Where's Jack?' The thought suddenly occurred to Tom. He asked Carol about it at the station, but she just replied by saying he was safe. Safe? What did that mean? Where the fuck was his son?

'Don't change the subject,' Carol fumed.

Tom squeezed his eyebrows together in frustration. 'I just want to know where my son is, ' he said, raising his voice at her.

Carol started pacing, 'Are you kidding me? I thought you were going to explain how in God's name you ended up getting arrested for the murder of a young eighteen-year-old and how a witness has seen you leaving the toilet together at that bar you went to with your idiot, irresponsible brother!' Carol took a huge breath, taking off her coat after her rant.

'I was angry at you. Really angry and really fed up,' Tom almost whined. There was no way he was taking all the blame for this. 'I didn't know how old she was. I thought she was twenty-two or something. I really didn't know she was eighteen and still in school. How would I? She was in a bar, for Christ's sake,' Tom braced himself for Carol's reaction. But instead, her vein stopped pulsating, and tears started to run down her cheeks.

'You hate me that much?' Carol sobbed, walking over to the sofa and sitting down. She put her face into her hands.

'No, I was just fed up with everything. I lost my job. You were working all the time. I never went out anywhere. Then, when I did, it just felt so good. I didn't plan it. I was drunk and high. She was just there. It didn't mean anything.'

Carol continued to cry. Tom didn't know what to do. Should he comfort her? Would she want him to? He shifted his weight to the side awkwardly.

'What happened then?' Carol muttered, looking at the ground. It didn't seem like she wanted to look at Tom. And who could blame her?

'I don't know! I can't remember! I thought you said I was at home at midnight. So, everything is cool, right? I didn't do it. Thank God because I really...,' Tom rambled.

'I lied,' Carol mumbled quietly. But Tom heard every word clearly. His heart flickered with a vague terror at the sheer mention of those two words Carol spoke. What? She lied? So, does that mean he could have done it?

'What do you mean you lied, what the fuck did happen then?' Tom questioned.

'I don't know what time you got in. I told them that's when you got in. I told the police I looked at the clock, and it was midnight,' Carol took a deep breath, looking up at him. 'But I don't know what time you got in. I just woke up early in the morning, and you were there. More or less naked. After putting your clothes in the wash, I went to work.'

Tom's worst nightmare had come true. It was becoming more evident that he attacked Jasmin whilst being off his face. But why?

'You do tend to get a bit rowdy when you're drinking vodka and those Red Bull drinks, even more so when you've had cocaine inside you. Oh, Tom, what have you done?' Carol's face fell forward into her hands again, and she continued to sob once more.

Tom rolled his eyes. How was she making this about her? He was the one finding out that he was most likely a murderer. 'Why did you lie?' he demanded.

'Because you're my husband....because you're Jack's father and a good one at that. Plus, I kind of panicked. I knew you were back at some point in the night. I just don't know if it was before midnight,' Carol cried, looking back at Tom. He could see the fear shining out of her eyes. Was she scared of him? Or scared for him?

'Oh my God, Carol, what have you done?' Tom contested.

Carol suddenly jumped up from the sofa. 'What have I done? What have you done, Tom?' she yelled, shoving Tom backwards.

He didn't retaliate. Instead, he collapsed on the sofa where Carol had been sitting. 'This is such a mess. I don't remember anything after I left the bar. I've tried to remember. But I don't even remember leaving the bar. I obviously got home at some point.'

Carol sat beside him, 'I've taken Jack to my mother's. I think he should stay there for a few days.'

'Your mother, why have you taken him to your mother's?!' Tom howled, and suddenly, he felt angry again. Oh, not that bloody cow. Any excuse! She was always looking down her nose at Tom. He knew full well Carol's mother thought Tom wasn't good enough for her daughter, and she could do better. If Carol's mother had it her way, she would be off marrying some lord.

'I think it is for the best, I don't think our son should be around this, do you?' Carol exclaimed, her voice condescending. She loved to be the one who was so perfect all the time.

'You think I did it, don't you?!' Tom yelled as he stood up, backing away from her, 'You think I killed that girl!'

'Well, Tom, to be fair. What am I supposed to think? The evidence is all flowing your way. Plus your history...' Carol stated.

'My history? What's that got anything to do with it?' Tom interrupted.

'I don't want to believe that's what really happened. But now I'm not so sure, looking back.'

'Carol, I didn't do that. You were one of the few people who I thought believed me. That girl back in our first year of uni made it up.'

'Yes, and I stuck by you then. Now I....'

'Go on!' Tom shrieked.

'Now I...Tom, I don't know what to believe anymore. I feel like I don't know you. Maybe I never knew you. It was there, and maybe I chose to ignore it. I'm the only reason you got away with it back then.'

'CAROL!' Tom screamed. 'I didn't rape that girl Suzie back in university, and I didn't fucking kill Jasmin!' Steam was coming out of Tom's ears. No matter what she thought, there was no way she was going to take away his son. No way in hell!

TWENTY-SIX

Lily

That murdering bastard. How could he? He wasn't Lily's friend. Nor was it likely that he actually was ever into her. She was such a lousy judge of character. Lily was muttering to herself as she slammed the pots on the drying rack. There were so many emotions raging through Lily. After burning a hole in the living room carpet with her pacing, Lily had decided she needed to do something. So, she had opted to do the washing up.

It was Lily's attempt to shake off the fathomless depths of suffering that were gripping her soundly. Was it working? Well, the pots and pans were positively feeling her pain.

'Mummy, are you okay?' Meghan ran in. She was making quite a racket.

'Yes, I'm okay, honey. I just thought I would do the dishes,' Lily plastered a forced smile across her face.

'Are you sure you're okay, Mummy?' Meghan spoke timidly. She was too smart for her own good.

'Yes, I'm fine,' Lily answered through gritted teeth. She really needed to be alone right now. 'Just go and play, Meghan. Leave mummy alone, okay?' Meghan's eyes were wide with extreme apprehension before she quickly ran out of the kitchen.

Lily sighed. She shouldn't be taking her anger out on Meghan. Lily stopped what she was doing and collapsed to the floor. Floods of tears came streaming down her face. The last thing Lily wanted to do was upset her daughter. To be honest, Lily was surprised there were any tears left after the amount of crying she had done over the past week. What was going to come next? Just when she thought things couldn't get any worse, they had. Her sister was dead, and Lily was still finding it hard to get her head around it.

Her mother was like Sleeping Beauty since she was released from the hospital. Dosed up and out of it. Part of Lily wished this were her. Taken away from reality for just a little bit. Then she wouldn't have to deal with her sister's murder on her own, as that's what it felt like. And the one person whom Lily thought she might actually be able to lean on was now the lead suspect in her sister's murder case. How the hell did that happen?

But that would leave Meghan alone. Lily was all she had, and she'd just told Meghan to leave her alone. What kind of mother was she?

But Lily couldn't deal with any questions or noise right now. Meghan's antics just irritated her. She didn't know how to be a good mother right now. Part of her personality was shutting down one by one, and Lily's once glistening personality became more like that of a figure in the distance. She could see it, yet she couldn't grab hold of it, and with each passing day, it appeared to be getting further and further away.

The doorbell rang, making Lily jump out of her thoughts. Great, what was it now? Lily ignored it. She didn't want to get up. But the next thing Lily knew, Tom stood in the kitchen doorway.

'Get away from me!' Lily shouted. 'Meghan, Meghan!' Meghan came running in.

'Mummy, you're scaring me,' Meghan cried, clinging to Lily.

'I promise, Lily, it wasn't me. I came here to tell you what happened. Please let me explain?' Lily darted her eyes over him. Should she hear him out?

'Meghan, go and play in the living room,' she instructed. Meghan did as her mother told her.

Tom reached out his hand to Lily. She ignored him and pushed herself off the floor, so she was now face to face with Tom.

'Okay, explain,' Lily ordered, crossing her arms. 'Didn't stay in jail long, then I see?'

Tom's eyes widened like a doe-eyed puppy. 'No, they released me. Look, I didn't know it was your sister. Things have been bad with my wife for a long time. I left and went to a bar with my brother. I met Jasmin. I thought she was older, I swear. I was really drunk and high. She was there, and it just happened.'

'You what? You slept with my eighteen-year-old sister?!' Lily couldn't help but yell.

'Yes, Lily, please don't shout. I can't take any more shouting,' Tom said quietly.

'Then you probably shouldn't have come around here if you didn't want to hear any shouting!' She yelled, purposely.

Tom continued to stare at her with his big, brown, puppy-dog eyes.

Lily sighed. 'I get it. You didn't know who she was at the time. But you knew who she was when you saw me hand you some flyers and.....' she pondered for a moment. 'And that's why you ran out so abruptly that day,' Lily looked down at the floor as she came to the realisation and then back up at him.

Tom nodded in agreement. 'Yes, I was with your sister, I'm a bad fucking guy. But I didn't kill her. I need you to know that. Well, I don't think so anyway...' Tom mumbled.

'What do you mean, you don't think so?' Lily asked, puzzled. Both hands were firmly placed on her hips, lifting her eyebrows as she waited for his response. Part of her wanted to take a swing at him. She was just waiting for the moment she could land a huge, great punch in between his nose.

'I mean, I don't actually remember anything after that night,' Tom stuttered.

'Jesus, you need to leave,' Lily exclaimed.

'I don't want to lie to you. I want to be honest with you,' Tom fretted.

'Tom, what are you even doing here? I'm not your wife. I'm not anything to you. You came over here to do what? Explain that you may or may not have killed my sister. And then what?' Lily tilted her head to the side condescendingly. 'You thought I would say, there, there, Tom, it's okay. I understand. We would hug it out, and all sing Kumbaya together! What is wrong with you? You are one messed-up person!' Lily was practically screaming in his face.

'Lily, I like you. I'm attracted to you. I love my wife, but....'

'Go and use your lines on some other poor girl. AND GET OUT!' Tom simply wasn't getting the message. She pushed him hard on his chest with both her hands. But he barely moved. God, what was he made of bricks?

Tom stared at her intently, 'Okay, I'm going if that's what you want.'

'It is,' Lily snared. It wasn't what she wanted deep down, but how could she trust this man? He had more baggage than Heathrow's Terminal One. Lily dropped her shoulders and looked at the ground. She had nothing left to give. 'Please just go.' Her voice was stern but softer than her previous yelling.

Tom walked out the front door. Thank God he was gone.

Meghan approached Lily and asked, 'Are you sad because of Aunty Jasmin?'

She bent down onto her knees so she was level with Meghan. 'Yes, I am.' Lily nodded.

'Is Aunty Jasmin coming back? Is she still lost?' Meghan asked.

'She's not lost anymore. But Aunty Jasmin isn't coming back, darling. She's gone to heaven, baby,' Lily spoke softly, trying to hold back the tears. A lump had become apparent in her throat as if she had swallowed a sweet humbug whole.

'I miss her, Mummy,' Meghan cried, resting her head on Lily's shoulder.

'I know, I miss her too,' she put her arms around Meghan. Meghan swung her arms around Lily's neck in response. She had been so selfish. Her little girl was going through a tough time, too. It wasn't just about herself.

'Come on, let's get your pyjamas on, and I'll read you a story. How about your favourite, Little Red Riding Hood?'

'Yay!' Meghan exclaimed. Jumping up and down.

After putting a tired Meghan to bed, Lily collapsed onto the sofa. Every inch of her muscles was aching. But she needed to be brave and carry on. If not for her, for Meghan's sake. Lily didn't want this to affect her childhood any more than it already had. She was all

Meghan had in the world. Yes, from now on, she would be braver. Tougher.

The doorbell rang. Please say that twat hasn't come back. Lily thought twice about answering, but didn't want to wake up Meghan. She got up and strolled to the front door. But it wasn't Tom, it was DI Carter. Excellent. What brilliant news did he have to bring now?

TWENTY-SEVEN

Katherine

Katherine smiled as she looked at herself in the mirror. She was so excited to be going back to work as a lawyer. But equally, she was nervous about telling James the news. How would he react? He had not been so positive when she had mentioned it before. Katherine wasn't scared of her husband. But he was a control freak, and this was without doubt out of his control. James wasn't going to take the news that well. In his eyes, James liked the idea of Katherine solely looking after the home.

Or maybe James hadn't wanted Katherine to get her hopes up too much about going to work? It was a possibility. An unlikely one, but still a possibility. Now that it was official and Katherine had the job, James might support her decision. After all, she had given up her career long enough for him. But Katherine wanted her own life, too. In fact, she needed a life of her own. Katherine was going stir-crazy, rattling around in that big house of theirs. And it was about time she got one. So, whether James liked it or not. This was happening.

Katherine had waited until after dinner to talk to James. Just the two of them. No disruptions. She walked down the stairs after tucking the girls into bed. Maybe a glass of wine would help smooth over their talk. Yes, a glass of wine was definitely worth taking out to James. Katherine took the Whispering Angel wine bottle from the fridge and poured herself and James a glass.

'Drinking wine, are we? On a school night?' James interjected. 'Do you think that is appropriate, Katherine?'

James narrowed his eyes at her; his tone was very serious.

She turned around and put the wine back in the fridge, rolling her eyes. Lighten up, James. It's just one bloody glass of wine. She didn't dare to say that to his face, though.

'I just thought it would be nice. I have some exciting news,' Katherine beamed, flicking her blonde hair fiercely. 'Should we sit?' She was finding it hard to stay calm.

'Oh, okay then,' James said, picking up the glass of wine and taking a sip. He walked over to the living room and sat down. Katherine joined him by his side.

'So go on then? Don't leave me in suspense,' James piped.

'So....I got offered my old job back at the firm,' she smiled, sipping a glass of wine.

'You what?' James yelled. Standing over her. 'I thought you were going to tell me you were pregnant.'

'Pregnant?' Katherine elevated her eyebrows, puzzled. 'Why would I be pregnant? I'm on the pill. Plus, I'm holding a glass of wine.'

'I don't know, these things happen. I thought maybe you were just having one glass. Going back to work and leaving your children is not good news!' James was using his large build to lean over Katherine and intimidate her.

She was desperate to stand up and meet his gaze, but James's body prevented her. Katherine glared at him. Despite her trembling hands resting on the sofa, she was not afraid of him, and she would have it out with him. 'Why can't I go back to work? I want to. I do everything around the house. The cleaning, washing, ironing, and cooking. Bloody everything! It's my turn to have a life.

We live in the 21st century, where women do work, James.'

The adrenaline was pumping fiercely around Katherine's body. She had never really spoken to James that way before. Most of the time, Katherine gave in to him; it was just easier. But not this time. This was something she passionately wanted to do. Katherine took a sip of her wine. But without warning, James knocked it out of her hand with an all-mighty force, and it landed on the wall to the side of her, smashing into tiny pieces.

Katherine's face fell. James stood back slightly as if allowing her permission to get up. Shit, she needed to get away from him. What the hell was going on? She had not seen him this angry before. He was always so in control. Always so collected. But not tonight. Tonight, there was a fire dancing around in his eyes. He was shaking like a wild animal, finally freed from their cage. Katherine got up, but James threw her against the wall as she did. He gripped hold of her shoulders, pinning her tightly. Excruciating pain shot down her arms, and they went limp. James raised his fist. Katherine closed her eyes, bracing herself for what was about to happen. Bang. She opened her eyes. There was a hole in the wall next to her.

'You are mine, do you understand?' his eyes blazed like a campfire. Fiercely red. Fixed to hers. 'I don't want you going off, doing God knows what. If you want to do something, you ask for my permission first!' James exclaimed.

'Do you understand?!' James shouted. Katherine nodded in agreement. 'Good!' James let go of his hand. She rubbed her shoulders. Tears ran down her cheeks, and Katherine swiftly brushed them away. He didn't deserve her tears.

Katherine knew James was slightly on the possessive side. But she had quite liked that side of him. He had always looked out for her in the past, ensuring she was always safe. She was his woman, and he never seemed interested in anyone else. James had been her protector against annoying guys when they had first met. He looked after her. James was her security blanket when her mother died. Katherine wouldn't have gone through her death if it hadn't been for James.

But now hearing the words "you are mine". Those words didn't feel good. There was a pit at the bottom of her stomach. Katherine had never seen James this angry before. Then again, she couldn't remember the last time she disobeyed her husband. Like a good little wife, Katherine always did everything on James's terms. Had she been that desperate for love? But now, something had sparked off inside Katherine. She wanted her independence back.

Katherine slowly drifted over to the kitchen and grabbed the mop, dustpan, and brush. She didn't want glass everywhere. Katherine made every effort to turn her back to the wall in case James made a move on her again. Katherine's shoulder ached as she moved, but she would not let him know that. She continued to sweep.

James left the room. Katherine dropped the mop and was left quivering in the living room. Thank God he was gone. Did that really just happen? Did her calm and controlled husband actually just lose his cool? Katherine grabbed a glass from the counter and ran the cold water. She downed a glass of water back with a shaking hand. She coughed as it reached her oesophagus. It had gone down the wrong way.

James walked back into the room. Katherine froze. 'Stay away from me,' she warned. She held up her hand to distance herself from him.

'Katherine, I'm so very sorry. I really don't know what came over me. Work is really stressful at the moment, and something is going on with one of the lads. I just don't understand why you want to return to work so much.' James muttered, 'I guess I just feel threatened. You are going back to work, so you might leave us. Go off with some hot lawyer,' James bowed his head. He did look really sorry for himself.

Katherine relaxed her shoulders. 'Aww, James. I just gave up my career to raise the girls, and I know they are not grown up, but they are both in school full-time now, and I want to do something for myself. I don't even have to work full-time. I could just do the school hours and see how I go,' Katherine moved a step closer to him.

Katherine beckoned him to come nearer. 'Come here,' James fell into her arms, and she cuddled him like a child. 'I'm so sorry I hurt you. I can't believe I hurt my beautiful wife. Please say you will forgive me?' James looked up at Katherine with complete sorrow in his eyes. He slowly grabbed her arm and started to kiss it.

She felt a tingling sensation up her arm, and she smiled. 'Of course I do,' Katherine replied. But she had not seen him this vulnerable before. He was always so controlled usually. So sure of himself and what he wanted. But James had lost his cool, something he had not done with her in a long time. What was up with him?

James was actually not as tough as he had made out. He was just a vulnerable little boy underneath it all. But Katherine was secretly glad he was now crying into her lap. It meant she could now comfort him. The hairs stood up on Katherine's arms. She had the upper hand for once. It was powerful.

TWENTY-EIGHT

Lily

Lily reluctantly opened her front door. What news did DI Carter need to bring her now? The last time she had seen him, he had practically told her off, like some naughty little girl. Now, he was standing face to face with her in the rain. Lily stared at him. He had an impressive jaw structure that actually made him quite handsome.

'So are you going to let me in, Lily, or just watch me get drenched in the rain?' DI Carter said to her.

'Umm...yeah....sorry, come in. Is it just you? Or is Detective Millard with you?' She widened the door and placed her back against the door so he could get past. As DI Carter moved closer, she noticed his brown eyes were a beautiful honey colour that glowed as he stood under the hallway light. She hadn't noticed it before.

'No, it's just me,' he said, massaging the back of his neck.

Lily cleared her throat. 'Would you like a cup of tea?'

'Do you have coffee?' DI Carter asked.

'Yeah, sure, I think so. My Mum drinks it, so there should be some here,' Lily walked into the kitchen, her eyes searching the counter. 'You're in luck, yes, we do.'

'Thanks,' DI Carter replied and followed her into the kitchen. He still had his damp coat on, which was dripping wet. DI Carter took it off and hung it on the back of the kitchen chair. Lily looked at the coat. Her mum would have a fit if she saw water dripping on her kitchen floor.

There was a heavy silence between them. Why was he here? What was this visit about? Lily was dreading the answer. Maybe he was here to tell her off again.

'How is your mum?' DI Carter asked, breaking the tension between them.

'Yeah, she's doing much better, thanks,' Lily replied. But the truth was, her mum was not herself at the moment, especially with all the medication they had given her.

'Oh good,' he said with a half smile and took the cup of coffee that Lily was passing to him.

Would he tell her why he was there, or would they have small talk all evening? 'So...ummm....what brings you here?' Lily asked.

'I told you earlier I'd update you on the case. I know you were quite upset earlier when you saw Tom being arrested.'

Lily had almost forgotten about that.

'I just wanted to tell you in person that we don't believe Tom was involved with your sister's murder,' DI Carter informed. He took a sip of his coffee.

'Yes, I already know......well, he was just here, telling me he didn't do it.'

'He did what?' DI Carter exclaimed, nearly choking on his coffee. This was odd. Why did he care if Tom came over? It had nothing to do with him.

'Yeah, he came over earlier. Honestly, I thought it was him at the door again.'

'You know he has a wife, right?' DI Carter said, his voice was shrill. 'God damn low life,' he was shaking his head.

Lily tried to ignore his reaction. 'Yes, I know. Sorry, but what does this have to do with why you have come over? Plus, I don't really think this is any of your business.' He was meant to be a police officer. Surely, this was overstepping his professional duty.

'Maybe it was a mistake coming over here to update you on the case. I should probably go.' DI Carter moved back towards the back of the chair and grabbed hold of his coat.

He hesitated, 'It's just...I sort of know what you're going through, and it pains me to see pigs like him get away with it.'

'What do you mean?' Lily pursed her lips.

'My sister was murdered when we were both teenagers. I knew her boyfriend had done it. He even admitted it to me once. However, due to a lack of evidence and no witnesses, he got away with it. I don't want the same thing happening to Jasmin and you. And that Tom. I just had this feeling about him, like it was him. But I was wrong, letting my past feelings get in the way of this case.'

'Oh right, I'm really sorry about your sister. And thank you for coming over and telling me, DI Carter. It really does mean a lot that you're telling me,' Lily said softly. She had clearly been a bit harsh with him before, and now she felt bad. Her head was such a scrambled mess. She was going between reality and a daydream at the moment.

'That's okay, it was a long time ago,' he smiled warmly at her. I just thought you might want to know, as I know he's your friend. Also, please call me Alfie. I think we are on a first-name basis,' he walked towards the front door, and Lily followed to see him out.

DI Carter spun around before reaching the door. 'Look, I know Tom was not involved in your sister's murder, but there is something I don't like about that guy. You should stay away from him. A nice girl like you, he will take advantage,' DI Carter warned.

'He's harmless,' Lily told him. It was awful what happened to his sister, but still, this hadn't really anything to do with him. 'It is nice of you to be concerned, but really, that is up to me. Especially now I know he had nothing to do with my sister's murder.' She paused for a moment, looking him directly in the eye. 'But there's still the question of who did it.'

'Well, like I told you before, that's the police's job. So please do not get involved Lily. If there's an update in the case, I'm happy to come over and see you,' DI Carter ordered. My God, this man was bossy. What was wrong with wanting to do her own digging and research?

If it meant she would get answers, then that is what Lily would do. For all they knew, it could have been Dan, Jasmin's ex-boyfriend, who was involved. But Lily knew he had been on holiday. She had found that out before they did.

'Do you have any other leads then?' Lily asked.

'Not at the moment. But we will go back to the drawing board tomorrow. We are trying to get hold of the cab driver of the cab Jasmin got into. But it wasn't a company, it looked like a private cab, and unfortunately, the CCTV didn't pick up a number plate. But don't worry, we will find another way to chase him up.'

'Thank you, DI Carter. You really are doing everything you can to find who killed my sister. And sorry for being a pain,' Lily apologised. But that wasn't going to stop her from doing her own digging.

'Well, it's my job, but thanks for saying that,' DI Carter said. 'Please, Lily, call me Alfie.'

'Sorry, Alfie,' Lily replied reluctantly.

'You're the one who should be put on a pedestal. You just lost your sister to a murderer, and now you are taking care of your mum, too, which can't be easy. Plus, despite everything, you are trying to raise your daughter by yourself,' DI Carter stated.

It was tough, and the truth was that she was struggling to keep it together. Tom was the only person she could lean on, but Lily wasn't sure if she could trust him. Finding out he wasn't the one who murdered her sister was such a huge relief, and a part of security had been restored in her life. Lily was grateful for this. Maybe she should give Tom a call. It can't have been easy being arrested for a murder you didn't commit. Tom had been there for her when she needed him at the morgue.

'Have you told Tom that you won't be charging him?' Lily asked.

'No, not yet. I think I'll wait until tomorrow to tell him. Keep him in his misery for a little longer.'

'Why would you do that? It wasn't him, so surely you could give him the same courtesy as you did me?' Lily demanded. Who did he think he was? 'I tell you what, don't worry yourself, I will just go and tell him.'

'Sorry, I didn't mean to upset you,' DI Carter's voice suddenly became more timid. His face dropped, and Lily knew he regretted making those comments.

'It's okay,' she muttered, although she was waiting for the moment he opened the door and was gone.

'Okay, I will leave you to it. Please be careful with that one, though. I don't want you getting hurt. You have been through enough as it is,' DI Carter stated.

'Yes, yes, okay.' Lily replied. Oh my God. He wasn't her dad. She was actually a grown woman.

'Okay, I'll leave you to it then,' DI Carter finally opened the front door to leave.

'Okay, bye, DI Carter,' Lily said. It didn't feel right calling him Alfie.

'Bye, Lily, take care of yourself,' she nodded and closed the door behind him. What a funny copper. He was most undoubtedly unusual and bossy. But Lily was also grateful he had come around.

Lily took out her phone as she strolled back into the kitchen. She texted Tom, "Please, can you come over? I need to talk to you. Sorry about earlier."

Lily placed her phone down on the kitchen counter next to her. She hoped he wasn't too upset from earlier. Tom deserved to know the truth sooner rather than later. It must be awful thinking you might have killed someone when you hadn't. Not being able to remember what happened because you were so wasted.

Lily's phone almost instantly pinged. There was a text message from Tom. "Okay, I'm on my way. You're not going to shout at me, are you?"

Lily laughed out. "No, I'm not. See you in a minute".

Lily walked across the living room and sat back on the couch. The TV was still playing, and an episode of Prime Suspect was on. Oh shit. It was one of her favourite programmes at the moment. Was it recording? Lily picked up the TV remote. Umm no. Damn it.

The doorbell rang, and Lily clicked the record button on her Sky remote before running to the door.

'Hi,' Tom stared up at her, smiling.

'Hi,' Lily greeted him. He was absolutely soaking. 'Let me take your coat,' she said, undoing it from his shoulders. Phew! It stank of dampness. He had only walked from around the corner, but it looked like it was really coming down out there. As Lily walked back into the living room, she was suddenly aware of the loud thumping of the rain hitting the living room window. She placed his coat on the radiator.

Tom followed her in. 'I know I'm soaking. Do you mind if I take off my socks and shoes? They're drenched too,' Tom declared.

'Yeah, sure, go ahead. You can put your socks on the radiator there,' Lily pointed out.

'Thanks,' he replied.

Lily shivered. She put on the electric fire her mum had installed where there had once been a fireplace. It was a pretty nice feature and looked nice to cuddle into on a night like this. The downpour was getting louder from outside, but Lily liked the sound of rain. It reminded her of being in a caravan as a child on holiday in West Wales. Jackie, Jasmin and she all snuggled inside, playing board games and listening to the sound of rain outside. The sound was comforting.

Lily sat down on the sofa, and Tom followed her into her living room, sitting next to her.

'So I just had a visit from the police, and they will not be charging you. I think they're formally going to tell you tomorrow, but I thought you should know,' Lily said excitedly to him.

'Oh wow, that's great. I wasn't expecting that. That's such a huge relief. I've been so worried,' Tom exclaimed. He collapsed onto the back of the sofa, looking up at the ceiling. 'I think I need a drink to celebrate!'

'I don't have any alcohol here, sorry,' Lily said.

Tom leaned forward on the sofa towards her, 'Are you still mad at me?'

'Yeah, I'm still annoyed that you slept with my sister. But I understand you didn't know who she was or her age, and that you have been going through a lot with your wife,' Lily sighed. 'But you've been there for me when I had no one else, and I'm so grateful for that. So thank you.' Lily leaned towards him and gave him a cuddle. Tom gently responded to her cuddle and stroked the back of her hair. As Lily pulled away from the hug, Tom softly stroked her face with the back of his hand.

'You're so beautiful,' Tom whispered to her. Lily's face tingled with delight as he stroked it. Is he coming on to her? Yes, she's sure he is. This wasn't right. It wasn't all that long ago that Tom was sleeping with her sister. Oh, how confusing. She wanted the comfort so much right now. More than anything. But she knew this man was not to be trusted with her emotions.

'Tom, we can't do this,' Lily whispered back to match his tone. 'You're married, remember? You're sorting things out. Plus, my sister.'

She was so mad at Tom for sleeping with her sister, who subsequently was murdered on the same night, and now he was trying to seduce her. Ah, what should she do?

'I know, it's wrong, but I badly want this. I'm attracted to you. I can't help it,' Tom spoke softly, grabbing the back of Lily's neck and gently edging her towards him. Oh God, he was always saying that to her. She could feel flutters inside her, and she knew if she didn't push him out the door right now, she would succumb to him.

'Do you feel the same?' he whispered gently in her ear.

'Yes,' Lily replied without thinking. She was so sick of feeling lonely. It would be so nice to be touched.

'But......' She didn't have the words to follow; the next thing Lily knew, they were kissing. He pushed his tongue inside her, and intense electricity shot up inside her as if her body had been awoken from a coma. It had been a while since Lily had been kissed. Lily had not been with anyone since her ex, Meghan's father, Chris. In the midst of all her suffering, it was so nice to feel something other than the horrendous pain Lily had been feeling since the murder of her sister.

She started to have a fight with herself as they stopped kissing, and Tom stared at her for a moment. Did she really want Tom? Probably not. In fact, if she had a choice, she would have Chris in front of her right now. But he wasn't. So Tom would have to do. She needed this. Lily just needed to feel something else, even for a moment, or she wasn't sure how much longer she would cope.

She grabbed hold of his face with both her hands and started to kiss him passionately. Her morals had gone out the window, and all she wanted was Tom to help her so she could forget her misery for even a short while.

Lily jumped on top of Tom, sitting on his lap on the sofa. She gripped onto his face, digging her fingernails into his face as she pushed her lips onto his hard. He reacted by kissing her back hard, too. Lily could feel the excitement running down into her vagina. This was precisely what she needed.

She stopped kissing him. Leaning back, she started unbuckling his trouser belt. She leant forward to kiss him again. Suddenly Tom reached into her trousers and knickers and began to touch her clit as they continued to kiss fiercely.

Oh shit. That felt good. Oh my God, really good. Lily started to tingle as he continued to caress her; over and over again, the pleasure kept coming. 'Do you want me to stop Lily?'

Lily was offended by this remark. Tom knew full well that she didn't want him to stop. If she wanted to stop, she would stop and tell Tom to f-off! 'No,' Lily furrowed her eyebrows at him. 'Why would I want you to stop?'

'Okay,' he smirked back at her.

Lily took his hand from her trousers and got off him. Standing over him, she pulled his trouser zipper down and pulled his trousers off as fast as she could. This needed to happen now. She couldn't wait. Lily went to take off his boxers, but Tom slipped them off before she had a chance. Tom sat in front of her, fully naked. That was more like it. Wow, that is quite an impressive penis as far as size goes. Much bigger than she had expected. No wonder he walked around all smug about life.

Lily was in no mood to strip tease. She started to undo the buttons of her top as quickly as she could, shrugging it off using her shoulders and letting it fall to the ground. Lily began to pull off her jeans, trying to do this in a sexy way. However, she tripped and landed on the living room floor. 'Ouch,' Lily cried as she fell to the ground. Oh, that was not sexy. She sprang up almost as quickly as she fell.

Tom started to laugh, 'Are you okay?'

'Yes, I am good,' Lily popped back up, her jeans off, so she was just standing in her underwear. Lily's cheeks burned up, and she knew they had gone bright red with humiliation. What a klutz.

Lily knew that she should probably take Tom upstairs. Her Mum could be home at any time. But she was so horny that she really wanted to just have him. Here and now. No waiting.

Lily moved back towards him, shaking the embarrassment out of her mind. She started to stroke his hard throbbing penis.

'I don't think you need to do that. I'm horny enough as it is,' Tom whispered to her. 'I just want you.'

Wanted her? Really? Lily just wanted a shag. It was now starting to irritate her that it was taking so long. 'Okay, let's just do this,' Lily pulled off her knickers and sat back on top of him, leaving just her bra on.

Tom tried to pick her backup. He wanted to go on top of her. But he had no chance. Lily wanted sex, and she wanted to do it her way. There was no way she was going to let Tom fuck her so he could cum and then leave her high and dry. If she was going to do this, then she wanted an orgasm.

Lily shook her head and pushed Tom; he hit the back of the sofa. 'Uh, Uh,' she shook her finger at him.

Lily slid her vagina onto his penis. The wetness inside her made it easy to slip right onto him. Tom bit his bottom lip as he gazed up at her. Tom started to slowly but firmly stroke the side of Lily's body. He stopped at her hips, gripping her tightly.

She moved up and down, slowly at first and let out a quiet moan. It had been a long time since Lily had sex with a man. Up until now, her only friend had been Willy, her vibrator. That just didn't give her the same comfort as a man's touch against her body.

'Stay still. Don't move. Not an inch,' Tom ordered, looking up at her. Was he trying to take control? Well, maybe it was worth seeing what he had. If only for a little while. Tom moved his hand around her ass, intensely gripping him deeper inside her. He moved his hand to her bra and tugged at the strap. It gave way with ease and dropped onto her lap in front of her. Tom grabbed hold of her breasts and started to suck hard on her left breast and then the other. Tom grabbed hold of Lily's hips, coaching her up and down. Oh God, the pleasure was so immense. It had been that long that Lily almost forgot what sex was like. Hell, she couldn't remember having sex as good as this. Ever.

Tom moved her hips faster and faster. Again, then again. To Lily's surprise, an orgasm started to immediately build up inside her. Tom briefly kissed her hard on the lips, their tongues locking. He moved his lips over her breasts once more, sucking hard on them. But as Tom continued to bounce Lily on his hard pulsating penis, Lily could feel her reaching to that almighty point. Screaming out, she let out an uncontrollable shudder as she came. Tom gave her a cocky grin as Lily could feel his breathing getting quicker, then before she knew it, his penis was vibrating inside her as he let out a huge moan, closing his eyes.

Lily collapsed her head on his shoulder, panting, assuming they were done with their sexual encounter. She felt somewhat satisfied with Tom's work. She brushed a sweaty strand of hair from her face. Tom's breathing was still hard and loud in her ear. He grabbed hold of her face and planted a passionate kiss on her lips.

As Lily stood up, fully naked, about to run to the toilet, Tom leaned forward, grabbing hold of her by her hips once more. Tom clamped his fingers back into her swollen clit. Lily raised an eyebrow as he then started to kiss her vagina. This was a bit embarrassing. They had already had sex. She was satisfied. He didn't really need to do more. But Tom's kissing had given Lily a tingling sensation, and she could feel herself becoming aroused once more. Lily collapsed on top of him, knees apart, panting with exhaustions as she let his face stay underneath her vagina.

Tom pushed his mouth into her sodden clit once more. Lily was unable to control the loud cry that followed his touch. She closed her eyes, feeling every lick that brought her closer to the time bomb that was about to explode once again. Tom moved his tongue away from her clit and shoved his fingers hard into her vagina.

'One more time for me,' Tom growled as he stopped to look up at her. His fingers started to vigorously thrust inside her once again.

But it didn't take long for that 2nd bomb to go off inside her. Lily shuddered, legs turning to jelly, cum seeping out of her. Okay, that was some session. Lily was powerless to move as if she had been paralysed.

Tom rolled away and looked up at her, sweat pouring from his forehead. He gave another cocky grin. It was only then that he seemed convinced she was fully satisfied. And he was right. She most certainly was.

But despite his tremendous sexual achievement, he needed to get out. Lily searched to the side of her, looking for her knickers. Where the bloody hell had her knickers gone? She knew they were around here somewhere. They were there, on the floor next to the sofa.

'You need to go,' Lily ordered coldly, pulling her knickers on.

Tom moved his head back, shocked. 'What?'

'My Mum will be back any minute. You need to leave. Now!' Lily was almost yelling at him. He had still slept with her sister. He was still a prick.

What did he expect? A cuddle and a night at the inn? No way! He needed to leave and pronto.

Lily found her bra and slipped it back on. Tom is still in the same position, just watching her. What was he waiting for? The fury was starting to latch onto her emotions. 'Get fucking dressed then!' Lily exclaimed.

'Okay, okay,' Tom breathed. 'Geez,' he pulled on his boxers.

Lily shook her head. 'My mum will be back any minute; you need to get out now. Lily picked up his trousers and threw them at him. He gracefully took his time to put them back on.

Lily continued to get dressed, and just as she finished buttoning up her jeans, the front door opened. Shit. Tom was still pulling his top over his head. Lily quickly grabbed the blanket that was half hanging on the back of the chair and chucked it over the cushion. She was sure there had to be some of their sweat and Tom's semen soaking their way into it. There was no time to clean it now. Jackie walked into the living room.

'Oh, hi,' she said, her voice shrill. 'Who's this, Lily? Her mother ignored Tom and looked directly at Lily, waiting for an answer to her question.

'This is Tom,' she introduced. 'He's one of the dads at the school. He lives just down the street, too. He was actually just leaving.'

'Hi,' Tom said, holding out his hand to shake her mum's hand. Lily felt a pit in her stomach. What was he doing? They must stink.

'Hello,' Jackie said to him, ignoring his hand held out and turning to face Lily. Her mum didn't like strangers in her house. It made her feel nervous. Suspicious even. It had been bad enough when the police had been rummaging around their house.

'Do you always leave the TV on, Lily, when you have company? I'm sure Tom here doesn't want to watch your crime dramas,' her mother continued.

Lily had completely forgotten that the TV was still on in the background. 'He was only popping in Mum. Like I said, Tom was just going,' Lily gave him a look that said, get-the-fuck-out! Then, she twiddled her fingers nervously as she started to walk towards the door, hoping he would follow. She wanted him out of there as soon as possible before she died of embarrassment. 'Come on, Tom, I'll see you out.'

Tom waved at Jackie. 'It's nice to meet you, Ms Knowell.'

'You too, dear,' Jackie replied. But Lily could tell from her Mum’s tone of voice that she was not happy to meet him.

'Wow,' Tom whispered while safely out in the hallway.

Lily opened the front door. 'Yes, it was,' Lily spluttered. 'Now please go,' she pushed him out of the house.

Tom leaned in to kiss her, but she turned her face, so he kissed Lily on her cheek instead.

'What's wrong. I thought we had a nice time?' Tom questioned. Lily could see from the look on his face that this was not a usual response for him after sex. But what did he expect? It was just sex, nothing more. He was a distraction from the constant pain she felt.

'Yes, we did. And now you need to leave.'

'Okay, I'll see you around at school then,' Tom mumbled as he stepped away from her, his eyes filled with sorrow. Oh God, he wasn't going to get all sentimental over this, was he?

'Yeah, bye,' Lily said, shutting the door in his face.

As the door slammed shut behind her, Lily leaned back on it. What had she just done? Tears filled Lily's eyes. She didn't feel any better after having sex with Tom. If anything, she just felt dirty, like she was some sort of dirty whore. He had slept with her sister and now her. Oh God! Lily stopped herself from crying as a bitter pool of anger built up inside her.

Then the thought hit her of Tom's wife. His poor wife. She didn't deserve what they had just done. Even though it was a nice distraction from what was going on for Lily, it was still wrong. She was not in the habit of sleeping with married men. When she saw him next, she would make it clear to Tom that she wanted nothing further to do with him.

TWENTY-NINE

Tom

Tom sipped his coffee as he looked out the living room window.

Not that he was waiting for anyone. It helped him think. His head was a complete mess. After having sex with Lily two nights previously, she was all he could think of. Lily wasn't like any of the women Tom had been with.

She was different. Mesmerising even. Lily intrigued him like no other woman had ever done before. There was something about Lily that drew Tom towards her. However, he couldn't begin to describe why. Yet she was not answering Tom's calls or replying to his messages. He forcefully ran his hand through his hair and sipped more coffee. His hands shook with agitation as he did so. They'd had a good time. So why was she ignoring him? She was driving him crazy.

Jack ran into the living room. Tom turned from the window to face his son. 'Hey buddy, ready for school?' he said to his son gently.

'Yup! Teeth brushed and ready to go.' Jack bounced up and down on the spot. Jack absolutely loved school and was always so eager to go. He must take after his mother because she loves to learn, too.

Carol had insisted on taking Jack to school the past couple of days. Today is no exception. What was with the doting mother act? After a week of playing Mrs Doubtfire, it wouldn't give her "The Mother of the Year" award. Who had been there day in, day out, the past six months whilst she built a career? Him. That was who.

'Ready, love?' Carol suddenly appeared at his side. ''Finish your coffee. We need to go, or we'll be late,' she practically ordered him.

Tom rolled his eyes behind Carol's retreating back. 'Yes, okay, dear, I'm coming,' he retaliated. Tom shook his head and grabbed his coat from the hallway hanger before following Jack and Carol out the door.

He put his arms into his coat and reluctantly walked next to Carol as Jack ran ahead towards Kitterton Academy. Jack's hair waved crazily about in the wind as he ran, despite Tom using his gel to stick it down earlier that morning. That was a pointless exercise because now it had sprung back up, making his son look like some kind of nutty professor. Tom puffed. Oh, brilliant, now he was going into school looking like a tramp.

'This is nice, isn't it?' Carol said whilst grabbing Tom's hand.

'Yeah,' Tom lied. But the truth was, he was dreading bumping into Katherine. Or even Lily, for that matter, but especially that blackmailing bitch Katherine. Hopefully, they could get in and out without seeing anyone.

Soon enough, they approached the school. Tom couldn't spot Katherine. They were in the clear to walk across the playground. Jack had wandered over to the climbing frame.

'Come on, Jack, don't mess around,' Tom called. There was tension in his voice. His eyes narrowed as he searched the playground for her. He didn't want to be caught off guard.

'What's the rush?' Carol said calmly. Fucking hell, she was as relaxed as a cucumber. Tom just wanted to get Jack into school as soon as possible so they could get out of there.

'I just don't want Jack to be late,' Tom said, still scouring the playground. He needs to get into his classroom before the bell goes. ' There was still no sign of Katherine. Whew!

Jack ran across towards them.

'Bye, sweety,' Carol bent over and kissed him.

'Yeah, bye, son,' he said. He hugged Jack goodbye.

Jack ran towards his classroom.

'Come on then, let's go,' Tom insisted before Jack had even reached Miss Norton's classroom door.

'What's going on with you?' Carol questioned; her hand was on her hip, and her eyebrows creased.

'Nothing is going on. Jack's gone to school. So let's get going,' Tom pulled his wife away from the classroom door. He squared his shoulders uncomfortably and turned to walk towards the gate.

'Are you trying to get me back home so we can have round two of the other night?' Carol chuckled.

What sex? With her? That was the last thing on Tom's mind. But he would tell her anything she wanted to hear so they could get out of there. 'You got me!' Tom agreed and gave her the most convincing smile he could muster. 'Now, can we please get going?'

Carol stared at Jack's classroom as he disappeared inside. 'Aww, bless him,' she said, placing her hand on her chest. 'Yeah, come on, let's get out of here and return home,' Carol laughed.

Carol and Tom were both at the gate when someone grabbed Tom's arm. He spun around to find Katherine facing him. Fuck! What did that stupid cow want?

'Hey you,' Katherine stroked Tom's arm. Tom flinched, trying to shrug her off. Katherine let go but pinched his arse discreetly. He jumped.

'And you must be Carol. Tom's wife. I've heard so much about you,' Katherine plastered a Stepford wife smile over her stupid, smug face and held out her hand for Carol to shake. 'Nice to meet you, I'm Katherine.'

THIRTY

Katherine

'Come on, Ellie, we're going to be late for school,' Katherine called up the stairs. 'What are you doing?' She was tapping her black and red Christian Louboutin stilettoes in the doorway as she and Sophie waited for Ellie to come down the stairs.

'I'm coming, mum, stop yelling at me!' Ellie screamed from up the stairs.

'Don't yell at me, Ellie Louise Lippet!' Katherine screamed back at her daughter. Right, that was it. She was going to find out what the hell Ellie was playing at. Katherine stomped up the stairs, but as she reached halfway up, Ellie appeared.

'What took you so long?' Katherine demanded, frowning at her. Ellie didn't reply.

Ellie walked down the stairs past her with her arms wrapped around her stomach. What was up with this attitude? She was usually such a sweet little girl.

'What's wrong? You're not getting your period, are you? Katherine queried. 'Although you're probably a bit young for that.'

'No, I'm fine, Mum. Get off my case,' Ellie stormed out of the house, barging past Sophie.

Sophie was knocked into the wall. 'Ow!' she let out.

'You're such a baby,' Ellie snarled.

'I'm not a baby!' yelled Sophie.

'Yes, you are!' Ellie continued.

Sophie started to cry.

Katherine sighed. 'Please don't be so nasty to your sister,' Katherine sometimes worried about Ellie's behaviour. She hoped it was just down to sibling rivalry and nothing more.

On their way to school, Ellie strolled behind, glued to her phone as Sophie skipped ahead. Why couldn't they just walk together at the same pace? Being a parent was such hard work sometimes. Especially when you had a bitchy vain nine-year-old. God only knew where she got that from.

As Katherine approached the school gates, Ellie wandered off with her friends. 'Ellie, I think you're missing something, ' Ellie said, passing her phone to Katherine.

'Bye, dear,' she leaned in to hug Ellie, but she stepped back so Katherine was left hanging. Then she turned around and walked off. What was going on with her lately? She was so moody. It was like she was a teenager. Most nine-year-olds weren't this stroppy, were they? Was this normal?

'Come on, darling,' Katherine grabbed Sophie's hand, who had now stopped, so she could catch up with her. Katherine continued to walk around the playground to Miss Norton's door. She spotted Tom across the playground amongst the crowd of parents. Shit, it looked like he was with his wife, Carol. Katherine smirked, rubbing her hands together. This was going to be interesting. If he thought he could just pick her up and drop her whenever he saw fit, he had another thing coming. She was a human being, not a puppet he could play with.

'Okay, go and run into your class, Sophie dear,' Katherine pushed Sophie along towards the class door quite hard. She was desperate to get to Tom, but Sophie stumbled, nearly falling flat on her face.

'But mummy, you haven't gone to the door,' Sophie said in a whiny voice.

'That's okay. I'll watch from here. Go on,' she quickly kissed Sophie and pushed her forward again. This time, Sophie ran straight towards the door.

Katherine quickly spun around and briskly walked across the playground, catching up with Tom and Carol. The crowd of parents ahead had slowed the pair down. Katherine shuffled in between them. Grabbing Tom's arm.

'Hey, you?' Katherine threw back her head in amusement. Tom's face dropped. She was going to enjoy this.

'Hi, I'm Katherine, a friend of Tom's. You must be Tom's wife, Carol. Tom has told me so much about you,' she said to the woman whose husband she'd recently had rough, dirty sex with in her kitchen. Just the thought of what they'd done made Katherine shudder with excitement.

She moved towards Tom. She wanted to be near him. Feel his breath on her skin as much as she could. The waft of his luring aftershave was streaming off of him. It instantly took her back to the morning they had sex. Ass cheeks on the kitchen counter and he pushed himself inside her like she was some sort of sex goddess. Katherine could daydream about that moment all day, but not now. Now was not the time. She had to focus.

'Hi, yes, lovely to meet you,' Carol greeted with a bright face. Was she always this stupidly happy?

'Oh my God, I love your top,' Katherine lied. In fact, Carol was far from glamorous. She definitely had the upper hand in terms of glamour compared to her. Carol's plain black top and ugly matching black trousers made her look like some sort of depressed teenager. Who dressed like that? If Katherine could be bothered, she would take Carol shopping one day. Add a bit of colour to her life. No wonder Tom had a wandering eye. She probably fucked the same as she dressed; boring.

'Aww, thank you,' Carol graciously replied.

'So, how are you coping after they put you in that awful prison cell?' Katherine asked Tom, stroking his arm. She was getting immense pleasure from this.

Watching Tom squirm was fun. He obviously had no idea Richard, his solicitor, had told Katherine he had been arrested. So he must be racking his brain trying to figure out how she knew. Katherine chuckled to herself.

'I didn't know people knew,' Carol responded, concerned.

'Oh, they don't. It's just Tom and I who have become quite close these past two weeks, and he trusted me enough to tell me.' She looked up at him. His eyes were cold. Tom didn't look impressed. But she didn't give two shits. It was what he bloody deserved.

'You should both come to my party this Saturday and celebrate,' Katherine smirked at Tom. He nudged Katherine in her ribs. But she wanted him at her party, and inviting them in front of his wife was the best way to do it. Especially as she was so lovely and innocent. Katherine wanted more of him, and she knew Tom felt the same. This was a way to get her claws into him at her birthday party.

'That sounds great,' Carol replied.

On the other hand, Tom didn't look too keen on going. He was hiding his genuine emotions again. Just as Katherine expected, he was a coward.

'We don't have a babysitter,' Tom tried to insist. But Tom didn't realise he was coming to the party whether he liked it or not. She was going to see to that.

'Don't be silly,' Carol piped up. 'My mum will babysit,' Katherine smiled. It looked like she didn't need to. Carol was seeing to it on his behalf. Tom gave a half-shrug.

Well, that looked like an agreement. 'That's settled then. See you at my house at seven o'clock on Saturday. Oh, and by the way, it's 1920s themed, so bring your costumes,' Katherine beamed.

Luckily, Susan was walking past the three of them, and for once, she was thankful to see her. She needed to get away before Tom had a chance to try and wriggle his way out of her party. Plus, anything to get away from that vulgar woman Tom called a wife. 'I've just spotted a friend, and I need a word with her. I'll see you at the party,' Katherine chased after Susan before they could say another word.

'Hey Susan,' she panted. It was harder than it looked to briskly walk across the uneven playground in her skinny stilettoes. 'So. Change of plan, we're not having the usual dinner this year. I'm inviting some other friends over, and it will be more of a party. A 1920s theme party, to be exact.'

'Have you spoken to James about this, Katherine?' Susan asked. By the look on her face, she was in shock that Katherine had even suggested a party.

'No, not yet, but it's my birthday party, and I'm doing what I want this year,' Katherine insisted. How dare she? She didn't need permission from her husband. She was no longer taking orders from him. Even if she got a beating for it. Katherine was having her own bloody birthday party the way she wanted, and that was that.

'Well, I think you should speak to him before you go inviting people and saying things like that,' Susan snubbed.

'Please, Susan, I don't want to get into another fight over this. Anyway, it's a bit late for that as I've already invited other people,' Katherine pouted.

'Who were those people you were just talking to when I walked past?' Susan demanded, changing the subject.

'My friends,' she replied, crossing her arms and shifting her body away from Susan. 'The decision is final, Susan. If you don't like it, don't come,' Katherine said, giving a dismissive wave of the hand. Who did this woman think she was? Susan pretended to be Katherine's friend, yet she always had her head so far up James's arse she could probably see his tonsils. When did James get his own personal spy? Susan was such a pretentious cow. And despite them being "made up", she was still no friend of Katherine's.

'Katherine!' Susan exclaimed, raising her eyebrows. 'Where's this coming from? You have not been acting like your usual self lately. You haven't even given me a response for the decoration display for the Halloween fete at the school. Oh, and please don't tell me you have invited that treacherous woman Alison to this so-called party of yours?'

'Yup!' Katherine nodded, faking a smile at her. 'See you Saturday. Come or don't come. That's what's happening,' Katherine stormed off, stomping her heels like some spoilt princess. 'Oh, and I'll get back to you on the fete when I'm good and ready,' she spun around to face Susan one last time before leaving the school gates behind her.

Katherine skipped down the road, laughing to herself as she thought back to Tom's reaction. He was so hilarious, sweating his pants off. That face was so irresistible that she could eat him all up. Oh, Katherine wished so much that Tom was hers. If only they weren't both married. But then again, that wasn't about to stop her getting what she wanted from Tom. Sex, and lots of it.

It was no more than ten minutes later when Katherine reached her front door, and her mobile phone was ringing. She scrunched up her face as she read the caller ID. "James."

'Hello,' Katherine answered in a cool, casual tone.

'What do you think you're doing?' James exclaimed over the phone. She immediately gulped, even though he was miles away from her.

'What do you mean?' Katherine answered, but she knew full well what was going on. That traitor, Susan, had phoned James, stabbing her in the back. Katherine was sure Susan had a crush on James. Susan adored James. He could do no wrong in her eyes. Plus, Susan constantly flutters her eyelashes at him and agrees with him whenever she is in James's company. *Just gross!*

Although Katherine didn't blame her, she was sure Susan's husband, Bruce, was gay. Whenever Katherine saw Bruce, he always complimented her on her designer labels. Now, what straight man knew what designer was what? So Susan probably wasn't getting any in the bedroom department.

'Throwing a fucking party like some sort of irresponsible teenager, that's not how we do things, Katherine, and you know it. And inviting Alison Pierce.

I'll be the laughingstock of the office,' James exclaimed. He was mad. Katherine envisioned him at his office now, veins waiting to pop out of his head.

'Well, don't invite them. Cancel it. James, it's my birthday, and I just want a party. What's so wrong with that?' Katherine paused. Should she say the next sentence? It was one way to get her party. 'James, you said you wanted to make up for the other night with me. This is how. Please give me this party for my birthday? It would mean the world to me,' she pleaded.

James sighed. 'This isn't what I had in mind for your party. You're only trying to punish me,' James moaned at her. He knew she had him and was trying to get her to change her mind with sympathy.

'James, I'm not. I don't ask for much. We always do what you want. I don't mind a dinner party the rest of the time, but I want something more than that for my birthday. Plus, you wouldn't want your friends at the office to find out you're going around throwing your wife against the walls, would we?' Katherine ridiculed. The words had flooded out of her mouth before she could stop herself. Katherine clasped her hand over her mouth. Her heart was racing. What was he going to say?

There was a long pause before he spoke. 'Katherine, I don't know what you have turned into lately. First the job and now this,' James huffed. Katherine knew this must be killing him. Normally, he was her puppet master. But things were different. For her, anyway. The tables had turned, and it suddenly dawned on Katherine that she was not this boxed housewife imprisoned in this life. She could do more if she wanted to.

'James, I'm still your wife. I just want a party for my birthday. Jesus, why doesn't anyone get this!' Katherine clicked off the phone. Shit. That was going too far, and she would probably regret saying that to James later. But part of her didn't care. It was worth it to get to her party and see Tom.

However, little did Katherine know that she would regret ever having a party for her birthday.

THIRTY-ONE

Tom

Carol skipped up the drive, humming the tune to "Call Me Maybe" by Carly Rae Jepsen. Tom tutted. How was he going to get out of having sex with her? He wasn't in the mood. Not with her anyway. As much as Tom wanted them to stay together for Jack's sake, her being around every second of the day was driving Tom crazy with her consistent nagging. It was more like living with his mother than his wife. He hadn't realised it before, but her working and being apart was probably what made their relationship work. Now he had no space from her.

The only thing Carol was good for was her financial security. Tom wasn't sure how much more of Carol's annoyance he could take. But Carol would be back at work soon, and it couldn't come a minute sooner. Then Tom and she could get a bit of distance between themselves. Or rather, Tom could get his distance from Carol.

Tom strolled in after her, tugging at his hair again, which was becoming a habit whenever he was stressed. He needed a way to get her out of the house so he could have some space on his own. But how?

'Why did you go and agree to that party on the weekend?' Tom demanded, clenching his jaw.

'What are you talking about? She's your friend,' Carol replied calmly. 'Plus, you did say you wanted to get out of the house more. So what better way than for us to go to a party and enjoy ourselves like we used to. Plus, it will give me a chance to catch up and get to know the parents at our son's school,' she added.

'Yes, but... ' Tom began, not really knowing what to say next.

'I want a night out, Thomas,' Carol interrupted.

Tom huffed, gripping hold of the sofa tightly. Stop calling me Thomas, he said to himself. 'Well, no, I don't want to go,' Tom replied abruptly.

'Come on, stop being so childish. It'll be fun. We haven't had a night out in ages.'

A darkened thought entered Tom's mind. This was going to be a disaster. 'Why don't we cancel and stay home instead. You and I have a night in with takeaway and a few drinks.'

'No, we're going to that party!' Carol shouted at him. This was clearly not going to be easy.

'But Carol...' Tom tried again to come up with an excuse before being abruptly cut off once again.

'This is happening, Tom. Plus, after what I've done to clean up your mess, I would have thought you would be grateful to go and have a night out together. You know, enjoy ourselves,' Carol glared at him.

Was she threatening him? If Tom didn't go to the party, would she tell the police that her alibi was false? Part of Tom didn't want to find out the answer.

'Yeah, fine, I'll go,' Tom mumbled. But he already knew this was a disaster waiting to happen. Somehow, Katherine would corner him and expect him to 'perform' for her. But he didn't want to have sex with her, just as he didn't want to have sex with his wife.

'I'm not forcing you to go, Thomas,' Carol said. She was really starting to piss him off.

He had no choice, though. Go to the party and withstand a gruesome night with Katherine. Or go to prison for the rest of his life. Did this mean he now had to do everything she said?

Tom took a deep breath and stared directly into her eyes. 'No, I want to go, Carol. You're right, though. I said we should get out. I'm sure I will enjoy it when we go,' Tom nodded as he spoke, trying to convey his seriousness.

'Brilliant, that's settled then. I'd better go to town and get a nice dress to wear. It's been ages since I went shopping,' Carol beamed. 'Rain check on the sex?'

Tom nodded. Thank God for that. 'Yeah, great. You go. Take your time, and I'll pick Jack up from school,' Tom insisted.

'Aww, thanks, love. I'll see you later. I know it's a couple of days away, but I'm excited to be going out now,' Carol said, picking up her purse and heading back to the front door. Tom let out a sigh of relief as the front door closed. Now he could relax.

Tom wasn't sure how long he could keep this up. He was trapped now more than ever. There was no way that Tom could leave. Even if she suddenly decided she had mistakenly guessed the time Tom had gotten home that night. There was his son to think of. Jack meant everything to Tom. Carol could take his son, but Tom would never see him again. What would he do then? He had no money to fight her? Or any money to live on? So, there was no way a judge would want to give him custody. Yet all he could think of was Lily and being with her. She was just so incredible, and the best part of all, she didn't even know it. My god, what was he going to do?

***

Later that day, Tom was on his way to pick up Jack from school. He lifted his chin up as he walked and let in the fresh air. She was suffocating him. The fresh air entered his lungs like a gentle, flowing river. The branches on the trees bounced as if they were dancing to a tune. More leaves fell from their summer place and covered the floor beneath.

Tom turned the corner of his street. He hoped he would bump into Lily. She wouldn't be able to ignore him then if he were face-to-face with her. But she wasn't there. She usually walked to school about this time. Well, maybe he would hang about for a few moments. This was his window of opportunity to catch Lily while Carol was shopping.

Tom nearly gave up after a few minutes, but eventually, Lily strolled up the street. Tom moved back around the corner so Lily wouldn't see him. After a few seconds, Tom started to walk, pretending to bump into her. Tom waved as Lily got closer. She looked down, ignoring him. Charming!

'Hi Lily, you okay?' Tom asked as he joined her side, his tone gentle.

'Oh yeah, Tom, I'm brilliant!' Lily responded sarcastically.

'Hey, what's up?' Tom asked. He put his arm around her back and gently pulled Lily towards him. But to Tom's surprise, Lily pushed him away.

'Get off me!' Lily spat. 'And stop ringing me too while you're at it! There's a reason I'm not picking up Tom.'

'What have I done?' Tom lifted an eyebrow, puzzled by her remarks. Why was Lily acting like this? He thought there was something between them.

'Tom, I'm sorry. But the other night was a mistake.'

Was she saying this because of Carol?

'I know what I said about giving it another go with my wife, but it's not working. There's nothing there between us anymore. We tried, and it's just not working. I want to be with you, Lily,' Tom explained. 'It's just....Jack.'

Lily looked at him for a moment, not saying anything. What was she thinking? Despite Lily throwing him out of the house the other night, Tom knew there was a special connection between them. That wasn't just from his end. There was so much fire and electricity between them when they had sex. It wasn't possible for her to fake that. It was the best sex he'd ever had. Lily blatantly wanted him, so why not carry on? See where it goes. Lily was like no other woman Tom had ever met. She was beautiful, strong and above all, she was cool.

'Look, Tom,' Lily finally said, stopping in her tracks and turning her whole body to face him. 'I just wanted some comfort from you the other night. I just wanted to feel anything other than the pain I'm feeling right now. And you were there. Ready and waiting. You slept with my sister, for Christ's sake. My dead sister and then me. How messed up is that? I have enough to deal with without the complication of you, too. Let's just leave it as a one-off, okay? God, if I knew you were going to stalk me, I would never have bothered!'

Tom stood, grounded to the spot. Bewildered by her words. What could he say to that? She had made her feelings perfectly clear. 'Okay,' Tom replied. 'If that's how you feel. Fuck off then!' he yelled. Lily jumped back, shaking her head. Her eyes gave him a chilling glare, telling him she was repulsed by him. Then she stormed off down the road to the school without him. Great. That's not how he envisioned the conversation going.

THIRTY-TWO

Lily

'Mum, my legs are tired. I can't walk very far,' Meghan moaned as she and Lily walked home from school.

'Oh, Meghan, stop your whining. There are worse things going on in the world,' Lily snapped.

'Lily, Lily,' a voice called from behind. Lily spun around to find Katherine beating her heels towards her. Why was it that every time she turned a corner, there Katherine was? In her face, banging on about some petty little thing that she really didn't care about. And if it wasn't her, it was that twat Tom, who she should never have slept with. That was something she really regretted now.

'What is it, Katherine?' Lily sighed. She really wasn't in the mood.

'Oh, what's wrong, Lily?' Katherine pulled that face again as if she were full of concern, but really, it was all an act. Did these people keep forgetting her sister was murdered?

'Why does everyone keep asking me that? You do realise my sister has been murdered, right?' Lily spat out the words a little too harshly.

'Oh, sorry, Lily. I was only coming over to invite you to my birthday party tomorrow. It's at my house at seven. I thought you might like to come.'

'The last time you invited me to something, you interrogated me about a man who wasn't your husband. So what if I wanted to have sex with Tom? I'm a free woman. And if he wants to cheat on his wife, then that's his issue, not mine!' Lily raged. She could feel herself losing control. Unravelling in front of a woman she hardly knew or trusted.

Katherine gasped. She took a step back from Lily, her big blue eyes were wide with horror, as if Lily had just told her Santa Claus wasn't real.

It was becoming more apparent to Lily that she was not the only one who had gotten involved with Tom. 'Oh, I see....you slept with him, didn't you?' Lily gave Katherine a knowing smile.

'What? Ummm...no.' Katherine's face had gone as red as a beetroot. It had to be true with a response like that.

Lily shook her head. 'You're pathetic, you know that? I wouldn't waste your breath on him because, believe me, he doesn't care about you.' Lily took hold of Meghan's hand and dragged her down the street towards their house, leaving Katherine speechless, which pleased Lily even more.

'Ow, mum, you're hurting me,' Meghan complained as both she and Lily walked.

'I just want to get home Meghan, and you're not making it any easier,' Lily snapped at her daughter.

Shit. She was being so hard on her. But she just couldn't help it. There was so much rage firing around her body, like a demon possessing her. Lily was finding it harder and harder to control.

As both Lily and Meghan approached the front door of their flat. Lily stopped, bending down to Meghan. The force of reporters that were once there, showering Lily and her mother with their presence, had now disappeared. All that remained was the police tape fluttering in the wind like a lost spirit.

Lily lifted up Meghan's chin. 'I'm sorry, I shouted Meghan. Mummy shouldn't have done that.'

Meghan nodded and wrapped her arms around Lily. Lily felt like such a bad person, and even worse, she felt like a bad mother.

Suddenly, the front door swung open. 'Daddy!' Meghan cried. Lily froze. Entranced by the person she was facing, Chris, her ex-boyfriend. The one who abandoned her for a social life. Correction, he abandoned her and his daughter for a social life. What in God's name was he doing here?

'Hey princess,' Chris cheered, embracing Meghan in a hug. 'I thought I heard voices out here.'

'Look who's here, Lily. It's Chris,' Jackie exclaimed as Lily walked into the house. Jackie always had a soft spot for Chris. Well, of course, she did; he was so bloody charming. That was the reason she got knocked up in the first place.

'Mummy said you had gone away. I've missed you so much, Daddy!' Meghan was squeezing him tightly.

Lily slammed the door behind her. 'Meghan, go and watch TV with Nanny,' Lily ordered. Her voice was stern. 'You, in the kitchen!' Lily pointed her finger at Chris.

Jackie grabbed Meghan's hand and said, 'Come on, dear, let your Mum and Dad talk.'

Lily stormed into the kitchen, spun around with her arms folded, and tapped her trainer on the floor. Chris entered the kitchen with his head down.

'What are you doing here, Chris?' Lily said through gritted teeth.

'I'm sorry to hear about Jasmin,' Chris said. 'You must be beside yourself,' he moved closer to Lily, trying to stroke her arm.

'Why do you care?' She shrugged him off, not wanting any part of him to touch her. 'You haven't been here. Unlike me, who has been here grieving for my poor little sister. My murdered little sister,' Lily's hands were shaking with fury. Her adrenaline was coursing around her body.

'I know, I've been a dick......' Chris muttered, not looking her in the eye.

'Save it, Chris. I don't want to hear your pathetic excuses. Just get out!' Lily yelled. Except that wasn't what she wanted. Lily wanted Chris to stay. She still loved him. But he had swanned off with his mates for months on end, not giving a toss about her or Meghan and buggered off to Ibiza to top it all off.

'Please, Lily, just hear me out. I'm not proud of what I've done. I lost sight of what was important, which is you and Meghan. I've been so selfish,' he took hold of Lily's hand. She wrenched her hand away from him. 'All I can think of is you and her. I would literally take it all back if I could.'

'It's not that simple, Chris. I've been on my own. Raising our daughter. Looking after mum whilst there is a murdering bastard loose!' Lily screamed. Her whole body was shaking uncontrollably. Lily gave a high-pitched agonising scream and picked up a plate from the kitchen table, launching it at the wall. All the pain and anguish was draining out of her like a plug being pulled from a bath.

Jackie came running in. 'It's okay, Mum. We're fine,' Lily said. Jackie nodded and disappeared from the kitchen.

'She was eighteen, Chris, fucking eighteen! What sick bastard would want to beat her to death? Why? Why would they want to do that?' Lily slammed her fists down on the kitchen table. Tears were starting to fill up her eyelids, threatening to spill over at any second. She was struggling to hold them back.

'You made your choice! You've been living it up in fucking Ibiza, with the boys having a wail of time. Not giving a second thought about us. You left us! You left me!' Tears were now exploding down her face like a tidal wave. The tightness in her chest made it hard to breathe, as the suffering made it too hard to bear anyone.

'That's true, I have. I can't believe I thought going out and partying with my mates was more important. I've been so stupid.' Chris took a step forward towards her.

'Don't!' Lily cried.

'I'm really sorry, Lily. I love you and Meghan. You are both the most important things in my life.' Chris ignored her warning and grabbed hold of her, clutching her tightly in his arms. Lily punched his chest as more tears began to stream down her face.

Releasing part of the demon that had built up inside her. 'It's all my fault!' Lily wailed. 'I wasn't there for her.'

'There, there, it's okay. I'm here now. I'm going to look after you. I'm not going anywhere ever again,' Chris stroked her soft brunette hair. Lily gave in, collapsing her head into his chest and letting his warm hug comfort her as she continued to sob hard.

Lily wiped the snot away with the back of her hand as she looked up at Chris. 'And what about the next time one of your friends knocks on the door and asks you to go on a night out?'

'Then, I'll tell them I'm going out for the day with my girlfriend and daughter.'

'And what about when they want you to go on another lad's holiday?'

'I'll tell them I'm going on holiday with my family instead,' Chris said, pulling Lily back into his arms and cradling her. He kissed Lily on her head.

She continued to sob, letting the comfort he gave her in. They stood like that for a few minutes.

She looked at him, 'You can stay here for Meghan's sake, Chris. But this doesn't mean we're getting back together. You really hurt me when you left, and it was me who had to pick up all the pieces. Then Jasmin...' Lily took a step back and out of Chris's hold, taking a deep breath. She composed herself. 'It's going to take a while to trust you again.'

'Okay, I understand,' Chris bowed his head.

'Listen, Chris, I need to find Jasmin's killer,' Lily said, pulling her hair back.

'What, you can't?' Chris objected. 'You need to let the police do their job and find Jasmin's murderer.'

'If you don't want to help Chris, you know where the door is!' Lily snapped

Chris held up his hands.

'You don't understand, Chris,' Lily continued. 'I need to find justice for her. Her killer needs to pay for what they have done. I owe her that much. Are you going to help me?' She looked up into his eyes with as much hope as she could muster.

'If that's what you want, of course I will help you,' Chris nodded.

'Then it's time. It's time I finally got the courage to go inside Jasmin's room. Maybe there might be some clues in there,' Lily narrowed her eyes at Chris. 'Jasmine's killer deserves to die for what they did to my sister!'

THIRTY-THREE

Katherine

Finally, it was the day of Katherine's birthday party. And there was a lot to organise. But first things first, the house needed to be cleaned. It was a tip. Katherine thought it was best to start in the bedrooms. Although nobody was staying the night, she wanted to make sure everything looked presentable for her guests. Might as well start with the girl's bedroom and get the worst out of the way.

Katherine walked into Ellie's bedroom. 'Only me, I just......'

'Mum, what are you doing? Get out!' Ellie exclaimed.

Katherine froze. 'What are you doing, Ellie?' Ellie was scrunching up her sheet from her bed.

'Nothing, mum, just get out,' Ellie yelled.

'No, what is going on, Ellie Louise Lippet?' Katherine placed her hand on her hip. Waiting for an explanation. Ellie didn't reply. Katherine could tell by the look on her face that something was up.

Katherine stormed towards her, grabbing the sheet off her. But as she stepped closer, the smell suddenly became obvious. Katherine put her finger up to her nose and turned away from the sheet. Wow, that was some stench. Katherine moved her eyes towards the mattress. There was a wet patch. Ellie had wet the bed.

'Oh, honey, did you wet the bed?' Katherine spoke softly. She couldn't make heads or tails out of it.

'Mum, just get out of my room,' Ellie shouted. Katherine wasn't quite sure what to do. She spun around and walked out of the room, still holding the sheet of urine in her hand. Katherine's head was spinning as she stood on the landing. Wet the bed? My Ellie. She was nine. She hadn't wet the bed since she was three years old. Now, this most definitely wasn't normal. Katherine needed to speak to James about this.

Katherine trotted downstairs and put the sheet into the washing machine.

Katherine approached James' office door. She cleared her throat and then knocked hard on the door.

'Wait a minute,' James called. A few moments passed. God, what's he doing? Jerking off? Although the funny thing was, he probably was.

James took his office seriously. When he was in there, there were usually no disturbances. But this was an emergency. Katherine needed to talk to James about Ellie.

'Okay, come in,' James instructed.

'Hi Honey. You busy? I need a word,' Katherine shuffled in and closed the office door behind her.

James pushed his laptop down. 'You have my attention dear,' rubbing his hands together.

'It's Ellie. She's wet the bed,' Katherine lowered her chin submissively. What was going on with her baby that she would wet the bed?

'Wet the bed?' James scoffed. 'Don't be so stupid Katherine. She's nine years old. She wouldn't have wet the bed.'

'She has,' Katherine insisted. 'I have just caught her changing her bed sheets.'

James stood up, moving closer to her face. Katherine stepped back, holding her hands behind her back, feeling for the wall behind her. 'Are you telling me you are doing such a shit job at being a mother that you have let our nine-year-old daughter wet the fucking bed!' James leant into her face.

'No....James. I'm not. I'm just saying she....' Katherine quivered away from James. He was starting to scare her again. James reached for her face, squashing her cheeks in his right hand so her face was now screwed up. His grip was strong, and his hold was like iron. He then pushed her back, so she hit the wall with a solid smack. Pain shot into her back and shoulder like a lightning bolt as she crumbled on the ground against James's office wall.

James stood over her and grabbed her hair, pulling her back onto her feet. Then yanked it back down hard. Katherine screamed out. 'You stupid fucking bitch!' he seethed. The excruciating pain of her roots being pulled away from her scalp sent shockwaves through her head. It hurt. It really hurt. She tried desperately not to cry, but the tears came down her face anyway. James let go, and Katherine collapsed to her knees, momentarily relieving her from the misery.

James stood over her like a predator preying on its prey. Katherine continued to bow her head. Should she get up? Was he going to do anything else? Katherine placed her hand on her knee and pushed herself to her feet. But before she could stand up properly, she felt what could only have been James's knee bury itself in her stomach. Katherine coughed and toppled back to the floor. The pain riveted inside Katherine's stomach as she curled into a ball on the ground. How long was this going to go on for? Katherine decided she would stay down until James had finished what he'd started before attempting to get up again.

'Mum,' Sophie called.

Shit Sophie. Please don't come in. She didn't want Sophie to see her like this. Katherine was trying to teach her kids to be strong, independent women. Not weak like their mother was right now. James stepped away from her, sitting back on his office chair.

Katherine took a deep breath, but the wind had been knocked out of her, and all she could accomplish was shallow breathing. You can do this. Just get up, she told herself. Go see your daughter. 'I'm coming, just a minute, darling,' Katherine replied, in the most normal-sounding voice she could manage.

Katherine was fairly confident James was finished, so she got up and held onto her side as she escaped James's office. Katherine leant on the back of the door briefly as she shut it behind herself.

Katherine closed her eyes for a moment before opening them again. Katherine stroked down her blonde hair and shook off the pain as best as possible. 'I'm coming, sweety,' Katherine called as she walked into the living room to carry out her motherly duties.

***

Katherine stepped out of the shower and walked into her bedroom. She opened her dressing table and swivelled through the pile of knickers until Katherine saw the new pair of black lace cheekies and matching black lace bra she had bought from Victoria's Secret. Katherine dropped her towel and slipped them on. Katherine looked at her beaten body in front of the full-length mirror. Her side throbbed, and Katherine knew all the thick purple bruises over her stomach and shoulders would only darken as the night went on.

James had not been home when Katherine returned from dropping off the children at Alison's for the night with Jean. Katherine was grateful, as it gave her time to get ready in peace.

Katherine strolled over to her wardrobe and picked up her long, silver-fringed 1920s flapper dress. After placing her birthday costume on, Katherine looked over her shoulder to see if her bruises were noticeable. They were. Shit. Katherine grabbed some of her concealer from her vanity dresser. Katherine cried out repeatedly as she dabbed it down over her swollen skin. It was still visible. She was going to need a shawl to cover her shoulders. There was one in the wardrobe. Katherine wrapped it over her, along with her silver gloves and matching sequinned headband.

Despite the agony that only appeared to grow, nothing would stop Katherine from having her fabulous party. The decorations had been elegantly placed, Alison was downstairs sorting out the alcohol, and in one hour's time, her guests would start arriving. Katherine would make sure she had a night to remember—and that she would.

THIRTY-FOUR

Tom

'Come on, Tom, we're going to be late,' Carol called from downstairs. 'What are you doing up there?'

'There's no rush, is there?' Tom called back from the bathroom.

'Yes, it's already seven o'clock. The party has started.'

'Well, we'll be fashionably late,' Tom answered.

'We have a babysitter, so I want to make the most of the night. So just hurry up,' Carol yelled.

'Alright. Alright. I'm nearly ready, woman,' Tom retaliated. Bloody hell!

The truth was, however, Tom was sitting on top of the toilet, having a secret cigarette while he tried to waste some time. The less time he had to spend at this party, the better. Tom's theory was that the later he and Carol turned up, the more crowded the party would be. This would give Tom a better chance of blending in and avoiding Katherine.

Tom finished his cigarette and flicked it out of the window. Then, he flushed the toilet as if he had actually used it. Tom looked into the bathroom mirror. Okay, Tom, you can do this, he coached himself. Then he headed downstairs to meet Carol.

'Wow, don't you look handsome,' Carol admired as Tom walked down the stairs. Carol had bought him a 1920s pinstripe gangster costume for Katherine's birthday party. It actually didn't look too bad on him. Tom wasn't sure if that was a good thing or a bad thing. Well, it was done now.

'Thanks, you too,' Tom replied, not even looking up to see what Carol was wearing. Tom didn't really give a toss about what she was wearing. He was too busy looking for his phone. She could be wearing a bin bag for all Tom cared. He just wanted to get this night over with as fast as possible. Tom was sure he'd put it down when getting dressed upstairs, but it hadn't been in the bedroom.

'Looking for something?' Carol asked. Tom glanced up. Her forehead was creased, and she held his phone between her fingers. Twiddling it about. Fuck. What messages were on there? He was sure he had deleted any to Lily.

'Oh great. You found it. Where was it?' Tom inquired.

'In the bedroom,' Carol replied, observing him intently with her eyes.

Why did she go upstairs and get his phone while he was in the bathroom? Did she know something? 'Thanks,' he said, grabbing the phone out of her hand and giving her a quick once-over. She actually looked quite nice. For a change, she was wearing heels, which were nice. Seeing a woman wearing heels and making an effort was always nice.

'So, are we going or not?' he questioned.

'Yes, Tom. Let's go,' Carol sighed.

'What's wrong?' Tom asked.

'Nothing. Tom. Nothing is wrong,' Carol replied.

What was her deal? He was going to this stupid party. What more did she want from him? Carol stormed out the front door. Tom reluctantly trailed behind.

THIRTY-FIVE

Lily

Lily crept down the landing. You can do this, Lily, she coached herself. It's just a room. Just go in there and see what you can find. Something the police might have missed. It was worth a try. Lily's heart sped up as she crept closer. This was tougher than she had imagined.

Lily gently pushed open the door. Taking a deep breath, she stepped inside. Everything was exactly how Jasmin had left it. Her bed was only half made, with clothes sprawled across it. It looked like Jasmin had been undecided on which dress to wear before leaving the night she died. Her hair dryer, make-up, and everything else were plastered across her bedroom like any other teen her age. Yet she would never use any of it again. Lily sighed. Nothing of hers in this room would ever be used by her again. She was gone.

Lily took a deep breath and softly shuffled across her room. There were pictures of Jasmin and her friends hanging on the wall. She looked so happy. Lily had to turn away before she started crying. She needed to be practical about this and started with Jasmin's chest of drawers. She brushed her hand over Jasmin's things scattered on top. Lily picked up Jasmin's perfume and smelled it. The scent instinctively reminded Lily of her. Like she was still there. In the room with her. But she wasn't. She was gone.

Pull yourself together, Lily, she told herself. Lily bent down, rummaging her hands through each drawer. Lily wasn't exactly sure what she was looking for. Anything. Anything that would give Lily a clue as to who had killed her sister. But there was nothing in her drawers. Just clothes.

Lily shuffled through her sister's stuff on the nightstand and then through her wardrobe. But nothing was there either. All completely normal teenage stuff. Maybe there wouldn't be anything that would help Lily find the answers she was looking for. After all, the police had already been in here. Lily placed her head on Jasmin's white vintage wardrobe and slid down to the floor. Just staring across Jasmin's room.

Which was when she noticed that the carpet had been turned up at the corner of the bedroom. Lily crawled across and pulled it back. The floorboard underneath was loose. Lily pulled it away, and there was a box. Bingo! What was this? Lily pushed open the box and found lots of strange bits inside. Movie tickets. Some hair. Ew! A used condom. Why did she have this inside the box? How random. Lily continued to look. At the bottom were some photographs. Lily turned them over and felt her jaw drop as she stared at the picture. She instantly recognised the man with his arm draped over Jasmin's shoulder. Lily stared at the photo. Not able to comprehend what she was seeing. It couldn't be him. It wasn't possible. Or was it? She looked again. It had to be him. He was the one who murdered Jasmin. Lily needed to get to Katherine's party. Now!

Lily ran into her bedroom, ransacking her room. There weren't many 1920s-style dresses in there. Lily shuffled through her wardrobe desperately until she came to a maroon V-neck maxi dress. That would have to do. She just needed a dress so she wouldn't stand out too much in, as everyone would be in their costumes. Grabbing her silver heels, she sprang down the stairs.

'You're going out?" Chris asked, screwing up his face like the neighbour's pug.

'I need to go to a party. It's about Jasmin,' Lily said while doing up her shoe strap.

Well, you're not going by yourself. I said I would be there for you, and I meant it. Give me two minutes, and I'll get dressed,' Chris bounded off the sofa.

'It's meant to be a 1920s theme. But I haven't got anything like that. So don't worry, just grab anything smartish you have,' Lily shouted after him as he took two steps at a time up the stairs.

'Mum,' Lily ran into the kitchen. 'I need a huge favour. Can you just keep an eye on Meghan? She's already in bed. There's just something I need to do. It's really important, Mum. I won't be long.'

Her Mum stared at her. 'Ummm....I guess so.....ummm, yes, okay. If you won't be too long,' she mumbled.

Lily threw her arms around Jackie, gripping her tightly. 'Thanks, Mum. I won't be long.'

'Chris!' Lily shouted. 'How are you getting on?' Lily approached the living room mirror and grabbed her brush and straighteners. She quickly pulled the straighteners through her hair and chucked some mascara on as fast as she could.

'I'm ready,' Chris appeared in the living room.

'Okay, let's go confront a murderer,' Lily said with a face as cool as steel.

'What?' Chris replied, with a look of confusion plastered all over his face.

THIRTY-SIX

Katherine

Katherine stood at the front door with her blue lagoon cocktail carefully placed in her hand. She tapped her foot. It was seven o'clock, and hardly anyone had turned up yet. Not even James was there, although that really didn't bother her. It was Tom whom she wanted to see. Suddenly, the doorbell rang. Katherine leapt forward, swinging open the door.

'Hey, good looking,' James grinned. Katherine sighed.

'Oh hi, where have you been?' Katherine asked.

'Getting myself looking gorgeous for you,' James beamed. Katherine nodded in response. Somehow, James was already dressed in his pinstriped gangster costume. Where had he got dressed? Katherine couldn't be bothered to ask. Did she really want to know anyway? Probably not. Plus, Katherine didn't want an argument with him. She was already bruised enough. Hopefully, the throbbing in her side would ease up with one more cocktail.

'Well, someone looks handsome,' Alison said, joining Katherine by her side.

'Alison,' James said formally. 'Always lovely to see you, my dear.'

'Likewise,' Alison replied. However, the tension between them could be cut with a knife.

James stepped into their house. 'So where is the bar girls? I need a good drink.'

'Come on, I'll take you. I've set up a special bar out here in the garden,' Alison gestured for James to follow her.

'I better go get drunk then,' James raised one eyebrow at Katherine cheekily before following Alison out into the garden.

Katherine leaned on the wall in the hallway. She took a sip of her cocktail. More people continued to show up, but none of them were who she wanted to see on her birthday. Maybe Tom wasn't going to come. Perhaps he had been so determined not to see Katherine that he had managed to get out of attending. Katherine hoped she was wrong.

Katherine swirled the last of her drink and made her way outside to get a top-up. As Katherine filled up her drink, she spun around to find Carol and Tom standing in front of her. Katherine immediately straightened up and embraced the cartwheels, turning inside her stomach. He's here. Tom is actually here at her party. Katherine didn't want to make too much eye contact at first. She didn't want Tom to know how much she had looked forward to his arrival.

But the cocktail had gone to Katherine's head more than she thought, and before Katherine could stop herself, she was grabbing hold of Carol and swinging her towards her chest. 'Thanks for coming,' Katherine said. She shifted her body and looked up at Tom. Staring intently at him. Tom scratched his short, sexy beard and shook his head at her. One way or another, Katherine was going to have him tonight. She was going to make sure of it. Katherine let go of Carol.

'So, who's this then, Katherine?' James suddenly appeared out of nowhere next to her. 'Aren't you going to introduce me to your friends?'

'Yes, of course. Sorry, James, this is Tom and Carol. Friends from school. They live on Forest Lane too.'

Katherine introduced, using her hand to point them out. 'They have a little boy called Jack in the same class as Sophie. They've become friends.'

'Ah, right, lovely to meet you both,' James gave them his I-don't-really-give-a-fuck-who-these-people-are smile. But Katherine knew he was as fake as she was, and really, he was still pissed off Katherine had brought strangers into their home. They were no friends of James. Which meant they were no friends of Katherine either.

But Katherine didn't care. She wanted Tom to be here. No matter how hard Katherine tried, she couldn't shake that feeling he gave her—the feeling of being wanted, a feeling of desire. It was a sensation Katherine had never experienced before Tom.

'Come on, Tom, let's get you a drink,' James said, putting his arm around Tom and dragging him towards the bar behind them. Oh, no! What did James want with Tom? This wasn't good.

Katherine didn't want to be stuck talking to Carol. 'Sorry, excuse me, Carol, I think I heard the doorbell. I'll be back in a minute. Please help yourself to a drink.'

'Oh, okay, thank you,' Carol muttered.

Katherine dashed around her before Carol had a chance to say anything else. Katherine looked over her shoulder. James was deep in conversation with Tom. Katherine bit into her fingernails. What were they talking about? No doubt, James was probably doing his best to make her look like a fool.

Katherine walked into the house, nodding to a few of her guests. Where is Alison? Katherine's hand trembled. Now that Tom was here, she was suddenly nervous in his presence. This was a really important moment. Katherine wanted to give Tom the best impression possible. He was obviously attracted to her, or he wouldn't have had sex with her. So Katherine needed to convince Tom that she was a great catch and they should be together.

Katherine spotted Alison in the living room. Alison made a gesture with her hand for Katherine to come towards her. Katherine strolled over.

'Is that him?' Alison asked, cupping her hand over her and Katherine's faces like they were twelve and talking about a secret crush. 'Is that the guy you...you know...you shagged?'

'Shhhh,' Katherine shushed her friend. 'Yes, that's him.'

'Ah yes, I think I've seen him at Kitterton. He's cute,' Alison admired, looking out of the garden through the French glass doors at Tom and James. There was a loud bang. What was that? Was it their front door?

'Hang on a minute, Ali, was that the door?' Katherine walked out of the living room into the hallway. Lily stood next to a young, good-looking guy roughly the same age as her. What was she doing here? The last time Katherine spoke to Lily, she made it quite clear she didn't want to come to her party. What was wrong with her? Lily's eyes were darting from one place to the next as if she were looking for something. But Lily's eyes also looked bloodshot, as if she had been crying. This looked like a recipe for disaster. She was not going to come here causing trouble, was she? Ruining her perfect birthday party.

'Hi, Lily. Thought you couldn't make it?' Katherine questioned, folding her arms across her chest. 'Thought this party was too good for you?' Katherine was now tapping her heel, waiting for an answer. But Lily didn't even look like she was listening.

'Not now, Katherine,' Lily snapped.

'You do realise you have just walked into my house? To my birthday party,' Katherine retaliated. Who did she think she was? Lily was such a moody bitch. Dead sister aside.

'Is Tom here Katherine? I know you invited him.' Lily squinted her eyes, finally directing her gaze at Katherine.

'Tom? Why do you want to speak to Tom? What's going on?' Katherine insisted. This girl had a nerve. 'I think maybe you should just leave Lily if you're going to start trouble.'

'Lily, just tell her.' The young lad Lily came with said, lightly touching Lily on her shoulder. Now, something was definitely going on, and Katherine wanted to know what it was.

'Okay. Katherine, can we go somewhere quiet?' Lily asked, her voice a lot lower yet creepy.

Did Katherine really want to know? Katherine didn't even know Lily that well. She could be a right weirdo for all Katherine knew. 'Yeah, we can go into James's office. Come on.'

Katherine walked through the hallway and opened James's office door.

'I'll go get us some drinks,' Chris said to Lily, touching her again on the shoulder. 'Do you want a cocktail?'

Lilly nodded. 'Yeah, thanks Chris. I really need a drink.' Who was this random stranger Lily was suddenly hanging around with? He seemed like a boyfriend. But Lily didn't have one.

'Who's that?' Katherine asked as soon as he disappeared.

'Oh, that's Chris. Meghan's father. Forget about that, Katherine. I need to tell you something,' Lily said, practically pushing Katherine into James's office.

'Yeah, okay, okay. Let me get some more of my cocktail down me first. By the look of your face, I think I will have to down the rest of this after you tell me what is up.'

'I need to tell you something,' Lily said coldly.

'What are you going on about, Lily?' Katherine staggered back as she tried to finish the rest of her cocktail. This better be good. All she wanted to do was get out of this office and return to her party. She had endured enough of this office as it was for one day. And she didn't want round two if James found them.

'Maybe I should just show you,' Lily said, taking out a picture and showing it to Katherine. She stared at the picture. No, surely not!

Lily opened her mouth to say something, but the office door flew open as she did.

'What are you doing in here?' James asked, and Katherine could tell from the tone of his voice that he was going berserk inside.

'Sorry, James,' Katherine muttered. 'We're just leaving.'

'Yeah, just leaving,' Lily repeated, and she dashed out of the office before Katherine could stop her.

'Are you coming to host your party or what?' James glared at her. 'Yes, I'm coming, James; I'll be there now. Just give me a moment,' Katherine knew he wouldn't make a scene with all these people around. He would wait until afterwards to do that.

'I'll see to our guests then, shall I? While you sit here ignoring them.' James stormed out of his office before Katherine could say anything in response.

As Katherine stood alone, she breathed a sigh of relief and collapsed onto James's office chair. As she leaned back, so many questions burned their way through her head. There had to be a reasonable explanation for what Lily had just shown her.

Katherine shoved her hands into her face momentarily. But she couldn't sit here. She needed to look for Lily and find out what was happening. Just as Katherine got up from the chair, James's laptop caught the corner of her eye; it wasn't quite closed.

Katherine leaned forward and opened it. Katherine glanced at the door. James would kill her if he knew what Katherine was about to do. Maybe he thought she wouldn't have the guts to look at his laptop. If he had, he probably wouldn't have left his computer on display. Or maybe he had forgotten.

Katherine pulled open the laptop and peered at the screen. It was unlocked. Katherine opened up his picture files and scrolled through them. Just photos of Katherine and the girls. Nothing suspicious. Katherine leaned back again.

Katherine observed the desk drawer. She tried the drawer, thinking it would be locked, but it wasn't. Katherine poked through it. She came across a USB stick. What was this for? Work presumably. Hmmm. Let's have a look, she thought. Katherine plugged it into the side of the computer. There on the screen, up flashed files, all with different girls on there. Isabelle, Emma, Olivia and Jasmin. Katherine cautiously moved the mouse over the file and clicked on it.

Surely it wasn't the same Jasmin? Katherine clicked back out and clicked on the file named "Jasmin." Sure enough, it was a picture of that young teenage girl who had been brutally murdered. Oh, sick. They were naked pictures. Why were there pictures of this girl? Who had put that USB stick there? Was it James, or had someone planted it there? Surely, James had locked his office drawer.

There was something else, too—a reflection of someone, a reflection of a woman. Katherine looked more closely at the screen. She recognised that woman. Why was she there? In the background of these sick photos?

A wave of sickness suddenly overcame Katherine. She didn't want to see it anymore. But another name caught her eye just as Katherine was about to pull out the USB stick. "Ellie". Oh, please, God, no. Please don't let that be their Ellie. Please no. Katherine looked away. She didn't want to see. But she had to. She had to know. For her daughter's sake, she had to find out. Katherine clicked on the file and shut her eyes. Exhaling deeply, she opened them again and stared at the computer.

'No!' Katherine cried out. Oh, God, no! Not my Ellie. Tears washed down Katherine's face. What were they doing to her baby? Katherine yanked out the USB drive. She couldn't look anymore. Her mind was spinning, unable to comprehend what she'd just seen.

Katherine needed to get out of the house. Fuck this party. She needed to speak to Tom. Pronto. Katherine took out her phone and texted Tom, "Meet me at the park across the road. I need to speak to you. It's important."

Katherine opened the office door as quietly as she could. No one was in the hallway, so she could try to make a run for it. Katherine quickly shoved the USB stick down her bra and ran for the front door.

THIRTY-SEVEN

Tom

The strain from James's arm was uncomfortable on Tom's neck. James gripped him tightly around the shoulder, which was supposed to be a pally gesture, but Tom knew differently. As James babbled on about his contracts for work and building sites, Tom was more keen than ever to get away from the party. He had nothing in common with this man.

James kept staring at him closely as if they were sharing a secret between them. If they did, Tom had no idea what it was. He didn't even know James. However, he did look somewhat familiar. He had a bit of a Ryan Gosling look going on about him, the same blonde comb-over and goatee. Although James probably didn't look quite as good-looking as him. Not that Tom was gay or anything. But James did remind him of the actor nonetheless. Now how the fuck could he get away from this arrogant prick. He couldn't listen to another one of his stories. Tom could see why Katherine slept with him the other day in this tosser's kitchen. With a husband at home like that. Who could blame her? Tom looked around for Carol. But she was nowhere to be seen. Shit, where had she gone? Who was she with? Tom hoped Carol hadn't bumped into Katherine.

'Sorry, James,' Tom interrupted before James could say another word. 'I need to go and find my wife. Excuse me.'

'Oh, sorry, mate. I didn't mean to keep you from your wife. If you find mine along the way. Push her in my direction. She appears to have disappeared too.' James said and walked towards the house.

'Umm, yeah, sure. Of course,' Tom replied as he briskly headed towards the house. A sly cigarette would be nice right about now. Maybe he could get through the house and out the front without being spotted by Carol or Katherine. Hiding sounded like a perfect choice.

However, as Tom stepped into the kitchen, he quickly stopped in his tracks when he noticed Lily walking into a room with Katherine. Tom had to do a double-take at first. What on earth was she doing here? They disappeared into the room, and Tom walked past them to the front door. Outside, the air was getting chillier as the sun had officially set. There was something about the nightfall that Tom quite liked, maybe because it felt so peaceful. So quiet without anyone yapping away. Tom puffed on his cigarette and flicked it over the fence into the neighbour's garden. Hiding any evidence of the cigarette butt.

Tom walked back into the hallway. Lily was standing there. He was glad. But wait, who was this guy next to her, looking all macho and buff? Stupid twat! Maybe he was just a relative or a friend, Tom told himself. But then the guy put his arm around Lily. The rage built up deep inside Tom but quickly blew over and turned to anguish like a storm breaking through his chest. He was given relief when Lily pulled his arm away from her. That's my girl.

That should be him holding Lily. Not this stupid Ken doll, spawned to perfection. She couldn't be with someone else already, though. She didn't have the time. She didn't go out anywhere. Where had she met a new man? Tom needed to get Lily away from him.

Tom marched over to Lily. 'Can I have a word?' he requested, disregarding the guy she was with.

'Umm....' Lily tried to reply.

'Excuse me....' Chris held out his arm, blocking Tom from getting near Lily. 'And who are you, mate?' puffing out his chest.

Really, who was this joker? 'Mate? I'm no mate of yours.'

Tom grabbed a shot placed on a tray on the kitchen counter. He necked one back and then another. Ah, that was better. It was harsh, but Tom felt better for it.

'Lily,' Tom protested, holding out his hand. Lily looked at Chris. His eyes were wide open, clearly waiting for her to tell Tom to back off.

She turned back to face Tom. 'Come on then. I've been looking for you anyway.'

'Lily!' Chris exclaimed. 'You don't need to go upstairs with him to talk.'

'I'll be back in a minute Chris.'

Tom followed Lily as he walked up the stairs first. He glanced over his shoulder and grinned at Chris in victory. Chris scowled back at him.

Tom and Lily both reached the top of the landing.

He took her hand in his. 'Why have you been ignoring me since our night together?' Tom asked. He wanted to get out what he had to say before she could say anything.

'Tom, I haven't got time for this right now; there's something important I need to talk to you about,' Lily crossed her arms across her chest; Tom could see she was pissed off.

Tom ignored her baffling behaviour. 'Who's that you're with? I have a right to know,' Tom demanded.

'No, you don't have a right to know. It's not really any of your business. Listen, Tom...' Lily shook her hand out of his.

'I thought we had something going on between us,' Tom said, moving closer to Lily, grabbing her arm this time and looking deep into her hazel eyes. God, she had no idea how beautiful she was.

Lily turned away from his gaze. 'Tom, I'm only here for one thing, and it's not for us to fuck like rabbits. So I think you should just move on and forget that any of this has ever happened between us. Okay?' She puffed. 'God, you're so infuriating. I'm trying to tell you something.'

Tom gripped Lily's arm even tighter, causing Lily to give out a small yelp, 'But I'm crazy about you, Lily,' Tom pleaded.

Lily shook him away. 'Look, Tom, I'm sure you are a nice guy. But like I said, I used you.'

'I don't believe you.' Tom grabbed hold of her hand and entwined his fingers with hers. 'There was something special between us.'

Lily shrugged him away again. Lily narrowed her eyes. 'Listen Tom, this is getting beyond a joke. Hear me when I say there is positively nothing between us. I'm back with my ex. Please get the fucking message!' What! Her ex? That gimp downstairs?

'And does your ex know about us, Lily? How would he feel if he found out?' He didn't mean to sound like he was blackmailing her, but the words were tumbling out before he had time to think. Tom really just wanted Lily to be with him and nobody else.

'Tom, he already knows. I tell you what. Forget our talk. You're not listening to me anyway,' Lily pushed Tom aside.

'No, wait, Lily... I'm sorry. What did you want to tell me?'

'Forget it!' She walked past him, returning down the stairs.

Tom's phone vibrated in his pocket. He took it out. It read,

"Meet me at the park across the road. I need to speak to you. It's important."

Oh great, what did this crazy bitch want now? However, the fear of Katherine telling Carol their secret was enough for him to consider meeting her. If he didn't and Carol found out, she would retract her police statement, leave him, and even take away his son, which wasn't worth the risk. Katherine was a psycho bitch, and who's telling what she would say.

Tom ran down the stairs; he peeked out from the bannister. Carol was nowhere to be seen. He wouldn't be long. Tom would just go and have it out with Katherine once and for all. Then, be back to enjoy the rest of this fake evening. Tom shut the front door behind him and took out his cigarettes from inside his pocket. He had bought them earlier that day, and Tom had only meant to have one, but he had already passed half the packet. Screw it, another one won't hurt.

He put his arms to his sides to try to gain some warmth from the ice-cold weather. Tom extended one arm from his pocket. His fingers were bright red as he toked on his cigarette. Tom really picked the wrong woman to shag. Look what mess he had gotten himself into. There was something wrong with him. After this, he would need to go to therapy. He just couldn't help it. Tom couldn't say no to women. In fact, Tom had a hard time saying no to most things. Now, this was the result.

Still, the situation was rectifiable as long as he could sweet-talk Katherine into making sure she didn't say anything to Carol. Even if Carol still agreed to testify on his behalf, he couldn't lose her. What would he do with himself? He wouldn't be able to look after himself financially. He needed Carol and her money to keep him secure. He needed her to keep him out of trouble.

As Tom crossed the road, he stepped onto the slightly muddy path to the park. He looked across and saw a figure sitting on a bench.

'Took your time, didn't you?' A voice burst out. Tom recognised the voice. It was definitely that smug bitch Katherine. He was already annoyed with her, and her sarky comment really riled him up.

'Actually, I thought I came over straight away,' Tom growled, clenching his fists. God, short of teleporting, Tom really couldn't have got there any quicker.

'Relax, I was only joking,' Katherine bit her bottom lip, touching his arm. Tom flinched. 'Come on, Tom. I'm not going to bite.'

'This isn't a game, Katherine.'

'Well, you didn't seem to mind playing games the other day,' Katherine said with a smile on her lips. 'You do realise these are people's emotions you are messing with? Do I need to remind you what your wife would say about us shagging on my kitchen counter?'

'Yes, well, it seemed like a good idea at the time. A momentary lapse in judgment,' Tom knew that dismissing her like that could be the wrong thing to do, but he couldn't help himself. She was just such an awful human being. 'I was just in a bad place at the time with my wife, Katherine. I seem to have this problem with saying no,' Tom needed to be straight with her. But he also had to remember to tread carefully. He wasn't sure how unstable she was, and there was no telling what she might do.

Katherine suddenly burst into tears, burying her hands in her face.

Tom took a step towards her. He suddenly felt sorry for her. 'I'm really sorry, Katherine. I know I'm a dick. I shouldn't have done what I did. Just please don't tell Carol. Can we just forget about it and move on?'

Katherine continued to sob, not saying anything. 'It's not just you I'm upset about. I just made the mistake of thinking I might be able to talk to you about something."

God, what was so important that everyone had to talk to him? 'What did you want to talk about?' Tom asked softly, taking a step closer towards Katherine. He didn't really want to put his arm around her. Still, she looked so lost, sobbing away. Plus, what did she want to tell him?

'Well, well. Isn't this cosy?' a voice from behind them suddenly sounded.

Tom spun around. It was James. Tom's eyes widened, and he stumbled back. How much had he heard? By the look of James's face, it was a lot. There was steam practically coming out of James's ears. He was clenching his fists. Tom laid out his hands in a bid to protect himself. Tom expected a fight to happen.

'Sorry mate, it was a mistake,' as if Tom saying those words would make James bow down and shake his hand in forgiveness. But the words had already fallen out of his mouth.

'Shagging my wife was a mistake? You're going to know what a mistake feels like,' James's face was red with fury. James pushed out his chest, and his shoulders went back. Somehow, James now looked bigger than he did previously at the party. Fuck. How had Tom not noticed before?

'James, please no,' Tom squealed, stepping back. But James grew closer to him. Then, before Tom could react, a fist came towards him and plunged into his nose. Tom heard the crack of the cartilage in his nose explode! Tom leant forward, grabbing hold of his nose with both hands. Then another blow came. This time, Tom went down like a sack of potatoes. His nose tingled with tenderness. Fuck. It felt like his nose was broken.

'James, leave him alone,' Katherine pleaded; she grabbed hold of his arm, but James just shrugged her off.

James started laughing. 'She doesn't even know what you did, does she?'

Tom scrambled to his feet, clutching his nose as blood poured over his mouth and down his chin. 'What are you talking about?' Tom gasped.

Tom had it wrong. James was more of a lunatic than Katherine. He had never met James in his life before tonight.

'Okay then, if you're going to play dumb, I'll just tell her what you did,' he turned to Katherine. 'So, my dearest, it appears that your lover is actually the one who killed that girl, Jasmin.' James stood tall, waving a finger at Tom.

What was James on about? Surely he hadn't killed Jasmin? There was no way he was capable of doing that.

'Me? No, I didn't. Plus, how would you know? I don't even know you,' Tom contested. Did this James know something Tom didn't, or was he just plain insane and blaming Tom? Tom decided to go with the latter.

But then, something happened. The memory came flooding into his mind like a Tsunami. James was right. He had killed Jasmin. Fuck. He was a murderer.

Then, before Tom could think anymore, James's fist came flying his way again. Everything went dark.

THIRTY-EIGHT

Katherine

Tom's body lay motionless on the ground, like a possum playing dead.

'What have you done?' Katherine demanded. Oh my God, this was crazy. Was Tom okay? 'Why would you say that? You're a really nasty piece of work, you know that.' Katherine was so angry that she wasn't even thinking of the consequences of talking to James this way.

'Because it's true,' James replied smugly. The bastard was enjoying this. Was this his way of trying to get Tom against Katherine? Because if it were so, it wasn't working!

Katherine's stomach churned. She couldn't believe she had been sleeping next to this man after all these years. Having sex with him and sharing bodily fluids. Her body shuddered. She couldn't be more repulsed by him. Katherine turned her head as she thought about all the terrible, vile things her husband had been doing. And now, on top of this, he was trying to frame Tom for the murder of that poor girl.

In fact, where had James even been that night? He stayed out late so often, working and God knows what else. She couldn't keep track of his comings and goings.

Katherine thought long and hard. It was Monday the 4th. The first day of term was the night that poor girl died. He had not been at home. He had not been there all night. James had been at a networking event but had left a message on her phone to say he was crashing at the office as he had an early start.

'It was you,' Katherine mumbled. 'It was you who killed Jasmin.'

James started to laugh.

'Stay away from me,' Katherine raised her hand, gesturing for him to stay away from her as she took a step backwards.

'Katherine, baby. Come on, let's get out of here. Let's go home,' James pulled out his hand for Katherine to take it. But Katherine stepped back away from him.

'No, it was you. You're a monster. You make me sick,' Katherine yelled.

'You're blinded by this joke of a man. What, you're gonna believe this womaniser over your devoted husband? Father of your children. He doesn't give a shit about you. You're just some silly old slut to him,' James said coldly. 'Come on, let's go home so we can talk about this,' his hand still out for her to grab.

'You're not fit to be a father. I know what you have been doing. I know what you have been doing to our poor little girl. And with that woman! I saw her on your computer. I know what you and her have been doing to Ellie. And Jasmin. And those other poor girls.' Tears were surging down Katherine's face. 'Was she ever my friend? Or was she pretending all along?'

'She couldn't stand you, Katherine, Oh and yes...I know about your fight in the school playground.'

'Oh God, poor Ellie. Those photos of her and....' Katherine gulped '.....And you! And Susan! How could you both do that to her? You've scarred her for life. You're an abuser and a murderer. Why would I want to go anywhere with you? Stay the fuck away from me,' Katherine screamed. Anyone who does that to a child, to their child, is just pure evil. The lying prick. He did kill Jasmin, not Tom.

James ignored her warning and stepped forward anyway. His shoulders were back, and his chin was up. He was such an arrogant dick. He really thought he was God. Taking what he can for himself.

'What you gonna do, baby?' Leaning forward, James poked his face forward into hers. 'Nothing!' he grinned, grabbing hold of her. 'You're mine!' his eyes burned into hers fiercely.

James started to drag her by the arm. She was not his. She wasn't his property. A piece of meat he could play around with. Abusing their daughter and killing young teenage girls. The flashes of disturbing thoughts tumbled around in her head. Katherine jittered. A breathtaking surge of hatred strung out of Katherine like a volcano erupting. Katherine raised her knee with an almighty force, straight into James's balls. James cried out. This was her chance. She needed to get away from him. Katherine briefly glanced down at Tom and ran through the forest park.

'Ah, you bitch!' James yelled behind her, but she kept running through the forest. Running deeper and deeper into the woods. Her heels made it hard to run. But Katherine just kept going. Not turning around to see if he was behind her. Katherine headed to a large bush in front of her. She needed a breather. She couldn't run any longer. Katherine crouched down behind the bush. Her panting was loud. The mixture of alcohol and running was making her head spin. But there was nothing she could do. Katherine had to get away from this man, or he was going to kill her. Make her pay the same way he made Jasmin pay. What did that girl do to make James kill her? But what did Katherine ever do to make him hit her? Nothing.

Katherine peered over the bush. He was gone. But he was out there somewhere, and soon, the running would have to start again. Her legs were like jelly, but she had to dig deep. Somewhere deep inside her, Katherine needed to find the strength to get away and tell others what her husband was really like. Or he would get away with it. Katherine clutched onto the bush, still searching the darkness for James. Waiting for him to spring up at any moment. Come on, Katherine, she told herself. Get hold of your breathing. It was so loud. The woods were quiet, yet her panting overshadowed the stillness surrounding her. Come on, Katherine, if you're not quiet, he will find you. And kill you. Katherine trembled. This was really happening. She was being hunted. Hunted down by her own husband. People would say, 'How had she not known?' When the other mums went to her funeral. *Silly cow*, they would call her. How could she not have known her husband was a complete and utter monster?

There were slashes on her hands, and blood had found its way onto them. Katherine's trembling, frightened hands had been gripping hold of the bush too tightly. Shit. There he was. In the distance. His back was turned to Katherine. She ducked back down sharply, holding her breath.

Katherine's stomach tightened, and her head continued to spin. She would give anything to have a gallon of water right now. Katherine had indulged in way too many cocktails, and she was not geared up to be running for her life. Thick teardrops flowed down Katherine's cheek. This could be it. She would never see her children again. Her friends again. All because she married the wrong guy. They would be right to judge her. She was a silly cow. And a crappy mother.

Katherine slapped herself. Get a grip, girl. You need to start running again, and now! Or he would find your hiding place. Katherine kicked off her muddy heals and tossed them to her side. Katherine stood up. She gripped hold of her head to keep it steady, attempting to focus on what was in front of her.

She could make it. She had to make it. Katherine gulped, making an effort to forget the horror that lay behind her. This was her chance to make it. Katherine started to run barefoot across the forest. Getting rid of the heels made it faster to run, but the ground was so harsh on her delicate, soft feet. The branches beneath her dug into them, and Katherine was sure there was blood pouring out of them.

Her tight, long dress made it hard to run. She hitched it up to try and make it easier. Whose stupid idea was it to wear a flapper dress? Yet, how was she to know she would be running through a forest in the middle of the night? With each step, the branches thrashed at her feet, the pain shot through her like a bolt of lightning, but she had to keep going.

This was not trying to beat a stupid girl on the treadmill at the gym. This was life or death. If she got caught, the consequence would be death. But her legs were so heavy, and Katherine wasn't sure how long they would run for. They were aching so much. Her chest burned, and she was struggling more than ever to take in each breath.

Suddenly, she wasn't running anymore as Katherine toppled over a branch onto the soggy ground. Jumping to her knees, Katherine spun around. Searching in the darkness for James. She couldn't see him anywhere. Oh god. Where was he? The blackness made it impossible to see. Katherine scrambled back up to her feet. Maybe he had gone? Maybe he was back at the house, given up on his hunt for her blood. The sweat dripped from her face, and Katherine wiped it out of her eyes with a trembling hand.

Katherine leant on a tree. She needed to take a breather for a moment. Her legs were struggling to stay upright, and she was screaming at Katherine to collapse to the floor. Her tightened stomach finally gave way. Katherine projectile vomited. Cocktails from earlier splashed onto the ground below. Her mouth was now drier than ever. Her head began to spin again. She needed fluid. Katherine's mouth drooled, and she imagined a cold glass of water hitting her lips. Her body was weak, and she didn't know if she could run anymore.

Blood pooled down her hands. God, she was in one hell of a state. Mud and scratches covered the length of her body. Katherine could not feel her fingers anymore, the coldness catching hold of them. There was just no energy left inside her. She just wanted to give up. Katherine raised her head to look up. She could see light. It was a road. It was just up ahead. Katherine had been so frantically trying to escape her husband that she hadn't realised which direction she was running in. But there was a glimmer of hope. She could make it out. Getting away from that demon once and for all.

Just as Katherine was about to run, something grabbed her from behind, forcing their hand across her mouth so no screams would come out. Katherine spun around. Was she facing her killer? But as Katherine looked more closely. It wasn't James. It wasn't even a man. It was a woman. Katherine focused her eyes, trying to make out who it was. The woman put her finger to her lips, gesturing for Katherine to be quiet. Suddenly, Katherine could make out the figure. It was Lily. Katherine nodded in response. Lily was pointing behind her. Katherine turned. It was James.

'Come out, Come out. Wherever you are. I know you're here, baby,' James sang, mocking her at every turn. How she hated this man. A man she once thought she loved. 'I could hear you spewing your guts up Katherine. What a weak, pathetic woman you are. You're not fit to be a mother,' James called out, creeping slowly towards them. Lily and Katherine were hiding behind a big oak tree.

James moved closer towards them. 'Come on, we can talk about this, my dear,' he chirped.

Katherine leaned her back against the tree alongside Lily. "Please just go away," she thought. "Please just let this God-forsaken nightmare be over." Katherine peered out from the tree to see where James had gone. He had been quiet for a few minutes. Maybe he had walked off in the other direction. Then, she and Lily could make a run for it across the road and back home to safety, where there was a crowd of people.

'Gotcha!' James grinned. Katherine jumped. He was close against her face, and she could smell his whiskey breath in her mouth. She was a goner now.

THIRTY-NINE

Lily

Lily peeked out from the tree. Katherine was on her knees, pleading with James. He had her face in his hand.

'James, please just let me go. Please don't kill me like you killed Jasmin. I'm the mother of your children. Think about them,' Katherine's arms were wide open as she tried to reason with her husband.

'Kill you?' James stepped back, his eyes raised.

'I fucking knew it!' Lily stepped out from the tree, reacting before she had time to take in what Katherine had just said. 'I knew when I saw that photo of you with your arm around my sister. That it was you!'

Lily searched the ground and grabbed a thick branch, clutching it tightly in her hand. Lily's heart was racing. She had no time to think, just actions. He was her sister's killer, and he was going to pay for what he did. Lily's body quivered as she cautiously took steps toward James. The branch shook uncontrollably in her hands, and her consciousness butted in for a moment. You shouldn't be doing this. He's not worth it. But the rage that roared inside her was too overpowering to control. Lily just wanted him dead—cruel bastard.

James started to laugh, letting go of Katherine's face. 'What you gonna do with that little girl? There's no way you will use that on me,' he was in fits of laughter. But this just angered Lily even more. Was he really just going to stand there and laugh at her? Did he just laugh at Jasmin when he killed her? Not this time, mate!

The venom inside her body was overpowering. She clenched the branch tighter. The splinters started to pierce the palms of her hands. Yet Lily felt no pain from it. 'You killed my sister!' Lily screamed at him.

'Why does everyone keep saying that?' James replied. 'I didn't kill anyone. I'm not saying that slut didn't deserve it. But I didn't kill her. It was that guy Tom.'

Lily's chin was jutting. 'What! How dare you call my sister a slut! She was a beautiful eighteen-year-old!' she continued to yell. 'You're really going to deny what you did?!'

'Don't listen to him, Lily. He's a manipulator and a liar,' Katherine begged, still collapsed on her knees in front of James.

'Ha. And you're not Katherine,' James turned to Lily. 'My wife is just protecting her lover. You do know my wife has been fucking Tom? So naturally, she would stick up for him and abandon her loving husband.'

'I knew it! Katherine, are you covering for Tom?' Lily demanded. She had raised the branch high over her shoulder, ready to swing it if needed. Who should she believe? Who was lying?

'Well, yes, but I'm not sticking up for Tom. It was James. I know it was. He wasn't at home the night Jasmin was murdered,' Katherine started. 'I didn't think anything of it then, but now it all makes sense.'

Lily didn't know who to believe. Who was telling the truth? She didn't know. One thing was for certain: Tom had slept with Jasmin that night, followed by Katherine and her. Now, James was telling Lily it was Tom who killed her sister. How did he know this? One thing was for sure, though: Tom was nowhere near as innocent as he made out and nowhere near the man she thought he was. In fact, she didn't know him at all.

'How do you know it was Tom?' Lily asked James. Her arms were shaking from the exertion of holding the branch above her head.

But Katherine responded instead. 'He doesn't, Lily. He's just trying to get into your head. I found pictures on his computer. He has been abusing our little girl, Ellie.' Katherine's eyes welled up. 'She's only nine. Plus, there are loads of photos of other girls on there too, including Jasmin. I have the evidence to prove it.'

'You stupid fucking bitch,' James ran and kicked Katherine in the stomach. She screamed out. Katherine curled into a ball.

How could Lily have doubted her thoughts? It was him. James was the killer. Keeping pictures of Jasmin on his computer. Abusing girls. Abusing his own daughter? What kind of sick fuck does that? Then she realised something. Jasmin had been pregnant. It was James. He was the father. Lily's heart rate picked up once more. The rage shimmered through her body like an intense wave.

James continued to stomp on Katherine's stomach with his foot. She sputtered and started to retch from the beating. Oh my God. He's going to kill her too. Kill his own wife. The same way he killed her sister. She had to do something. Lily had to stop him.

'It was you. She had been pregnant, and that's why you killed her! You bastard!' Lily yelled. 'Get off her!' Lily ran forward with the branch still raised over her head, intent on swinging it at him. She swung the branch as hard as she could towards his face. But it stopped dead in James's hand, missing him completely. James's force was too strong. He ripped the branch from her hand and tossed it to the ground. Shit. Shit. What was she going to do now? Run? Yes, run.

James stopped beating his wife and turned to face Lily. Katherine was spluttering on the ground and panting deeply. She was still alive. For now. Lily stepped back from James, her body trembling. What was he going to do? Flashes of Meghan flew through Lily's head. How could Lily have gotten herself into this situation? If she died, her daughter would grow up without a mother.

James stood tall over Lily, his eyes filled with evil. His eyes were enough to kill alone. Lily tried to turn and make a run for it, but he gripped the back of her hair, yanking Lily towards him. Lily screamed. But there was no one else coming. Why had she come here? Why had she followed James to the park? Lily was so intent on avenging her sister's murderer. She was so blinded by grief that she was willing to put herself in harm's way and leave her four-year-old daughter without a mother. No. She wasn't going to make it easy for him.

James punched Lily in the stomach, and she dropped to her knees. She grabbed some dirt from the cold ground and spun around, throwing it on his face.

'Fucking bitch!' James yelled out, slapping Lily hard in the face. Lily grabbed hold of her throbbing cheek. He hit her again on the other side. This time, he flung Lily onto her back. Her long brunette hair covered her face. Lily couldn't see him, but she could smell his harsh whiskey breath as he placed his heavy frame on top of her.

Lily wriggled her body as much as she could. But it was no use. Her tiny physique against his manly torso wouldn't budge. He ran his hand underneath her dress. Tugging at her knickers until they gave way and ripped open. Giving him full access to her.

'Oh God no. Please, no,' Lily cried out. Part of Lily wished she were already dead. So she wouldn't have to witness this. No, please don't let this happen, she pleaded to herself.

'It's easier if you don't struggle, my dear,' James whispered into her ear. The sound of James unbuckling his belt made Lily quiver. Then she heard the zip of his trousers being pulled down. Oh God, this really is going to happen. James wasn't going to kill her. He was going to rape her like he had all his other victims Katherine had seen on his computer. Or was he going to rape her, then kill her? Is that what he had done to Jasmin? Lily continued to squirm, scuffing her feet on the soil. Trying anything to get his dead weight off her. But it was no use. He didn't budge one bit. It was as if he were made of stone.

'Please don't,' Lily screamed out. 'Please don't.'

'Stop struggling, you stupid bitch,' James slapped Lily across the face.

It burnt. The tears ran down her face. Lily started to sob loudly. She didn't care any more about what he thought of her. There was nothing Lily could do to stop the inevitable from happening. This was going to happen whether she liked it or not. Lily closed her eyes tightly and turned her head to the side. The tears fell down her face into the hard ground beneath her. Lily took a deep breath. Bracing herself for him to do what he was about to do. Lily felt James's trousers wriggle down his legs as they brushed against hers.

But the inevitable didn't happen. A loud cracking noise sounded, and James fell on top of her like a dead weight. Lily opened her eyes. Who was that? Someone was standing over her. Lily blinked. It was so dark. Lily's eyes adjusted to the lights. It was Carol. She was standing with a stiletto in her hand, up over her shoulder. The heel dripping with blood. Hands shaking. Eyes wide open with horror. Gasping heavily for air like she was hyperventilating.

Lily managed to push James's body to the side of her with an almighty force. Then, somehow, she managed to wriggle out from underneath him. She rolled onto the dirt, scuffing her knee. Lily pulled down her dress, closing her knees tightly and snugly wrapping her arms around her legs as if protecting herself. Lily continued to feel exposed.

James lay motionless on the ground. Was he dead? Lily didn't want to look. She couldn't look. Carol dropped her shoe. It hit the park floor with a thud.

'Is he...ummm,' Carol cleared her throat. 'Is he... er.....is he dead?' Carol gulped.

'I don't know,' Lily muttered.

Sticks crackled behind the tree in front of Lily. Who else was there? Lily stared in the direction of the sound. It was too dark to see. Carol quickly picked up her shoe again, spinning around, ready to attack whoever it was.

FORTY

Tom

Tom rose from the ground. He rubbed the back of his head. It was sore. Shit. That bastard.

Then, the reality struck Tom like he had been knocked over the head by it. It was him. Tom had been the one who killed Jasmin. The memories of that night flooded back into his mind as Tom became more conscious. It was an accident. An awful accident. Tom was just trying to help. But she ended up dead. Tears shuffled their way down his ice-cold face. Tom buried his hands in his face as he recalled that night.

He had been almost home when Tom had spewed in the taxi. Naturally, the taxi driver had shoved him out of his cab. So Tom had stumbled through the park to reach Forest Lane.

But if he hadn't vomited that night, none of this would have happened, and Jasmin would still be alive. It was at the park that Tom saw a man on top of a girl. He was shouting at her for being pregnant. The man was James.

As Tom drew closer, he decided to confront James, but his heroic actions were deeply let down, as James punched Tom in the face.

However, it distracted James and allowed the girl to jump to her feet. When Tom looked again, he noticed that it was Jasmin from the bar.

This set Tom off into a drunk rage, and he started to swing punches at James. But for some reason, Jasmin had gotten involved. Screaming at Tom. Telling him to get off James. But Tom was entranced in his rage and wasn't listening. Anger was not something he was good at controlling when he was drunk, especially around abusive grown men. At that point, the cocaine had worn off, and Tom was feeling the full force of his drunken state.

Tom had pushed Jasmin away from him as he continued to land punches on the man. But he must have pushed her too hard. Because suddenly she went quiet. Tom had stopped swinging and turned to find Jasmin had hit her head on a big rock behind her. Blood trickling down her face. So still. And so lifeless. It was then and there that Tom knew what he had done.

James had checked for a pulse and said he couldn't feel for one. Tom had taken out his phone to phone for an ambulance, but James had said it was too late. He wasn't sure what happened after that. He must have left her. He had flashes of staggering inside the house. He was with someone. Had it been James? He wasn't sure. It didn't really matter. He had been the one who had killed her.

For some reason, Tom had blocked this tragic event from his mind until now. Tom wasn't sure if it was being back at the scene of the crime or being in the same company as James. But now Tom knew. The blood was on his hands. His subconscious had revealed the tragedies of that awful night to his conscious mind. And now he had to live with them.

A woman's scream in the distance shook Tom from his thoughts. Oh God, not again. What was going on? He had to help. Tom started to run through the forest, going deeper and deeper, running towards the sound, jumping over branches and brushing the bushes out of his face. What was James doing now? Tom jumped from behind a tree to find Lily, Carol, James, and Katherine.

'What happened?' Tom asked frantically. He scratched his head as he stood over James's body.

Carol was firmly gripping her shoe above her head as she faced Tom. He slowly walked over to her, gently taking the shoe from Carol's hand. She looked up at Tom, her eyes wide with alarm. She released her grip, allowing Tom to take hold of the shoe. Once in his hand, he released it, allowing it to drop to the ground.

'He was....he was...' Carol stuttered as she turned to face Lily. Tom looked over at Lily, who was still clutching her knees tightly together for dear life. There was no need for Carol to explain. Tom knew what James had tried to do to Lily.

Tom nodded. 'There, there, it's okay. Come here,' Tom grabbed Carol's hand and hugged her tightly.

Tom turned to Lily. 'Are you okay?' He walked over to Lily and held out his hand. Lily rose to her feet and stepped behind Tom.

Was he dead? Tom tiptoed towards James's motionless body nervously. He bent down and touched his neck with two fingers. He couldn't feel a pulse. Tom laid his head on his chest. There was no sound of a beating heart.

This was more up Carol's street. But she looked in no fit state to check if James was still alive. Carol was used to saving lives, not taking them away.

Nope, there was definitely no trace of a pulse or a heartbeat. 'He's dead,' Tom announced, gazing up at Carol and Lily.

FORTY-ONE

Katherine

Immense stabbing pains were coming from Katherine's stomach as she sat up from the cold, muddy floor, and then the cramping came from her abdomen. It felt like she was having the worst period of her life. The pain was so bad that it took Katherine several moments to realise that James was lying on the floor with blood pouring from his head.

She looked up, and Carol, Lily, and Tom stood over his body.

'I'm so sorry Katherine,' Carol sobbed. 'He's dead.'

Katherine blinked in disbelief as she stared at James's dead body. She didn't know whether to jump for joy or cry with sorrow. Was he really dead? On one hand, she felt sad that he was gone. He was her husband, and she had loved him for many years. But she hadn't been in love with him for a long time, and he was the reason she had become so weak. And on top of that, learning he was sexually abusing girls, including their own precious daughter, just made Katherine sick to her stomach. Katherine's visions of him doing stuff that she just couldn't get out of her head.

Pregnant, Lily had said. Just before Katherine had blacked out. Is that why James had killed her? To cover up the baby? Was it because of her? So she wouldn't find out? Maybe Jasmin had threatened to tell Katherine, and that's why James had done it. Her mind felt scrambled as she tried to make sense of it all.

Katherine breathed out a sigh of relief. She decided she was glad he was gone. James didn't deserve to be alive. But who killed him? Was it Lily? The last thing she remembered, Lily was holding a branch, ready to swing for him.

'Lily?' Katherine said. Lily shook her head.

'It was me,' Carol said, her eyes raw and red and her face pale. 'I did it. I er....' Tears fell down her cheeks, her hands shaking, and Katherine could see she was completely distraught by what she had just done.

Katherine bent forward onto her knees, and with a forceful push, she scrambled to her feet, holding onto her stomach in agony as she moved. Katherine stepped towards Carol. 'It's okay,' Katherine whispered, touching her arm gently. 'He was a monster.'

Carol started to weep. Tom stepped in between them and grabbed hold of Carol, hugging her.

'One thing I can't understand....' Lily started. 'Why was James so intent on saying it was you who killed Jasmin?' she glared at Tom.

'I've no idea!' Tom said blankly.

'Right,' Lily was eyeing Tom up suspiciously. She had a point. James had been so intent on saying it was Tom. Now, thinking back, why would he say it? Was there some truth to what James was saying? Had Katherine been too full of hate, focusing on what he and Susan had done to Ellie, to ignore what he had been saying?

'Your wife saved my life. I wouldn't be here if it weren't for her,' Lily continued. Tears shimmered in her eyes.

Tom turned back towards Carol and hugged her closer, placing her head on his shoulder with his hand.

Did this mean he was staying with his wife, tossing Katherine to the side? Like nothing had ever happened between them? She needed to say something to her, but she felt sorry for Carol, sobbing away.

Lily rolled her eyes at them. 'We're going to have to ring the police,' Lily piped up. 'And we need to get our story straight about who did it?'

'We know who did,' Tom protested.

What, and you'll let your wife go down for it, will you?' Lily exclaimed. Wow, she was really going at Tom. Maybe Katherine was wrong about them too? Her tone was cold.

'Well, what do you propose I do then, Lily?' Tom narrowed his eyes at her.

'You should take the fall for her,' Lily said to him.

'What!' he uttered.

'I agree,' Katherine blurted out. Tom turned towards her coldly.

'Stay out of it, you!' he yelled at Katherine. God, he was such a prick. Katherine couldn't quite believe she had fallen for such a dick.

Maybe Katherine had just felt so miserable with James that she wanted to hold onto someone other than her husband. And Tom was there, sweeping Katherine off her feet and making her feel wanted. She had missed that feeling of being wanted, seduced in a way that made her feel special. It had been nice, even though it had only lasted a moment.

But now she saw Tom for who he was. 'You are such a self-centred prick who doesn't care about anyone but himself! I can't believe I ever fell for you!' Katherine suddenly yelled at him, so much so that Lily jumped back in surprise.

'What!' Carol stepped away from him, rubbing her eyes. 'What else have you been up to, Thomas?' she screamed.

Tom looked at the floor.

'You can't get out of this one, Tom; you slept with me too.' Lily confessed.

Katherine swung her head to face Lily, as did Carol. Oh God, he was a tosser!

Carol's face flushed red. 'For once in your scrawny life, tell the truth. Did you have anything to do with Jasmin's death? Was James lying or telling the truth when he said it was you?' Carol demanded. She had planted her hand on her hip sharply. Her eyes were fierce as she stared at Tom. She was one scary lady when she wanted to be!

Tom didn't say anything. Carol continued to glare at him, almost coaching him to confess. Was it him, though? After all, even though James had denied killing Jasmin, he was the monster, not Tom.

'It was an accident,' Tom blurted out. 'I was trying to help. He was attacking her. I tried to help, but she got in the way.' Carol stepped back and away from him.

Katherine raised her eyes in astonishment. What! Tom? No. She had been so convinced it was her husband who did it.

Tom turned to Lily. 'Lily, I'm so sorry. I tried to help her. Really, I did.'

'I can't believe I ever had you anywhere near me, you murdering bastard!' Lily yelled, shaking her head. 'Right, here's what's going to happen, Tom,' she took a deep breath, straightening herself up. 'You're going to say it was you who killed James. And we will all confirm that it was James who killed Jasmin.'

Well, that was a bit hasty. To assume she and Carol would just back her up, giving a false statement. Except Katherine would. She was well and truly done siding with men. Despite Lily sleeping with him, she clearly hated his guts. And Tom seemed to hate hers. So yes, why not? Why shouldn't he be the one to suffer?

'I...errrr,' Tom mumbled.

'Don't you think you owe her that?' Katherine barked.

'Stay out of it, you!' Tom scolded her. God, really, what did Katherine see in him?

'Don't speak to her like that, ' Lily exploded. 'Accident or no accident, my sister is dead because of you.'

Tom turned to Carol, 'Carol, please,' he pleaded with her.

Carol looked at him for a moment without saying anything. 'I've stuck by you so much, Tom. But how many chances do you want? You've hurt me so much,' she exhaled heavily, but her chest was still rapidly rising and dropping. 'I think you should do it. If you loved me at all, then you would put Jack and me first for once in your life.'

Lily took a step towards him. 'Are you really going to let the mother of your child go down for murder, Tom? Especially when she was trying to protect me, and you claimed you were doing the same thing for Jasmin. Wouldn't you rather go down for one murder rather than two?' Was Lily threatening Tom? Saying if he didn't do it, then she would out him for both murders? She was craftier than Katherine first thought.

'You won't keep Jack from me?' Tom said softly, turning to face Carol. Tears were welling up in his eyes.

'No,' she said.

'Okay,' he muttered, looking at the ground. 'I'll do it.'
'I'll call the police,' Lily stated.

FORTY-TWO

Tom

DI Carter walked up to Tom. 'So what happened here?' he asked, holding out his notepad, ready to ask for questions.

Tom sighed. He had already rehearsed the scene in his head as they waited for the police and ambulance to arrive. Katherine was getting medical attention in the back of the ambulance for her beating from James.

Tom's eyes darted from Lily to Carol. They both nodded at him. It was either go down for one murder or two murders. Carol had promised he wouldn't lose his son. And that he couldn't cope with.

Tom cleared his throat. 'He was on top of Lily and trying to attack her. James was going to rape her. I had no choice. Carol's heel was on the floor. I picked it up and launched it at his head. I was just trying to get him off her,' Tom clarified. He swallowed hard, but it felt like a golf ball was stuck in his throat. 'The one blow seemed to have killed him.' Tom looked down at the floor; he couldn't believe these words were coming out of his mouth. But he had to.

DI Carter stopped writing. He looked up at Tom and turned to face Lily. 'Is that true?' Lily nodded. Carol had bowed her head. She reluctantly agreed that Tom should take the fall. But had agreed nonetheless. Carol knew everything. All three women knew everything. Oh, Tom, you have made such a mess of everything, he told himself.

The way Tom saw it, it was either take the rap for Carol and do a couple of years in prison for involuntary manslaughter, hopefully, then see his son when he got out. Or go down for two murders without ever seeing his son. Tom had no choice. Lily was orchestrating this and there wasn't a damn thing he could do about it.

DI Carter turned to Carol, 'And you saw Thomas here hit James over the head?' Carol nodded.

Katherine was sitting in the back of the ambulance. Although she hadn't actually witnessed what had happened to James, she was willing to testify that it was Tom, too, and go along with the same story as Lily and Carol.

Still, at least that psycho James was dead.

'It was me. I whacked James over the head. I killed him,' Tom asserted to DI Carter.

'Okay, and Katherine says James admitted to killing Jasmin Knowell?' DI Carter muttered.

'Yes, now are you going to arrest me or not?' Tom laid out his hands, ready.

DI Carter put his notepad away. 'I will need you both to give statements,' he pointed his finger at both Carol and Lily. They both nodded in agreement, their lips still silent.

'Okay then. Thomas Dwelling. I'm arresting you on suspicion of murder. You do not have to say anything, but it may hurt your defence if you do not mention, when questioned, something which you later rely on in court. Anything you say may be given in evidence.' DI Carter took out his cuffs. 'Turn around, please.'

Tom slowly turned around as DI Carter placed the cuffs on his wrists. He looked up at Lily and Carol. Lily's eyes were cold and heartless. Whilst Carol was a mess, tears streaming down her face as she stared at him. She looked utterly crushed. He was an idiot.

FORTY-THREE

Tom

Tom stood waiting for the gates to open to the prison cells so he could go into the visitor room. He scrunched the bottom of his plain grey jumper. He tried not to look too nervous, even though his heart hadn't stopped racing since entering prison. But he couldn't show any weakness in here. Some scary characters were around, and one wrong look could mean a beating. Or worse. Knifed. Tom shuddered at the thought. Since arriving, he'd tried to get his head down. How on earth was he going to survive prison long term?

One eye started to twitch; Tom rubbed it in order to try and stop it from flickering. He had not slept well at all the previous night. The only thing that had allowed him to finally fall asleep was the thought of seeing Jack. Although he wished they were not meeting in prison. God knows what kind of scarring he was giving him right about now. However, it was the only thing that could comfort him right now.

The doors opened, and Tom immediately spotted Carol sitting on one of the seats. He quickly walked over to her. He practically ran towards her, giving her a huge hug as he reached her.

'No touching,' a guard shouted at him.

'Sorry,' he mumbled. Sitting down, suddenly realising she was alone.

'Where's Jack?' he asked nervously. He hoped she was coming in separately and that he would be along any minute.

Carol avoided his eye contact, staring at the floor next. 'Tom, I don't think it is a good idea for you to see Jack,' Carol said.

'What?!' He shouted louder than he meant to. The guard across the room gave him daggers. Warning him with his eyes to stay quiet.

Carol looked around the room tensely. 'You're on trial for a murder charge,' she spoke quietly as if it were a secret.

Tom crinkled his nose and gripped the side of the table. 'Involuntary manslaughter, actually,' he corrected.

'Still murder Tom,' her voice still quiet.

'And are you kidding me, after what I did for you? You're going to stop me from seeing my son? How fucking dare you,' Tom objected through gritted teeth. 'You promised!' his hands started shaking from the adrenaline pumping around his body. But he knew he had to stay calm or the guards would likely make him leave.

'Come on, Tom, don't pretend you are Mr Innocent in all of this,' Carol began. 'You are the reason why Jasmin is dead after you slept with her behind my back. Then went on to have an affair with Katherine, then Lily,' Carol reminded. 'You didn't give us a second thought then.'

She looked down at the floor, twiddling her fingers like something was on her mind.

'Go on, spit it out, Carol! What is it you want to say?'

She looked up at him. 'I want a divorce, Tom,' she said, tears starting to creep down her face.

'A divorce?' Tom questioned, furrowing his eyebrows. 'I know, I've made a mess of things. I'm so sorry, Carol. But divorce?' Tom grabbed her hand, looked into her eyes, and used them to try to plead for her forgiveness. She needed him now more than ever. He couldn’t survive this place without her support.

Carol brushed the tears away from her eyes. 'I'm so sorry, Tom. But you only have yourself to blame,' Carol paused momentarily, her lip curling up. 'What goes around comes around, Thomas,' she brushed herself out of his grip and stood up, she walked toward the door, before glancing back at him briefly one last time. The guards opened the door for her, and she was gone. Fuck.

FORTY-FOUR

Katherine

There were large gusts of wind in the air as Katherine pushed open the gate of the children's playground. She could distinctly smell the cold Autumn air; the temperature was dropping with each passing day. Katherine scrunched up her nose as it stung from the bitter cold. She tucked her face into her Karen Millen coat. But the weather didn't bother her. Nothing could bring her down today. The nightmare was over. That bastard was gone. And for the first time in a long time, she felt free. Knowing James wouldn't be taking another breath. It was over for her, and it was over for her daughter. They were all completely safe with that man out of her life. Katherine took a deep breath, exhaling deeply. Her mouth curved into a smile as she thought about their new life ahead.

'How'd it go?' Lily beamed at Katherine.

Katherine darted her eyes at Lily and Carol sheepishly, keeping them in suspense momentarily. 'Really well. I passed. I'm now officially a barrister!'

'Well done!' Carol beamed; her whole face lit up.

'Yes, well done, Katherine,' Lily exclaimed. 'I also have some news of my own,' she paused, giving them a lopsided grin.

'Well, don't leave us in suspense. What is it?' Katherine urged.

'So, I have applied to be a police officer,' Lily revealed coyly. A flush crept onto her face as she spoke, as if she was somewhat in disbelief at her own news. Her hands were firmly tucked into her oversized, puffy black coat, and she slowly moved from side to side as if waiting to see the reaction between Katherine and Carol.

'Oh, no way. That's brilliant. Good for you,' Carol answered.

'Yes, Lily, that's brilliant news,' Katherine exclaimed.

'Really?' Lily's eyebrows raised. She took her hands out of her pocket and stood confidently.

'Yes, of course. You'll make one hell of a copper,' Katherine walked up to Lily and hugged her.'

'You'll make one hell of a barrister. I wouldn't want to go up against you,' Katherine smiled. They both chuckled. It was funny. If you had asked Katherine a few weeks ago if she would be sitting in the park with Lily and Carol laughing, genuinely laughing, Katherine wouldn't have believed it. But now Katherine couldn't imagine having any other friends around her.

'I'm just going to see if Ellie is okay,' she told Carol and Lily. They nodded. Still chatting amongst themselves.

'Hey.' Katherine said, sitting on the swing next to her. 'How are you doing?' Katherine didn't want to invade her space too much. She had been really quiet after Katherine had told her the news of her father. How would she get over this? Would she be the same ever again? Maybe James had got inside Ellie's head that much she would resent Katherine?

Ellie looked at the floor. 'Okay.'

'I'm so sorry, Ellie, for everything. You know you can tell me anything, and I will always be here for you. No matter what,' Katherine assured. 'I'm your mother and will always be here for you. I love you. You and Sophie are the most important things to me in the world.'

Ellie suddenly jumped up from the swing and tightly wrapped her arms around Katherine. It had been the first time in a long time since Katherine had hugged her daughter, and it had comforted Katherine. She stroked Ellie's hair like she did when she was younger. Ellie was so vulnerable at the moment, and whether Ellie knew it or not, she had been through a great ordeal.

Katherine continued to stroke Ellie's hair as she sat on Katherine's lap, leaning her head into her chest. Ellie was her little girl, and having her soft, sweet smell back in her arms was so lovely. Katherine knew there and then that she and Ellie would be able to face anything together, and everything would be okay.

Sophie was running around with Jack and Meghan. It was so nice to see them all playing so nicely together. Full of life. Not a care in the world. Happy and safe. Because, at the end of the day, that is all any mother wants for their children.

All a woman really wants is to have some true friends along the way; after all, what's life if you don't have friends to back you up when you need them the most? Tom was still hot, though. If only.

FORTY-FIVE

Lily

Lily sat at the kitchen table, twiddling her fingers back and forth on her pen. She was preparing for her interview for the police constable entry programme. Chris had taken Meghan to the park. So far, he had been true to his work and was desperately trying to get himself in her good books. She wanted to believe him. But equally, she was not getting her hopes up too much.

Lily looked down at the paper. What were they going to say? Would they ask why she wanted to become a police officer? Is it too much to tell them her sister was murdered in cold blood, and she wanted to dedicate her life to catching lowlifes? Maybe that would be too much. She could say she was hard-working and not shy about getting stuck. It was true she was ready to work hard. And ready to catch criminals. She hated that people walked around thinking they could do what they wanted without repercussions. Well, not on her watch.

The door knocked, interrupting her thoughts. She put her pen down and strolled over to the door. DI Carter was looking serious at her on the other side of the door.

'Hi Lily,' he said, straightening his long black trench coat. 'Can I come in?'

'Yeah, sure,' Lily beckoned him inside. She had a pit in the bottom of her stomach and wondered if DI Carter had found out the truth about what happened that night.

'Can I get you a coffee?' she said breezily, walking back towards the kitchen.

DI Carter followed her 'Oh no, I'm good, thanks. I can't stay too long. I just wanted to tell you that we have closed the case on Jasmin. After James had confessed the truth to you, and we have no other leads to say otherwise.'

'Oh right,' she sat down at the kitchen table. Suddenly hearing the words out loud made it all seem too real.

He raised his eyebrows at her. Did he expect her to say something different? There was something about his expression that said he didn't quite believe her. And he was right, too.

'Yes, it's hard to believe he killed Jasmin with just one push. One fateful hit of the head killed her.' Lily said, looking down at the floor. The thought of it was making her want to well up with tears.

'There wasn't just one blow to the head that killed her?'

Lily glanced up suddenly, looking directly at DI Carter. 'What!' She exclaimed.

'Yes, she was still alive after she hit her head the first time. There was a second blow to her head. The coroner confirmed it.'

Lily gulped. The blood had drained from her body.

'What exactly did James say to you? As far as we could tell, there was no record of him being there anywhere. That's not to say he was and that he killed her. But we can't be sure if it was him either.'

Lily just stared at him in silence. She had no words. Did that mean Tom went back and finished her off? He lied?

'It wasn't Tom who killed her either. Mrs Pattison, your neighbour, came to the station and said she had helped him get up from the floor and into his house. She said she was coming home from a shift at work when she really ran him over. That was around 12.30 am, she had said. The coroner confirmed Lily was still alive then. Plus, her Fitbit had stopped working at around 1.34 am, and the coroner confirmed it was highly likely this was around the time she died.

Well, if Tom hadn't killed her. Who did?

FORTY - SIX

Carol

Carol watched the door slam shut behind Tom. She couldn't believe he had just walked out. He never walked out. This wasn't what she wanted. The last time he'd walked out, Carol had to make sure he needed her. To make sure he came back and to make sure he'd stay. That was when they were at university. And it has worked. Suzie had seen to that. Tom was so predictable. She knew he found it hard to say no to temptation. All she had to do was put Suzie in his path. Get him drunk and high. Then Suzie was to come onto him. But Tom had held out better than she thought. So, Suzie had to improvise. She had to wait until he was completely wasted before getting him hard so she could climb on top of him. He had to cum for there to be evidence. Then the next day cry rape. She was good. Carol had to give her that. So good that Carol had paid for her entire year at university rather than just the one term she needed. Worth every penny. She swooped in and was her saviour. Forever in her debt. Bonded together. It had worked. Since that day, he knew he needed her. And wouldn't be going anywhere, until just that moment when he walked out on her. She could tell he was pulling away from her. And she didn't want him getting any ideas that he didn't need her.

But what to do now? She needed to follow him. That was the first thing she needed to do. Carol had a tracker on Tom's phone, so she knew he wouldn't get far. But what about Jack? She couldn't leave him alone. Could she? Carol thought about ringing her mother. But then that would raise suspicion. She didn't want anyone to know she had left the house.

Carol went to the cupboard instead and started rummaging around. She knew it was in here somewhere. She started throwing things out behind her. Then she saw it. The baby monitor. It was a video monitor. She could plug it in and watch Jack on her phone. He never got up, and if he did, she could rush back.

She quietly crept upstairs, plugged it into his room as he slept soundly and linked it back up to her app on the phone. She was now so glad she hadn't gotten rid of it.

Carol went downstairs and put on her long back coat. She opened the box in the hallway, looking through the winter hats and scarves they had. She found a black hat and pulled it over her head. She needed to blend in and not be seen as much as possible.

She grabbed her keys and slid her phone inside her pocket before closing the front door gently behind her.

The cold air hit her cheeks. She felt a great rush of anxiety. Her heart was pounding hard. It had been around an hour or so since he'd left. She took out her phone from her pocket. This was not her usual phone. It was a burner phone. She wanted no trace of her being out. As far as the world was concerned, she was at home with her son while her husband had stormed out on her. She'd left her normal phone in the house with the location tracker on. It would be her alibi if she needed one later. However, she didn't have a plan for what she was going to do yet. All she knew was that she needed to spy on Tom. She needed to make sure he would not be going anyway. He was her husband, and she planned on keeping it that way.

She looked down at the tracking app on her phone. It looked like he had just arrived in town at a bar. Carol walked down the road from her house before phoning for a taxi. It arrived quickly, and she arrived at the place where Tom's phone said he was: "The Smoking Gun."

It was fairly busy when she arrived. That was good. It made it easier for her to blend in. She kept her hood up as she was inside and made sure to keep herself against the walls. She kept her eyes peeled for Tom. As she moved through the bar, she noticed Damian swaying on the dance floor, with a beer swishing around as he moved.

Carol scanned the bar meticulously, her eyes darting from shadowed corners to crowded pockets of patrons. Yet, Tom was nowhere in sight. She moved cautiously toward the restroom area, her pulse quickening with every step. Suddenly, she caught a glimpse of him just as he disappeared into the toilets, accompanied by someone else. Carol froze, her breath hitching as a wave of dread swept over her.

Summoning every ounce of composure, she crept closer to the door, her movements light. As she approached, sounds began filtering through the gaps—a mixture of moans and whispers that confirmed her worst fear. Her heart felt like it might shatter.

Steadying herself, Carol gently pressed her hand against the toilet door, allowing it to close softly without drawing attention. With trembling hands, she stepped back, her mind swirling with emotions too chaotic to name.

Carol ran out of the bar. She found an alleyway and crouched down onto the floor. She sat there for some time before deciding to get up. Maybe it was time to let him go if that's what he wanted.

As Carol came out of the alleyway and made her way to the taxi rank on the corner, she noticed the girl Tom had been with. She was alone. She was on the phone to someone. She heard her mention Forest Lane. There's no way. There is no way she lived on the same street as her. Or is it? Maybe she had mentioned it because of Tom. Either way, she needed to follow this girl. Tom was her husband. She wasn't going to let him go without a fight. There was no way she was going to sleep with her husband and get away with it. She wanted to see why she knew her street and where she was going. As his wife, she had a duty to.

Carol stepped into the taxi, instructing the driver to follow the vehicle ahead. She explained, with casualness, that it carried a friend she'd argued with, and they were heading to the same destination. It was a story that seemed to convince him. Adding lightly, she mentioned alcohol as the probable cause of their disagreement.

Carol checked her phone. Jack was still safely tucked up in his bed. "Don't worry baby", she said to herself. Mummy will be home shortly.

As the vibrant city lights faded into the tranquil suburbs of Cardiff, the surroundings became quieter, with fewer people in sight. The realisation struck Carol like a cold gust of wind—this girl was heading towards her neighbourhood, perhaps even her street. Was this mere coincidence, or something far more unsettling?

The taxi abruptly stopped near the park entrance close to Forest Lane.

'Please pull over here,' Carol instructed quickly, her voice firm. The driver complied, glancing at the fare meter.

'That'll be £25.50,' he announced with a neutral tone.

Carol reached into her purse and handed him £30. 'Keep the change,' she said hastily, stepping out of the car, her movements quick and deliberate. She didn't want him to turn around and see her.

Carol hoped the girl wouldn't notice her, although they were a little up the street, the taxi had its lights on, and the car was running. Thankfully, she didn't turn around; she seemed to be distracted by something else and disappeared instead into the park's darkened pathways.

Carol pulled her hood up, blending into the night as she followed at a distance. She kept her movements stealthy, sticking to the shadows of the trees, careful not to crunch the brittle branches and leaves under her feet. Every step was deliberate, her mind racing, her pulse pounding as she crept closer, determined to find out what she was doing.

As Carol got closer, she could hear the girl talking to someone. It was a man.

'I thought you would be pleased,' the girl said.

'Pleased that you are pregnant,' the man said.

'Yes,' she uttered. 'Now that I am eighteen. We can be a family together.'

'Are you mad?' He shouted. 'I have a family. One that I love very much. You need to get rid of it. And pronto.' He raised his voice.

'I'm not getting rid of it,' she shouted. 'It's my baby and you can't make me.'

'Oh yes, I bloody well can!' He was now in her face, shouting.

What a bloody slut, thought Carol. This girl liked going around and shagging people's husbands. She deserved what she got from this guy.

Suddenly, lights flashed through the park, and she saw a man stumble out. Carol watched intently. Was that

Tom? He stumbled into the park, not noticing that this argument was unfolding between the girl and her lover. Carol felt a rush of excitement. She was curious to see how this went.

Carol stepped closer so she could see better. By now, the argument had heated up, and the man had hold of the girl. Gripping her tightly and shouting in her face. Tom finally noticed and ran over. He got between the two of them. Tom was hitting the man all over the place. Carol moved so she was more or less in touching distance. Carol picked up a large branch on the floor. Should she intervene? She was not meant to be here. But she didn't want anything to happen to Tom. Carol stopped and waited. Hiding behind a tree but watching intently with her branch still in her hand.

The girl suddenly went quiet as she was flung to the floor. Carol gasped and she watched as Tom checked her and tried to phone for an ambulance. The man was panicking, saying she was dead.

'We should phone the police,' Tom said.

'No!' the man interjected. 'We will both get done. Our lives will be over. Go home. We were never here. You never saw me. It will look like she was coming home from a night out. She tripped and hit her head.'

All of a sudden, Tom started to vomit all over the floor.

'Oh mate!' The man said, turning away from Tom and holding his nose.

Carol almost stepped forward to check he was okay before remembering she couldn't be seen. Tom then staggered out of the woods and towards their street. She would need to get home. Before he noticed she wasn't there.

Just as Carol started to move backwards into the darkness of the woods and away from the man, the twigs snapped beneath her, signalling her presence.

She quickly hid behind the tree. Holding her breath and keeping as still as she possibly could.

She heard his footsteps walk away. Carol sighed in relief.

Carol turned around and walked towards the girl. Should she leave her? Do nothing?

Maybe that was the best thing to do. Tom had killed her. This meant he'd be forever in her debt if he wanted to get away with it. He would never be able to leave now.

Carol decided she would leave her and go home. She walked past her towards Forest Lane. But as she did, she heard a groan. Oh God, she thought. She's still alive?

Carol spun back towards her. She leant over her. 'Hello? Are you ok?'

'You,' she said. 'Why are you following me?'

Carol's heart raced. She saw her?

'You were in town and now you're here.' Maybe Carol hadn't been as inconspicuous as she had originally thought.

'That guy, he tried to kill me. They both left me for dead. Please help me.'

Carol wasn't sure what to do. She didn't want anyone to know she had left the house. She didn't want anyone to know she'd left her son alone to go and stalk her husband. And most all she didn't want Tom to know.

Equally, she didn't want Tom to go down for attempted murder. She just wanted Tom to think he was a killer. She wanted to be his saviour. She wanted him to need her. This girl would tell them what he did. She didn't want her to say anything.

Without thinking any further, Carol picked up a rock beside her and hurled it down on the girl's head with all her might. Blood streamed down her face. Carol collapsed backwards onto her bum, hitting the hard ground beneath her, her hands trembling. She looked down at them in horror. What had she done? Why had she done that? Oh god!

There was no going back now – she was a murderer.

COMING SOON.....

......The Forest Lane Killer

(Sequel to The Secrets of Forest Lane)

To keep updated with news about my upcoming book or for free giveaways. Please follow me on the below:

TikTok:

www.tiktok.com/@sianmorganauthor

Instagram: www.instagram.com/sianmorganauthor/

Facebook: www.facebook.com/SEMorganAuthor

Printed in Dunstable, United Kingdom

67057806R00201